PENGUIN CLASSICS

A NEW ENGLAND NUN AND OTHER STORIES

MARY E. WILKINS FREEMAN was born in Randolph, Massachusetts, in 1852 and at fifteen moved with her family to Brattleboro, Vermont. In 1884, left without any immediate family, she returned to Randolph, where she lived for almost twenty years with her childhood friend Mary Wales. She began to write seriously in the 1870s, and in the early 1880s her work began to appear in such popular magazines as *Harper's Bazar* and *Harper's Monthly Magazine*. Her first published book was *A Humble Romance and Other Stories* (1887). At forty-nine Mary E. Wilkins married Charles Manning Freeman, a New Jersey physician, and moved to Metuchen. Thereafter she wrote under the name Mary E. Wilkins Freeman. The marriage became troubled by his increasing alcoholism, the couple separated formally in 1921, and Charles died in 1923. Freeman wrote prolifically throughout her career, publishing short stories, novels (among them *Pembroke* in 1894 and *The Portion of Labor* in 1901), children's books, a play, and poetry. Her last book was *Edgewater People* (1918), a collection of village sketches. In April 1926, she received the William Dean Howells Medal for Fiction from the American Academy of Arts and Letters; later that year she and Edith Wharton were among the first women to be elected to membership in the National Institute of Arts and Letters. Mary E. Wilkins Freeman died in 1930.

SANDRA A. ZAGARELL is a professor of English at Oberlin College. She is coeditor of the Penguin Classics edition of *The Morgesons* by Elizabeth Stoddard, as well as the editor of *A New Home—Who'll Follow?* by Caroline Kirkland and author of numerous articles on American literature.

A NEW ENGLAND NUN
AND OTHER STORIES

MARY E. WILKINS FREEMAN

EDITED WITH AN INTRODUCTION AND NOTES
BY SANDRA A. ZAGARELL

PENGUIN BOOKS

To my parents,
Milton and Olivia I. Abelson,
and the memory of my aunt, Esther I. Kahn   —S.A.Z.

PENGUIN BOOKS
Published by the Penguin Group
Penguin Putnam Inc., 375 Hudson Street,
New York, New York 10014, U.S.A.
Penguin Books Ltd, 27 Wrights Lane, London W8 5TZ, England
Penguin Books Australia Ltd, Ringwood, Victoria, Australia
Penguin Books Canada Ltd, 10 Alcorn Avenue,
Toronto, Ontario, Canada M4V 3B2
Penguin Books (N.Z.) Ltd, 182–190 Wairau Road,
Auckland 10, New Zealand

Penguin Books Ltd, Registered Offices:
Harmondsworth, Middlesex, England

This volume first published in Penguin Books 2000

3 5 7 9 10 8 6 4 2

LIBRARY OF CONGRESS CATALOGING IN PUBLICATION DATA
Freeman, Mary Eleanor Wilkins, 1852–1930.
A New England nun and other stories / Mary E. Wilkins Freeman ;
edited with an introduction and notes by Sandra A. Zagarell.
p.   cm.
Includes bibliographical references (p.   ).
ISBN 0 14 04.3739 8
1. New England—Social life and customs—Fiction.   I. Zagarell, Sandra A.
II. Title.
PS1712.N4   2000
813´.4—dc21   99-056635

Printed in the United States of America
Set in Stempel Garamond

ACKNOWLEDGMENTS

My thanks to Oberlin College for awarding me McGregor-Oresman funds for employing a research assistant, and to Hillary Lamson Chute for filling that role ideally and for being an enthusiastic and discriminating reader of the fiction of Mary E. Wilkins Freeman. Thanks, too, to Helen Black and Cynthia Comer of the Reference Department of the Oberlin College library, for help in tracking down hard-to-locate information, and to Linda Pardee for secretarial assistance. I am grateful to Caroline White, of Penguin Books, for suggesting this project to me, and to Joanne Dobson, June Howard, Augusta Rohrbach, Paula Richman, and Eve Sandberg, from whose adroit critiques my introduction has profited. To June Howard I am also indebted for several illuminating conversations about Freeman. Finally, I want to thank the Northeast Nineteenth-Century American Women Writers Discussion Group, whose vibrant, savvy, and searching discussions continue to deepen my understanding and appreciation of American literature and culture.

—*Sandra A. Zagarell*

CONTENTS

INTRODUCTION

MARY E. WILKINS FREEMAN once asked another New England regionalist, Sarah Orne Jewett, if "it seems to you as it does to me that everything you have heard, seen, or done, since you opened your eyes on the world, is coming back to you sooner or later, to go into stories" (December 10, 1889). Imaginative and observant, a consummate and committed artist, Freeman also ardently pursued commercial success. She came of age at a time when literature in America was becoming both a hallowed art and a branch of commerce, and was adept at negotiating lucrative payment for her work. She often wrote to editors' specifications of length and even subject matter, producing many commissioned stories for Thanksgiving and Christmas publication. Still, her best work—of which there is a great deal—not only creatively reworks the literary formulas it sometimes uses, but also often actively disputes or complicates standard "regionalist" images of rural life as the sanctuary of a "traditional" America untouched by industrialism or commodity culture.

Freeman's life, too, is marked by intriguing complexities. For nearly half a century she lived in rural New England; its culture, history, and people were her main subject matter. Success, however, afforded her considerable cosmopolitanism, as it did many regionalist writers of her era: she was part of a northeastern network of editors, writers, and artists and spent much time in Boston, New York, and Chicago. But her public image was that of a rural New Englander, and she habitually identified herself as such.

Her personal life also resists ready classification. At thirty she entered into an intimate domestic relationship with her childhood friend Mary Wales that would endure for almost two decades (whether or not the relationship was sexual we cannot know). Then, at forty-nine, she left Wales and New England to marry Dr. Charles Manning Freeman and would spend the rest of her life in his hometown of Metuchen, New Jersey.

Although Freeman's life and writing are at once highly individual and deeply engaged in her era, by the end of her life critical and scholarly commentators saw both mainly as holdovers from an outmoded past. In 1926, presenting her with the first William Dean Howells Medal for distinguished work in American fiction, writer Hamlin Garland adopted a patronizing tone that would typify evaluation of Freeman for decades. He cast her as a mere transcriber of New England provincial life, the producer "of a record which was all the better, perhaps, for being unconsciously historical." Only in the early 1970s, particularly as feminist literary critics began to elucidate the accomplished nature of her artistry and subject matter, did a more fully dimensioned Freeman emerge. Freeman's many-sided depictions of women, on which feminist criticism initially cast light—of women single as well as married; old as well as young; often struggling for livelihood and determined to preserve their independence—spoke eloquently to late twentieth century readers and underwrote the current Freeman revival.

Building especially on feminist scholarship, we may expand our understanding of Freeman's life and work, and the corresponding relevance to both of such matters as the consolidation of literature as a business and the emergence of authorial celebrity, the nature of postbellum regionalism, and possibilities for fluid relationships between gender and sexuality. The first section of this introduction recounts Freeman's life, placing it within historical/cultural context. The second section provides a framework for reading her short fiction, focusing especially on the often subtle and variegated ways in which her work inscribed the confluence of the modern and the traditional in postbellum rural New England.

The fiction included here represents the breadth of Freeman's work. The most familiar Freeman, whose stories center on questions of women's integrity, courage, and, often, privation, is represented by "A Moral Exigency," "A Mistaken Charity," "A New England Nun," "Louisa," "The Revolt of 'Mother,'" and "Old Woman Magoun." The volume also collects some of the short fiction Freeman wrote during her middle and later years. Much of her work from this time has been unavailable in modern anthologies but is at least as fine as that which is well-known today. Included are a ghost story, "The Lost Ghost," two stories exploring cultural constructions of masculinity ("The Love of Parson Lord," "A Retreat to the Goal"), several stories which emphasize the interconnection of rural New England with modern culture and commerce, also focusing on femininity (the often-anthologized "A Poetess," as well as the lesser-known "One Good Time" and the generally neglected "The Winning Lady," "The Amethyst Comb," and "Dear

Annie"). Selections have also been made with an eye toward presenting Freeman's tonal scope: her use of pathos and sentimentality,
of dry reserve, and of humor, satire, irony, these last most vividly
expressed in *The Jamesons*, a series of sketches about village life.
Also represented are her many modes: romantic, gothic, and—dra-
matically expressed by "The Parrot"—psychologically symbolic.
Taking these works together, readers will encounter an appealingly
complex artistry, and a highly accomplished one.

Mary E. Wilkins was born in 1852 in Randolph, Massachusetts, a
village whose economic base of agriculture and shoe manufacturing
was eroding by the end of the Civil War. In 1867 her father, War-
ren, a builder, moved his wife, Eleanor, and two children to the
more prosperous village of Brattleboro, Vermont. There they par-
ticipated in a rich culture with ties to New York and Boston, but
also experienced increasingly precarious finances. By 1877 matters
were so bad that Eleanor Wilkins became the housekeeper of a local
family, with whom the Wilkinses resided.
    Shy and delicate as a child, Mary was always an ardent reader.
She received a good formal education, graduating from Brattleboro
High School in 1870 and attending Mt. Holyoke Seminary (later
College) for a year. By the mid-1870s, when it became imperative
that she earn money, she did a stint of schoolteaching and gave music lessons. As she had since childhood, she also wrote poetry. Some
of it was published—though without renumeration—in a Boston
magazine in the late 1870s, inaugurating so seamless a shift to authorship as a profession that she later said, "I am a little vague . . .
about the number of years I have been writing . . . because I wrote
when I was not *really* writing" (May 11, 1905). In the late 1870s she
began a de facto literary apprenticeship, concentrating initially on
poetry and stories for children's magazines, then on short fiction
for adults. In 1882, she submitted a story, "The Shadow Family," to
a contest in a Boston newspaper and won first prize. In 1883,
Harper's Bazar (only later was the spelling changed to *Bazaar*)
accepted "Two Old Lovers," an accomplished story about the
decades-long courtship between two New England villagers, and
her career as a writer of short fiction about New England was
launched. So, too, was a lifelong association with the prominent
publishing firm of Harper Brothers. Soon her stories appeared not
only in the *Bazar*, a magazine directed to women, but in the presti-
gious *Harper's Monthly Magazine*. Her status as an author of adult

fiction solidified in 1887, when Harper's issued *A Humble Romance and Other Stories*, a collection of fiction originally published in the *Bazar* or the *Monthly Magazine*. The book was well received. Novelist William Dean Howells, America's most influential editor and reviewer, identified Wilkins's (this was before her marriage) writing as "peculiarly American" and distinctly regional, and praised its "directness and simplicity"—qualities Howells prized for their realism—as on a level with "the best modern work everywhere."

New publishing opportunities, not just artistic excellence, enabled this little-known woman from Randolph, Massachusetts, to place her fiction in one of America's best magazines shortly after breaking into print, and soon to become a highly esteemed, well-paid author. By the late 1870s, developments in the production of print material, along with the professionalization of editorial work and authorship, expanding networks of distribution, and the emergence of proto-modern marketing techniques, had all helped transform the business of literature into the first successful culture industry. These circumstances underwrote the flourishing of postbellum regionalist literature. Readers devoured material featuring the cultures and peoples of locales where life seemed untouched by the accelerating changes so visible in the nation's cities. Regionalist literature's commercial appeal, in combination with its readily mastered conventions, created unprecedented opportunities for writers with few or no initial literary connections, among them Jewett, Garland, Charles Chesnutt, and Mary Noailles Murfree as well as Wilkins.

Wilkins's success came at a critical point in her life. By early 1883, she was without immediate family. Her sister Anna had died in 1876, followed by her mother in 1880; her father died just after the publication of "Two Old Lovers." After his meager estate was settled, Mary returned to Randolph, moving in with her childhood friend Mary Wales and Wales's parents. With Harper's providing professional stability and Mary Wales providing a supportive domestic environment, Wilkins's writing blossomed. During her years with Wales, she expanded her generic repertoire, writing a play, a collaborative detective story, more children's fiction and verse, and five novels, as well as numerous, often excellent short stories for adults. The once-retiring Mary Wilkins also flourished socially, becoming part of an extensive northeastern social circle that included writers, artists, and editors. By the mid-1880s she could comment to Louisa Maria Booth, editor of *Harper's Bazar* and by then a close friend, "There is one beautiful thing which comes from this kind of work, and the thing I have the most need of, I think. One is going to find friends because of it" (April 21, 1885).

While social-professional networks often enriched postbellum writers' lives, Wilkins's experiences indicate that—as was true also for their male counterparts—literary celebrity could present women with a degree of public intrusion unimaginable for even the most popular female writers before the Civil War. Though as a "lady" Wilkins was unlikely to capitalize on celebrity as Mark Twain did, she struggled to balance personal privacy with the avid interest in her life of the readership on which her livelihood depended. Many of the impositions to which she was subject are commonplace nowadays, but her efforts to keep them in check highlight the link between the establishment of literature as a culture industry and the development of authorial celebrity.

The impositions began when Wilkins's work was just becoming well-known. Not only was she barraged with requests for autographs and advice from would-be writers, but she also received a steady stream of invitations to speak publicly and to attend public and private events, such as receptions, club meetings, and lunch and dinner parties. Journalists and others wanted to interview her. Like most writers, she had no private secretary and had to respond to these solicitations while preserving time for writing. Once her work became popular, she also had to respond to frequent professional requests. Her standing as a Harper's author allowed her to reject some of these, but since she was financially dependent on writing she had to accept some, try (often unsuccessfully) to avoid overwork, and maintain friendly business relations. Her response to an acquaintance who was an editor with the S. S. McClure publishing syndicate shows how careful she was to preserve good professional relationships. She promises "not a half a dozen [stories] at once for my own peace of mind, for I am *so* busy, but . . . two before long." Asking for details about the readers' age, the fiction's length, and deadlines, she adds, "Dear Mrs. Pratt . . . if my little stories are of use to you, I will write you all I can" (August 16, 1891).

Wilkins had also to parry a new assumption about public access to authors: that her *likeness* was available for popular consumption. Her career was launched at a time when the technology of photography and image production had become quite advanced and having one's picture taken was commonplace. When her network of friends began to expand, she wanted to send her photo to those at a distance. As was common, her picture also appeared as the frontispiece of many of her books. But she grew increasingly uneasy about public circulation of her image and disliked the trend, encouraged by publishers, to promote work by cultivating public interest in the author. Eventually she decided that her work, not her face, should be the focus of public attention. Expressing a resolution "to have no picture of myself appear in connection with my work" (August 2, 1906), she began to resist editors' and publishers' requests for recent photographs. Like many an author since, however, she found that her wishes made little difference. She could prevent neither the reuse of images already circulating nor the creation of new ones, and drawings and photographs of her continued to be printed in newspapers and magazines.

By the late 1890s, Mary Wilkins had even more personal reasons to try to control public intrusion. She had become involved in an on-again, off-again courtship with Charles Freeman, a handsome physician with a reputation as a ladies' man whom she had met at the Metuchen, New Jersey, home of *Harper's Monthly Magazine* editor Henry Alden. Little information about the courtship is available, though her apparent ambivalence about marrying has been plausibly attributed to her attachment to Mary Wales, to apprehension about losing her independence, to her conviction that she could write only in New England, and to the need to focus on her work. What is indisputable is that newspaper coverage made a public spectacle out of a personal matter. Reporters trailed Dr. Freeman to Randolph; they announced the marriage as impending several times before it actually took place. Scholar Brent Kendrick quotes this fairly typical passage from the *New York Telegraph* in the late 1890s: "The public is really tired of the love affairs of the literary old maid, and the sooner she marries the doctor and takes him out of the public view the more highly will the action be appreciated." Distressed by such publicity, Wilkins was silent not only to the press but to close friends. To Evelyn Sawyer Severance, one of her closest, she finally announced her engagement on December 22, 1901: "At this extremely late hour of the day, I am about to be married. Early in January, the day I don't even mention in my prayers, on account of the newspapers. . . . The unfortunate man's name is Dr. Chas. Freeman. . . . We are very old friends, but have not been engaged as long as the papers state. They have married and postponed at their discretion."

It is her aversion to celebrity, in part, that makes Mary E. Wilkins Freeman—as she instructed her publishers to title her after she married—so unavailable to later generations. She went to extremes to maintain her privacy, but our knowledge of her culture sheds considerable light on the circumstances within which she had to negotiate her life and her sense of identity. The *Telegraph*'s unabashed reference to her as a "literary old maid" expresses the social stigma that still attached to single women over thirty and the assumption that a woman's social, emotional, and sexual self corresponded with her marital status. As a (literary) "old maid," Miss Wilkins appeared somewhat comical; marriage would transform her into the more socially acceptable—and presumably fulfilled—"Mrs. Freeman."

What we know suggests that for Mary E. Wilkins, as for numerous other women of her era, including Jewett, commonly held images like "old maid" obscured the richness and complexity of their lives. The aspects of self inherent in gender presentation, gender identity, sexuality, and experiences of intimacy did not match the abrasive stereotype. Wilkins's self-presentation was very feminine in the conventional manner of the day. Proud of her light-haired, blue-eyed prettiness (for which she was nicknamed "Dolly," for doll-like, as a child), she was always fashionably dressed. She was soft-spoken and reserved, and in business letters and letters to acquaintances she is extremely solicitous and gracious. But while the culture at large presumed that heterosexual romance was the point and purpose of a "feminine" woman's existence, for much of her life Wilkins did not live out that presumption. Although her biographer, Edward Foster, speculates that in her early twenties she was in love with a good-looking, flirtatious naval ensign named Hanson Tyler, she had no lasting romantic relationship with Tyler, nor is there evidence that she was involved with any other man before her engagement to Charles Freeman. Her femininity did, however, coexist with powerful bonds with women. Mary Wales provided emotional sustenance, encouraged her to write, read her work-in-progress, and took care of domestic and financial arrangements. Many of her other close associates were women. Yet neither she nor Wales lived in the kind of "female world" that some historians have seen as the primary environment of many nineteenth-century women. Wilkins also had close male friends, including editors Edgar Joseph Chamberlain and Henry Alden, and for years the two Marys hosted two Randolph bachelors for Saturday evening get-togethers of supper and card games. Moreover, Wilkins's attraction to the flirtatious, prank-loving, hard-drinking, good-looking Charles Freeman—a man rather in the Hanson Tyler mode, Foster suggests—indicates that she may have been drawn to a conventionally "bad boy," rather brash kind of masculinity. An added complexity is that, despite a deep love of children, Wilkins severed both femininity and sexuality from childbearing. Any sexual relationship she may have had with Mary Wales, of course, could not have resulted in pregnancy, nor did her marriage to Charles Freeman at age forty-nine.

At least once Mary Wilkins Freeman expressed the opinion that a woman could be feminine, mature, sexual, heterosexually appealing, childless, *and* single. In the early twentieth century, she upset William Dean Howells's plan for a collaborative novel, *The Whole Family*, by making the thirty-something "Old Maid Aunt"—the title of her assigned chapter—highly attractive and by suggesting that the young fiancé of one of the heroines was actually in love with the aunt. When informed by *Harper's Bazar* editor Elizabeth Jordan of Howells's old-fashioned concept of "old maid," Freeman (for by this time she was married) responded with a brief for the vibrancy and sexuality of the contemporary single older women: "In these days of voluntary celibacy on the part of women an old maid only fifteen years older than a young girl is a sheer impossibility, if she is an educated woman with a fair amount of brains. Moreover, a young man is really more apt to fall in love with her. . . . To-day [such women] look as pretty and up-to-date as their young nieces. . . . Their single state is deliberate choice on their own part." Freeman is explicit in her identification of a historical change centering on the sexual appeal of older women exempt from childbearing. "Mr. Howells," she declares, "is thinking of the time when women of thirty put on caps, and renounced the world. That was because [most women] married at fifteen and sixteen, and at thirty had about a dozen children" (August 1, 1906).

Once she married Charles, Freeman appears to have been content with him for many years. Though she found Metuchen uninspiring and continued to set most of her writing in New England—and to spend time with Mary Wales until Wales's death in 1916—she appreciated Charles's support of her work and enthusiastically embraced such aspects of married life as her husband's companionship and their sometimes hectic social activity. She continued to write prolifically, partly because, although Charles had means, the Freemans required a good deal of money to maintain their desired standard of living. They built a home designed according to their own luxurious specifications, traveled and vacationed, and by 1912 had owned six automobiles. Charles remained a heavy drinker and in 1908 was briefly institutionalized for alcoholism, but according to Freeman's account the marriage began to unravel only in the late teens, when his drinking and an addiction to sleeping medicine became unmanageable. In 1921 she had him committed to a hospital for the insane; after his release, she obtained a legal separation. When he died in 1923, she had to go to court to overturn his will, in which she was left one dollar. A letter to a friend captures her complex feelings about Charles: "It is a wonderful thing to be able to feel that your husband was your unshattered ideal. I cannot feel badly because I can hardly say that of my husband, for I doubt very much if I ever had an ideal to shatter anyway, and I reckon Charles may have thought I smashed his to smithereens. After all my husband had splendid traits. . . . Sometimes I think [Prohibition] was what really finished him. If he could have had good whiskey he might have weathered the gale. But that is over, and if I can hold on to my religion, he may have better [whiskey] now." She ends this pained, honest, and characteristically sardonic reflection with a jokey challenge: "And if you dare laugh at that!!" (Fragment. After October 15, 1925.)

As her marriage and then her health deteriorated, Mary E. Wilkins Freeman published relatively little. *Edgewater People* (1918), a collection of linked village sketches, was her last book. But her determination to keep her writing independent of her life redoubled during her last years. She was energetic about maintaining the stature of her published work, communicating frequently with Harper's about arrangements for its reproduction and the renewal of copyrights, asking the firm to permit textbooks' inclusion of her stories. Conscious that her health was declining, she destroyed unpublished work she deemed inferior. A 1928 letter in which she pressed Harper's to step up advertisement for *The Best Short Stories of Mary E. Wilkins Freeman* captures her final assessment of her life: "Aside from the financial aspect [what matters is] the life of my work. I feel that is all I came into the world for, and have failed dismally if it is not a success" (February 1, 1928). She died in 1930.

While recognizably a part of the literary movement now known as regionalism, Freeman's short fiction questions the common regionalist premise that rural New England was cut off from modernity and modernization. In a host of ways, some direct, some implied, her work portrays rural New England and "modern" America as dynamically connected. Freeman often suggests that modernization is ubiquitous throughout city and country, although not the same in one as in the other. In "Two Old Lovers," a shoe factory forms the village's economic foundation. In much of her fiction, village life is affected by the railroad and other forms of modern technology, and in some respects, like much New England regionalism, her work regrets the changes wrought by modernization. "Dear Annie" (1910) reflects on the selfishness of a new generation of "modern" women represented by the self-centered, anti-domestic sisters who exploit the generous Annie (still, a telephone is essential to Annie's eventual self-preservation). On balance, though, Freeman's fiction depicts modernization's consequences for rural New England as multifarious. It highlights the commodities that modern capitalism has brought but also shows how it has relegated much of New England to the periphery of growth rather than the center. Much of her work brilliantly dramatizes modernization and the creation of "regions" as one complicated, uneven process that continues to affect not only rural America, but, at least by implication, urban America as well.

Freeman often conveys her take on rural New England and its relationship with "modern" America obliquely, engaging in what might be called critical regionalism. Her stories tend to put regionalism's stock conventions and motifs into play in unusual, sometimes off-center ways that unsettle the presumption that rural life is fully separate from modern life. Characterization is a case in point. Many of Freeman's characters superficially conform to stock figures that cast regions as unalterably old-fashioned. Deciding not to marry, prim Louisa Ellis confirms her status as a "New England Nun" (1887)—a village "old maid"; Betsey Dole of "A Poetess" (1890) is the kind of spinster versifier of which Twain's Emmeline Grangerford is a southern spoof; Ruben Lord ("The Love of Parson Lord," 1899) is the kind of Puritan-descended man tormented by an iron sense of duty featured in some of Hawthorne's fiction; David Dunn ("A Retreat to the Goal," 1915–16) is the standard prodigal son returning to his upstanding country family from the corrupt city. But unlike fully stereotypical characters, which are generally portrayed in an exterior manner, Freeman's characters also exist on a subjective plane. Betsey Dole, for instance, writes poetry when neighbors request that she commemorate major events in their lives: the plot of "A Poetess" is precipitated by a grieving mother's request for an elegy for her dead child. Betsey's verse is clichéd doggerel, relying on stock rhymes such as "flowers" and "vernal bowers," and the story hinges on her devastation when she learns that the village minister has pronounced her poems "as poor as . . . could be." But unlike Twain's account of Emmeline Grangerford, whose death, precipitated by her inability to find a rhyme for "whistler," reinforces her status as an incarnation of the untalented, maudlin "lady poet," Betsey Dole's experience of poetic inspiration is spiritual. When Betsey discovers that despite her joy in poetic expression she has no ability, her expression of anguish conveys the magnitude of her tragedy: "I'd like to know if it's fair. . . . Had I ought to have been born with the wantin' to write poetry if I couldn't write it—had I? . . . Would it be fair if that canary-bird there, that ain't never done anything but sing, should turn out not to be singin'?"

Here, as in much of her fiction, Freeman potentially complicates metropolitan readers' habitual processing of rural New Englanders and their environs. Through depth of characterization she decreases the sense of distance that stock types often evoked, whether of patronizing sympathy or of amusement. Betsey Dole is not merely a pathetic rural "poetess": readers may identify with her imaginative vision, love of beauty, and devastation. On the other hand, she is not "universal" only. She is fundamentally the product of a rural village at a historical moment when highbrow taste, modern literature, and literary magazines are beginning, but only beginning, to alter the local culture. Through Betsey, "A Poetess" also works against the proclivity to view regional and modern life as polar opposites. It suggests that individuals—Betsey, her callow minister, readers themselves—are capable of negotiating, perhaps affecting, the changing mix of the traditional and the new. Betsey's final injunction that the minister, who has published poetry "in a magazine," commemorate her in poetry puts him in the position of promising to write just the kind of sentimental verse for which he had mocked her. With this turn, her characterization similarly enjoins readers to reflect on the possibility that dynamic, two-way relationships do, or can, exist between seemingly anachronistic and up-to-date aspects of American life. Exploring such dimensions of character and situation will illuminate how in other stories too Freeman's work endeavors to undo regionalism's habitual casting of rural New England as separated from the rest of the nation.

Like her characters, Freeman's narrative structures tend to disrupt suppositions that rural New England was seamlessly "traditional." While many regionalist writers conveyed the autonomy of village life through linked stories about life in a single village, only a few of Freeman's story collections celebrate life in one place. Likewise, she rarely employs the kind of participant/observer narrator that Stowe, Jewett, and many other regionalists used in evoking country cultures as "indigenous." And she makes little use of the sketch, a genre that facilitated the representation of rural life as dynamic but essentially unchanging and that was used with great effect by Stowe, Jewett, Alice Brown, and others. Freeman's preferred form, the short story, accentuates change and conflict. With it she often suggests difficulties in her characters' lives that are both individual and historically based. Thus "A Poetess" is plotted around the consequences of the slow penetration of remote New England villages by "modern" literature and taste. In "The Amethyst Comb" (1914) one protagonist, Jane Carew, embraces the self-sufficiency, dignity, and celibacy traditionally appropriate to New England spinsters; the modernity of the other, Viola Longstreet, is tied to a campaign to preserve her youthful appearance and have a chance at romantic love. While the story pivots on the painful consequences of Viola's path, it presents each woman with great sympathy, highlighting the gains and losses of each as well as the mutual incompatibility of their ways of life, and it ends by maintaining, not dispelling, the tension it has developed.

Freeman's fiction does sometimes counteract its evocation of historical/cultural tensions with stock sentimental conclusions that recast these tensions as personal matters resolved through romantic love. Of the work included here, this is most true of *The Jamesons* (1898–99), a canny satire of urbanites' attitudes toward rural life in which a young couple's love functions formulaically to reconcile an intrusive urbanite tourist with the inhabitants of a New England village. Sometimes, however, Freeman's romantic endings have an edge that underscores the story's historical/cultural conflicts. At the end of "One Good Time" (1897), William Crane, the worthy if dull fiancé of protagonist Narcissa Stone, acknowledges the restrictiveness of the village life to which Narcissa returns after the single "good time" of her life, a magical shopping trip to New York.

William picks up on the metaphor of leaping over a wall which Narcissa had used to express her need for her fling. Full of love and compassion, he asks, "Do you think you can be contented to—stay on my side of the wall now, Narcissa?" His question and her answer—"I wouldn't go out again if the bars were down"—affirm William's understanding of Narcissa and the couple's mutual devotion and compatibility, yet the language also registers the insuperable limitations of a way of life that had already nearly suffocated Narcissa. Love cannot alter a culture and economy that have been constricted by modernization; it can simply help sustain William and Narcissa in the life available to them.

Freeman occasionally took open exception to the regionalist premise that New England villages were the preserves of richly traditional cultures. *The Jamesons*, reprinted here for the first time since the turn of the century, is a satire of the narrative of community, a form that Jewett and others used in portraying rural villages as repositories of New England's cultural heritage. The predominating tone of many narratives of community, including Jewett's *The Country of the Pointed Firs* (1896), was unalloyed nostalgia for the satisfyingly old-fashioned quality of country life. *The Jamesons* satirizes such nostalgia by suggesting that it is a metropolitan construct. Freeman here presents village life as a mixture of the provincial, the traditional, and the modern, and in the characterization of New Yorker Mrs. H. Boardman Jameson, she spoofs the notion, complementary to nostalgia, that country villages are sadly behind the times.

Like the narrator of *Country*, *The Jamesons'* narrator, Sophia Lane, is a participant/observer. But Lane is no summer visitor. She is a native resident of Linnville, the village in which the narrative's six sketches are set. What Lane conveys is not the delectable old-fashionedness of village life, but the absurdity of Mrs. Jameson's efforts at "improving" Linnville by importing fads like dress reform, bicycling, and hiking. Much of the satire stems from the gap between Mrs. Jameson's assumptions and the real Linnville. Unaware that, like women all over the country, Linnville women have a literary society and are well read, she tries to bring them up to date by reading Robert Browning's poetry aloud. Failing to recognize that their varied and appetizing food contributes to their good health, she promotes fat-free crackers and biscuits.

The last chapter, "The Centennial," is arguably the funniest and most satirical. Playing off the rituals prominent in many narratives of community (a family reunion is the high point of *Country*), it also sends up the late-nineteenth-century fervor for "authentic" Americana which had antique dealers scouring rural New England for colonial artifacts and tourists flocking there to enjoy newly organized "traditional" ceremonies. Detailing Mrs. Jameson's re-arrangement of Linnville's oldest home so that it appears "authentically" colonial, *The Jamesons* lampoons a widespread urban fantasy, the identification of the colonial past with contemporaneous rural New England. Freeman's first readers would probably have recognized the "colonial" kitchen Mrs. Jameson is shown to assemble as a takeoff on re-creations of colonial kitchens featured at several celebrated fairs, including the 1876 American Centennial in Philadelphia and the 1893 Chicago Exposition. That Centennial Linnville is an urbanite's construction is underscored by the fact that most of the people seated on the dignitaries' dais are visitors, not Linnville inhabitants. As the touristy character of the celebration's "authenticity" is emphasized, Mrs. Jameson's other premise, that Linnville is cut off from modernity, is mocked: the dignitaries have to leave before the celebration is over to catch their train at a nearby village.

Although the presence of the modern in rural New England is evident in many stories in the present volume, some do seem to depict a New England so self-sufficient as to be immune from either "progress" or marginalization: "Louisa" (1890), "The Revolt of 'Mother'" (1890), and certainly "A New England Nun," viewed in Freeman's day and ours as a hallmark of her work. "A New England Nun" has in fact usually been read as a story about the cloistering of its protagonist: its final words characterize Louisa as an "uncloistered nun." Excellent commentary has variously illuminated Louisa Ellis's decision to preserve her way of life by not marrying her fiancé as Freeman's endorsement of Louisa's self-sustenance and independence; as the exposé of a pathology; as an irreducibly ambiguous rendering in which Louisa is simultaneously confined and autonomous. These interpretations all approach "A New England Nun" as cloistered—separate from modernity—and rely on methods of readings that are themselves cloistered, in that they largely focus on the inner workings of the text: tone of the narrator, ambiguity, inner tension, symbolism, characterization.

The story shifts startlingly if we also consider the context of its initial appearance, *Harper's Bazar*. As Freeman knew, the *Bazar* was a print emporium for middle-class women. The cover of the

May 7, 1887, number, which included "A New England Nun," characteristically features women in the latest fashion; dress and other patterns are prominent among the magazine's offerings. Two back pages of advertisement promote corsets, skin creams, depilatories, cocoa, and other consumer goods and announce the services of personal shoppers. "A New England Nun" is in a complicated dialogue with the *Bazar*. The story's emphasis on the austere neatness of Louisa Ellis's parlor, her homemade aprons and "flat straw hat," her pleasure in domestic work for its own sake, counterpoint the magazine's enthusiasm for commodity consumption, even as the story takes shape as yet another item to be consumed. Moreover, the placement of Freeman's story accentuates its appeal to the metropolitanism of its original readers. Given the place of honor at the magazine's center, with its first page laid out top to bottom, not horizontally, "A New England Nun" is set opposite the reproduction of a section of the painting "Full Speed" by Julius I. Stewart. This painting, which depicts two fashionably dressed young women and a young man aboard a yacht on the Seine, pays tribute to the increased postbellum cosmopolitanism of wealthy Americans by celebrating the merging of two leisure-time pursuits that had recently become markers of upper- and upper-middle-class life: yachting and tourism.

Its pairing with "Full Speed" may have cast "A New England Nun" as the medium of a kind of tourism that allowed readers to participate vicariously in the life of a rural New England woman, with Louisa's old-fashionedness providing temporary respite from the "fashion, pleasure and instruction" to which the *Bazar*'s banner proclaimed its devotion. Perhaps, on the other hand, readers in 1887 saw Louisa more negatively, as the embodiment of provincial privations from which they were happily exempt. Surely, however its initial readers may have processed "A New England Nun," it appealed to their metropolitan constructs of the rural in complicated, perhaps self-contradictory ways.

The kind of contextual overtones that sound in "A New England Nun" reverberate throughout Freeman's fiction. They form an important dimension of her work's complex involvement with the discourses and social formations of her America. Recognizing this involvement, as well as savoring the seeming simplicity complicated by layers of subtlety; powerful characterization; selective, quasi-symbolic emphasis on detail; and finely tuned sense of literary form, can contribute significantly to contemporary readers' appreciation of Freeman's writing. Her aesthetic achievements enhance our recognition of much American writing in her day. The substance of her work attests to that literature's concern with issues that, while historically particular, continue to speak across a century and more. Whether approached simply as a good read or on other levels as well, Freeman's fiction thus stands to delight readers today at least as much as it did her most enthusiastic contemporaries.

SUGGESTIONS FOR FURTHER READING

Works by Mary E. Wilkins Freeman

VOLUMES OF SHORT FICTION

The Givers. New York: Harper and Brothers, 1904.
Six Trees. New York: Harper and Brothers, 1901.

ANTHOLOGIES OF SHORT FICTION

The Best Short Stories of Mary E. Wilkins. Selected, with introduction, by
  H. W. Lanier. New York: Harper and Brothers, 1927.
The Revolt of "Mother" and Other Stories. Edited, with afterword, by Michelle
  Clark. Old Westbury, N.Y.: Feminist Press, 1974.
Selected Stories of Mary E. Wilkins Freeman. Edited, with introduction and af-
  terword, by Marjorie Pryse. New York: W. W. Norton, 1983.
Mary E. Wilkins Freeman Reader. Edited, with introduction, by Mary R.
  Reichardt. Lincoln: University of Nebraska Press, 1997.

NOVELS

Pembroke. New York: Harper and Brothers, 1894.
Madelon. New York: Harper and Brothers, 1896.
Jerome, A Poor Man. New York: Harper and Brothers, 1897.
The Portion of Labor. New York: Harper and Brothers, 1901.
The Whole Family: A Novel by Twelve Authors. New York: Harper and Broth-
  ers, 1908. Collaborative novel of which Freeman wrote chapter two.

MISCELLANEOUS PROSE

"Good Wits, Pen and Paper." In *What Women Can Earn: Occupations of
  Women and Their Compensation.* By Grace H. Dodge, Thomas Hunter and
  others. New York: Frederick A. Stokes, 1899, 28–29.
"Mary E. Wilkins Freeman." In *My Maiden Effort: Being Personal Confessions
  of Well-Known American Authors as to Their Literary Beginnings.* Introduc-
  tion, G. Burgess. Garden City, N.Y.: Doubleday, Page, 1902, 265–67.
"The Girl Who Wants to Write: Things to Do and Avoid." *Harper's Bazar* 47
  (June 1913), 272.

Related Works

Brodhead, Richard H. *Cultures of Letters. Scenes of Reading and Writing in Nineteenth-Century America.* Chicago: University of Chicago Press, 1993.

Brooks, Van Wyck. *New England Indian Summer: 1865–1915.* New York: E. P. Dutton, 1940.

Brown, Dona. *Inventing New England: Regional Tourism in the Nineteenth Century.* Washington, D.C.: Smithsonian Institution Press, 1995.

Donovan, Josephine. *New England Local Color Literature: A Women's Tradition.* New York: Frederick Ungar, 1983.

Fetterley, Judith, and Marjorie Pryse, eds. *American Women Regionalists, 1850–1910.* New York: W. W. Norton, 1992.

Fienberg, Lorne. "Mary E. Wilkins Freeman's 'Soft Diurnal Commotion': Women's Work and Strategies of Containment," in *New England Quarterly* 62:2 (1989), 483–504.

Fisher, Benjamin F. "The Supernatural Stories of Mary Wilkins Freeman and Edith Wharton." In *American Supernatural Fiction from Edith Wharton to the* Weird Tales *Writers.* Douglas Robillard, ed. New York: Garland Publishing, 1996.

Foster, Edward. *Mary E. Wilkins Freeman.* New York: Hendricks House, 1956.

Garvey, Ellen Gruber. *The Adman in the Parlor: Magazines and the Gendering of Consumer Culture, 1880s to 1910s.* New York: Oxford University Press, 1996.

Glasser, Leah Blatt. *In a Closet Hidden: The Life and Work of Mary E. Wilkins Freeman.* Amherst, Mass.: University of Massachusetts Press, 1996.

Glazener, Nancy. *Reading for Realism: The History of a Literary Institution, 1850–1910.* Durham, N.C.: Duke University Press, 1997.

Hamblen, Abigail Ann. *The New England Art of Mary E. Wilkins Freeman.* Amherst, Mass.: Green Knight Press, 1966.

Howard, June. "Introduction: Sarah Orne Jewett and the Traffic in Words." In *New Essays on* The Country of the Pointed Firs. June Howard, ed. Cambridge: Cambridge University Press, 1994, 1–38.

———. "Unraveling Regions, Unsettling Periods: Sarah Orne Jewett and American Literary History." In *American Literature* 68 (1996), 365–84.

Johanningsmeier, Charles. "Sarah Orne Jewett and Mary E. Wilkins (Freeman): Two Shrewd Businesswomen in Search of New Markets." In *New England Quarterly* 70:1 (March 1997), 57–81.

Kendrick, Brent L., ed. *The Infant Sphinx: Collected Letters of Mary E. Wilkins Freeman.* Metuchen, N.J.: Scarecrow Press, 1983.

Marchalonis, Shirley, ed. *Critical Essays on Mary E. Wilkins Freeman.* Boston: G. K. Hall, 1991.

Ohmann, Richard. *Selling Culture: Magazines, Markets, and Class at the Turn of the Century.* London: Verso, 1996.

Pattee, Fred Lewis. "On the Terminal Moraine of New England Puritanism. In *Sidelights in American Literature.* New York: Century, 1915, 175–209.

Reichardt, Mary. *Mary Wilkins Freeman: A Study of the Short Fiction.* New York: Twayne Publishers, 1997.

———. *A Web of Responsibility: Women in the Short Stories of Mary E. Wilkins Freeman.* Jackson: University Press of Mississippi, 1992.

Schlereth, Thomas J. "Country Stores, Country Fairs, and Mail-Order Catalogues: Consumption in Rural America." In *Consuming Visions: Accumulation and Display of Goods in America, 1880–1920.* Simon J. Bronner, ed. New York: W. W. Norton, 1989, 339–75.

Shumway, David R. "The Star System in Literary Studies." In *PMLA* 112:1 (January 1997), 85–100.

Westbrook, Perry D. *Mary Wilkins Freeman.* Rev. ed. Boston: G. K. Hall, 1988.

Zagarell. Sandra A. "Narrative of Community: The Identification of a Genre." In *Signs* 13:3 (1988), 498–527.

———. "Crosscurrents: Registers of Nordicism, Community, and Culture in Jewett's *Country of the Pointed Firs.*" In *Yale Journal of Criticism* 10:2 (1997), 355–70.

A NOTE ON THE TEXTS

Listed below are the books in which the stories collected here first appeared; these collections are the sources for the stories in the present text. Since almost all of Freeman's stories initially appeared in magazines, the magazine citations are also given where possible.

A Humble Romance and Other Stories (New York: Harper and Brothers, 1887): "A Mistaken Charity," "A Moral Exigency" (*Harper's Bazar*, July 1887).

A New England Nun and Other Stories (New York: Harper and Brothers, 1891): "A New England Nun" (*Harper's Bazar*, May 7, 1887), "A Poetess" (*Harper's Monthly Magazine*, July 1890), "Louisa" (*Harper's Bazar*, September 13, 1890), "The Revolt of 'Mother'" (*Harper's Monthly Magazine*, September 1890).

The Jamesons (New York: Doubleday, McClure, 1899; *Ladies' Home Journal*, November 1898–April 1899).

The Love of Parson Lord and Other Stories (New York: Harper and Brothers, 1900): "One Good Time" (*Harper's Monthly Magazine*, January 1897), "The Love of Parson Lord" (*Harper's Monthly Magazine*, December 1898).

Understudies (New York: Harper and Brothers, 1901): "The Parrot" (*Harper's Monthly Magazine*, September 1900).

The Wind in the Rose-Bush and Other Stories of the Supernatural (New York: Doubleday, Page, 1903): "The Lost Ghost" (*Everybody's*, May 1903).

The Winning Lady and Others (New York: Harper and Brothers, 1909): "Old Woman Magoun" (*Harper's Monthly Magazine*, October 1905), "The Winning Lady" (*Harper's Monthly Magazine*, November 1909).

The Copy-Cat and Other Stories (New York: Harper and Brothers, 1914): "Dear Annie" (*Harper's Monthly Magazine*, October–November 1910), "The Amethyst Comb" (*Harper's Monthly Magazine*, February 1914).

Edgewater People (New York: Harper Brothers, 1918): "A Retreat to the Goal" (*Harper's Monthly Magazine*, December 1915–January 1916).

A NEW ENGLAND NUN
AND OTHER STORIES

A Moral Exigency

AT FIVE O'CLOCK, Eunice Fairweather went up-stairs to dress herself for the sociable and Christmas-tree to be given at the parsonage that night in honor of Christmas Eve. She had been very busy all day, making preparations for it. She was the minister's daughter, and had, of a necessity, to take an active part in such affairs.

She took it, as usual, loyally and energetically, but there had always been seasons from her childhood—and she was twenty-five now—when the social duties to which she had been born seemed a weariness and a bore to her. They had seemed so to-day. She had patiently and faithfully sewed up little lace bags with divers-colored worsteds, and stuffed them with candy. She had strung pop-corn, and marked the parcels which had been pouring in since day-break from all quarters. She had taken her prominent part among the corps of indefatigable women always present to assist on such occasions, and kept up her end of the line as minister's daughter bravely. Now, however, the last of the zealous, chattering women she had been working with had bustled home, with a pleasant importance in every hitch of her shawled shoulders, and would not bustle back again until half-past six or so; and the tree, fully bedecked, stood in unconscious impressiveness in the parsonage parlor.

Eunice had come up-stairs with the resolution to dress herself directly for the festive occasion, and to hasten down again to be in readiness for new exigencies. Her mother was delicate, and had kept to her room all day in order to prepare herself for the evening, her father was inefficient at such times, there was no servant, and the brunt of everything came on her.

But her resolution gave way; she wrapped herself in an old plaid shawl and lay down on her bed to rest a few minutes. She did not close her eyes, but lay studying idly the familiar details of the room. It was small, and one side ran in under the eaves; for the parsonage was a cottage. There was one window, with a white cotton curtain trimmed with tasselled fringe, and looped up on an old porcelain knob with a picture painted on it. That knob, with its tiny bright landscape, had been one of the pretty wonders of Eunice's childhood. She looked at it even now with interest, and the marvel and

1

the beauty of it had not wholly departed for her eyes. The walls of
the little room had a scraggly-patterned paper on them. The first
lustre of it had departed, for that too was one of the associates of
Eunice's childhood, but in certain lights there was a satin sheen and
a blue line visible. Blue roses on a satin ground had been the original pattern. It had never been pretty, but Eunice had always had
faith in it. There was an ancient straw matting on the floor, a home-
made braided rug before the cottage bedstead, and one before the
stained-pine bureau. There were a few poor attempts at adornment
on the walls; a splint letter-case, a motto worked in worsteds, a gay
print of an eminently proper little girl holding a faithful little dog.

This last, in its brilliant crudeness, was not a work of art, but Eunice believed in it. She was a conservative creature. Even after her
year at the seminary, for which money had been scraped together
five years ago, she had the same admiring trust in all the revelations
of her childhood. Her home, on her return to it, looked as fair to
her as it had always done; no old ugliness which familiarity had
caused to pass unnoticed before gave her a shock of surprise.

She lay quietly, her shawl shrugged up over her face, so only her
steady, light-brown eyes were visible. The room was drearily cold.
She never had a fire; one in a sleeping-room would have been sinful
luxury in the poor minister's family. Even her mother's was only
warmed from the sitting-room.

In sunny weather Eunice's room was cheerful, and its look, if
not actually its atmosphere, would warm one a little, for the windows faced southwest. But to-day all the light had come through
low, gray clouds, for it had been threatening snow ever since morning, and the room had been dismal.

A comfortless dusk was fast spreading over everything now.
Eunice rose at length, thinking that she must either dress herself
speedily or go down-stairs for a candle.

She was a tall, heavily-built girl, with large, well-formed feet and
hands. She had a full face, and a thick, colorless skin. Her features
were coarse, but their combination affected one pleasantly. It was a
stanch, honest face, with a suggestion of obstinacy in it.

She looked unhappily at herself in her little square glass, as she
brushed out her hair and arranged it in a smooth twist at the top of
her head. It was not becoming, but it was the way she had always
done it. She did not admire the effect herself when the coiffure was
complete, neither did she survey her appearance complacently
when she had gotten into her best brown cashmere dress, with its

ruffle of starched lace in the neck. But it did not occur to her that any change could be made for the better. It was her best dress, and it was the way she did up her hair. She did not like either, but the simple facts of them ended the matter for her.

After the same fashion she regarded her own lot in life, with a sort of resigned disapproval.

On account of her mother's ill-health, she had been encumbered for the last five years with the numberless social duties to which the wife of a poor country minister is liable. She had been active in Sunday-school picnics and church sociables, in mission bands and neighborhood prayer-meetings. She was a church member and a good girl, but the rôle did not suit her. Still she accepted it as inevitable, and would no more have thought of evading it than she would have thought of evading life altogether. There was about her an almost stubborn steadfastness of onward movement that would forever keep her in the same rut, no matter how disagreeable it might be, unless some influence outside of herself might move her.

When she went down-stairs, she found her mother seated beside the sitting-room stove, also arrayed in her best—a shiny black silk, long in the shoulder-seams, the tops of the sleeves adorned with pointed caps trimmed with black velvet ribbon.

She looked up at Eunice as she entered, a complacent smile on her long, delicate face; she thought her homely, honest-looking daughter charming in her best gown.

A murmur of men's voices came from the next room, whose door was closed.

"Father's got Mr. Wilson in there," explained Mrs. Fairweather, in response to Eunice's inquiring glance. "He came just after you went up-stairs. They've been talking very busily about something. Perhaps Mr. Wilson wants to exchange."

Just at that moment, the study door opened and the two men came out, Eunice's father, tall and round-shouldered, with grayish sandy hair and beard, politely allowing his guest to precede him. There was a little resemblance between the two, though there was no relationship. Mr. Wilson was a younger man by ten years; he was shorter and slighter; but he had similarly sandy hair and beard, though they were not quite so gray, and something the same cast of countenance. He was settled over a neighboring parish; he was a widower with four young children; his wife had died a year before.

He had spoken to Mrs. Fairweather on his first entrance, so he stepped directly towards Eunice with extended hand. His ministerial affability was slightly dashed with embarrassment, and his thin cheeks were crimson around the roots of his sandy beard.

Eunice shook the proffered hand with calm courtesy, and inquired after his children. She had not a thought that his embarrassment betokened anything, if, indeed, she observed it at all.

Her father stood by with an air of awkward readiness to proceed to action, waiting until the two should cease the interchanging of courtesies.

When the expected pause came he himself placed a chair for Mr. Wilson. "Sit down, Brother Wilson," he said, nervously, "and I will consult with my daughter concerning the matter we were speaking of. Eunice, I would like to speak with you a moment in the study."

"Certainly, sir," said Eunice. She looked surprised, but she followed him at once into the study. "Tell me as quickly as you can what it is, father," she said, "for it is nearly time for people to begin coming, and I shall have to attend to them."

She had not seated herself, but stood leaning carelessly against the study wall, questioning her father with her steady eyes.

He stood in his awkward height before her. He was plainly trembling. "Eunice," he said, in a shaking voice, "Mr. Wilson came—to say—he would like to marry you, my dear daughter."

He cleared his throat to hide his embarrassment. He felt a terrible constraint in speaking to Eunice of such matters; he looked shamefaced and distressed.

Eunice eyed him steadily. She did not change color in the least. "I think I would rather remain as I am, father," she said, quietly.

Her father roused himself then. "My dear daughter," he said, with restrained eagerness, "don't decide this matter too hastily, without giving it all the consideration it deserves. Mr. Wilson is a good man; he would make you a worthy husband, and he needs a wife sadly. Think what a wide field of action would be before you with those four little motherless children to love and care for! You would have a wonderful opportunity to do good."

"I don't think," said Eunice, bluntly, "that I should care for that sort of an opportunity."

"Then," her father went on, "you will forgive me if I speak plainly, my dear. You—are getting older; you have not had any other visitors. You would be well provided for in this way—"

"Exceedingly well," replied Eunice, slowly. "There would be six hundred a year and a leaky parsonage for a man and woman and four children, and—nobody knows how many more." She was almost coarse in her slow indignation, and did not blush at it.

"The Lord would provide for his servants."

"I don't know whether he would or not. I don't think he would be under any obligation to if his servant deliberately encumbered himself with more of a family than he had brains to support."

Her father looked so distressed that Eunice's heart smote her for her forcible words. "You don't want to get rid of me, surely, father," she said, in a changed tone.

Mr. Fairweather's lips moved uncertainly as he answered: "No, my dear daughter; don't ever let such a thought enter your head. I only—Mr. Wilson is a good man, and a woman is best off married, and your mother and I are old. I have never laid up anything. Sometimes— Maybe I don't trust the Lord enough, but I have felt anxious about you, if anything happened to me." Tears were standing in his light-blue eyes, which had never been so steady and keen as his daughter's.

There came a loud peal of the door-bell. Eunice started. "There! I must go," she said. "We'll talk about this another time. Don't worry about it, father dear."

"But, Eunice, what shall I say to him?"

"Must something be said to-night?"

"It would hardly be treating him fairly otherwise."

Eunice looked hesitatingly at her father's worn, anxious face. "Tell him," she said at length, "that I will give him his answer in a week."

Her father looked gratified. "We will take it to the Lord, my dear."

Eunice's lip curled curiously, but she said, "Yes, sir," dutifully, and hastened from the room to answer the door-bell.

The fresh bevies that were constantly arriving after that engaged her whole attention. She could do no more than give a hurried "Good-evening" to Mr. Wilson when he came to take leave, after a second short conference with her father in the study. He looked deprecatingly hopeful.

The poor man was really in a sad case. Six years ago, when he married, he had been romantic. He would never be again. He was not thirsting for love and communion with a kindred spirit now, but for a good, capable woman who would take care of his four clamorous children without a salary.

He returned to his shabby, dirty parsonage that night with, it seemed to him, quite a reasonable hope that his affairs might soon be changed for the better. Of course he would have preferred that the lady should have said yes directly; it would both have assured him and shortened the time until his burdens should be lightened; but he could hardly have expected that, when his proposal was so sudden, and there had been no preliminary attention on his part. The week's probation, therefore, did not daunt him much. He did not really see why Eunice should refuse him. She was plain, was getting older; it probably was her first, and very likely her last, chance of marriage. He was a clergyman in good standing, and she would not lower her social position. He felt sure that he was now about to be relieved from the unpleasant predicament in which he had been ever since his wife's death, and from which he had been forced to make no effort to escape, for decency's sake, for a full year. The year, in fact, had been up five days ago. He actually took credit to himself for remaining quiescent during those five days. It was rather shocking, but there was a good deal to be said for him. No wife and four small children, six hundred dollars a year, moderate brain, and an active conscience, are a hard combination of circumstances for any man.

To-night, however, he returned thanks to the Lord for his countless blessings with pious fervor, which would have been lessened had he known of the state of Eunice's mind just at that moment.

The merry company had all departed, the tree stood dismantled in the parlor, and she was preparing for bed, with her head full, not of him, but another man.

Standing before her glass, combing out her rather scanty, lustreless hair, her fancy pictured to her, beside her own homely, sober face, another, a man's, blond and handsome, with a gentle, almost womanish smile on the full red lips, and a dangerous softness in the blue eyes. Could a third person have seen the double picture as she did, he would have been struck with a sense of the incongruity, almost absurdity, of it. Eunice herself, with her hard, uncompromising common-sense, took the attitude of a third person in regard to it, and at length blew her light out and went to bed, with a bitter amusement in her heart at her own folly.

There had been present that evening a young man who was a comparatively recent acquisition to the village society. He had been in town about three months. His father, two years before, had purchased one of the largest farms in the vicinity, moving there from an

adjoining state. This son had been absent at the time; he was reported to be running a cattle ranch in one of those distant territories
which seem almost fabulous to New-Englanders. Since he had
come home he had been the cynosure of the village. He was thirty
and a little over, but he was singularly boyish in his ways, and took
part in all the town frolics with gusto. He was popularly supposed
to be engaged to Ada Harris, Squire Harris's daughter, as she was
often called. Her father was the prominent man of the village, lived
in the best house, and had the loudest voice in public matters. He
was a lawyer, with rather more pomposity than ability, perhaps, but
there had always been money and influence in the Harris family,
and these warded off all criticism.

The daughter was a pretty blonde of average attainments, but
with keen wits and strong passions. She had not been present at the
Christmas tree, and her lover, either on that account, or really from
some sudden fancy he had taken to Eunice, had been at her elbow
the whole evening. He had a fashion of making his attentions
marked: he did on that occasion. He made a pretence of assisting
her, but it was only a pretence, and she knew it, though she thought
it marvellous. She had met him, but had not before exchanged two
words with him. She had seen him with Ada Harris, and he had
seemed almost as much out of her life as a lover in a book. Young
men of his kind were unknown quantities heretofore to this steady,
homely young woman. They seemed to belong to other girls.

So his devotion to her through the evening, and his asking permission to call when he took leave, seemed to her well-nigh incredible. Her head was not turned, in the usual acceptation of the
term—it was not an easy head to turn—but it was full of Burr Mason, and every thought, no matter how wide a starting-point it had,
lost itself at last in the thought of him.

Mr. Wilson's proposal weighed upon her terribly through the
next week. Her father seemed bent upon her accepting it; so did her
mother, who sighed in secret over the prospect of her daughter's remaining unmarried. Either through unworldliness, or their conviction of the desirability of the marriage in itself, the meagreness of
the financial outlook did not seem to influence them in the least.

Eunice did not once think of Burr Mason as any reason for her
reluctance, but when he called the day but one before her week of
probation was up, and when he took her to drive the next day, she
decided on a refusal of the minister's proposal easily enough. She
had wavered a little before.

So Mr. Wilson was left to decide upon some other worthy, reliable woman as a subject for his addresses, and Eunice kept on with her new lover.

How this sober, conscientious girl could reconcile to herself the course she was now taking, was a question. It was probable she did not make the effort; she was so sensible that she would have known its futility and hypocrisy before-hand.

She knew her lover had been engaged to Ada Harris; that she was encouraging him in cruel and dishonorable treatment of another woman; but she kept steadily on. People even came to her and told her that the jilted girl was breaking her heart. She listened, her homely face set in an immovable calm. She listened quietly to her parents' remonstrance, and kept on.

There was an odd quality in Burr Mason's character. He was terribly vacillating, but he knew it. Once he said to Eunice, with the careless freedom that would have been almost insolence in another man: "Don't let me see Ada Harris much, I warn you, dear. I mean to be true to you, but she has such a pretty face, and I meant to be true to her, but you have—I don't know just what, but something she has not."

Eunice knew the truth of what he said perfectly. The incomprehensibleness of it all to her, who was so sensible of her own disadvantages, was the fascination she had for such a man.

A few days after Burr Mason had made that remark, Ada Harris came to see her. When Eunice went into the sitting-room to greet her, she kept her quiet, unmoved face, but the change in the girl before her was terrible. It was not wasting of flesh or pallor that it consisted in, but something worse. Her red lips were set so hard that the soft curves in them were lost, her cheeks burned feverishly, her blue eyes had a fierce light in them, and, most pitiful thing of all for another woman to see, she had not crimped her pretty blond hair, but wore it combed straight back from her throbbing forehead.

When Eunice entered, she waited for no preliminary courtesies, but sprang forward, and caught hold of her hand with a strong, nervous grasp, and stood so, her pretty, desperate face confronting Eunice's calm, plain one.

"Eunice!" she cried, "Eunice! why did you take him away from me? Eunice! Eunice!" Then she broke into a low wail, without any tears.

Eunice released her hand, and seated herself. "You had better take a chair, Ada," she said, in her slow, even tones. "When you say *him*, you mean Burr Mason, I suppose."

"You know I do. Oh, Eunice, how could you? how could you? I thought you were so good!"

"You ask me why *I* do this and that, but don't you think he had anything to do with it himself?"

Ada stood before her, clinching her little white hands. "Eunice Fairweather, you know Burr Mason, and I know Burr Mason. You know that if you gave him up, and refused to see him, he would come back to me. You know it."

"Yes, I know it."

"You know it; you sit there and say you know it, and yet you do this cruel thing—you, a minister's daughter. You understood from the first how it was. You knew he was mine, that you had no right to him. You knew if you shunned him ever so little, that he would come back to me. And yet you let him come and make love to you. You knew it. There is no excuse for you: you knew it. It is no better for him. You have encouraged him in being false. You have dragged him down. You are a plainer girl than I, and a soberer one, but you are no better. You will not make him a better wife. You cannot make him a good wife after this. It is all for yourself—yourself!"

Eunice sat still.

Then Ada flung herself on her knees at her side, and pleaded, as for her life. "Eunice, O Eunice, give him up to me! It is killing me! Eunice, dear Eunice, say you will!"

As Eunice sat looking at the poor, dishevelled golden head bowed over her lap, a recollection flashed across her mind, oddly enough, of a certain recess at the village school they two had attended years ago, when she was among the older girls, and Ada a child to her: how she had played she was her little girl, and held her in her lap, and that golden head had nestled on her bosom.

"Eunice, O Eunice, he loved me first. You had better have stolen away my own heart. It would not have been so wicked or so cruel. How could you? O Eunice, give him back to me, Eunice, *won't you?*"

"No."

Ada rose, staggering, without another word. She moaned a little to herself as she crossed the room to the door. Eunice accompanied her to the outer door, and said good-bye. Ada did not return it. Eunice saw her steady herself by catching hold of the gate as she passed through.

Then she went slowly up-stairs to her own room, wrapped herself in a shawl, and lay down on her bed, as she had that Christmas Eve. She was very pale, and there was a strange look, almost of horror, on her face. She stared, as she lay there, at all the familiar objects in the room, but the most common and insignificant of them had a strange and awful look to her. Yet the change was in herself, not in them. The shadow that was over her own soul overshadowed them and perverted her vision. But she felt also almost a fear of all those inanimate objects she was gazing at. They were so many reminders of a better state with her, for she had gazed at them all in her unconscious childhood. She was sickened with horror at their dumb accusations. There was the little glass she had looked in before she had stolen another woman's dearest wealth away from her, the chair she had sat in, the bed she had lain in.

At last Eunice Fairweather's strong will broke down before the accusations of her own conscience, which were so potent as to take upon themselves material shapes.

Ada Harris, in her pretty chamber, lying worn out on her bed, her face buried in the pillow, started at a touch on her shoulder. Some one had stolen into the room unannounced—not her mother, for she was waiting outside. Ada turned her head, and saw Eunice. She struck at her wildly with her slender hands. "Go away!" she screamed.

"Ada!"

"Go away!"

"Burr Mason is down-stairs. I came with him to call on you."

Ada sat upright, staring at her, her hand still uplifted.

"I am going to break my engagement with him."

"Oh, Eunice! Eunice! you blessed—"

Eunice drew the golden head down on her bosom, just as she had on that old school-day.

"Love me all you can, Ada," she said. "I want—something."

A Mistaken Charity

THERE WERE IN A green field a little, low, weather-stained cottage, with a foot-path leading to it from the highway several rods distant, and two old women—one with a tin pan and old knife searching for dandelion greens among the short young grass, and the other sitting on the door-step watching her, or, rather, having the appearance of watching her.

"Air there enough for a mess, Harriét?" asked the old woman on the door-step. She accented oddly the last syllable of the Harriet, and there was a curious quality in her feeble, cracked old voice. Besides the question denoted by the arrangement of her words and the rising inflection, there was another, broader and subtler, the very essence of all questioning, in the tone of her voice itself; the cracked, quavering notes that she used reached out of themselves, and asked, and groped like fingers in the dark. One would have known by the voice that the old woman was blind.

The old woman on her knees in the grass searching for dandelions did not reply; she evidently had not heard the question. So the old woman on the door-step, after waiting a few minutes with her head turned expectantly, asked again, varying her question slightly, and speaking louder:

"Air there enough for a mess, do ye s'pose, Harriét?"

The old woman in the grass heard this time. She rose slowly and laboriously; the effort of straightening out the rheumatic old muscles was evidently a painful one; then she eyed the greens heaped up in the tin pan, and pressed them down with her hand.

"Wa'al, I don't know, Charlotte," she replied, hoarsely. "There's plenty on 'em here, but I 'ain't got near enough for a mess; they do bile down so when you get 'em in the pot; an' it's all I can do to bend my j'ints enough to dig 'em."

"I'd give consider'ble to help ye, Harriét," said the old woman on the door-step.

But the other did not hear her; she was down on her knees in the grass again, anxiously spying out the dandelions.

So the old woman on the door-step crossed her little shrivelled

11

hands over her calico knees, and sat quite still, with the soft spring wind blowing over her.

The old wooden door-step was sunk low down among the grasses, and the whole house to which it belonged had an air of settling down and mouldering into the grass as into its own grave.

When Harriet Shattuck grew deaf and rheumatic, and had to give up her work as tailoress, and Charlotte Shattuck lost her eyesight, and was unable to do any more sewing for her livelihood, it was a small and trifling charity for the rich man who held a mortgage on the little house in which they had been born and lived all their lives to give them the use of it, rent and interest free. He might as well have taken credit to himself for not charging a squirrel for his tenement in some old decaying tree in his woods.

So ancient was the little habitation, so wavering and mouldering, the hands that had fashioned it had lain still so long in their graves, that it almost seemed to have fallen below its distinctive rank as a house. Rain and snow had filtered through its roof, mosses had grown over it, worms had eaten it, and birds built their nests under its eaves; nature had almost completely overrun and obliterated the work of man, and taken her own to herself again, till the house seemed as much a natural ruin as an old tree-stump.

The Shattucks had always been poor people and common people; no especial grace and refinement or fine ambition had ever characterized any of them; they had always been poor and coarse and common. The father and his father before him had simply lived in the poor little house, grubbed for their living, and then unquestioningly died. The mother had been of no rarer stamp, and the two daughters were cast in the same mould.

After their parents' death Harriet and Charlotte had lived alone in the old place from youth to old age, with the one hope of ability to keep a roof over their heads, covering on their backs, and victuals in their mouths—an all-sufficient one with them.

Neither of them had ever had a lover; they had always seemed to repel rather than attract the opposite sex. It was not merely because they were poor, ordinary, and homely; there were plenty of men in the place who would have matched them well in that respect; the fault lay deeper—in their characters. Harriet, even in her girlhood, had a blunt, defiant manner that almost amounted to surliness, and was well calculated to alarm timid adorers, and Charlotte had always had the reputation of not being any too strong in her mind.

Harriet had gone about from house to house doing tailor-work after the primitive country fashion, and Charlotte had done plain sewing and mending for the neighbors. They had been, in the main, except when pressed by some temporary anxiety about their work or the payment thereof, happy and contented, with that negative kind of happiness and contentment which comes not from gratified ambition, but a lack of ambition itself. All that they cared for they had had in tolerable abundance, for Harriet at least had been swift and capable about her work. The patched, mossy old roof had been kept over their heads, the coarse, hearty food that they loved had been set on their table, and their cheap clothes had been warm and strong.

After Charlotte's eyes failed her, and Harriet had the rheumatic fever, and the little hoard of earnings went to the doctors, times were harder with them, though still it could not be said that they actually suffered.

When they could not pay the interest on the mortgage they were allowed to keep the place interest free; there was as much fitness in a mortgage on the little house, anyway, as there would have been on a rotten old apple-tree; and the people about, who were mostly farmers, and good friendly folk, helped them out with their living. One would donate a barrel of apples from his abundant harvest to the two poor old women, one a barrel of potatoes, another a load of wood for the winter fuel, and many a farmer's wife had bustled up the narrow foot-path with a pound of butter, or a dozen fresh eggs, or a nice bit of pork. Besides all this, there was a tiny garden patch behind the house, with a straggling row of currant bushes in it, and one of gooseberries, where Harriet contrived every year to raise a few pumpkins, which were the pride of her life. On the right of the garden were two old apple-trees, a Baldwin and a Porter, both yet in a tolerably good fruit-bearing state.

The delight which the two poor old souls took in their own pumpkins, their apples and currants, was indescribable. It was not merely that they contributed largely towards their living; they were their own, their private share of the great wealth of nature, the little taste set apart for them alone out of her bounty, and worth more to them on that account, though they were not conscious of it, than all the richer fruits which they received from their neighbors' gardens.

This morning the two apple-trees were brave with flowers, the currant bushes looked alive, and the pumpkin seeds were in the ground. Harriet cast complacent glances in their direction from time to time, as she painfully dug her dandelion greens. She was a short, stoutly built old woman, with a large face coarsely wrinkled, with a suspicion of a stubble of beard on the square chin.

When her tin pan was filled to her satisfaction with the sprawling, spidery greens, and she was hobbling stiffly towards her sister on the door-step, she saw another woman standing before her with a basket in her hand.

"Good-morning, Harriet," she said, in a loud, strident voice, as she drew near. "I've been frying some doughnuts, and I brought you over some warm."

"I've been tellin' her it was real good in her," piped Charlotte from the door-step, with an anxious turn of her sightless face towards the sound of her sister's footstep.

Harriet said nothing but a hoarse "Good-mornin', Mis' Simonds." Then she took the basket in her hand, lifted the towel off the top, selected a doughnut, and deliberately tasted it.

"Tough," said she. "I s'posed so. If there is anything I 'spise on this airth it's a tough doughnut."

"Oh, Harriét!" said Charlotte, with a frightened look.

"They air tough," said Harriet, with hoarse defiance, "and if there is anything I 'spise on this airth it's a tough doughnut."

The woman whose benevolence and cookery were being thus ungratefully received only laughed. She was quite fleshy, and had a round, rosy, determined face.

"Well, Harriet," said she, "I am sorry they are tough, but perhaps you had better take them out on a plate, and give me my basket. You may be able to eat two or three of them if they are tough."

"They air tough—turrible tough," said Harriet, stubbornly; but she took the basket into the house and emptied it of its contents nevertheless.

"I suppose your roof leaked as bad as ever in that heavy rain day before yesterday?" said the visitor to Harriet, with an inquiring squint towards the mossy shingles, as she was about to leave with her empty basket.

"It was turrible," replied Harriet, with crusty acquiescence— "turrible. We had to set pails an' pans everywheres, an' move the bed out."

"Mr. Upton ought to fix it."

"There ain't any fix to it; the old ruff ain't fit to nail new shingles on to; the hammerin' would bring the whole thing down on our heads," said Harriet, grimly.

"Well, I don't know as it can be fixed, it's so old. I suppose the wind comes in bad around the windows and doors too?"

"It's like livin' with a piece of paper, or mebbe a sieve, 'twixt you an' the wind an' the rain," quoth Harriet, with a jerk of her head.

"You ought to have a more comfortable home in your old age," said the visitor, thoughtfully.

"Oh, it's well enough," cried Harriet, in quick alarm, and with a complete change of tone; the woman's remark had brought an old dread over her. "The old house'll last as long as Charlotte an' me do. The rain ain't so bad, nuther is the wind; there's room enough for us in the dry places, an' out of the way of the doors an' windows. It's enough sight better than goin' on the town." Her square, defiant old face actually looked pale as she uttered the last words and stared apprehensively at the woman.

"Oh, I did not think of your doing that," she said, hastily and kindly. "We all know how you feel about that, Harriet, and not one of us neighbors will see you and Charlotte go to the poorhouse while we've got a crust of bread to share with you."

Harriet's face brightened. "Thank ye, Mis' Simonds," she said, with reluctant courtesy. "I'm much obleeged to you an' the neighbors. I think mebbe we'll be able to eat some of them doughnuts if they air tough," she added, mollifyingly, as her caller turned down the foot-path.

"My, Harriét," said Charlotte, lifting up a weakly, wondering, peaked old face, "what did you tell her them doughnuts was tough fur?"

"Charlotte, do you want everybody to look down on us, an' think we ain't no account at all, just like any beggars, 'cause they bring us in vittles?" said Harriet, with a grim glance at her sister's meek, unconscious face.

"No, Harriét," she whispered.

"Do you want *to go to the poor-house?*"

"No, Harriét." The poor little old woman on the doorstep fairly cowered before her aggressive old sister.

"Then don't hender me agin when I tell folks their doughnuts is tough an' their pertaters is poor. If I don't kinder keep up an' show some sperrit, I sha'n't think nothing of myself, an' other folks won't nuther, and fust thing we know they'll kerry us to the poorhouse. You'd 'a been there before now if it hadn't been for me, Charlotte."

Charlotte looked meekly convinced, and her sister sat down on a chair in the doorway to scrape her dandelions.

"Did you git a good mess, Harriét?" asked Charlotte, in a humble tone.

"Toler'ble."

"They'll be proper relishin' with that piece of pork Mis' Mann brought in yesterday. O Lord, Harriét, it's a chink!"

Harriet sniffed.

Her sister caught with her sensitive ear the little contemptuous sound. "I guess," she said, querulously, and with more pertinacity than she had shown in the matter of the doughnuts, "that if you was in the dark, as I am, Harriét, you wouldn't make fun an' turn up your nose at chinks. If you had seen the light streamin' in all of a sudden through some little hole 'that you hadn't known of before when you set down on the door-step this mornin', and the wind with the smell of the apple blows in it came in your face, an' when Mis' Simonds brought them hot doughnuts, an' when I thought of the pork an' greens jest now— O Lord, how it did shine in! An' it does now. If you was me, Harriét, you would know there was chinks."

Tears began starting from the sightless eyes, and streaming pitifully down the pale old cheeks.

Harriet looked at her sister, and her grim face softened.

"Why, Charlotte, hev it that thar *is* chinks if you want to. Who cares?"

"Thar *is* chinks, Harriét."

"Wa'al, thar *is* chinks, then. If I don't hurry, I sha'n't get these greens in in time for dinner."

When the two old women sat down complacently to their meal of pork and dandelion greens in their little kitchen they did not dream how destiny slowly and surely was introducing some new colors into their web of life, even when it was almost completed, and that this was one of the last meals they would eat in their old home for many a day. In about a week from that day they were established in the "Old Ladies' Home" in a neighboring city. It came about in this wise: Mrs. Simonds, the woman who had brought the gift of hot doughnuts, was a smart, energetic person, bent on doing good, and she did a great deal. To be sure, she always did it in her own way. If she chose to give hot doughnuts, she gave hot doughnuts; it made not the slightest difference to her if the recipients of her charity would infinitely have preferred ginger cookies. Still, a great many would like hot doughnuts, and she did unquestionably a great deal of good.

She had a worthy coadjutor in the person of a rich and childless elderly widow in the place. They had fairly entered into a partnership in good works, with about an equal capital on both sides, the widow furnishing the money, and Mrs. Simonds, who had much the better head of the two, furnishing the active schemes of benevolence.

The afternoon after the doughnut episode she had gone to the widow with a new project, and the result was that entrance fees had been paid, and old Harriet and Charlotte made sure of a comfortable home for the rest of their lives. The widow was hand in glove with officers of missionary boards and trustees of charitable institutions. There had been an unusual mortality among the inmates of the "Home" this spring, there were several vacancies, and the matter of the admission of Harriet and Charlotte was very quickly and easily arranged. But the matter which would have seemed the least difficult—inducing the two old women to accept the bounty which Providence, the widow, and Mrs. Simonds were ready to bestow on them—proved the most so. The struggle to persuade them to abandon their tottering old home for a better was a terrible one. The widow had pleaded with mild surprise, and Mrs. Simonds with benevolent determination; the counsel and reverend eloquence of the minister had been called in; and when they yielded at last it was with a sad grace for the recipients of a worthy charity.

It had been hard to convince them that the "Home" was not an almshouse under another name, and their yielding at length to anything short of actual force was only due probably to the plea, which was advanced most eloquently to Harriet, that Charlotte would be so much more comfortable.

The morning they came away, Charlotte cried pitifully, and trembled all over her little shrivelled body. Harriet did not cry. But when her sister had passed out the low, sagging door she turned the key in the lock, then took it out and thrust it slyly into her pocket, shaking her head to herself with an air of fierce determination.

Mrs. Simonds's husband, who was to take them to the depot, said to himself, with disloyal defiance of his wife's active charity, that it was a shame, as he helped the two distressed old souls into his light wagon, and put the poor little box, with their homely clothes in it, in behind.

Mrs. Simonds, the widow, the minister, and the gentleman from the "Home" who was to take charge of them, were all at the depot, their faces beaming with the delight of successful benevolence. But the two poor old women looked like two forlorn prisoners in their midst. It was an impressive illustration of the truth of the saying "that it is more blessed to give than to receive."

Well, Harriet and Charlotte Shattuck went to the "Old Ladies' Home" with reluctance and distress. They stayed two months, and then—they ran away.

The "Home" was comfortable, and in some respects even luxurious; but nothing suited those two unhappy, unreasonable old women.

The fare was of a finer, more delicately served variety than they had been accustomed to; those finely flavored nourishing soups for which the "Home" took great credit to itself failed to please palates used to common, coarser food.

"O Lord, Harriét, when I set down to the table here there ain't no chinks," Charlotte used to say. "If we could hev some cabbage, or some pork an' greens, how the light would stream in!"

Then they had to be more particular about their dress. They had always been tidy enough, but now it had to be something more; the widow, in the kindness of her heart, had made it possible, and the good folks in charge of the "Home," in the kindness of their hearts, tried to carry out the widow's designs.

But nothing could transform these two unpolished old women into two nice old ladies. They did not take kindly to white lace caps and delicate neckerchiefs. They liked their new black cashmere dresses well enough, but they felt as if they broke a commandment when they put them on every afternoon. They had always worn calico with long aprons at home, and they wanted to now; and they wanted to twist up their scanty gray locks into little knots at the back of their heads, and go without caps, just as they always had done.

Charlotte in a dainty white cap was pitiful, but Harriet was both pitiful and comical. They were totally at variance with their surroundings, and they felt it keenly, as people of their stamp always do. No amount of kindness and attention—and they had enough of both—sufficed to reconcile them to their new abode. Charlotte pleaded continually with her sister to go back to their old home.

"O Lord, Harriét," she would exclaim (by the way, Charlotte's "O Lord," which, as she used it, was innocent enough, had been heard with much disfavor in the "Home," and she, not knowing at all why, had been remonstrated with concerning it), "let us go home. I can't stay here no ways in this world. I don't like their vittles, an' I don't like to wear a cap; I want to go home and do different. The currants will be ripe, Harriét. O Lord, thar was almost a chink, thinking about 'em. I want some of 'em; an' the Porter apples will be gittin' ripe, an' we could have some apple-pie. This here ain't good; I want merlasses fur sweeting. Can't we get back no ways, Harriét? It ain't far, an' we could walk, an' they don't lock us in, nor nothin'. I don't want to die here; it ain't so straight up to heaven from here. O Lord, I've felt as if I was slantendicular from heaven ever since I've been here, an' it's been so awful dark. I ain't had any chinks. I want to go home, Harriét."

"We'll go to-morrow mornin'," said Harriet, finally; "we'll pack up our things an' go; we'll put on our old dresses, an' we'll do up the new ones in bundles, an' we'll jest shy out the back way to-morrow mornin'; an' we'll go. I kin find the way, an' I reckon we kin git thar, if it is fourteen mile. Mebbe somebody will give us a lift."

And they went. With a grim humor Harriet hung the new white lace caps with which she and Charlotte had been so pestered, one on each post at the head of the bedstead, so they would meet the eyes of the first person who opened the door. Then they took their bundles, stole slyly out, and were soon on the high-road, hobbling along, holding each other's hands, as jubilant as two children, and chuckling to themselves over their escape, and the probable astonishment there would be in the "Home" over it.

"O Lord, Harriét, what do you s'pose they will say to them caps?" cried Charlotte, with a gleeful cackle.

"I guess they'll see as folks ain't goin' to be made to wear caps agin their will in a free kentry," returned Harriet, with an echoing cackle, as they sped feebly and bravely along.

The "Home" stood on the very outskirts of the city, luckily for them. They would have found it a difficult undertaking to traverse the crowded streets. As it was, a short walk brought them into the free country road—free comparatively, for even here at ten o'clock in the morning there was considerable travelling to and from the city on business or pleasure.

People whom they met on the road did not stare at them as curiously as might have been expected. Harriet held her bristling chin high in air, and hobbled along with an appearance of being well aware of what she was about, that led folks to doubt their own first

opinion that there was something unusual about the two old
women.

Still their evident feebleness now and then occasioned from one
and another more particular scrutiny. When they had been on the
road a half-hour or so, a man in a covered wagon drove up behind
them. After he had passed them, he poked his head around the front
of the vehicle and looked back. Finally he stopped, and waited for
them to come up to him.

"Like a ride, ma'am?" said he, looking at once bewildered and
compassionate.

"Thankee," said Harriet, "we'd be much obleeged."

After the man had lifted the old women into the wagon, and established them on the back seat, he turned around, as he drove
slowly along, and gazed at them curiously.

"Seems to me you look pretty feeble to be walking far," said he.
"Where were you going?"

Harriet told him with an air of defiance.

"Why," he exclaimed, "it is fourteen miles out. You could never
walk it in the world. Well, I am going within three miles of there,
and I can go on a little farther as well as not. But I don't see— Have
you been in the city?"

"I have been visitin' my married darter in the city," said Harriet,
calmly.

Charlotte started, and swallowed convulsively.

Harriet had never told a deliberate falsehood before in her life,
but this seemed to her one of the tremendous exigencies of life
which justify a lie. She felt desperate. If she could not contrive to
deceive him in some way, the man might turn directly around and
carry Charlotte and her back to the "Home" and the white caps.

"I should not have thought your daughter would have let you
start for such a walk as that," said the man. "Is this lady your sister?
She is blind, isn't she? She does not look fit to walk a mile."

"Yes, she's my sister," replied Harriet, stubbornly: "an' she's
blind; an' my darter didn't want us to walk. She felt reel bad about
it. But she couldn't help it. She's poor, and her husband's dead, an'
she's got four leetle children."

Harriet recounted the hardships of her imaginary daughter with
a glibness that was astonishing. Charlotte swallowed again.

"Well," said the man, "I am glad I overtook you, for I don't
think you would ever have reached home alive."

About six miles from the city an open buggy passed them

swiftly. In it were seated the matron and one of the gentlemen in charge of the "Home." They never thought of looking into the covered wagon—and indeed one can travel in one of those vehicles, so popular in some parts of New England, with as much privacy as he could in his tomb. The two in the buggy were seriously alarmed, and anxious for the safety of the old women, who were chuckling maliciously in the wagon they soon left far behind. Harriet had watched them breathlessly until they disappeared on a curve of the road; then she whispered to Charlotte.

A little after noon the two old women crept slowly up the footpath across the field to their old home.

"The clover is up to our knees," said Harriet; "an' the sorrel and the white-weed; an' there's lots of yaller butterflies."

"O Lord, Harriét, thar's a chink, an' I do believe I saw one of them yaller butterflies go past it," cried Charlotte, trembling all over, and nodding her gray head violently.

Harriet stood on the old sunken door-step and fitted the key, which she drew triumphantly from her pocket, in the lock, while Charlotte stood waiting and shaking behind her.

Then they went in. Everything was there just as they had left it. Charlotte sank down on a chair and began to cry. Harriet hurried across to the window that looked out on the garden.

"The currants air ripe," said she; "*an'* them pumpkins hev run all over everything."

"O Lord, Harriét," sobbed Charlotte, "thar is so many chinks that they air all runnin' together!"

A New England Nun

IT WAS LATE in the afternoon, and the light was waning. There was a difference in the look of the tree shadows out in the yard. Somewhere in the distance cows were lowing and a little bell was tinkling; now and then a farm-wagon tilted by, and the dust flew; some blue-shirted laborers with shovels over their shoulders plodded past; little swarms of flies were dancing up and down before the peoples' faces in the soft air. There seemed to be a gentle stir arising over everything for the mere sake of subsidence—a very premonition of rest and hush and night.

This soft diurnal commotion was over Louisa Ellis also. She had been peacefully sewing at her sitting-room window all the afternoon. Now she quilted her needle carefully into her work, which she folded precisely, and laid in a basket with her thimble and thread and scissors. Louisa Ellis could not remember that ever in her life she had mislaid one of these little feminine appurtenances, which had become, from long use and constant association, a very part of her personality.

Louisa tied a green apron round her waist, and got out a flat straw hat with a green ribbon. Then she went into the garden with a little blue crockery bowl, to pick some currants for her tea. After the currants were picked she sat on the back door-step and stemmed them, collecting the stems carefully in her apron, and afterwards throwing them into the hen-coop. She looked sharply at the grass beside the step to see if any had fallen there.

Louisa was slow and still in her movements; it took her a long time to prepare her tea; but when ready it was set forth with as much grace as if she had been a veritable guest to her own self. The little square table stood exactly in the centre of the kitchen, and was covered with a starched linen cloth whose border pattern of flowers glistened. Louisa had a damask napkin on her tea-tray, where were arranged a cut-glass tumbler full of teaspoons, a silver cream-pitcher, a china sugar-bowl, and one pink china cup and saucer. Louisa used china every day—something which none of her neighbors did. They whispered about it among themselves. Their daily tables were laid with common crockery, their sets of best china

stayed in the parlor closet, and Louisa Ellis was no richer nor better
bred than they. Still she would use the china. She had for her supper
a glass dish full of sugared currants, a plate of little cakes, and one of
light white biscuits. Also a leaf or two of lettuce, which she cut up
daintily. Louisa was very fond of lettuce, which she raised to per-
fection in her little garden. She ate quite heartily, though in a delicate, pecking way; it seemed almost surprising that any considerable
bulk of the food should vanish.

After tea she filled a plate with nicely baked thin corn-cakes, and
carried them out into the back-yard.

"Cæsar!" she called. "Cæsar! Cæsar!"

There was a little rush, and the clank of a chain, and a large
yellow-and-white dog appeared at the door of his tiny hut, which
was half hidden among the tall grasses and flowers. Louisa patted
him and gave him the corn-cakes. Then she returned to the house
and washed the tea-things, polishing the china carefully. The twilight had deepened; the chorus of the frogs floated in at the open
window wonderfully loud and shrill, and once in a while a long
sharp drone from a tree-toad pierced it. Louisa took off her green
gingham apron, disclosing a shorter one of pink and white print.
She lighted her lamp, and sat down again with her sewing.

In about half an hour Joe Dagget came. She heard his heavy step
on the walk, and rose and took off her pink-and-white apron. Under that was still another—white linen with a little cambric edging
on the bottom; that was Louisa's company apron. She never wore it
without her calico sewing apron over it unless she had a guest. She
had barely folded the pink and white one with methodical haste and
laid it in a table-drawer when the door opened and Joe Dagget entered.

He seemed to fill up the whole room. A little yellow canary that
had been asleep in his green cage at the south window woke up and
fluttered wildly, beating his little yellow wings against the wires.
He always did so when Joe Dagget came into the room.

"Good-evening," said Louisa. She extended her hand with a kind
of solemn cordiality.

"Good-evening, Louisa," returned the man, in a loud voice.

She placed a chair for him, and they sat facing each other, with
the table between them. He sat bolt-upright, toeing out his heavy
feet squarely, glancing with a good-humored uneasiness around the
room. She sat gently erect, folding her slender hands in her white-
linen lap.

"Been a pleasant day," remarked Dagget.

"Real pleasant," Louisa assented, softly. "Have you been haying?" she asked, after a little while.

"Yes, I've been haying all day, down in the ten-acre lot. Pretty hot work."

"It must be."

"Yes, it's pretty hot work in the sun."

"Is your mother well to-day?"

"Yes, mother's pretty well."

"I suppose Lily Dyer's with her now?"

Dagget colored. "Yes, she's with her," he answered, slowly.

He was not very young, but there was a boyish look about his large face. Louisa was not quite as old as he, her face was fairer and smoother, but she gave people the impression of being older.

"I suppose she's a good deal of help to your mother," she said, further.

"I guess she is; I don't know how mother'd get along without her," said Dagget, with a sort of embarrassed warmth.

"She looks like a real capable girl. She's pretty-looking too," remarked Louisa.

"Yes, she is pretty fair looking."

Presently Dagget began fingering the books on the table. There was a square red autograph album, and a Young Lady's Gift-Book[1] which had belonged to Louisa's mother. He took them up one after the other and opened them; then laid them down again, the album on the Gift-Book.

Louisa kept eying them with mild uneasiness. Finally she rose and changed the position of the books, putting the album underneath. That was the way they had been arranged in the first place.

Dagget gave an awkward little laugh. "Now what difference did it make which book was on top?" said he.

Louisa looked at him with a deprecating smile. "I always keep them that way," murmured she.

"You do beat everything," said Dagget, trying to laugh again. His large face was flushed.

He remained about an hour longer, then rose to take leave. Going out, he stumbled over a rug, and trying to recover himself, hit Louisa's work-basket on the table, and knocked it on the floor.

He looked at Louisa, then at the rolling spools; he ducked himself awkwardly toward them, but she stopped him. "Never mind," said she; "I'll pick them up after you're gone."

She spoke with a mild stiffness. Either she was a little disturbed, or his nervousness affected her, and made her seem constrained in her effort to reassure him.

When Joe Dagget was outside he drew in the sweet evening air with a sigh, and felt much as an innocent and perfectly well-intentioned bear might after his exit from a china shop.

Louisa, on her part, felt much as the kind-hearted, long-suffering owner of the china shop might have done after the exit of the bear.

She tied on the pink, then the green apron, picked up all the scattered treasures and replaced them in her work-basket, and straightened the rug. Then she set the lamp on the floor, and began sharply examining the carpet. She even rubbed her fingers over it, and looked at them.

"He's tracked in a good deal of dust," she murmured. "I thought he must have."

Louisa got a dust-pan and brush, and swept Joe Dagget's track carefully.

If he could have known it, it would have increased his perplexity and uneasiness, although it would not have disturbed his loyalty in the least. He came twice a week to see Louisa Ellis, and every time, sitting there in her delicately sweet room, he felt as if surrounded by a hedge of lace. He was afraid to stir lest he should put a clumsy foot or hand through the fairy web, and he had always the consciousness that Louisa was watching fearfully lest he should.

Still the lace and Louisa commanded perforce his perfect respect and patience and loyalty. They were to be married in a month, after a singular courtship which had lasted for a matter of fifteen years. For fourteen out of the fifteen years the two had not once seen each other, and they had seldom exchanged letters. Joe had been all those years in Australia, where he had gone to make his fortune, and where he had stayed until he made it. He would have stayed fifty years if it had taken so long, and come home feeble and tottering, or never come home at all, to marry Louisa.

But the fortune had been made in the fourteen years, and he had come home now to marry the woman who had been patiently and unquestioningly waiting for him all that time.

Shortly after they were engaged he had announced to Louisa his determination to strike out into new fields, and secure a competency before they should be married. She had listened and assented with the sweet serenity which never failed her, not even when her lover set forth on that long and uncertain journey. Joe, buoyed up as he was by his sturdy determination, broke down a little at the last, but Louisa kissed him with a mild blush, and said good-by.

"It won't be for long," poor Joe had said, huskily; but it was for fourteen years.

In that length of time much had happened. Louisa's mother and brother had died, and she was all alone in the world. But greatest happening of all—a subtle happening which both were too simple to understand—Louisa's feet had turned into a path, smooth maybe under a calm, serene sky, but so straight and unswerving that it could only meet a check at her grave, and so narrow that there was no room for any one at her side.

Louisa's first emotion when Joe Dagget came home (he had not apprised her of his coming) was consternation, although she would not admit it to herself, and he never dreamed of it. Fifteen years ago she had been in love with him—at least she considered herself to be. Just at that time, gently acquiescing with and falling into the natural drift of girlhood, she had seen marriage ahead as a reasonable feature and a probable desirability of life. She had listened with calm docility to her mother's views upon the subject. Her mother was remarkable for her cool sense and sweet, even temperament. She talked wisely to her daughter when Joe Dagget presented himself, and Louisa accepted him with no hesitation. He was the first lover she had ever had.

She had been faithful to him all these years. She had never dreamed of the possibility of marrying any one else. Her life, especially for the last seven years, had been full of a pleasant peace, she had never felt discontented nor impatient over her lover's absence; still she had always looked forward to his return and their marriage as the inevitable conclusion of things. However, she had fallen into a way of placing it so far in the future that it was almost equal to placing it over the boundaries of another life.

When Joe came she had been expecting him, and expecting to be married for fourteen years, but she was as much surprised and taken aback as if she had never thought of it.

Joe's consternation came later. He eyed Louisa with an instant confirmation of his old admiration. She had changed but little. She still kept her pretty manner and soft grace, and was, he considered, every whit as attractive as ever. As for himself, his stent was done; he had turned his face away from fortune-seeking, and the old winds of romance whistled as loud and sweet as ever through his ears. All the song which he had been wont to hear in them was

Louisa; he had for a long time a loyal belief that he heard it still, but finally it seemed to him that although the winds sang always that one song, it had another name. But for Louisa the wind had never more than murmured; now it had gone down, and everything was still. She listened for a little while with half-wistful attention; then she turned quietly away and went to work on her wedding clothes.

Joe had made some extensive and quite magnificent alterations in his house. It was the old homestead; the newly-married couple would live there, for Joe could not desert his mother, who refused to leave her old home. So Louisa must leave hers. Every morning, rising and going about among her neat maidenly possessions, she felt as one looking her last upon the faces of dear friends. It was true that in a measure she could take them with her, but, robbed of their old environments, they would appear in such new guises that they would almost cease to be themselves. Then there were some peculiar features of her happy solitary life which she would probably be obliged to relinquish altogether. Sterner tasks than these graceful but half-needless ones would probably devolve upon her. There would be a large house to care for; there would be company to entertain; there would be Joe's rigorous and feeble old mother to wait upon; and it would be contrary to all thrifty village traditions for her to keep more than one servant. Louisa had a little still, and she used to occupy herself pleasantly in summer weather with distilling the sweet and aromatic essences from roses and peppermint and spearmint. By-and-by her still must be laid away. Her store of essences was already considerable, and there would be no time for her to distil for the mere pleasure of it. Then Joe's mother would think it foolishness; she had already hinted her opinion in the matter. Louisa dearly loved to sew a linen seam, not always for use, but for the simple, mild pleasure which she took in it. She would have been loath to confess how more than once she had ripped a seam for the mere delight of sewing it together again. Sitting at her window during long sweet afternoons, drawing her needle gently through the dainty fabric, she was peace itself. But there was small chance of such foolish comfort in the future. Joe's mother, domineering, shrewd old matron that she was even in her old age, and very likely even Joe himself, with his honest masculine rudeness, would laugh and frown down all these pretty but senseless old maiden ways.

Louisa had almost the enthusiasm of an artist over the mere order and cleanliness of her solitary home. She had throbs of genuine triumph at the sight of the window-panes which she had polished until they shone like jewels. She gloated gently over her orderly bureau-drawers, with their exquisitely folded contents redolent with lavender and sweet clover and very purity. Could she be sure of the endurance of even this? She had visions, so startling that she half repudiated them as indelicate, of coarse masculine belongings strewn about in endless litter; of dust and disorder arising necessarily from a coarse masculine presence in the midst of all this delicate harmony.

Among her forebodings of disturbance, not the least was with regard to Cæsar. Cæsar was a veritable hermit of a dog. For the greater part of his life he had dwelt in his secluded hut, shut out from the society of his kind and all innocent canine joys. Never had Cæsar since his early youth watched at a woodchuck's hole; never had he known the delights of a stray bone at a neighbor's kitchen door. And it was all on account of a sin committed when hardly out of his puppyhood. No one knew the possible depth of remorse of which this mild-visaged, altogether innocent-looking old dog might be capable; but whether or not he had encountered remorse, he had encountered a full measure of righteous retribution. Old Cæsar seldom lifted up his voice in a growl or a bark; he was fat and sleepy; there were yellow rings which looked like spectacles around his dim old eyes; but there was a neighbor who bore on his hand the imprint of several of Cæsar's sharp white youthful teeth, and for that he had lived at the end of a chain, all alone in a little hut, for fourteen years. The neighbor, who was choleric and smarting with the pain of his wound, had demanded either Cæsar's death or complete ostracism. So Louisa's brother, to whom the dog had belonged, had built him his little kennel and tied him up. It was now fourteen years since, in a flood of youthful spirits, he had inflicted that memorable bite, and with the exception of short excursions, always at the end of the chain, under the strict guardianship of his master or Louisa, the old dog had remained a close prisoner. It is doubtful if, with his limited ambition, he took much pride in the fact, but it is certain that he was possessed of considerable cheap fame. He was regarded by all the children in the village and by many adults as a very monster of ferocity. St. George's dragon[2] could hardly have surpassed in evil repute Louisa Ellis's old yellow dog. Mothers charged their children with solemn emphasis not to go too near to him, and the children listened and believed greedily, with a fascinated appetite for terror, and ran by Louisa's house

stealthily, with many sidelong and backward glances at the terrible
dog. If perchance he sounded a hoarse bark, there was a panic.
Wayfarers chancing into Louisa's yard eyed him with respect, and
inquired if the chain were stout. Cæsar at large might have seemed a
very ordinary dog, and excited no comment whatever; chained, his
reputation overshadowed him, so that he lost his own proper outlines and looked darkly vague and enormous. Joe Dagget, however,
with his good-humored sense and shrewdness, saw him as he was.
He strode valiantly up to him and patted him on the head, in spite
of Louisa's soft clamor of warning, and even attempted to set him
loose. Louisa grew so alarmed that he desisted, but kept announc-
ing his opinion in the matter quite forcibly at intervals. "There
ain't a better-natured dog in town," he would say, "and it's down-
right cruel to keep him tied up there. Some day I'm going to take
him out."

Louisa had very little hope that he would not, one of these days,
when their interests and possessions should be more completely
fused in one. She pictured to herself Cæsar on the rampage through
the quiet and unguarded village. She saw innocent children bleeding
in his path. She was herself very fond of the old dog, because he had
belonged to her dead brother, and he was always very gentle with
her; still she had great faith in his ferocity. She always warned people not to go too near him. She fed him on ascetic fare of corn-mush
and cakes, and never fired his dangerous temper with heating and
sanguinary diet of flesh and bones. Louisa looked at the old dog
munching his simple fare, and thought of her approaching marriage
and trembled. Still no anticipation of disorder and confusion in lieu
of sweet peace and harmony, no forebodings of Cæsar on the rampage, no wild fluttering of her little yellow canary, were sufficient
to turn her a hair's-breadth. Joe Dagget had been fond of her and
working for her all these years. It was not for her, whatever came to
pass, to prove untrue and break his heart. She put the exquisite little
stitches into her wedding-garments, and the time went on until it
was only a week before her wedding day. It was a Tuesday evening,
and the wedding was to be a week from Wednesday.

There was a full moon that night. About nine o'clock Louisa
strolled down the road a little way. There were harvest-fields on
either hand, bordered by low stone walls. Luxuriant clumps of
bushes grew beside the wall, and trees—wild cherry and old apple-
trees—at intervals. Presently Louisa sat down on the wall and
looked about her with mildly sorrowful reflectiveness. Tall shrubs

of blueberry and meadow-sweet, all woven together and tangled with blackberry vines and horsebriers, shut her in on either side. She had a little clear space between them. Opposite her, on the other side of the road, was a spreading tree; the moon shone between its boughs, and the leaves twinkled like silver. The road was bespread with a beautiful shifting dapple of silver and shadow; the air was full of a mysterious sweetness. "I wonder if it's wild grapes?" murmured Louisa. She sat there some time. She was just thinking of rising, when she heard footsteps and low voices, and remained quiet. It was a lonely place, and she felt a little timid. She thought she would keep still in the shadow and let the persons, whoever they might be, pass her.

But just before they reached her the voices ceased, and the footsteps. She understood that their owners had also found seats upon the stone wall. She was wondering if she could not steal away unobserved, when the voice broke the stillness. It was Joe Dagget's. She sat still and listened.

The voice was announced by a loud sigh, which was as familiar as itself. "Well," said Dagget, "you've made up your mind, then, I suppose?"

"Yes," returned another voice; "I'm going day after to-morrow."

"That's Lily Dyer," thought Louisa to herself. The voice embodied itself in her mind. She saw a girl tall and full-figured, with a firm, fair face, looking fairer and firmer in the moonlight, her strong yellow hair braided in a close knot. A girl full of a calm rustic strength and bloom, with a masterful way which might have beseemed a princess. Lily Dyer was a favorite with the village folk; she had just the qualities to arouse the admiration. She was good and handsome and smart. Louisa had often heard her praises sounded.

"Well," said Joe Dagget, "I ain't got a word to say."

"I don't know what you could say," returned Lily Dyer.

"Not a word to say," repeated Joe, drawing out the words heavily. Then there was a silence. "I ain't sorry," he began at last, "that that happened yesterday—that we kind of let on how we felt to each other. I guess it's just as well we knew. Of course I can't do anything any different. I'm going right on an' get married next week. I ain't going back on a woman that's waited for me fourteen years, an' break her heart."

"If you should jilt her to-morrow, I wouldn't have you," spoke up the girl, with sudden vehemence.

"Well, I ain't going to give you the chance," said he; "but I don't believe you would, either."

"You'd see I wouldn't. Honor's honor, an' right's right. An' I'd never think anything of any man that went against 'em for me or any other girl; you'd find that out, Joe Dagget."

"Well, you'll find out fast enough that I ain't going against 'em for you or any other girl," returned he. Their voices sounded almost as if they were angry with each other. Louisa was listening eagerly.

"I'm sorry you feel as if you must go away," said Joe, "but I don't know but it's best."

"Of course it's best. I hope you and I have got common-sense."

"Well, I suppose you're right." Suddenly Joe's voice got an undertone of tenderness. "Say, Lily," said he, "I'll get along well enough myself, but I can't bear to think— You don't suppose you're going to fret much over it?"

"I guess you'll find out I sha'n't fret much over a married man."

"Well, I hope you won't—I hope you won't, Lily. God knows I do. And—I hope—one of these days—you'll—come across somebody else—"

"I don't see any reason why I shouldn't." Suddenly her tone changed. She spoke in a sweet, clear voice, so loud that she could have been heard across the street. "No, Joe Dagget," said she, "I'll never marry any other man as long as I live. I've got good sense, an' I ain't going to break my heart nor make a fool of myself; but I'm never going to be married, you can be sure of that. I ain't that sort of a girl to feel this way twice."

Louisa heard an exclamation and a soft commotion behind the bushes; then Lily spoke again—the voice sounded as if she had risen. "This must be put a stop to," said she. "We've stayed here long enough. I'm going home."

Louisa sat there in a daze, listening to their retreating steps. After a while she got up and slunk softly home herself. The next day she did her housework methodically; that was as much a matter of course as breathing; but she did not sew on her wedding-clothes. She sat at her window and meditated. In the evening Joe came. Louisa Ellis had never known that she had any diplomacy in her, but when she came to look for it that night she found it, although meek of its kind, among her little feminine weapons. Even now she could hardly believe that she had heard aright, and that she would not do Joe a terrible injury should she break her troth-plight. She wanted to sound him without betraying too soon her own inclinations in the matter. She did it successfully, and they finally came to an understanding; but it was a difficult thing, for he was as afraid of betraying himself as she.

She never mentioned Lily Dyer. She simply said that while she had no cause of complaint against him, she had lived so long in one way that she shrank from making a change.

"Well, I never shrank, Louisa," said Dagget. "I'm going to be honest enough to say that I think maybe it's better this way; but if you'd wanted to keep on, I'd have stuck to you till my dying day. I hope you know that."

"Yes, I do," said she.

That night she and Joe parted more tenderly than they had done for a long time. Standing in the door, holding each other's hands, a last great wave of regretful memory swept over them.

"Well, this ain't the way we've thought it was all going to end, is it, Louisa?" said Joe.

She shook her head. There was a little quiver on her placid face.

"You let me know if there's ever anything I can do for you," said he. "I ain't ever going to forget you, Louisa." Then he kissed her, and went down the path.

Louisa, all alone by herself that night, wept a little, she hardly knew why; but the next morning, on waking, she felt like a queen who, after fearing lest her domain be wrested away from her, sees it firmly insured in her possession.

Now the tall weeds and grasses might cluster around Cæsar's little hermit hut, the snow might fall on its roof year in and year out, but he never would go on a rampage through the unguarded village. Now the little canary might turn itself into a peaceful yellow ball night after night, and have no need to wake and flutter with wild terror against its bars. Louisa could sew linen seams, and distil roses, and dust and polish and fold away in lavender, as long as she listed. That afternoon she sat with her needle-work at the window, and felt fairly steeped in peace. Lily Dyer, tall and erect and blooming, went past; but she felt no qualm. If Louisa Ellis had sold her birthright she did not know it, the taste of the pottage was so delicious, and had been her sole satisfaction for so long. Serenity and placid narrowness had become to her as the birthright itself. She gazed ahead through a long reach of future days strung together like pearls in a rosary, every one like the others, and all smooth and flawless and innocent, and her heart went up in thankfulness. Outside was the fervid summer afternoon; the air was filled with the sounds of the busy harvest of men and birds and bees; there were halloos, metallic clatterings, sweet calls, and long hummings. Louisa sat, prayerfully numbering her days, like an uncloistered nun.

A Poetess

THE GARDEN-PATCH at the right of the house was all a gay spangle with sweet-peas and red-flowering beans, and flanked with feathery asparagus. A woman in blue was moving about there. Another woman, in a black bonnet, stood at the front door of the house. She knocked and waited. She could not see from where she stood the blue-clad woman in the garden. The house was very close to the road, from which a tall evergreen hedge separated it, and the view to the side was in a measure cut off.

The front door was open; the woman had to reach to knock on it, as it swung into the entry. She was a small woman and quite young, with a bright alertness about her which had almost the effect of prettiness. It was to her what greenness and crispness are to a plant. She poked her little face forward, and her sharp pretty eyes took in the entry and a room at the left, of which the door stood open. The entry was small and square and unfurnished, except for a well-rubbed old card-table against the back wall. The room was full of green light from the tall hedge, and bristling with grasses and flowers and asparagus stalks.

"Betsey, you there?" called the woman. When she spoke, a yellow canary, whose cage hung beside the front door, began to chirp and twitter.

"Betsey, you there?" the woman called again. The bird's chirps came in a quick volley; then he began to trill and sing.

"She ain't there," said the woman. She turned and went out of the yard through the gap in the hedge; then she looked around. She caught sight of the blue figure in the garden. "There she is," said she.

She went around the house to the garden. She wore a gay cashmere-patterned calico dress with her mourning bonnet, and she held it carefully away from the dewy grass and vines.

The other woman did not notice her until she was close to her and said, "Good-mornin', Betsey." Then she started and turned around.

"Why, Mis' Caxton! That you?" said she.

"Yes. I've been standin' at your door for the last half-hour. I was jest goin' away when I caught sight of you out here."

In spite of her brisk speech her manner was subdued. She drew down the corners of her mouth sadly.

"I declare I'm dreadful sorry you had to stan' there so long!" said the other woman.

She set a pan partly filled with beans on the ground, wiped her hands, which were damp and green from the wet vines, on her apron, then extended her right one with a solemn and sympathetic air.

"It don't make much odds, Betsey," replied Mrs. Caxton. "I ain't got much to take up my time nowadays." She sighed heavily as she shook hands, and the other echoed her.

"We'll go right in now. I'm dreadful sorry you stood there so long," said Betsey.

"You'd better finish pickin' your beans."

"No; I wa'n't goin' to pick any more. I was jest goin' in."

"I declare, Betsey Dole, I shouldn't think you'd got enough for a cat!" said Mrs. Caxton, eying the pan.

"I've got pretty near all there is. I guess I've got more flowerin' beans than eatin' ones, anyway."

"I should think you had," said Mrs. Caxton, surveying the row of bean-poles topped with swarms of delicate red flowers. "I should think they were pretty near all flowerin' ones. Had any peas?"

"I didn't have more'n three or four messes. I guess I planted sweet-peas mostly. I don't know hardly how I happened to."

"Had any summer squash?"

"Two or three. There's some more set, if they ever get ripe. I planted some gourds. I think they look real pretty on the kitchen shelf in the winter."

"I should think you'd got a sage bed big enough for the whole town."

"Well, I have got a pretty good-sized one. I always liked them blue sage-blows. You'd better hold up your dress real careful goin' through here, Mis' Caxton, or you'll get it wet."

The two women picked their way through the dewy grass, around a corner of the hedge, and Betsey ushered her visitor into the house.

"Set right down in the rockin-chair," said she. "I'll jest carry these beans out into the kitchen."

"I should think you'd better get another pan and string 'em, or you won't get 'em done for dinner."

"Well, mebbe I will, if you'll excuse it, Mis' Caxton. The beans had ought to boil quite a while; they're pretty old."

Betsey went into the kitchen and returned with a pan and an old knife. She seated herself opposite Mrs. Caxton, and began to string and cut the beans.

"If I was in your place I shouldn't feel as if I'd got enough to boil a kettle for," said Mrs. Caxton, eying the beans. "I should 'most have thought when you didn't have any more room for a garden than you've got that you'd planted more real beans and peas instead of so many flowerin' ones. I'd rather have a good mess of green peas boiled with a piece of salt pork than all the sweet peas you could give me. I like flowers well enough, but I never set up for a butterfly, an' I want something else to live on." She looked at Betsey with pensive superiority.

Betsey was near-sighted; she had to bend low over the beans in order to string them. She was fifty years old, but she wore her streaky light hair in curls like a young girl. The curls hung over her faded cheeks and almost concealed them. Once in a while she flung them back with a childish gesture which sat strangely upon her.

"I dare say you're in the right of it," she said, meekly.

"I know I am. You folks that write poetry wouldn't have a single thing to eat growin' if they were left alone. And that brings to mind what I come for. I've been thinkin' about it ever since—our—little Willie—left us." Mrs. Caxton's manner was suddenly full of shame-faced dramatic fervor, her eyes reddened with tears.

Betsey looked up inquiringly, throwing back her curls. Her face took on unconsciously lines of grief so like the other woman's that she looked like her for the minute.

"I thought maybe," Mrs. Caxton went on, tremulously, "you'd be willin' to—write a few lines."

"Of course I will, Mis' Caxton. I'll be glad to, if I can do 'em to suit you," Betsey said, tearfully.

"I thought jest a few—lines. You could mention how—handsome he was, and good, and I never had to punish him but once in his life, and how pleased he was with his little new suit, and what a sufferer he was, and—how we hope he is at rest—in a better land."

"I'll try, Mis' Caxton, I'll try," sobbed Betsey. The two women wept together for a few minutes.

"It seems as if—I couldn't have it so sometimes," Mrs. Caxton said, brokenly. "I keep thinkin' he's in the other—room. Every time I go back home when I've been away it's like—losin' him again. Oh, it don't seem as if I could go home and not find him there—it don't, it don't! Oh, you don't know anything about it, Betsey. You never had any children!"

"I don't s'pose I do, Mis' Caxton; I don't s'pose I do."

Presently Mrs. Caxton wiped her eyes. "I've been thinkin'," said she, keeping her mouth steady with an effort, "that it would be real pretty to have—some lines printed on some sheets of white paper with a neat black border. I'd like to send some to my folks, and one to the Perkinses in Brigham, and there's a good many others I thought would value 'em."

"I'll do jest the best I can, Mis' Caxton, an' be glad to. It's little enough anybody can do at such times."

Mrs. Caxton broke out weeping again. "Oh, it's true, it's true, Betsey!" she sobbed. "Nobody can do anything, and nothin' amounts to anything—poetry or anything else—when he's *gone*. Nothin' can bring him back. Oh, what shall I do, what shall I do?"

Mrs. Caxton dried her tears again, and arose to take leave. "Well, I must be goin', or Wilson won't have any dinner," she said, with an effort at self-control.

"Well, I'll do jest the best I can with the poetry," said Betsey. "I'll write it this afternoon." She had set down her pan of beans and was standing beside Mrs. Caxton. She reached up and straightened her black bonnet, which had slipped backward.

"I've got to get a pin," said Mrs. Caxton, tearfully. "I can't keep it anywheres. It drags right off my head, the veil is so heavy."

Betsey went to the door with her visitor. "It's dreadful dusty, ain't it?" she remarked, in that sad, contemptuous tone with which one speaks of discomforts in the presence of affliction.

"Terrible," replied Mrs. Caxton. "I wouldn't wear my black dress in it nohow; a black bonnet is bad enough. This dress is 'most too good. It's enough to spoil everything. Well, I'm much obliged to you, Betsey, for bein' willin' to do that."

"I'll do jest the best I can, Mis' Caxton."

After Betsey had watched her visitor out of the yard she returned to the sitting-room and took up the pan of beans. She looked doubtfully at the handful of beans all nicely strung and cut up. "I declare I don't know what to do," said she. "Seems as if I should kind of relish these, but it's goin' to take some time to cook 'em, tendin' the fire an' everything, an' I'd ought to go to work on that poetry. Then, there's another thing, if I have 'em to-day, I can't to-morrow. Mebbe I shall take more comfort thinkin' about 'em. I guess I'll leave 'em over till to-morrow."

Betsey carried the pan of beans out into the kitchen and set them away in the pantry. She stood scrutinizing the shelves like a veritable Mother Hubbard.[1] There was a plate containing three or four potatoes and a slice of cold boiled pork, and a spoonful of red jelly in a tumbler; that was all the food in sight. Betsey stooped and lifted the lid from an earthen jar on the floor. She took out two slices of bread. "There!" said she. "I'll have this bread and that jelly this noon, an' to-night I'll have a kind of dinner-supper with them potatoes warmed up with the pork. An' then I can sit right down an' go to work on that poetry."

It was scarcely eleven o'clock, and not time for dinner. Betsey returned to the sitting-room, got an old black portfolio and pen and ink out of the chimney cupboard, and seated herself to work. She meditated, and wrote one line, then another. Now and then she read aloud what she had written with a solemn intonation. She sat there thinking and writing, and the time went on. The twelve-o'clock bell rang, but she never noticed it; she had quite forgotten the bread and jelly. The long curls drooped over her cheeks; her thin yellow hand, cramped around the pen, moved slowly and fitfully over the paper. The light in the room was dim and green, like the light in an arbor, from the tall hedge before the windows. Great plumy bunches of asparagus waved over the tops of the looking-glass; a framed sampler, a steel engraving of a female head taken from some old magazine, and sheaves of dried grasses hung on or were fastened to the walls; vases and tumblers of flowers stood on the shelf and table. The air was heavy and sweet.

Betsey in this room, bending over her portfolio, looked like the very genius of gentle, old-fashioned, sentimental poetry. It seemed as if one, given the premises of herself and the room, could easily deduce what she would write, and read without seeing those lines wherein flowers rhymed sweetly with vernal bowers, home with beyond the tomb, and heaven with even.

The summer afternoon wore on. It grew warmer and closer; the air was full of the rasping babble of insects, with the cicadas shrilling over them; now and then a team passed, and a dust cloud floated over the top of the hedge; the canary at the door chirped and trilled, and Betsey wrote poor little Willie Caxton's obituary poetry.

Tears stood in her pale blue eyes; occasionally they rolled down her cheeks, and she wiped them away. She kept her handkerchief in her lap with her portfolio. When she looked away from the paper she seemed to see two childish forms in the room—one purely human, a boy clad in his little girl petticoats, with a fair chubby face; the other in a little straight white night-gown, with long, shining wings, and the same face. Betsey had not enough imagination to change the face. Little Willie Caxton's angel was still himself to her, although decked in the paraphernalia of the resurrection.

"I s'pose I can't feel about it nor write about it anything the way I could if I'd had any children of my own an' lost 'em. I s'pose it *would* have come home to me different," Betsey murmured once, sniffing. A soft color flamed up under her curls at the thought. For a second the room seemed all aslant with white wings, and smiling with the faces of children that had never been. Betsey straightened herself as if she were trying to be dignified to her inner consciousness. "That's one trouble I've been clear of, anyhow," said she; "an' I guess I can enter into her feelin's considerable."

She glanced at a great pink shell on the shelf, and remembered how she had often given it to the dead child to play with when he had been in with his mother, and how he had put it to his ear to hear the sea.

"Dear little fellow!" she sobbed, and sat awhile with her handkerchief at her face.

Betsey wrote her poem upon backs of old letters and odd scraps of paper. She found it difficult to procure enough paper for fair copies of her poems when composed; she was forced to be very economical with the first draft. Her portfolio was piled with a loose litter of written papers when she at length arose and stretched her stiff limbs. It was near sunset; men with dinner-pails were tramping past the gate, going home from their work.

Betsey laid the portfolio on the table. "There! I've wrote sixteen verses," said she, "an' I guess I've got everything in. I guess she'll think that's enough. I can copy it off nice to-morrow. I can't see to-night to do it, anyhow."

There were red spots on Betsey's cheeks; her knees were unsteady when she walked. She went into the kitchen and made a fire, and set on the tea-kettle. "I guess I won't warm up them potatoes to-night," said she; "I'll have the bread an' jelly, an' save 'em for breakfast. Somehow I don't seem to feel so much like 'em as I did, an' fried potatoes is apt to lay heavy at night."

When the kettle boiled, Betsey drank her cup of tea and soaked her slice of bread in it; then she put away her cup and saucer and plate, and went out to water her garden. The weather was so dry and hot it had to be watered every night. Betsey had to carry the water from a neighbor's well; her own was dry. Back and forth she went in the deepening twilight, her slender body strained to one side with the heavy water-pail, until the garden-mould looked dark and wet. Then she took in the canary-bird, locked up her house, and soon her light went out. Often on these summer nights Betsey went to bed without lighting a lamp at all. There was no moon, but it was a beautiful starlight night. She lay awake nearly all night, thinking of her poem. She altered several lines in her mind.

She arose early, made herself a cup of tea, and warmed over the potatoes, then sat down to copy the poem. She wrote it out on both sides of note-paper, in a neat, cramped hand. It was the middle of the afternoon before it was finished. She had been obliged to stop work and cook the beans for dinner, although she begrudged the time. When the poem was fairly copied, she rolled it neatly and tied it with a bit of black ribbon; then she made herself ready to carry it to Mrs. Caxton's.

It was a hot afternoon. Betsey went down the street in her thinnest dress—an old delaine, with delicate bunches of faded flowers on a faded green ground. There was a narrow green belt ribbon around her long waist. She wore a green barège bonnet, stiffened with rattans, scooping over her face, with her curls pushed forward over her thin cheeks in two bunches, and she carried a small green parasol with a jointed handle. Her costume was obsolete, even in the little country village where she lived. She had worn it every summer for the last twenty years. She made no more change in her attire than the old perennials in her garden. She had no money with which to buy new clothes, and the old satisfied her. She had come to regard them as being as unalterably a part of herself as her body.

Betsey went on, setting her slim, cloth-gaitered feet daintily in the hot sand of the road. She carried her roll of poetry in a black-mitted hand. She walked rather slowly. She was not very strong; there was a limp feeling in her knees; her face, under the green shade of her bonnet, was pale and moist with the heat.

She was glad to reach Mrs. Caxton's and sit down in her parlor, damp and cool and dark as twilight, for the blinds and curtains had been drawn all day. Not a breath of the fervid out-door air had penetrated it.

"Come right in this way; it's cooler than the sittin'-room," Mrs. Caxton said; and Betsey sank into the hair-cloth rocker and waved a palm-leaf fan.

Mrs. Caxton sat close to the window in the dim light, and read the poem. She took out her handkerchief and wiped her eyes as she read. "It's beautiful, beautiful," she said, tearfully, when she had finished. "It's jest as comfortin' as it can be, and you worked that in about his new suit so nice. I feel real obliged to you, Betsey, and you shall have one of the printed ones when they're done. I'm goin' to see to it right off."

Betsey flushed and smiled. It was to her as if her poem had been approved and accepted by one of the great magazines. She had the pride and self-wonderment of recognized genius. She went home buoyantly, under the wilting sun, after her call was done. When she reached home there was no one to whom she could tell her triumph, but the hot spicy breath of the evergreen hedge and the fervent sweetness of the sweet-peas seemed to greet her like the voices of friends.

She could scarcely wait for the printed poem. Mrs. Caxton brought it, and she inspected it, neatly printed in its black border. She was quite overcome with innocent pride.

"Well, I don't know but it does read pretty well," said she.

"It's beautiful," said Mrs. Caxton, fervently. "Mr. White said he never read anything any more touchin', when I carried it to him to print. I think folks are goin' to think a good deal of havin' it. I've had two dozen printed."

It was to Betsey like a large edition of a book. She had written obituary poems before, but never one had been printed in this sumptuous fashion. "I declare I think it would look pretty framed!" said she.

"Well, I don't know but it would," said Mrs. Caxton. "Anybody might have a neat little black frame, and it would look real appropriate."

"I wonder how much it would cost?" said Betsey.

After Mrs. Caxton had gone, she sat long, staring admiringly at the poem, and speculating as to the cost of a frame. "There ain't no use; I can't have it nohow, not if it don't cost more'n a quarter of a dollar," said she.

Then she put the poem away and got her supper. Nobody knew how frugal Betsey Dole's suppers and breakfasts and dinners were. Nearly all her food in the summer came from the scanty vegetables which flourished between the flowers in her garden. She ate scarcely more than her canary-bird, and sang as assiduously. Her income was almost infinitesimal: the interest at a low per cent. of a tiny sum in the village savings-bank, the remnant of her father's little hoard after his funeral expenses had been paid. Betsey had lived upon it for twenty years, and considered herself well-to-do. She had never received a cent for her poems; she had not thought of such a thing as possible. The appearance of this last in such shape was worth more to her than its words represented in as many dollars.

Betsey kept the poem pinned on the wall under the looking-glass; if any one came in, she tried with delicate hints to call attention to it. It was two weeks after she received it that the downfall of her innocent pride came.

One afternoon Mrs. Caxton called. It was raining hard. Betsey could scarcely believe it was she when she went to the door and found her standing there.

"Why, Mis' Caxton!" said she. "Ain't you wet to your skin?"

"Yes, I guess I be, pretty near. I s'pose I hadn't ought to come 'way down here in such a soak; but I went into Sarah Rogers's a minute after dinner, and something she said made me so mad, I made up my mind I'd come down here and tell you about it if I got drowned." Mrs. Caxton was out of breath; rain-drops trickled from her hair over her face; she stood in the door and shut her umbrella with a vicious shake to scatter the water from it. "I don't know what you're goin' to do with this," said she; "it's drippin'."

"I'll take it out an' put it in the kitchen sink."

"Well, I'll take off my shawl here too, and you can hang it out in the kitchen. I spread this shawl out. I thought it would keep the rain off me some. I know one thing, I'm goin' to have a waterproof if I live."

When the two women were seated in the sitting-room, Mrs. Caxton was quiet for a moment. There was a hesitating look on her face, fresh with the moist wind, with strands of wet hair clinging to the temples.

"I don't know as I had ought to tell you," she said, doubtfully.

"Why hadn't you ought to?"

"Well, I don't care; I'm goin' to, anyhow. I think you'd ought to know, an' it ain't so bad for you as it is for me. It don't begin to be. I put considerable money into 'em. I think Mr. White was pretty high, myself."

Betsey looked scared. "What is it?" she asked, in a weak voice.

"*Sarah Rogers says that the minister told her Ida that that poetry you wrote was jest as poor as it could be, an' it was in dreadful bad taste to have it printed an' sent round that way.* What do you think of that?"

Betsey did not reply. She sat looking at Mrs. Caxton as a victim whom the first blow had not killed might look at her executioner. Her face was like a pale wedge of ice between her curls.

Mrs. Caxton went on. "Yes, she said that right to my face, word for word. An' there was something else. She said the minister said that you had never wrote anything that could be called poetry, an' it was a dreadful waste of time. I don't s'pose he thought 'twas comin' back to you. You know he goes with Ida Rogers, an' I s'pose he said it to her kind of confidential when she showed him the poetry. There! I gave Sarah Rogers one of them nice printed ones, an' she acted glad enough to have it. Bad taste! H'm! If anybody wants to say anything against that beautiful poetry, printed with that nice black border, they can. I don't care if it's the minister, or who it is. I don't care if he does write poetry himself, an' has had some printed in a magazine. Maybe his ain't quite so fine as he thinks 'tis. Maybe them magazine folks jest took his for lack of something better. I'd like to have you send that poetry there. Bad taste! I jest got right up. 'Sarah Rogers,' says I, 'I hope you won't never do anything yourself in any worse taste.' I trembled so I could hardly speak, and I made up my mind I'd come right straight over here."

Mrs. Caxton went on and on. Betsey sat listening, and saying nothing. She looked ghastly. Just before Mrs. Caxton went home she noticed it. "Why, Betsey Dole," she cried, "you look as white as a sheet. You ain't takin' it to heart as much as all that comes to, I hope. Goodness, I wish I hadn't told you!"

"I'd a good deal ruther you told me," replied Betsey, with a certain dignity. She looked at Mrs. Caxton. Her back was as stiff as if she were bound to a stake.

"Well, I thought you would," said Mrs. Caxton, uneasily; "and you're dreadful silly if you take it to heart, Betsey, that's all I've got to say. Goodness, I guess I don't, and it's full as hard on me as 'tis on you!"

Mrs. Caxton arose to go. Betsey brought her shawl and umbrella from the kitchen, and helped her off. Mrs. Caxton turned on the door-step and looked back at Betsey's white face. "Now don't go to thinkin' about it any more," said she. "I ain't goin' to. It ain't worth mindin'. Everybody knows what Sarah Rogers is. Good-by."

"Good-by, Mis' Caxton," said Betsey. She went back into the sitting-room. It was a cold rain, and the room was gloomy and chilly. She stood looking out of the window, watching the rain pelt on the hedge. The bird-cage hung at the other window. The bird watched her with his head on one side; then he begun to chirp.

Suddenly Betsey faced about and began talking. It was not as if she were talking to herself; it seemed as if she recognized some other presence in the room. "I'd like to know if it's fair," said she. "I'd like to know if you think it's fair. Had I ought to have been born with the wantin' to write poetry if I couldn't write it—had I? Had I ought to have been let to write all my life, an' not know before there wa'n't any use in it? Would it be fair if that canary-bird there, that ain't never done anything but sing, should turn out not to be singin'? Would it, I'd like to know? S'pose them sweet-peas shouldn't be smellin' the right way? I ain't been dealt with as fair as they have, I'd like to know if I have."

The bird trilled and trilled. It was as if the golden down on his throat bubbled. Betsey went across the room to a cupboard beside the chimney. On the shelves were neatly stacked newspapers and little white rolls of writing-paper. Betsey began clearing the shelves. She took out the newspapers first, got the scissors, and cut a poem neatly out of the corner of each. Then she took up the clipped poems and the white rolls in her apron, and carried them into the kitchen. She cleaned out the stove carefully, removing every trace of ashes; then she put in the papers, and set them on fire. She stood watching them as their edges curled and blackened, then leaped into flame. Her face twisted as if the fire were curling over it also. Other women might have burned their lovers' letters in agony of heart. Betsey had never had any lover, but she was burning all the love-letters that had passed between her and life. When the flames died out she got a blue china sugar-bowl from the pantry and dipped the ashes into it with one of her thin silver teaspoons; then she put on the cover and set it away in the sitting-room cupboard.

The bird, who had been silent while she was out, began chirping again. Betsey went back to the pantry and got a lump of sugar, which she stuck between the cage wires. She looked at the clock on the kitchen shelf as she went by. It was after six. "I guess I don't want any supper to-night," she muttered.

She sat down by the window again. The bird pecked at his sugar. Betsey shivered and coughed. She had coughed more or less for years. People said she had the old-fashioned consumption. She sat at the window until it was quite dark; then she went to bed in her little bedroom out of the sitting-room. She shivered so she could not hold herself upright crossing the room. She coughed a great deal in the night.

Betsey was always an early riser. She was up at five the next morning. The sun shone, but it was very cold for the season. The leaves showed white in a north wind, and the flowers looked brighter than usual, though they were bent with the rain of the day before. Betsey went out in the garden to straighten her sweet-peas.

Coming back, a neighbor passing in the street eyed her curiously. "Why, Betsey, you sick?" said she.

"No; I'm kinder chilly, that's all," replied Betsey.

But the woman went home and reported that Betsey Dole looked dreadfully, and she didn't believe she'd ever see another summer.

It was now late August. Before October it was quite generally recognized that Betsey Dole's life was nearly over. She had no relatives, and hired nurses were rare in this little village. Mrs. Caxton came voluntarily and took care of her, only going home to prepare her husband's meals. Betsey's bed was moved into the sitting-room, and the neighbors came every day to see her, and brought little delicacies. Betsey had talked very little all her life; she talked less now, and there was a reticence about her which somewhat intimidated the other women. They would look pityingly and solemnly at her, and whisper in the entry when they went out.

Betsey never complained; but she kept asking if the minister had got home. He had been called away by his mother's illness, and returned only a week before Betsey died.

He came over at once to see her. Mrs. Caxton ushered him in one afternoon.

"Here's Mr. Lang come to see you, Betsey," said she, in the tone she would have used towards a little child. She placed the rocking-chair for the minister, and was about to seat herself, when Betsey spoke:

"Would you mind goin' out in the kitchen jest a few minutes, Mis' Caxton?" said she.

Mrs. Caxton arose, and went out with an embarrassed trot. Then there was silence. The minister was a young man—a country boy who had worked his way through a country college. He was gaunt and awkward, but sturdy in his loose clothes. He had a homely, impetuous face, with a good forehead.

He looked at Betsey's gentle, wasted face, sunken in the pillow, framed by its clusters of curls; finally he began to speak in the stilted fashion, yet with a certain force by reason of his unpolished honesty, about her spiritual welfare. Betsey listened quietly; now and then she assented. She had been a church member for years. It seemed now to the young man that this elderly maiden, drawing near the end of her simple, innocent life, had indeed her lamp, which no strong winds of temptation had ever met, well trimmed and burning.

When he paused, Betsey spoke. "Will you go to the cupboard side of the chimney and bring me the blue sugar-bowl on the top shelf?" said she, feebly.

The young man stared at her a minute; then he went to the cupboard, and brought the sugar-bowl to her. He held it, and Betsey took off the lid with her weak hand. "Do you see what's in there?" said she.

"It looks like ashes."

"It's—the ashes of all—the poetry I—ever wrote."

"Why, what made you burn it, Miss Dole?"

"I found out it wa'n't worth nothin'."

The minister looked at her in a bewildered way. He began to question if she were not wandering in her mind. He did not once suspect his own connection with the matter.

Betsey fastened her eager, sunken eyes upon his face. "What I want to know is—if you'll 'tend to—havin' this—buried with me."

The minister recoiled. He thought to himself that she certainly was wandering.

"No, I ain't out of my head," said Betsey. "I know what I'm sayin'. Maybe it's queer soundin', but it's a notion I've took. If you'll—'tend to it, I shall be—much obliged. I don't know anybody else I can ask."

"Well, I'll attend to it, if you wish me to, Miss Dole," said the minister, in a serious, perplexed manner. She replaced the lid on the sugar-bowl, and left it in his hands.

"Well, I shall be much obliged if you will 'tend to it; an' now there's something else," said she.

"What is it, Miss Dole?"

She hesitated a moment. "You write poetry, don't you?"

The minister colored. "Why, yes; a little sometimes."

"It's good poetry, ain't it? They printed some in a magazine."

The minister laughed confusedly. "Well, Miss Dole. I don't know how good poetry it may be, but they did print some in a magazine."

Betsey lay looking at him. "I never wrote none that was—good," she whispered, presently; "but I've been thinkin'—if you would jest write a few—lines about me—afterward— I've been thinkin' that— mebbe my—dyin' was goin' to make me—a good subject for—poetry, if I never wrote none. If you would jest write a few lines."

The minister stood holding the sugar-bowl; he was quite pale with bewilderment and sympathy. "I'll—do the best I can, Miss Dole," he stammered.

"I'll be much obliged," said Betsey, as if the sense of grateful obligation was immortal like herself. She smiled, and the sweetness of the smile was as evident through the drawn lines of her mouth as the old red in the leaves of a withered rose. The sun was setting; a red beam flashed softly over the top of the hedge and lay along the opposite wall; then the bird in his cage began to chirp. He chirped faster and faster until he trilled into a triumphant song.

Louisa

"I DON'T SEE what kind of ideas you've got in your head, for my part." Mrs. Britton looked sharply at her daughter Louisa, but she got no response.

Louisa sat in one of the kitchen chairs close to the door. She had dropped into it when she first entered. Her hands were all brown and grimy with garden-mould; it clung to the bottom of her old dress and her coarse shoes.

Mrs. Britton, sitting opposite by the window, waited, looking at her. Suddenly Louisa's silence seemed to strike her mother's will with an electric shock; she recoiled, with an angry jerk of her head. "You don't know nothin' about it. You'd like him well enough after you was married to him," said she, as if in answer to an argument.

Louisa's face looked fairly dull; her obstinacy seemed to cast a film over it. Her eyelids were cast down; she leaned her head back against the wall.

"Sit there like a stick if you want to!" cried her mother.

Louisa got up. As she stirred, a faint earthy odor diffused itself through the room. It was like a breath from a ploughed field.

Mrs. Britton's little sallow face contracted more forcibly. "I s'pose now you're goin' back to your potater patch," said she. "Plantin' potaters out there jest like a man, for all the neighbors to see. Pretty sight, I call it."

"If they don't like it, they needn't look," returned Louisa. She spoke quite evenly. Her young back was stiff with bending over the potatoes, but she straightened it rigorously. She pulled her old hat farther over her eyes.

There was a shuffling sound outside the door and a fumble at the latch. It opened, and an old man came in, scraping his feet heavily over the threshold. He carried an old basket.

"What you got in that basket, father?" asked Mrs. Britton.

The old man looked at her. His old face had the round outlines and naïve grin of a child.

"Father, what you got in that basket?"

Louisa peered apprehensively into the basket. "Where did you get those potatoes, grandfather?" said she.

"Digged 'em." The old man's grin deepened. He chuckled hoarsely.

"Well, I'll give up if he ain't been an' dug up all them potaters you've been plantin'!" said Mrs. Britton.

"Yes, he has," said Louisa. "Oh, grandfather, didn't you know I'd jest planted those potatoes?"

The old man fastened his bleared blue eyes on her face, and still grinned.

"Didn't you know better, grandfather?" she asked again.

But the old man only chuckled. He was so old that he had come back into the mystery of childhood. His motives were hidden and inscrutable; his amalgamation with the human race was so much weaker.

"Land sakes! don't waste no more time talkin' to him," said Mrs. Britton. "You can't make out whether he knows what he's doin' or not. I've give it up. Father, you jest set them pertaters down, an' you come over here an' set down in the rockin'-chair; you've done about 'nough work to-day."

The old man shook his head with slow mutiny.

"Come right over here."

Louisa pulled at the basket of potatoes. "Let me have 'em, grandfather," said she. "I've got to have 'em."

The old man resisted. His grin disappeared, and he set his mouth. Mrs. Britton got up, with a determined air, and went over to him. She was a sickly, frail-looking woman, but the voice came firm, with deep bass tones, from her little lean throat.

"Now, father," said she, "you jest give her that basket, an' you walk across the room, and you set down in that rockin'-chair."

The old man looked down into her little, pale, wedge-shaped face. His grasp on the basket weakened. Louisa pulled it away, and pushed past out of the door, and the old man followed his daughter sullenly across the room to the rocking-chair.

The Brittons did not have a large potato field; they had only an acre of land in all. Louisa had planted two thirds of her potatoes; now she had to plant them all over again. She had gone to the house for a drink of water; her mother had detained her, and in the meantime the old man had undone her work. She began putting the cut potatoes back in the ground. She was careful and laborious about it.

A strong wind, full of moisture, was blowing from the east. The smell of the sea was in it, although this was some miles inland. Louisa's brown calico skirt blew out in it like a sail. It beat her in the face when she raised her head.

"I've got to get these in to-day somehow," she muttered. "It 'll rain to-morrow."

She worked as fast as she could, and the afternoon wore on. About five o'clock she happened to glance at the road—the potato field lay beside it—and she saw Jonathan Nye driving past with his gray horse and buggy. She turned her back to the road quickly, and listened until the rattle of the wheels died away. At six o'clock her mother looked out of the kitchen window and called her to supper.

"I'm comin' in a minute," Louisa shouted back. Then she worked faster than ever. At half-past six she went into the house, and the potatoes were all in the ground.

"Why didn't you come when I called you?" asked her mother.

"I had to get the potatoes in."

"I guess you wa'n't bound to get 'em all in to-night. It's kind of discouragin' when you work, an' get supper all ready, to have it stan' an hour, I call it. An' you've worked 'bout long enough for one day out in this damp wind, I should say."

Louisa washed her hands and face at the kitchen sink, and smoothed her hair at the little glass over it. She had wet her hair too, and made it look darker: it was quite a light brown. She brushed it in smooth straight lines back from her temples. Her whole face had a clear bright look from being exposed to the moist wind. She noticed it herself, and gave her head a little conscious turn.

When she sat down to the table her mother looked at her with admiration, which she veiled with disapproval.

"Jest look at your face," said she; "red as a beet. You'll be a pretty-lookin' sight before the summer's out, at this rate."

Louisa thought to herself that the light was not very strong, and the glass must have flattered her. She could not look as well as she had imagined. She spread some butter on her bread very sparsely. There was nothing for supper but some bread and butter and weak tea, though the old man had his dish of Indian-meal porridge. He could not eat much solid food. The porridge was covered with milk and molasses. He bent low over it, and ate large spoonfuls with loud noises. His daughter had tied a towel around his neck as she would have tied a pinafore on a child. She had also spread a towel over the tablecloth in front of him, and she watched him sharply lest he should spill his food.

"I wish I could have somethin' to eat that I could relish the way he does that porridge and molasses," said she. She had scarcely tasted anything. She sipped her weak tea laboriously.

Louisa looked across at her mother's meagre little figure in its neat old dress, at her poor small head bending over the tea-cup, showing the wide parting in the thin hair.

"Why don't you toast your bread, mother?" said she. "I'll toast it for you."

"No, I don't want it. I'd jest as soon have it this way as any. I don't want no bread, nohow. I want somethin' to relish—a herrin', or a little mite of cold meat, or somethin'. I s'pose I could eat as well as anybody if I had as much as some folks have. Mis' Mitchell was sayin' the other day that she didn't believe but what they had butcher's meat up to Mis' Nye's every day in the week. She said Jonathan he went to Wolfsborough and brought home great pieces in a market-basket every week. I guess they have everything."

Louisa was not eating much herself, but now she took another slice of bread with a resolute air. "I guess some folks would be thankful to get this," said she.

"Yes, I s'pose we'd ought to be thankful for enough to keep us alive, anybody takes so much comfort livin'," returned her mother, with a tragic bitterness that sat oddly upon her, as she was so small and feeble. Her face worked and strained under the stress of emotion; her eyes were full of tears; she sipped her tea fiercely.

"There's some sugar," said Louisa. "We might have had a little cake."

The old man caught the word. "Cake?" he mumbled, with pleased inquiry, looking up, and extending his grasping old hand.

"I guess we ain't got no sugar to waste in cake," returned Mrs. Britton. "Eat your porridge, father, an' stop teasin'. There ain't no cake."

After supper Louisa cleared away the dishes; then she put on her shawl and hat.

"Where you goin'?" asked her mother.

"Down to the store."

"What for?"

"The oil's out. There wasn't enough to fill the lamps this mornin'. I ain't had a chance to get it before."

It was nearly dark. The mist was so heavy it was almost rain. Louisa went swiftly down the road with the oil-can. It was a half-mile to the store where the few staples were kept that sufficed the simple folk in this little settlement. She was gone a half-hour. When she returned, she had besides the oil-can a package under her arm. She went into the kitchen and set them down. The old man was asleep in the rocking-chair. She heard voices in the adjoining room. She frowned, and stood still, listening.

"Louisa!" called her mother. Her voice was sweet, and higher pitched than usual. She sounded the *i* in Louisa long.

"What say?"

"Come in here after you've taken your things off."

Louisa knew that Jonathan Nye was in the sitting-room. She flung off her hat and shawl. Her old dress was damp, and had still some earth stains on it; her hair was roughened by the wind, but she would not look again in the glass; she went into the sitting-room just as she was.

"It's Mr. Nye, Louisa," said her mother, with effusion.

"Good-evenin', Mr. Nye," said Louisa.

Jonathan Nye half arose and extended his hand, but she did not notice it. She sat down peremptorily in a chair at the other side of the room. Jonathan had the one rocking-chair; Mrs. Britton's frail little body was poised anxiously on the hard rounded top of the carpet-covered lounge. She looked at Louisa's dress and hair, and her eyes were stony with disapproval, but her lips still smirked, and she kept her voice sweet. She pointed to a glass dish on the table.

"See what Mr. Nye has brought us over, Louisa," said she.

Louisa looked indifferently at the dish.

"It's honey," said her mother; "some of his own bees made it. Don't you want to get a dish an' taste of it? One of them little glass sauce dishes."

"No, I guess not," replied Louisa. "I never cared much about honey. Grandfather 'll like it."

The smile vanished momentarily from Mrs. Britton's lips, but she recovered herself. She arose and went across the room to the china closet. Her set of china dishes was on the top shelves, the lower were filled with books and papers. "I've got somethin' to show you, Mr. Nye," said she.

This was scarcely more than a hamlet, but it was incorporated, and had its town books. She brought forth a pile of them, and laid them on the table beside Jonathan Nye. "There," said she, "I thought mebbe you'd like to look at these." She opened one and pointed to the school report. This mother could not display her daughter's accomplishments to attract a suitor, for she had none. Louisa did not own a piano or organ; she could not paint; but she had taught school acceptably for eight years—ever since she was sixteen—and in every one of the town books was testimonial to that effect, intermixed with glowing eulogy. Jonathan Nye looked soberly through the books; he was a slow reader. He was a few years older than Louisa, tall and clumsy, long-featured and long-necked. His face was a deep red with embarrassment, and it contrasted oddly with his stiff dignity of demeanor.

Mrs. Britton drew a chair close to him while he read. "You see, Louisa taught that school for eight year," said she; "an' she'd be teachin' it now if Mr. Mosely's daughter hadn't grown up an' wanted somethin' to do, an' he put her in. He was committee, you know. I dun' know as I'd ought to say so, an' I wouldn't want you to repeat it, but they do say Ida Mosely don't give very good satisfaction, an' I guess she won't have no reports like these in the town books unless her father writes 'em. See this one."

Jonathan Nye pondered over the fulsome testimony to Louisa's capability, general worth, and amiability, while she sat in sulky silence at the farther corner of the room. Once in a while her mother, after a furtive glance at Jonathan, engrossed in a town book, would look at her and gesticulate fiercely for her to come over, but she did not stir. Her eyes were dull and quiet, her mouth closely shut; she looked homely. Louisa was very pretty when pleased and animated, at other times she had a look like a closed flower. One could see no prettiness in her.

Jonathan Nye read all the school reports; then he arose heavily. "They're real good," said he. He glanced at Louisa and tried to smile; his blushes deepened.

"Now don't be in a hurry," said Mrs. Britton.

"I guess I'd better be goin'; mother's alone."

"She won't be afraid; it's jest on the edge of the evenin'."

"I don't know as she will. But I guess I'd better be goin'." He looked hesitatingly at Louisa.

She arose and stood with an indifferent air.

"You'd better set down again," said Mrs. Britton.

"No; I guess I'd better be goin'." Jonathan turned towards Louisa. "Good-evenin'," said he.

"Good-evenin'."

Mrs. Britton followed him to the door. She looked back and beckoned imperiously to Louisa, but she stood still. "Now come again, do," Mrs. Britton said to the departing caller. "Run in any time; we're real lonesome evenin's. Father he sets an' sleeps in his chair, an' Louisa an' me often wish somebody 'd drop in; folks round here ain't none too neighborly. Come in any time you happen to feel like it, an' we'll both of us be glad to see you. Tell your mother I'll send home that dish to-morrer, an' we shall have a real feast off that beautiful honey."

When Mrs. Britton had fairly shut the outer door upon Jonathan Nye, she came back into the sitting-room as if her anger had a propelling power like steam upon her body.

"Now, Louisa Britton," said she, "you'd ought to be ashamed of yourself—ashamed of yourself! You've treated him like a—hog!"

"I couldn't help it."

"Couldn't help it! I guess you could treat anybody decent if you tried. I never saw such actions! I guess you needn't be afraid of him. I guess he ain't so set on you that he means to ketch you up an' run off. There's other girls in town full as good as you an' better-lookin'. Why didn't you go an' put on your other dress? Comin' into the room with that old thing on, an' your hair all in a frowse! I guess he won't want to come again."

"I hope he won't," said Louisa, under her breath. She was trembling all over.

"What say?"

"Nothin'."

"I shouldn't think you'd want to say anything, treatin' him that way, when he came over and brought all that beautiful honey! He was all dressed up, too. He had on a real nice coat—cloth jest as fine as it could be, an' it was kinder damp when he come in. Then he dressed all up to come over here this rainy night an' bring this honey." Mrs. Britton snatched the dish of honey and scudded into the kitchen with it. "Sayin' you didn't like honey after he took all that pains to bring it over!" said she. "I'd said I liked it if I'd lied up hill and down." She set the dish in the pantry. "What in creation smells so kinder strong an' smoky in here?" said she, sharply.

"I guess it's the herrin'. I got two or three down to the store."

"I'd like to know what you got herrin' for?"

"I thought maybe you'd relish 'em."

"I don't want no herrin's, now we've got this honey. But I don't

know that you've got money to throw away." She shook the old
man by the stove into partial wakefulness, and steered him into his
little bedroom off the kitchen. She herself slept in one off the
sitting-rooms; Louisa's room was up-stairs.

Louisa lighted her candle and went to bed, her mother's scolding
voice pursuing her like a wrathful spirit. She cried when she was in
bed in the dark, but she soon went to sleep. She was too healthfully
tired with her out-door work not to. All her young bones ached
with the strain of manual labor as they had ached many a time this
last year since she had lost her school.

The Brittons had been and were in sore straits. All they had in
the world was this little house with the acre of land. Louisa's meagre school money had bought their food and clothing since her father died. Now it was almost starvation for them. Louisa was
struggling to wrest a little sustenance from their stony acre of land,
toiling like a European peasant woman, sacrificing her New England dignity. Lately she had herself split up a cord of wood which
she had bought of a neighbor, paying for it in instalments with
work for his wife.

"Think of a school-teacher goin' into Mis' Mitchell's house to
help clean!" said her mother.

She, although she had been of poor, hard-working people all her
life, with the humblest surroundings, was a born aristocrat, with
that fiercest and most bigoted aristocracy which sometimes arises
from independent poverty. She had the feeling of a queen for a
princess of the blood about her school-teacher daughter; her working in a neighbor's kitchen was as galling and terrible to her. The
projected marriage with Jonathan Nye was like a royal alliance for
the good of the state. Jonathan Nye was the only eligible young
man in the place; he was the largest land-owner; he had the best
house. There were only himself and his mother; after her death the
property would all be his. Mrs. Nye was an older woman than Mrs.
Britton, who forgot her own frailty in calculating their chances of
life.

"Mis' Nye is considerable over seventy," she said often to herself; "an' then Jonathan will have it all."

She saw herself installed in that large white house as reign-
ing dowager. All the obstacle was Louisa's obstinacy, which her
mother could not understand. She could see no fault in Jonathan
Nye. So far as absolute approval went, she herself was in love with

him. There was no more sense, to her mind, in Louisa's refusing him than there would have been in a princess refusing the fairy prince and spoiling the story.

"I'd like to know what you've got against him," she said often to Louisa.

"I ain't got anything against him."

"Why don't you treat him different, then, I want to know?"

"I don't like him." Louisa said "like" shamefacedly, for she meant love, and dared not say it.

"*Like!* Well, I don't know nothin' about such likin's as some pretend to, an' I don't want to. If I see anybody is good an' worthy, I like 'em, an' that's all there is about it."

"I don't—believe that's the way you felt about—father," said Louisa, softly, her young face flushed red.

"Yes, it was. I had some common-sense about it."

And Mrs. Britton believed it. Many hard middle-aged years lay between her and her own love-time, and nothing is so changed by distance as the realities of youth. She believed herself to have been actuated by the same calm reason in marrying young John Britton, who had had fair prospects, which she thought should actuate her daughter in marrying Jonathan Nye.

Louisa got no sympathy from her, but she persisted in her refusal. She worked harder and harder. She did not spare herself in doors or out. As the summer wore on her face grew as sunburnt as a boy's, her hands were hard and brown. When she put on her white dress to go to meeting on a Sunday there was a white ring around her neck where the sun had not touched it. Above it her face and neck showed browner. Her sleeves were rather short, and there were also white rings above her brown wrists.

"You look as if you were turnin' Injun by inches," said her mother.

Louisa, when she sat in the meeting-house, tried slyly to pull her sleeves down to the brown on her wrists; she gave a little twitch to the ruffle around her neck. Then she glanced across, and Jonathan Nye was looking at her. She thrust her hands, in their short-wristed, loose cotton gloves, as far out of the sleeves as she could; her brown wrists showed conspicuously on her white lap. She had never heard of the princess who destroyed her beauty that she might not be forced to wed the man whom she did not love, but she had something of the same feeling, although she did not have it for the sake of any tangible lover. Louisa had never seen anybody whom she would have preferred to Jonathan Nye. There was no other marriageable young man in the place. She had only her dreams, which she had in common with other girls.

That Sunday evening before she went to meeting her mother took some old wide lace out of her bureau drawer. "There," said she, "I'm goin' to sew this in your neck an' sleeves before you put your dress on. It'll cover up a little; it's wider than the ruffle."

"I don't want it in," said Louisa.

"I'd like to know why not? You look like a fright. I was ashamed of you this mornin'."

Louisa thrust her arms into the white dress sleeves peremptorily. Her mother did not speak to her all the way to meeting. After meeting, Jonathan Nye walked home with them, and Louisa kept on the other side of her mother. He went into the house and stayed an hour. Mrs. Britton entertained him, while Louisa sat silent. When he had gone, she looked at her daughter as if she could have used bodily force, but she said nothing. She shot the bolt of the kitchen door noisily. Louisa lighted her candle. The old man's loud breathing sounded from his room; he had been put to bed for safety before they went to meeting; through the open windows sounded the loud murmur of the summer night, as if that, too, slept heavily.

"Good-night, mother," said Louisa, as she went up-stairs; but her mother did not answer.

The next day was very warm. This was an exceptionally hot summer. Louisa went out early; her mother would not ask her where she was going. She did not come home until noon. Her face was burning; her wet dress clung to her arms and shoulders.

"Where have you been?" asked her mother.

"Oh, I've been out in the field."

"What field?"

"Mr. Mitchell's."

"What have you been doin' out there?"

"Rakin' hay."

"Rakin' hay with the men?"

"There wasn't anybody but Mr. Mitchell and Johnny. Don't, mother!"

Mrs. Britton had turned white. She sank into a chair. "I can't stan' it nohow," she moaned. "All the daughter I've got."

"Don't, mother! I ain't done any harm. What harm is it? Why can't I rake hay as well as a man? Lots of women do such things, if nobody round here does. He's goin' to pay me right off, and we need the money. Don't, mother!" Louisa got a tumbler of water. "Here, mother, drink this."

Mrs. Britton pushed it away. Louisa stood looking anxiously at her. Lately her mother had grown thinner than ever; she looked scarcely bigger than a child. Presently she got up and went to the stove.

"Don't try to do anything, mother; let me finish getting dinner," pleaded Louisa. She tried to take the pan of biscuits out of her mother's hands, but she jerked it away.

The old man was sitting on the door-step, huddled up loosely in the sun, like an old dog.

"Come, father," Mrs. Britton called, in a dry voice, "dinner's ready—what there is of it!"

The old man shuffled in, smiling.

There was nothing for dinner but the hot biscuits and tea. The fare was daily becoming more meagre. All Louisa's little hoard of school money was gone, and her earnings were very uncertain and slender. Their chief dependence for food through the summer was their garden, but that had failed them in some respects.

One day the old man had come in radiant, with his shaking hands full of potato blossoms; his old eyes twinkled over them like a mischievous child's. Reproaches were useless; the little potato crop was sadly damaged. Lately, in spite of close watching, he had picked the squash blossoms, piling them in a yellow mass beside the kitchen door. Still, it was nearly time for the pease and beans and beets; they would keep them from starvation while they lasted.

But when they came, and Louisa could pick plenty of green food every morning, there was still a difficulty: Mrs. Britton's appetite and digestion were poor; she could not live upon a green-vegetable diet; and the old man missed his porridge, for the meal was all gone.

One morning in August he cried at the breakfast-table like a baby, because he wanted his porridge, and Mrs. Britton pushed away her own plate with a despairing gesture.

"There ain't no use," said she. "I can't eat no more garden-sauce nohow. I don't blame poor father a mite. You ain't got no feelin' at all."

"I don't know what I can do; I've worked as hard as I can," said Louisa, miserably.

"I know what you can do, and so do you."

"No, I don't, mother," returned Louisa, with alacrity. "He ain't been here for two weeks now, and I saw him with my own eyes yesterday carryin' a dish into the Moselys', and I knew 'twas honey. I think he's after Ida."

"Carryin' honey into the Moselys'? I don't believe it."

"He was; I saw him."

"Well, I don't care if he was. If you're a mind to act decent now, you can bring him round again. He was dead set on you, an' I don't believe he's changed round to that Mosely girl as quick as this."

"You don't want me to ask him to come back here, do you?"

"I want you to act decent. You can go to meetin' tonight, if you're a mind to—I sha'n't go; I ain't got strength 'nough—an' 'twouldn't hurt you none to hang back a little after meetin', and kind of edge round his way. 'Twouldn't take more'n a look."

"Mother!"

"Well, I don't care. 'Twouldn't hurt you none. It's the way more'n one girl does, whether you believe it or not. Men don't do all the courtin'—not by a long shot. 'Twon't hurt you none. You needn't look so scart."

Mrs. Britton's own face was a burning red. She looked angrily away from her daughter's honest, indignant eyes.

"I wouldn't do such a thing as that for a man I liked," said Louisa; "and I certainly sha'n't for a man I don't like."

"Then me an' your grandfather 'll starve," said her mother; "that's all there is about it. We can't neither of us stan' it much longer."

"We could—"

"Could what?"

"Put a—little mortgage on the house."

Mrs. Britton faced her daughter. She trembled in every inch of her weak frame. "Put a mortgage on this house, an' by-an'-by not have a roof to cover us! Are you crazy? I tell you what 'tis, Louisa Britton, we may starve, your grandfather an' me, an' you can follow us to the graveyard over there, but there's only one way I'll ever put a mortgage on this house. If you have Jonathan Nye, I'll ask him to take a little one to tide us along an' get your weddin' things."

"Mother, I'll tell you what I'm goin' to do."

"What?"

"I am goin' to ask Uncle Solomon."

"I guess when Solomon Mears does anythin' for us you'll know it. He never forgave your father about that wood lot, an' he's hated the whole of us ever since. When I went to his wife's funeral he never answered when I spoke to him. I guess if you go to him you'll take it out in goin'."

Louisa said nothing more. She began clearing away the breakfast dishes and setting the house to rights. Her mother was actually so weak that she could scarcely stand, and she recognized it. She had settled into the rocking-chair, and leaned her head back. Her face looked pale and sharp against the dark calico cover.

When the house was in order, Louisa stole up-stairs to her own chamber. She put on her clean old blue muslin and her hat, then she went slyly down and out the front way.

It was seven miles to her uncle Solomon Mears's, and she had made up her mind to walk them. She walked quite swiftly until the house windows were out of sight, then she slackened her pace a little. It was one of the fiercest dog-days. A damp heat settled heavily down upon the earth; the sun scalded.

At the foot of the hill Louisa passed a house where one of her girl acquaintances lived. She was going in the gate with a pan of early apples. "Hullo, Louisa," she called.

"Hullo, Vinnie."

"Where you goin'?"

"Oh, I'm goin' a little way."

"Ain't it awful hot? Say, Louisa, do you know Ida Mosely's cuttin' you out?"

"She's welcome."

The other girl, who was larger and stouter than Louisa, with a sallow, unhealthy face, looked at her curiously. "I don't see why you wouldn't have him," said she. "I should have thought you'd jumped at the chance."

"Should you if you didn't like him, I'd like to know?"

"I'd like him if he had such a nice house and as much money as Jonathan Nye," returned the other girl.

She offered Louisa some apples, and she went along the road eating them. She herself had scarcely tasted food that day.

It was about nine o'clock; she had risen early. She calculated how many hours it would take her to walk the seven miles. She walked as fast as she could to hold out. The heat seemed to increase as the sun stood higher. She had walked about three miles when she heard wheels behind her. Presently a team stopped at her side.

"Good-mornin'," said an embarrassed voice.

She looked around. It was Jonathan Nye, with his gray horse and light wagon.

"Good-mornin'," said she.

"Goin' far?"

"A little ways."

"Won't you—ride?"

"No, thank you. I guess I'd rather walk."

Jonathan Nye nodded, made an inarticulate noise in his throat, and drove on. Louisa watched the wagon bowling lightly along. The dust flew back. She took out her handkerchief and wiped her dripping face.

It was about noon when she came in sight of her uncle Solomon Mears's house in Wolfsborough. It stood far back from the road, behind a green expanse of untrodden yard. The blinds on the great square front were all closed; it looked as if everybody were away. Louisa went around to the side door. It stood wide open. There was a thin blue cloud of tobacco smoke issuing from it. Solomon Mears sat there in the large old kitchen smoking his pipe. On the table near him was an empty bowl; he had just eaten his dinner of bread and milk. He got his own dinner, for he had lived alone since his wife died. He looked at Louisa. Evidently he did not recognize her.

"How do you do, Uncle Solomon?" said Louisa.

"Oh, it's John Britton's daughter! How d'ye do?"

He took his pipe out of his mouth long enough to speak, then replaced it. His eyes, sharp under their shaggy brows, were fixed on Louisa; his broad bristling face had a look of stolid rebuff like an ox; his stout figure, in his soiled farmer dress, surged over his chair. He sat full in the doorway. Louisa standing before him, the perspiration trickling over her burning face, set forth her case with a certain dignity. This old man was her mother's nearest relative. He had property and to spare. Should she survive him, it would be hers, unless willed away. She, with her unsophisticated sense of justice, had a feeling that he ought to help her.

The old man listened. When she stopped speaking he took the pipe out of his mouth slowly, and stared gloomily past her at his hay field, where the grass was now a green stubble.

"I ain't got no money I can spare jest now," said he. "I s'pose you know your father cheated me out of consider'ble once?"

"We don't care so much about money, if you have got something you could spare to—eat. We ain't got anything but garden-stuff."

Solomon Mears still frowned past her at the hay field. Presently he arose slowly and went across the kitchen. Louisa sat down on the door-step and waited. Her uncle was gone quite a while. She, too, stared over at the field, which seemed to undulate like a lake in the hot light.

"Here's some things you can take, if you want 'em," said her uncle, at her back.

She got up quickly. He pointed grimly to the kitchen table. He was a deacon, an orthodox believer; he recognized the claims of the poor, but he gave alms as a soldier might yield up his sword. Benevolence was the result of warfare with his own conscience.

On the table lay a ham, a bag of meal, one of flour, and a basket of eggs.

"I'm afraid I can't carry 'em all," said Louisa.

"Leave what you can't then." Solomon caught up his hat and went out. He muttered something about not spending any more time as he went.

Louisa stood looking at the packages. It was utterly impossible for her to carry them all at once. She heard her uncle shout to some oxen he was turning out of the barn. She took up the bag of meal and the basket of eggs and carried them out to the gate; then she returned, got the flour and ham, and went with them to a point beyond. Then she returned for the meal and eggs, and carried them past the others. In that way she traversed the seven miles home. The heat increased. She had eaten nothing since morning but the apples that her friend had given her. Her head was swimming, but she kept on. Her resolution was as immovable under the power of the sun as a rock. Once in a while she rested for a moment under a tree, but she soon arose and went on. It was like a pilgrimage, and the Mecca at the end of the burning, desert-like road was her own maiden independence.

It was after eight o'clock when she reached home. Her mother stood in the doorway watching for her, straining her eyes in the dusk.

"For goodness sake, Louisa Britton! where have you been?" she began; but Louisa laid the meal and eggs down on the step.

"I've got to go back a little ways," she panted.

When she returned with the flour and ham, she could hardly get into the house. She laid them on the kitchen table, where her mother had put the other parcels, and sank into a chair.

"Is this the way you've brought all these things home?" asked her mother.

Louisa nodded.

"All the way from Uncle Solomon's?"

"Yes."

Her mother went to her and took her hat off. "It's a mercy if you ain't got a sunstroke," said she, with a sharp tenderness. "I've got somethin' to tell you. What do you s'pose has happened? Mr. Mosely has been here, an' he wants you to take the school again when it opens next week. He says Ida ain't very well, but I guess that ain't it. They think she's goin' to get somebody. Mis' Mitchell says so. She's been in. She says he's carryin' things over there the whole time, but she don't b'lieve there's anything settled yet. She says they feel so sure of it they're goin' to have Ida give the school up. I told her I thought Ida would make him a good wife, an' she was easier suited than some girls. What do you s'pose Mis' Mitchell says? She says old Mis' Nye told her that there was one thing about it: if Jonathan had you, he wa'n't goin' to have me an' father hitched on to him; he'd look out for that. I told Mis' Mitchell that I guess there wa'n't none of us willin' to hitch, you nor anybody else. I hope she'll tell Mis' Nye. Now I'm a-goin' to turn you out a tumbler of milk—Mis' Mitchell she brought over a whole pitcherful; says she's got more'n they can use—they ain't got no pig now—an' then you go an' lay down on the sittin'-room lounge, an' cool off; an' I'll stir up some porridge for supper, an' boil some eggs. Father'll be tickled to death. Go right in there. I'm dreadful afraid you'll be sick. I never heard of anybody doin' such a thing as you have."

Louisa drank the milk and crept into the sitting-room. It was warm and close there, so she opened the front door and sat down on the step. The twilight was deep, but there was a clear yellow glow in the west. One great star had come out in the midst of it. A dewy coolness was spreading over everything. The air was full of bird calls and children's voices. Now and then there was a shout of laughter. Louisa leaned her head against the door-post.

The house was quite near the road. Some one passed—a man carrying a basket. Louisa glanced at him, and recognized Jonathan Nye by his gait. He kept on down the road toward the Moselys', and Louisa turned again from him to her sweet, mysterious, girlish dreams.

The Revolt of "Mother"

"FATHER!"

"What is it?"

"What are them men diggin' over there in the field for?"

There was a sudden dropping and enlarging of the lower part of the old man's face, as if some heavy weight had settled therein; he shut his mouth tight, and went on harnessing the great bay mare. He hustled the collar on to her neck with a jerk.

"Father!"

The old man slapped the saddle upon the mare's back.

"Look here, father, I want to know what them men are diggin' over in the field for, an' I'm goin' to know."

"I wish you'd go into the house, mother, an' 'tend to your own affairs," the old man said then. He ran his words together, and his speech was almost as inarticulate as a growl.

But the woman understood; it was her most native tongue. "I ain't goin' into the house till you tell what them men are doin' over there in the field," said she.

Then she stood waiting. She was a small woman, short and straight-waisted like a child in her brown cotton gown. Her forehead was mild and benevolent between the smooth curves of gray hair; there were meek downward lines about her nose and mouth; but her eyes, fixed upon the old man, looked as if the meekness had been the result of her own will, never of the will of another.

They were in the barn, standing before the wide open doors. The spring air, full of the smell of growing grass and unseen blossoms, came in their faces. The deep yard in front was littered with farm wagons and piles of wood; on the edges, close to the fence and the house, the grass was a vivid green, and there were some dandelions.

The old man glanced doggedly at his wife as he tightened the last buckles on the harness. She looked as immovable to him as one of the rocks in his pasture-land, bound to the earth with generations of blackberry vines. He slapped the reins over the horse, and started forth from the barn.

"*Father!*" said she.

The old man pulled up. "What is it?"

"I want to know what them men are diggin' over there in that field for."

"They're diggin' a cellar, I s'pose, if you've got to know."

"A cellar for what?"

"A barn."

"A barn? You ain't goin' to build a barn over there where we was goin' to have a house, father?"

The old man said not another word. He hurried the horse into the farm wagon, and clattered out of the yard, jouncing as sturdily on his seat as a boy.

The woman stood a moment looking after him, then she went out of the barn across a corner of the yard to the house. The house, standing at right angles with the great barn and a long reach of sheds and out-buildings, was infinitesimal compared with them. It was scarcely as commodious for people as the little boxes under the barn eaves were for doves.

A pretty girl's face, pink and delicate as a flower, was looking out of one of the house windows. She was watching three men who were digging over in the field which bounded the yard near the road line. She turned quietly when the woman entered.

"What are they digging for, mother?" said she. "Did he tell you?"

"They're diggin' for—a cellar for a new barn."

"Oh, mother, he ain't going to build another barn?"

"That's what he says."

A boy stood before the kitchen glass combing his hair. He combed slowly and painstakingly, arranging his brown hair in a smooth hillock over his forehead. He did not seem to pay any attention to the conversation.

"Sammy, did you know father was going to build a new barn?" asked the girl.

The boy combed assiduously.

"Sammy!"

He turned, and showed a face like his father's under his smooth crest of hair. "Yes, I s'pose I did," he said, reluctantly.

"How long have you known it?" asked his mother.

" 'Bout three months, I guess."

"Why didn't you tell of it?"

"Didn't think 'twould do no good."

"I don't see what father wants another barn for," said the girl, in her sweet, slow voice. She turned again to the window, and stared

out at the digging men in the field. Her tender, sweet face was full
of a gentle distress. Her forehead was as bald and innocent as a
baby's, with the light hair strained back from it in a row of curl-
papers. She was quite large, but her soft curves did not look as if
they covered muscles.

Her mother looked sternly at the boy. "Is he goin' to buy more
cows?" said she.

The boy did not reply; he was tying his shoes.

"Sammy, I want you to tell me if he's goin' to buy more cows."

"I s'pose he is."

"How many?"

"Four, I guess."

His mother said nothing more. She went into the pantry, and
there was a clatter of dishes. The boy got his cap from a nail behind
the door, took an old arithmetic from the shelf, and started for
school. He was lightly built, but clumsy. He went out of the yard
with a curious spring in the hips, that made his loose home-made
jacket tilt up in the rear.

The girl went to the sink, and began to wash the dishes that were
piled up there. Her mother came promptly out of the pantry, and
shoved her aside. "You wipe 'em," said she; "I'll wash. There's a
good many this mornin'."

The mother plunged her hands vigorously into the water, the girl
wiped the plates slowly and dreamily. "Mother," said she, "don't
you think it's too bad father's going to build that new barn, much
as we need a decent house to live in?"

Her mother scrubbed a dish fiercely. "You ain't found out yet
we're women-folks, Nanny Penn," said she. "You ain't seen
enough of men-folks yet to. One of these days you'll find it out, an'
then you'll know that we know only what men-folks think we do,
so far as any use of it goes, an' how we'd ought to reckon men-folks
in with Providence, an' not complain of what they do any more
than we do of the weather."

"I don't care; I don't believe George is anything like that, anyhow," said Nanny. Her delicate face flushed pink, her lips pouted
softly, as if she were going to cry.

"You wait an' see. I guess George Eastman ain't no better than
other men. You hadn't ought to judge father, though. He can't help
it, 'cause he don't look at things jest the way we do. An' we've been
pretty comfortable here, after all. The roof don't leak—ain't never
but once—that's one thing. Father's kept it shingled right up."

"I do wish we had a parlor."

"I guess it won't hurt George Eastman any to come to see you in a nice clean kitchen. I guess a good many girls don't have as good a place as this. Nobody's ever heard me complain."

"I ain't complained either, mother."

"Well, I don't think you'd better, a good father an' a good home as you've got. S'pose your father made you go out an' work for your livin'? Lots of girls have to that ain't no stronger an' better able to than you be."

Sarah Penn washed the frying-pan with a conclusive air. She scrubbed the outside of it as faithfully as the inside. She was a masterly keeper of her box of a house. Her one living-room never seemed to have in it any of the dust which the friction of life with inanimate matter produces. She swept, and there seemed to be no dirt to go before the broom; she cleaned, and one could see no difference. She was like an artist so perfect that he has apparently no art. To-day she got out a mixing bowl and a board, and rolled some pies, and there was no more flour upon her than upon her daughter who was doing finer work. Nanny was to be married in the fall, and she was sewing on some white cambric and embroidery. She sewed industriously while her mother cooked, her soft milk-white hands and wrists showed whiter than her delicate work.

"We must have the stove moved out in the shed before long," said Mrs. Penn. "Talk about not havin' things, it's been a real blessin' to be able to put a stove up in that shed in hot weather. Father did one good thing when he fixed that stove-pipe out there."

Sarah Penn's face as she rolled her pies had that expression of meek vigor which might have characterized one of the New Testament saints. She was making mince-pies. Her husband, Adoniram Penn, liked them better than any other kind. She baked twice a week. Adoniram often liked a piece of pie between meals. She hurried this morning. It had been later than usual when she began, and she wanted to have a pie baked for dinner. However deep a resentment she might be forced to hold against her husband, she would never fail in sedulous attention to his wants.

Nobility of character manifests itself at loop-holes when it is not provided with large doors. Sarah Penn's showed itself to-day in flaky dishes of pastry. So she made the pies faithfully, while across the table she could see, when she glanced up from her work, the sight that rankled in her patient and steadfast soul—the digging of the cellar of the new barn in the place where Adoniram forty years ago had promised her their new house should stand.

The pies were done for dinner. Adoniram and Sammy were home a few minutes after twelve o'clock. The dinner was eaten with serious haste. There was never much conversation at the table in the Penn family. Adoniram asked a blessing, and they ate promptly, then rose up and went about their work.

Sammy went back to school, taking soft sly lopes out of the yard like a rabbit. He wanted a game of marbles before school, and feared his father would give him some chores to do. Adoniram hastened to the door and called after him, but he was out of sight.

"I don't see what you let him go for, mother," said he. "I wanted him to help me unload that wood."

Adoniram went to work out in the yard unloading wood from the wagon. Sarah put away the dinner dishes, while Nanny took down her curl-papers and changed her dress. She was going down to the store to buy some more embroidery and thread.

When Nanny was gone, Mrs. Penn went to the door. "Father!" she called.

"Well, what is it!"

"I want to see you jest a minute, father."

"I can't leave this wood nohow. I've got to git it unloaded an' go for a load of gravel afore two o'clock. Sammy had ought to helped me. You hadn't ought to let him go to school so early."

"I want to see you jest a minute."

"I tell ye I can't, nohow, mother."

"Father, you come here." Sarah Penn stood in the door like a queen; she held her head as if it bore a crown; there was that patience which makes authority royal in her voice. Adoniram went.

Mrs. Penn led the way into the kitchen, and pointed to a chair. "Sit down, father," said she; "I've got somethin' I want to say to you."

He sat down heavily; his face was quite stolid, but he looked at her with restive eyes. "Well, what is it, mother?"

"I want to know what you're buildin' that new barn for, father?"

"I ain't got nothin' to say about it."

"It can't be you think you need another barn?"

"I tell ye I ain't got nothin' to say about it, mother; an' I ain't goin' to say nothin'."

"Be you goin' to buy more cows?"

Adoniram did not reply; he shut his mouth tight.

"I know you be, as well as I want to. Now, father, look here"—
Sarah Penn had not sat down; she stood before her husband in the
humble fashion of a Scripture woman—"I'm goin' to talk real plain
to you; I never have sence I married you, but I'm goin' to now. I
ain't never complained, an' I ain't goin' to complain now, but I'm
goin' to talk plain. You see this room here, father; you look at it
well. You see there ain't no carpet on the floor, an' you see the paper is all dirty, an' droppin' off the walls. We ain't had no new paper on it for ten year, an' then I put it on myself, an' it didn't cost
but ninepence a roll. You see this room, father; it's all the one I've
had to work in an' eat in an' sit in sence we was married. There ain't
another woman in the whole town whose husband ain't got half the
means you have but what's got better. It's all the room Nanny's got
to have her company in; an' there ain't one of her mates but what's
got better, an' their fathers not so able as hers is. It's all the room
she'll have to be married in. What would you have thought, father,
if we had had our weddin' in a room no better than this? I was married in my mother's parlor, with a carpet on the floor, an' stuffed
furniture, an' a mahogany card-table. An' this is all the room my
daughter will have to be married in. Look here, father!"

Sarah Penn went across the room as though it were a tragic stage.
She flung open a door and disclosed a tiny bedroom, only large
enough for a bed and bureau, with a path between. "There, father,"
said she—"there's all the room I've had to sleep in forty year. All
my children were born there—the two that died, an' the two that's
livin'. I was sick with a fever there."

She stepped to another door and opened it. It led into the small,
ill-lighted pantry. "Here," said she, "is all the buttery[1] I've got—
every place I've got for my dishes, to set away my victuals in, an' to
keep my milk-pans in. Father, I've been takin' care of the milk of
six cows in this place, an' now you're goin' to build a new barn, an'
keep more cows, an' give me more to do in it."

She threw open another door. A narrow crooked flight of stairs
wound upward from it. "There, father," said she, "I want you to
look at the stairs that go up to them two unfinished chambers that
are all the places our son an' daughter have had to sleep in all their
lives. There ain't a prettier girl in town nor a more ladylike one than
Nanny, an' that's the place she has to sleep in. It ain't so good as
your horse's stall; it ain't so warm an' tight."

Sarah Penn went back and stood before her husband. "Now, father," said she, "I want to know if you think you're doin' right an'

accordin' to what you profess. Here, when we was married, forty year ago, you promised me faithful that we should have a new house built in that lot over in the field before the year was out. You said you had money enough, an' you wouldn't ask me to live in no such place as this. It is forty year now, an' you've been makin' more money, an' I've been savin' of it for you ever since, an' you ain't built no house yet. You've built sheds an' cow-houses an' one new barn, an' now you're goin' to build another. Father, I want to know if you think it's right. You're lodgin' your dumb beasts better than you are your own flesh an' blood. I want to know if you think it's right."

"I ain't got nothin' to say."

"You can't say nothin' without ownin' it ain't right, father. An' there's another thing—I ain't complained; I've got along forty year, an' I s'pose I should forty more, if it wa'n't for that—if we don't have another house. Nanny she can't live with us after she's married. She'll have to go somewheres else to live away from us, an' it don't seem as if I could have it so, noways, father. She wa'n't ever strong. She's got considerable color, but there wa'n't never any backbone to her. I've always took the heft of everything off her, an' she ain't fit to keep house an' do everything herself. She'll be all worn out inside of a year. Think of her doin' all the washin' an' ironin' an' bakin' with them soft white hands an' arms, an' sweepin'! I can't have it so, noways, father."

Mrs. Penn's face was burning; her mild eyes gleamed. She had pleaded her little cause like a Webster[2]; she had ranged from severity to pathos; but her opponent employed that obstinate silence which makes eloquence futile with mocking echoes. Adoniram arose clumsily.

"Father, ain't you got nothin' to say?" said Mrs. Penn.

"I've got to go off after that load of gravel. I can't stan' here talkin' all day."

"Father, won't you think it over, an' have a house built there instead of a barn?"

"I ain't got nothin' to say."

Adoniram shuffled out. Mrs. Penn went into her bedroom. When she came out, her eyes were red. She had a roll of unbleached cotton cloth. She spread it out on the kitchen table, and began cutting out some shirts for her husband. The men over in the field had a team to help them this afternoon; she could hear their halloos. She had a scanty pattern for the shirts; she had to plan and piece the sleeves.

Nanny came home with her embroidery, and sat down with her needlework. She had taken down her curl-papers, and there was a soft roll of fair hair like an aureole over her forehead; her face was as delicately fine and clear as porcelain. Suddenly she looked up, and the tender red flamed all over her face and neck. "Mother," said she.

"What say?"

"I've been thinking—I don't see how we're goin' to have any—wedding in this room. I'd be ashamed to have his folks come if we didn't have anybody else."

"Mebbe we can have some new paper before then; I can put it on. I guess you won't have no call to be ashamed of your belongin's."

"We might have the wedding in the new barn," said Nanny, with gentle pettishness. "Why, mother, what makes you look so?"

Mrs. Penn had started, and was staring at her with a curious expression. She turned again to her work, and spread out a pattern carefully on the cloth. "Nothin'," said she.

Presently Adoniram clattered out of the yard in his two-wheeled dump cart, standing as proudly upright as a Roman charioteer. Mrs. Penn opened the door and stood there a minute looking out; the halloos of the men sounded louder.

It seemed to her all through the spring months that she heard nothing but the halloos and the noises of saws and hammers. The new barn grew fast. It was a fine edifice for this little village. Men came on pleasant Sundays, in their meeting suits and clean shirt bosoms, and stood around it admiringly. Mrs. Penn did not speak of it, and Adoniram did not mention it to her, although sometimes, upon a return from inspecting it, he bore himself with injured dignity.

"It's a strange thing how your mother feels about the new barn," he said, confidentially, to Sammy one day.

Sammy only grunted after an odd fashion for a boy; he had learned it from his father.

The barn was all completed ready for use by the third week in July. Adoniram had planned to move his stock in on Wednesday; on Tuesday he received a letter which changed his plans. He came in with it early in the morning. "Sammy's been to the post-office," said he, "an' I've got a letter from Hiram." Hiram was Mrs. Penn's brother, who lived in Vermont.

"Well," said Mrs. Penn, "what does he say about the folks?"

"I guess they're all right. He says he thinks if I come up country right off there's a chance to buy jest the kind of a horse I want." He stared reflectively out of the window at the new barn.

Mrs. Penn was making pies. She went on clapping the rolling-pin into the crust, although she was very pale, and her heart beat loudly.

"I dun' know but what I'd better go," said Adoniram. "I hate to go off jest now, right in the midst of hayin', but the ten-acre lot's cut, an' I guess Rufus an' the others can git along without me three or four days. I can't get a horse round here to suit me, nohow, an' I've got to have another for all that wood-haulin' in the fall. I told Hiram to watch out, an' if he got wind of a good horse to let me know. I guess I'd better go."

"I'll get out your clean shirt an' collar," said Mrs. Penn calmly.

She laid out Adoniram's Sunday suit and his clean clothes on the bed in the little bedroom. She got his shaving-water and razor ready. At last she buttoned on his collar and fastened his black cravat.

Adoniram never wore his collar and cravat except on extra occasions. He held his head high, with a rasped dignity. When he was all ready, with his coat and hat brushed, and a lunch of pie and cheese in a paper bag, he hesitated on the threshold of the door. He looked at his wife, and his manner was defiantly apologetic. "*If* them cows come to-day, Sammy can drive 'em into the new barn," said he; "an' when they bring the hay up, they can pitch it in there."

"Well," replied Mrs. Penn.

Adoniram set his shaven face ahead and started. When he had cleared the door-step, he turned and looked back with a kind of nervous solemnity. "I shall be back by Saturday if nothin' happens," said he.

"Do be careful, father," returned his wife.

She stood in the door with Nanny at her elbow and watched him out of sight. Her eyes had a strange, doubtful expression in them; her peaceful forehead was contracted. She went in, and about her baking again. Nanny sat sewing. Her wedding-day was drawing nearer, and she was getting pale and thin with her steady sewing. Her mother kept glancing at her.

"Have you got that pain in your side this mornin'?" she asked.

"A little."

Mrs. Penn's face, as she worked, changed, her perplexed forehead smoothed, her eyes were steady, her lips firmly set. She formed a maxim for herself, although incoherently with her unlettered thoughts. "Unsolicited opportunities are the guide-posts of the Lord to the new roads of life," she repeated in effect, and she made up her mind to her course of action.

"S'posin' I *had* wrote to Hiram," she muttered once, when she was in the pantry—"s'posin' I had wrote, an' asked him if he knew of any horse? But I didn't, an' father's goin' wa'n't none of my doin'. It looks like a providence." Her voice rang out quite loud at the last.

"What you talkin' about, mother?" called Nanny.

"Nothin'."

Mrs. Penn hurried her baking; at eleven o'clock it was all done. The load of hay from the west field came slowly down the cart track, and drew up at the new barn. Mrs. Penn ran out. "Stop!" she screamed—"stop!"

The men stopped and looked; Sammy upreared from the top of the load, and stared at his mother.

"Stop!" she cried out again. "Don't you put the hay in that barn; put it in the old one."

"Why, he said to put it in here," returned one of the haymakers, wonderingly. He was a young man, a neighbor's son, whom Adoniram hired by the year to help on the farm.

"Don't you put the hay in the new barn; there's room enough in the old one, ain't there?" said Mrs. Penn.

"Room enough," returned the hired man, in his thick, rustic tones. "Didn't need the new barn, nohow, far as room's concerned. Well, I s'pose he changed his mind." He took hold of the horses' bridles.

Mrs. Penn went back to the house. Soon the kitchen windows were darkened, and a fragrance like warm honey came into the room.

Nanny laid down her work. "I thought father wanted them to put the hay into the new barn?" she said, wonderingly.

"It's all right," replied her mother.

Sammy slid down from the load of hay, and came in to see if dinner was ready.

"I ain't goin' to get a regular dinner to-day, as long as father's gone," said his mother. "I've let the fire go out. You can have some bread an' milk an' pie. I thought we could get along." She set out some bowls of milk, some bread, and a pie on the kitchen table. "You'd better eat your dinner now," said she. "You might jest as well get through with it. I want you to help me afterward."

Nanny and Sammy stared at each other. There was something strange in their mother's manner. Mrs. Penn did not eat anything herself. She went into the pantry, and they heard her moving dishes while they ate. Presently she came out with a pile of plates. She got the clothes-basket out of the shed, and packed them in it. Nanny and Sammy watched. She brought out cups and saucers, and put them in with the plates.

"What you goin' to do, mother?" inquired Nanny, in a timid voice. A sense of something unusual made her tremble, as if it were a ghost. Sammy rolled his eyes over his pie.

"You'll see what I'm goin' to do," replied Mrs. Penn. "If you're through, Nanny, I want you to go up-stairs an' pack up your things; an' I want you, Sammy, to help me take down the bed in the bedroom."

"Oh, mother, what for?" gasped Nanny.

"You'll see."

During the next few hours a feat was performed by this simple, pious New England mother which was equal in its way to Wolfe's storming of the Heights of Abraham.[3] It took no more genius and audacity of bravery for Wolfe to cheer his wondering soldiers up those steep precipices, under the sleeping eyes of the enemy, than for Sarah Penn, at the head of her children, to move all their little household goods into the new barn while her husband was away.

Nanny and Sammy followed their mother's instructions without a murmur; indeed, they were overawed. There is a certain uncanny and superhuman quality about all such purely original undertakings as their mother's was to them. Nanny went back and forth with her light loads, and Sammy tugged with sober energy.

At five o'clock in the afternoon the little house in which the Penns had lived for forty years had emptied itself into the new barn.

Every builder builds somewhat for unknown purposes, and is in a measure a prophet. The architect of Adoniram Penn's barn, while he designed it for the comfort of four-footed animals, had planned better than he knew for the comfort of humans. Sarah Penn saw at a glance its possibilities. Those great box-stalls, with quilts hung before them, would make better bedrooms than the one she had occupied for forty years, and there was a tight carriage-room. The harness-room, with its chimney and shelves, would make a kitchen of her dreams. The great middle space would make a parlor, by-and-by, fit for a palace. Up stairs there was as much room as down. With partitions and windows, what a house would there be! Sarah looked at the row of stanchions before the allotted space for cows, and reflected that she would have her front entry there.

At six o'clock the stove was up in the harness-room, the kettle was boiling, and the table set for tea. It looked almost as home-like as the abandoned house across the yard had ever done. The young hired man milked, and Sarah directed him calmly to bring the milk to the new barn. He came gaping, dropping little blots of foam from the brimming pails on the grass. Before the next morning he had spread the story of Adoniram Penn's wife moving into the new barn all over the little village. Men assembled in the store and talked it over, women with shawls over their heads scuttled into each other's houses before their work was done. Any deviation from the ordinary course of life in this quiet town was enough to stop all progress in it. Everybody paused to look at the staid, independent figure on the side track. There was a difference of opinion with regard to her. Some held her to be insane; some, of a lawless and rebellious spirit.

Friday the minister went to see her. It was in the forenoon, and she was at the barn door shelling pease for dinner. She looked up and returned his salutation with dignity, then she went on with her work. She did not invite him in. The saintly expression of her face remained fixed, but there was an angry flush over it.

The minister stood awkwardly before her, and talked. She handled the pease as if they were bullets. At last she looked up, and her eyes showed the spirit that her meek front had covered for a lifetime.

"There ain't no use talkin', Mr. Hersey," said she. "I've thought it all over an' over, an' I believe I'm doin' what's right. I've made it the subject of prayer, an' it's betwixt me an' the Lord an' Adoniram. There ain't no call for nobody else to worry about it."

"Well, of course, if you have brought it to the Lord in prayer, and feel satisfied that you are doing right, Mrs. Penn," said the minister, helplessly. His thin gray-bearded face was pathetic. He was a sickly man; his youthful confidence had cooled; he had to scourge himself up to some of his pastoral duties as relentlessly as a Catholic ascetic, and then he was prostrated by the smart.

"I think it's right jest as much as I think it was right for our forefathers to come over from the old country 'cause they didn't have what belonged to 'em," said Mrs. Penn. She arose. The barn threshold might have been Plymouth Rock from her bearing. "I don't doubt you mean well, Mr. Hersey," said she, "but there are things people hadn't ought to interfere with. I've been a member of the church for over forty year. I've got my own mind an' my own feet, an' I'm goin' to think my own thoughts an' go my own ways, an' nobody but the Lord is goin' to dictate to me unless I've a mind to have him. Won't you come in an' set down? How is Mis' Hersey?"

"She is well, I thank you," replied the minister. He added some more perplexed apologetic remarks; then he retreated.

He could expound the intricacies of every character study in the Scriptures, he was competent to grasp the Pilgrim Fathers and all historical innovators, but Sarah Penn was beyond him. He could deal with primal cases, but parallel ones worsted him. But, after all, although it was aside from his province, he wondered more how Adoniram Penn would deal with his wife than how the Lord would. Everybody shared the wonder. When Adoniram's four new cows arrived, Sarah ordered three to be put in the old barn, the other in the house shed where the cooking-stove had stood. That added to the excitement. It was whispered that all four cows were domiciled in the house.

Towards sunset on Saturday, when Adoniram was expected home, there was a knot of men in the road near the new barn. The hired man had milked, but he still hung around the premises. Sarah Penn had supper all ready. There were brown-bread and baked beans and a custard pie; it was the supper that Adoniram loved on a Saturday night. She had on a clean calico, and she bore herself imperturbably. Nanny and Sammy kept close at her heels. Their eyes were large, and Nanny was full of nervous tremors. Still there was to them more pleasant excitement than anything else. An inborn confidence in their mother over their father asserted itself.

Sammy looked out of the harness-room window. "There he is," he announced, in an awed whisper. He and Nanny peeped around the casing. Mrs. Penn kept on about her work. The children watched Adoniram leave the new horse standing in the drive while he went to the house door. It was fastened. Then he went around to the shed. That door was seldom locked, even when the family was away. The thought how her father would be confronted by the cow flashed upon Nanny. There was a hysterical sob in her throat. Adoniram emerged from the shed and stood looking about in a dazed fashion. His lips moved; he was saying something, but they could not hear what it was. The hired man was peeping around a corner of the old barn, but nobody saw him.

Adoniram took the new horse by the bridle and led him across the yard to the new barn. Nanny and Sammy slunk close to their mother. The barn doors rolled back, and there stood Adoniram, with the long mild face of the great Canadian farm horse looking over his shoulder.

Nanny kept behind her mother, but Sammy stepped suddenly forward, and stood in front of her.

Adoniram stared at the group. "What on airth you all down here for?" said he. "What's the matter over to the house?"

"We've come here to live, father," said Sammy. His shrill voice quavered out bravely.

"What"—Adoniram sniffed—"what is it smells like cookin?" said he. He stepped forward and looked in the open door of the harness-room. Then he turned to his wife. His old bristling face was pale and frightened. "What on airth does this mean, mother?" he gasped.

"You come in here, father," said Sarah. She led the way into the harness-room and shut the door. "Now, father," said she, "you needn't be scared. I ain't crazy. There ain't nothin' to be upset over. But we've come here to live, an' we're goin' to live here. We've got jest as good a right here as new horses an' cows. The house wa'n't fit for us to live in any longer, an' I made up my mind I wa'n't goin' to stay there. I've done my duty by you forty year, an' I'm goin' to do it now; but I'm goin' to live here. You've got to put in some windows and partitions; an' you'll have to buy some furniture."

"Why, mother!" the old man gasped.

"You'd better take your coat off an' get washed—there's the wash-basin—an' then we'll have supper."

"Why, mother!"

Sammy went past the window, leading the new horse to the old barn. The old man saw him, and shook his head speechlessly. He tried to take off his coat, but his arms seemed to lack the power. His wife helped him. She poured some water into the tin basin, and put in a piece of soap. She got the comb and brush, and smoothed his thin gray hair after he had washed. Then she put the beans, hot bread, and tea on the table. Sammy came in, and the family drew up. Adoniram sat looking dazedly at his plate, and they waited.

"Ain't you goin' to ask a blessin', father?" said Sarah.

And the old man bent his head and mumbled.

All through the meal he stopped eating at intervals, and stared furtively at his wife; but he ate well. The home food tasted good to him, and his old frame was too sturdily healthy to be affected by his mind. But after supper he went out, and sat down on the step of the smaller door at the right of the barn, through which he had meant his Jerseys to pass in stately file, but which Sarah designed for her front house door, and he leaned his head on his hands.

After the supper dishes were cleared away and the milk-pans washed, Sarah went out to him. The twilight was deepening. There was a clear green glow in the sky. Before them stretched the smooth level of field; in the distance was a cluster of hay-stacks like the huts of a village; the air was very cool and calm and sweet. The landscape might have been an ideal one of peace.

Sarah bent over and touched her husband on one of his thin, sinewy shoulders. "Father!"

The old man's shoulders heaved: he was weeping.

"Why, don't do so, father," said Sarah.

"I'll—put up the—partitions, an'—everything you—want, mother."

Sarah put her apron up to her face; she was overcome by her own triumph.

Adoniram was like a fortress whose walls had no active resistance, and went down the instant the right besieging tools were used. "Why, mother," he said, hoarsely, "I hadn't no idee you was so set on't as all this comes to."

The Jamesons

I

THEY ARRIVE

UNTIL THAT SUMMER nobody in our village had ever taken boarders. There had been no real necessity for it, and we had always been rather proud of the fact. While we were certainly not rich—there was not one positively rich family among us—we were comfortably provided with all the necessities of life. We did not need to open our houses, and our closets, and our bureau drawers, and give the freedom of our domestic hearths, and, as it were, our household gods for playthings, to strangers and their children.

Many of us had to work for our daily bread, but, we were thankful to say, not in that way. We prided ourselves because there was no summer hotel with a demoralizing bowling-alley, and one of those dangerous chutes, in our village. We felt forbiddingly calm and superior when now and then some strange city people from Grover, the large summer resort six miles from us, travelled up and down our main street seeking board in vain. We plumed ourselves upon our reputation of not taking boarders for love or money.

Nobody had dreamed that there was to be a break at last in our long-established custom, and nobody dreamed that the break was to be made in such a quarter. One of the most well-to-do, if not the most well-to-do, of us all, took the first boarders ever taken in Linnville. When Amelia Powers heard of it she said, "Them that has, gits."

On the afternoon of the first day of June, six years ago, I was sewing at my sitting-room window. I was making a white muslin dress for little Alice, my niece, to wear to the Seventeenth-of-June picnic. I had been sitting there alone all the afternoon, and it was almost four o'clock when I saw Amelia Powers, who lives opposite, and who had been sewing at her window—I had noticed her arm moving back and forth, disturbing the shadows of the horse-chestnut tree in the yard—fling open her front door, run out on the piazza, and stand peering around the corner post, with her neck so stretched that it looked twice as long as before. Then her sister

Candace, who has poor health and seldom ventures out-of-doors, threw up the front chamber window and leaned out as far as she was able, and stared with her hand shading her eyes from the sun. I could just see her head through an opening in the horse-chestnut branches.

Then I heard another door open, and Mrs. Peter Jones, who lives in the house next below the Powers', came running out. She ran down the walk to her front gate and leaned over, all twisted sideways, to see.

Then I heard voices, and there were Adeline Ketchum and her mother coming down the street, all in a flutter of hurry. Adeline is slender and nervous; her elbows jerked out, her chin jerked up, and her skirts switched her thin ankles; Mrs. Ketchum is very stout, and she walked with a kind of quivering flounce. Her face was blazing, and I knew her bonnet was on hindside before—I was sure that the sprig of purple flowers belonged on the front.

When Adeline and her mother reached Mrs. Peter Jones' gate they stopped, and they all stood there together looking. Then I saw Tommy Gregg racing along, and I felt positive that his mother had sent him to see what the matter was. She is a good woman, but the most curious person in our village. She never seems to have enough affairs of her own to thoroughly amuse her. I never saw a boy run as fast as Tommy did—as if his mother's curiosity and his own were a sort of motor compelling him to his utmost speed. His legs seemed never to come out of their running crooks, and his shock of hair was fairly stiffened out behind with the wind.

Then I began to wonder if it were possible there was a fire anywhere. I ran to my front door and called:

"Tommy! Tommy!" said I, "where is the fire?"

Tommy did not hear me, but all of a sudden the fire-bell began to ring.

Then I ran across the street to Mrs. Peter Jones' gate, and Amelia Powers came hurrying out of her yard.

"Where is it? Oh, where is it?" said she, and Candace put her head out of the window and called out, "Where is it? Is it near here?"

We all sniffed for smoke and strained our eyes for a red fire glare on the horizon, but we could neither smell nor see anything unusual.

Pretty soon we heard the fire-engine coming, and Amelia Powers cried out: "Oh, it's going to Mrs. Liscom's! It's her house! It's Mrs. Liscom's house!"

Candace Powers put her head farther out of the window, and screamed in a queer voice that echoed like a parrot's, "Oh, 'Melia! 'Melia! it's Mrs. Liscom's, it's Mrs. Liscom's, and the wind's this way! Come, quick, and help me get out the best feather bed, and the counterpane that mother knit! Quick! Quick!"

Amelia had to run in and quiet Candace, who was very apt to have a bad spell when she was over-excited, and the rest of us started for the fire.

As we hurried down the street I asked Mrs. Jones how she had known there was a fire in the first place, for I supposed that was why she had run out to her front door and looked down the street. Then I learned about the city boarders. She and Amelia, from the way they faced at their sitting-room windows, had seen the Grover stage-coach stop at Mrs. Liscom's, and had run out to see the boarders alight. Mrs. Jones said there were five of them—the mother, grandmother, two daughters, and a son.

I said that I did not know Mrs. Liscom was going to take boarders; I was very much surprised.

"I suppose she thought she would earn some money and have some extra things," said Mrs. Jones.

"It must have been that," said Mrs. Ketchum, panting—she was almost out of breath—"for, of course, the Liscoms don't need the money."

I laughed and said I thought not. I felt a little pride about it, because Mrs. Liscom was a second cousin of my husband, and he used to think a great deal of her.

"They must own that nice place clear, if it ain't going to burn to the ground, and have something in the bank besides," assented Mrs. Peter Jones.

Ever so many people were running down the street with us, and the air seemed full of that brazen clang of the fire-bell; still we could not see any fire, nor even smell any smoke, until we got to the head of the lane where the Liscom house stands a few rods from the main street.

The lane was about choked up with the fire-engine, the hose-cart, the fire department in their red shirts, and, I should think, half the village. We climbed over the stone wall into Mrs. Liscom's oat-field; it was hard work for Mrs. Ketchum, but Mrs. Jones and I pushed and Adeline pulled, and then we ran along close to the wall toward the house. We certainly began to smell smoke, though we still could not see any fire. The firemen were racing in and out of the house, bringing out the furniture, as were some of the village boys, and the engine was playing upon the south end, where the kitchen is.

Mrs. Peter Jones, who is very small and alert, said suddenly that it looked to her as if the smoke were coming out of the kitchen chimney, but Mrs. Ketchum said of course it was on fire inside in the woodwork. "Oh, only to think of Mrs. Liscom's nice house being all burned up, and what a dreadful reception for those boarders!" she groaned out.

I never saw such a hubbub, and apparently over nothing at all, as there was. There was a steady yell of fire from a crowd of boys who seemed to enjoy it; the water was swishing, the firemen's arms were pumping in unison, and everybody generally running in aimless circles like a swarm of ants. Then we saw the boarders coming out. "Oh, the house must be all in a light blaze inside!" groaned Mrs. Ketchum.

There were five of the boarders. The mother, a large, fair woman with a long, massive face, her reddish hair crinkling and curling around it in a sort of ivy-tendril fashion, came first. Her two daughters, in blue gowns, with pretty, agitated faces, followed; then the young son, fairly teetering with excitement; then the grandmother, a little, tremulous old lady in an auburn wig.

The woman at the head carried a bucket, and what should she do but form her family into a line toward the well at the north side of the house where we were!

Of course, the family did not nearly reach to the well, and she beckoned to us imperatively. "Come immediately!" said she; "if the men of this village have no head in an emergency like this, let the women arise! Come immediately."

So Mrs. Peter Jones, Mrs. Ketchum, Adeline, and I stepped into the line, and the mother boarder filled the bucket at the well, and we passed it back from hand to hand, and the boy at the end flung it into Mrs. Liscom's front entry all over her nice carpet.

Then suddenly we saw Caroline Liscom appear. She snatched the bucket out of the hands of the boy boarder and gave it a toss into the lilac-bush beside the door; then she stood there, looking as I had never seen her look before. Caroline Liscom has always had the reputation of being a woman of a strong character; she is manifestly the head of her family. It is always, "Mrs. Liscom's house," and "Mrs. Liscom's property," instead of Mr. Liscom's.

It is always understood that, though Mr. Liscom is the nominal voter in town matters, not a selectman goes into office with Mr. Liscom's vote unless it is authorized by Mrs. Liscom. Mr. Liscom is, so to speak, seldom taken without Mrs. Liscom's indorsement.

Of course, Mrs. Liscom being such a character has always more or less authority in her bearing, but that day she displayed a real majesty which I had never seen in her before. She stood there a second, then she turned and made a backward and forward motion of her arm as if she were sweeping, and directly red-shirted firemen and boys began to fly out of the house as if impelled by it.

"You just get out of my house; every one of you!" said Caroline in a loud but slow voice, as if she were so angry that she was fairly reining herself in; and they got out. Then she called to the firemen who were working the engine, and they heard her above all the uproar.

"You stop drenching my house with water, and go home!" said she.

Everybody began to hush and stare, but Tommy Gregg gave one squeaking cry of fire as if in defiance.

"There is no fire," said Caroline Liscom. "My house is not on fire, and has not been on fire. I am getting tea, and the kitchen chimney always smokes when the wind is west. I don't thank you, any of you, for coming here and turning my house upside down and drenching it with water, and lugging my furniture out-of-doors. Now you can go home. I don't see what fool ever sent you here!"

The engine stopped playing, and you could hear the water dripping off the south end of the house. The windows were streaming as if there had been a shower. Everybody looked abashed, and the chief engineer of the fire department—who is a little nervous man who always works as if the river were on fire and he had started it—asked meekly if they shouldn't bring the furniture back.

"No," said Caroline Liscom, "I want you to go home, and that is all I do want of you."

Then the mother boarder spoke—she was evidently not easily put down. "I refuse to return to the house or to allow my family to do so unless I am officially notified by the fire department that the fire is extinguished," said she.

"Then you can stay out-of-doors," said Caroline Liscom, and we all gasped to hear her, though we secretly admired her for it.

The boarder glared at her in a curious kind of way, like a broadside of stoniness, but Caroline did not seem to mind it at all. Then the boarder changed her tactics like a general on the verge of defeat. She sidled up to Mr. Spear, the chief engineer, who was giving orders to drag home the engine, and said in an unexpectedly sweet voice, like a trickle of honey off the face of a rock: "My good man, am I to understand that I need apprehend no further danger from fire! I ask for the sake of my precious family."

Mr. Spear looked at her as if she had spoken to him in Choctaw,[1] and she was obliged to ask him over again. "My good man," said she, "*is* the fire out?"

Mr. Spear looked at her as if he were half daft then, but he answered: "Yes, ma'am, yes, ma'am, certainly, ma'am, no danger at all, ma'am." Then he went on ordering the men: "A leetle more to the right, boys! All together!"

"Thank you, my good man, your word is sufficient," said the boarder, though Mr. Spear did not seem to hear her.

Then she sailed into the house, and her son, her two daughters, and the grandmother after her. Mrs. Peter Jones and Adeline and her mother went home, but I ventured, since I was a sort of relation, to go in and offer to help Caroline set things to rights. She thanked me, and said that she did not want any help; when Jacob and Harry came home they would set the furniture in out of the yard.

"I am sorry for you, Caroline," said I.

"Look at my house, Sophia Lane," said she, and that was all she would say. She shut her mouth tight over that. That house was enough to make a strong-minded woman like Caroline dumb, and send a weak one into hysterics. It was dripping with water, and nearly all the furniture out in the yard piled up pell-mell. I could not see how she was going to get supper for the boarders: the kitchen fire was out and the stove drenched, with a panful of biscuits in the oven.

"What are you going to give them for supper, Caroline?" said I, and she just shook her head. I knew that those boarders would have to take what they could get, or go without.

When Caroline was in any difficulty there never was any help for her, except from the working of circumstances to their own salvation. I thought I might as well go home. I offered to give her some pie or cake if hers were spoiled, but she only shook her head again, and I knew she must have some stored away in the parlor china-closet, where the water had not penetrated.

I went through the house to the front entry, thinking I would go out the front door—the side one was dripping as if it were under a waterfall. Just as I reached it I heard a die-away voice from the front chamber say, "My good woman."

I did not dream that I was addressed, never having been called by that name, though always having hoped that I was a good woman.

So I kept right on. Then I heard a despairing sigh, and the voice said, "You speak to her, Harriet."

Then I heard another voice, very sweet and a little timid, "Will you please step upstairs? Mamma wishes to speak to you."

I began to wonder if they were talking to me. I looked up, and there discovered a pretty, innocent, rosy little face, peering over the balustrade at the head of the stairs. "Will you please step upstairs?" said she again, in the same sweet tones. "Mamma wishes to speak to you."

I have a little weakness of the heart, and do not like to climb stairs more than I am positively obliged to; it always puts me so out of breath. I sleep downstairs on that account. I looked at Caroline's front stairs, which are rather steep, with some hesitation. I felt shaken, too, on account of the alarm of fire. Then I heard the first voice again with a sort of languishing authority: "My good woman, will you be so kind as to step upstairs immediately?"

I went upstairs. The girl who had spoken to me—I found afterward that she was the elder of the daughters—motioned me to go into the north chamber. I found them all there. The mother, Mrs. H. Boardman Jameson, as I afterward knew her name to be, was lying on the bed, her head propped high with pillows; the younger daughter was fanning her, and she was panting softly as if she were almost exhausted. The grandmother sat beside the north window, with a paper-covered book on her knees. She was eating something from a little white box on the window-sill. The boy was at another window, also with a book in which he did not seem to be interested. He looked up at me, as I entered, with a most peculiar expression of mingled innocence and shyness which was almost terror. I could not see why the boy should possibly be afraid of me, but I learned afterward that it was either his natural attitude or natural expression. He was either afraid of every mortal thing or else appeared to be. The singular elevated arch of his eyebrows over his wide-open blue eyes, and his mouth, which was always parted a little, no doubt served to give this impression. He was a pretty boy, with a fair pink-and-white complexion, and long hair curled like a girl's, which looked odd to me, for he was quite large.

Mrs. Jameson beckoned me up to the bed with one languid finger, as if she could not possibly do more. I began to think that perhaps she had some trouble with her heart like myself, and the fire had overcome her, and I felt very sympathetic.

"I am sorry you have had such an unpleasant experience," I began, but she cut me short.

"My good woman," said she in little more than a whisper, "do you know of any house in a sanitary location where we can obtain board immediately? I am very particular about the location. There must be no standing water near the house, there must not be trees near on account of the dampness, the neighbors must not keep hens—of course, the people of the house must not keep hens—and the woman must have an even temper. I must particularly insist upon an even temper. My nerves are exceedingly weak; I cannot endure such a rasping manner as that which I have encountered to-day."

When she stopped and looked at me for an answer I was so astonished that I did not know what to say. There she was, just arrived; had not eaten one meal in the house, and wanting to find another boarding-place.

Finally I said, rather stupidly I suppose, that I doubted if she could find another boarding-place in our village as good as the one which she already had.

She gave another sigh, as if of the most determined patience. "Have I not already told you, my good woman," said she, "that I cannot endure such a rasping manner and voice as that of the woman of the house? It is most imperative that I have another boarding-place at once."

She said this in a manner which nettled me a little, as if I had boarding-places, for which she had paid liberally and had a right to demand, in my hand, and was withholding them from her. I replied that I knew of no other boarding-place of any kind whatsoever in the village. Then she looked at me in what I suppose was meant to be an ingratiating way.

"My good woman," said she, "you look very neat and tidy yourself, and I don't doubt are a good plain cook; I am willing to try your house if it is not surrounded by trees and there is no standing water near; I do not object to running water."

In the midst of this speech the elder daughter had said in a frightened way, "Oh, mamma!" but her mother had paid no attention. As for myself, I was angry. The memory of my two years at Wardville Young Ladies' Seminary in my youth and my frugally independent life as wife and widow was strong upon me. I had read and improved my mind. I was a prominent member of the Ladies' Literary Society of our village: I wrote papers which were read at the meetings; I felt, in reality, not one whit below Mrs. H. Boardman Jameson, and, moreover, large sleeves were the fashion, and my sleeves were every bit as large as hers, though she had just come from the city. That added to my conviction of my own importance.

"Madam," said I, "I do not take boarders. I have never taken boarders, and I never shall take boarders." Then I turned and went out of the room, and downstairs, with, it seemed to me, much dignity.

However, Mrs. Jameson was not impressed by it, for she called after me: "My good woman, will you please tell Mrs. Liscom that I must have some hot water to make my health food with immediately? Tell her to send up a pitcher at once, very hot."

I did not tell Caroline about the hot water. I left that for them to manage themselves. I did not care to mention hot water with Caroline's stove as wet as if it had been dipped in the pond, even if I had not been too indignant at the persistent ignoring of my own dignity. I went home and found Louisa Field, my brother's widow, and her little daughter Alice, who live with me, already there. Louisa keeps the district school, and with her salary, besides the little which my brother left her, gets along very comfortably. I have a small sum in bank, besides my house, and we have plenty to live on, even if we don't have much to spare.

Louisa was full of excitement over the false alarm of fire, and had heard a reason for it which we never fairly knew to be true, though nearly all the village believed it. It seems that the little Jameson boy, so the story ran, had peeped into the kitchen and had seen it full of smoke from Caroline's smoky chimney when she was kindling the fire; then had run out into the yard, and seeing the smoke out there too, and being of such an exceedingly timid temperament, had run

out to the head of the lane calling fire, and had there met Tommy
Gregg, who had spread the alarm and been the means of calling out
the fire department.

Indeed, the story purported to come from Tommy Gregg, who
declared that the boy at Liscom's had "hollered" fire, and when he
was asked where it was had told him at Liscom's. However that
may have been, I looked around at our humble little home, at the
lounge which I had covered myself, at the threadbare carpet on the
sitting-room floor, at the wallpaper which was put on the year before my husband died, at the vases on the shelf, which had belonged
to my mother, and I was very thankful that I did not care for "extra
things" or new furniture and carpets enough to take boarders who
made one feel as if one were simply a colonist of their superior
state, and the Republic was over and gone.

II

WE BECOME ACQUAINTED WITH THEM

It was certainly rather unfortunate, as far as the social standing of
the Jamesons among us was concerned, that they brought Grandma
Cobb with them.

Everybody spoke of her as Grandma Cobb before she had been
a week in the village. Mrs. H. Boardman Jameson always called her
Madam Cobb, but that made no difference. People in our village
had not been accustomed to address old ladies as madam, and they
did not take kindly to it. Grandma Cobb was of a very sociable disposition, and she soon developed the habit of dropping into the village houses at all hours of the day and evening. She was an early
riser, and all the rest of her family slept late, and she probably
found it lonesome. She often made a call as early as eight o'clock in
the morning, and she came as late as ten o'clock in the evening.
When she came in the morning she talked, and when she came in
the evening she sat in her chair and nodded. She often kept the
whole family up, and it was less exasperating when she came in the
morning, though it was unfortunate for the Jamesons.

If a bulletin devoted to the biography of the Jameson family had
been posted every week on the wall of the town house it could have
been no more explicit than was Grandma Cobb. Whether we would
or not we soon knew all about them; the knowledge was fairly
forced upon us. We knew that Mr. H. Boardman Jameson had been
very wealthy, but had lost most of his money the year before

through the failure of a bank. We knew that his wealth had all been inherited, and that he would never have been, in Grandma Cobb's opinion, capable of earning it himself. We knew that he had obtained, through the influence of friends, a position in the customhouse, and we knew the precise amount of his salary. We knew that the Jamesons had been obliged to give up their palatial apartments in New York and take a humble flat in a less fashionable part of the city. We knew that they had always spent their summers at their own place at the seashore, and that this was the first season of their sojourn in a little country village in a plain house. We knew how hard a struggle it had been for them to come here; we knew just how much they paid for their board, how Mrs. Jameson never wanted anything for breakfast but an egg and a hygienic biscuit, and had health food in the middle of the forenoon and afternoon.

We also knew just how old they all were, and how the H. in Mr. Jameson's name stood for Hiram. We knew that Mrs. Jameson had never liked the name—might, in fact, have refused to marry on that score had not Grandma Cobb reasoned with her and told her that he was a worthy man with money, and she not as young as she had been; and how she compromised by always using the abbreviation, both in writing and speaking. "She always calls him H," said Grandma Cobb, "and I tell her sometimes it doesn't look quite respectful to speak to her husband as if he were a part of the alphabet." Grandma Cobb, if the truth had been told, was always in a state of covert rebellion against her daughter.

Grandma Cobb was always dressed in a black silk gown which seemed sumptuous to the women of our village. They could scarcely reconcile it with the statement that the Jamesons had lost their money. Black silk of a morning was stupendous to them, when they reflected how they had, at the utmost, but one black silk, and that guarded as if it were cloth of gold, worn only upon the grandest occasions, and designed, as they knew in their secret hearts, though they did not proclaim it, for their last garment of earth. Grandma Cobb always wore a fine lace cap also, which should, according to the opinions of the other old ladies of the village, have been kept sacred for other women's weddings or her own funeral. She used her best gold-bowed spectacles every day, and was always leaving them behind her in the village houses, and little Tommy or Annie had to run after her with a charge not to lose them, for nobody knew how much they cost.

Grandma Cobb always carried about with her a paper-covered

novel and a box of cream peppermints. She ate the peppermints and freely bestowed them upon others; the novel she never read. She said quite openly that she only carried it about to please her daughter, who had literary tastes. "She belongs to a Shakespeare Club, and a Browning Club, and a Current Literature Club," said Grandma Cobb.

We concluded that she had, feeling altogether incapable of even carrying about Shakespeare and Browning, compromised with peppermints and current literature.

"That book must be current literature," said Mrs. Ketchum one day, "but I looked into it when she was at our house, and I should not want Adeline to read it."

After a while people looked upon Grandma Cobb's book with suspicion; but since she always carried it, thereby keeping it from her grandchildren, and never read it, we agreed that it could not do much harm.

The very first time that I saw Grandma Cobb, at Caroline Liscom's, she had that book. I knew it by the red cover and a baking-powder advertisement on the back; and the next time also—that was at the seventeenth-of-June picnic.

The whole Jameson family went to the picnic, rather to our surprise. I think people had a fancy that Mrs. H. Boardman Jameson would be above our little rural picnic. We had yet to understand Mrs. Jameson, and learn that, however much she really held herself above and aloof, she had not the slightest intention of letting us alone, perhaps because she thoroughly believed in her own nonmixable quality. Of course it would always be quite safe for oil to go to a picnic with water, no matter how exclusive it might be.

The picnic was in Leonard's grove, and young and old were asked. The seventeenth-of-June picnic is a regular institution in our village. I went with Louisa, and little Alice in her new white muslin dress; the child had been counting on it for weeks. We were nearly all assembled when the Jamesons arrived. Half a dozen of us had begun to lay the table for luncheon, though we were not to have it for an hour or two. We always thought it a good plan to make all our preparations in season. We were collecting the baskets and boxes, and it did look as if we were to have an unusual feast that year. Those which we peeped into appeared especially tempting. Mrs. Nathan Butters had brought a great loaf of her rich fruit cake, a kind for which she is famous in the village, and Mrs. Sim White had brought two of her whipped-cream pies. Mrs. Ketchum had

brought six mince pies, which were a real rarity in June, and Flora
Clark had brought a six-quart pail full of those jumbles she makes,
so rich that if you drop one it crumbles to pieces. Then there were
two great pinky hams and a number of chickens. Louisa and I had
brought a chicken; we had one of ours killed, and I had roasted it
the day before.

I remarked to Mrs. Ketchum that we should have an unusually
nice dinner; and so we should have had if it had not been for Mrs.
H. Boardman Jameson.

The Jamesons came driving into the grove in the Liscom carryall
and their buggy. Mr. Jacob Liscom was in charge of the carryall,
and the Jameson boy was on the front seat with him; on the back
seat were Grandma, or Madam Cobb, and the younger daughter.
Harry Liscom drove the bay horse in the buggy, and Mrs. Jameson
and Harriet were with him, he sitting between them, very uncom-
fortably, as it appeared—his knees were touching the dasher, as he
is a tall young man.

Caroline Liscom did not come, and I did not wonder at it for
one. She must have thought it a good chance to rest one day from
taking boarders. We were surprised that Mrs. Jameson, since she is
such a stout woman, did not go in the carryall, and let either her
younger daughter or the boy go with Harry and Harriet in the
buggy. We heard afterward that she thought it necessary that she
should go with them as a chaperon. That seemed a little strange to
us, since our village girls were all so well conducted that we thought
nothing of their going buggy-riding with a good young man like
Harry Liscom; he is a church member and prominent in the
Sunday-school, and this was in broad daylight and the road full of
other carriages. So people stared and smiled a little to see Harry
driving in with his knees braced against the dasher, and the buggy
canting to one side with the weight of Mrs. H. Boardman Jameson.
He looked rather shamefaced, I thought, though he is a handsome,
brave young fellow, and commonly carries himself boldly enough.
Harriet Jameson looked very pretty, though her costume was not,
to my way of thinking, quite appropriate. However, I suppose that
she was not to blame, poor child, and it may easily be more embar-
rassing to have old fine clothes than old poor ones. Really, Harriet
Jameson would have looked better dressed that day in an old calico
gown than the old silk one which she wore. Her waist was blue silk
with some limp chiffon at the neck and sleeves, and her skirt was
old brown silk all frayed at the bottom and very shiny. There were

a good many spots on it, too, and some mud stains, though it had not rained for two weeks.

However, the girl looked pretty, and her hair was done with a stylish air, and she wore her old Leghorn hat,[2] with its wreath of faded French flowers, in a way which was really beyond our girls.

And as for Harry Liscom, it was plain enough to be seen that, aside from his discomfiture at the close attendance of Mrs. H. Boardman Jameson, he was blissfully satisfied and admiring. I was rather sorry to see it on his account, though I had nothing against the girl. I think, on general principles, that it is better usually for a young man of our village to marry one of his own sort; that he has a better chance of contentment and happiness. However, in this case it seemed quite likely that there would be no chance of married happiness at all. It did not look probable that Mrs. H. Boardman Jameson would smile upon her eldest daughter's marriage with the son of "a good woman," and I was not quite sure as to what Caroline Liscom would say.

Mr. Jacob Liscom is a pleasant-faced, mild-eyed man, very tall and slender. He lifted out the Jameson boy, who did not jump out over the wheel, as boys generally do when arriving at a picnic, and then he tipped over the front seat and helped out Madam Cobb, and the younger daughter, whose name was Sarah. We had not thought much of such old-fashioned names as Harriet and Sarah for some years past in our village, and it seemed rather odd taste in these city people. We considered Hattie and Sadie much prettier. Generally the Harriets and Sarahs endured only in the seclusion of the family Bible and the baptismal records. Quite a number of the ladies had met Mrs. Jameson, having either called at Mrs. Liscom's and seen her there, or having spoken to her at church; and as for Grandma Cobb, she had had time to visit nearly every house in the village, as I knew, though she had not been to mine. Grandma Cobb got out, all smiling, and Jacob Liscom handed her the box of peppermints and the paper-covered novel, and then Harry Liscom helped out Harriet and her mother.

Mrs. Jameson walked straight up to us who were laying the table, and Harry followed her with a curiously abashed expression, carrying a great tin cracker-box in one hand and a large basket in the other. We said good-morning as politely as we knew how to Mrs. Jameson, and she returned it with a brisk air which rather took our breaths away, it was so indicative of urgent and very pressing business. Then, to our utter astonishment, up she marched to the nearest basket on the table and deliberately took off the cover and began taking out the contents. It happened to be Mrs. Nathan Butters' basket. Mrs. Jameson lifted out the great loaf of fruit cake and set it on the table with a contemptuous thud, as it seemed to us; then she took out a cranberry pie and a frosted apple pie, and set them beside it. She opened Mrs. Peter Jones' basket next, and Mrs. Jones stood there all full of nervous twitches and saw her take out a pile of ham sandwiches and a loaf of chocolate cake and a bottle of pickles. She went on opening the baskets and boxes one after another, and we stood watching her. Finally she came to the pail full of jumbles, and her hand slipped and the most of them fell to the ground and were a mass of crumbles.

Then Mrs. Jameson spoke; she had not before said a word. "These are enough to poison the whole village," said she, and she sniffed with a proud uplifting of her nose.

I am sure that a little sound, something between a groan and a gasp, came from us, but no one spoke. I felt that it was fortunate, and yet I was almost sorry that Flora Clark, who made those jumbles, was not there; she had gone to pick wild flowers with her Sunday-school class. Flora is very high-spirited and very proud of her jumbles, and I knew that she would not have stood it for a minute to hear them called poison. There would certainly have been words then and there, for Flora is afraid of nobody. She is a smart, handsome woman, and would have been married long ago if it had not been for her temper.

Mrs. Jameson did not attempt to gather up the jumbles; she just went on after that remark of hers, opening the rest of the things; there were only one or two more. Then she took the cracker-box which Harry had brought; he had stolen away to put up his horse, and it looked to me very much as if Harriet had stolen away with him, for I could not see her anywhere.

Mrs. Jameson lifted this cracker-box on to the table and opened it. It was quite full of thick, hard-looking biscuits, or crackers. She laid them in a pile beside the other things; then she took up the basket and opened that. There was another kind of a cracker in that, and two large papers of something. When everything was taken out she pointed at the piles of eatables on the table, and addressed us: "Ladies, attention!" rapping slightly with a spoon at the same time. Her voice was very sweet, with a curious kind of forced sweetness: "Ladies, attention! I wish you to carefully observe the food upon the table before us. I wish you to consider it from the standpoint of wives and mothers of families. There is the food which you have brought, unwholesome, indigestible; there is mine, approved of by the foremost physicians and men of science of the day. For ten years I have had serious trouble with the alimentary canal, and this food has kept me in strength and vigor. Had I attempted to live upon your fresh biscuits, your frosted cakes, your rich pastry, I should be in my grave. One of those biscuits which you see there before you is equal in nourishment to six of your indigestible pies, or every cake upon the table. The great cause of the insanity and dyspepsia so prevalent among the rural classes is rich pie and cake. I feel it my duty to warn you. I hope, ladies, that you will consider carefully what I have said."

With that, Mrs. Jameson withdrew herself a little way and sat down under a tree on a cushion which had been brought in the carryall. We looked at one another, but we did not say anything for a few minutes.

Finally, Mrs. White, who is very good-natured, remarked that she supposed that she meant well, and she had better put her pies back in the basket or they would dry up. We all began putting back the things which Mrs. Jameson had taken out, except the broken jumbles, and were very quiet. However, we could not help feeling astonished and aggrieved at what Mrs. Jameson had said about the insanity and dyspepsia in our village, since we could scarcely remember one case of insanity, and very few of us had to be in the least careful as to what we ate. Mrs. Peter Jones did say in a whisper that if Mrs. Jameson had had dyspepsia ten years on those hard biscuits it was more than any of us had had on our cake and pie. We left the biscuits, and the two paper packages which Mrs. Jameson had brought, in a heap on the table just where she had put them.

After we had replaced the baskets we all scattered about, trying to enjoy ourselves in the sweet pine woods, but it was hard work, we were so much disturbed by what had happened. We wondered uneasily, too, what Flora Clark would say about her jumbles. We were all quiet, peaceful people who dreaded altercation; it made our hearts beat too fast. Taking it altogether, we felt very much as if some great, overgrown bird of another species had gotten into our village nest, and we were in the midst of an awful commotion of strange wings and beak. Still we agreed that Mrs. Jameson had probably meant well.

Grandma Cobb seemed to be enjoying herself. She was moving about, her novel under her arm and her peppermint box in her hand, holding up her gown daintily in front. She spoke to every-body affably, and told a number confidentially that her daughter was very delicate about her eating, but she herself believed in eating what you liked. Harriet and Harry Liscom were still missing, and so were the younger daughter, Sarah, and the boy. The boy's name, by the way, was Cobb, his mother's maiden name. That seemed strange to us, but it possibly would not have seemed so had it been a prettier name.

Just before lunch-time Cobb and his sister Sarah appeared, and they were in great trouble. Jonas Green, who owns the farm next the grove, was with them, and actually had Cobb by the hair, hold-ing all his gathered-up curls tight in his fist. He held Sarah by one arm, too, and she was crying. Cobb was crying, too, for that matter, and crying out loud like a baby.

Jonas Green is a very brusque man, and he did look as angry as I had ever seen any one, and when I saw what those two were carry-ing I did not much wonder. Their hands were full of squash blos-soms and potato blossoms, and Jonas Green's garden is the pride of his life.

Jonas Green marched straight up to Mrs. Jameson under her tree, and said in a loud voice: "Ma'am, if this boy and girl are yours I think it is about time you taught them better than to tramp through folks' fields picking things that don't belong to them, and I expect what I've lost in squashes and potatoes to be made good to me."

We all waited, breathless, and Mrs. Jameson put on her eye-glasses and looked up. Then she spoke sweetly.

"My good man," said she, "if, when you come to dig your squashes, you find less than usual, and when you come to pick your potatoes the bushes are not in as good condition as they generally are, you may come to me and I will make it right with you."

Mrs. Jameson spoke with the greatest dignity and sweetness, and we almost felt as if she were the injured party, in spite of all those squash and potato blossoms. As for Jonas Green, he stared at her for the space of a minute, then he gave a loud laugh, let go of the boy and girl, and strode away. We heard him laughing to himself as he went; all through his life the mention of potato bushes and dig-ging squashes was enough to send him into fits of laughter. It was the joke of his lifetime, for Jonas Green had never been a merry man, and it was probably worth more than the vegetables which he had lost. I pitied Cobb and Sarah, they were so frightened, and got hold of them myself and comforted them. Sarah was just such another little timid, open-mouthed, wide-eyed sort of thing as her brother, and they were merely picking flowers, as they supposed.

"I never saw such beautiful yellow flowers," Sarah said, sobbing and looking ruefully at her great bouquet of squash blossoms. This little Sarah, who was only twelve, and very small and childish for her age, said sooner and later many ignorant, and yet quaintly innocent things about our country life, which were widely repeated. It was Sarah who said, when she was offered some honey at a village tea-drinking, "Oh, will you please tell me what time you drive home your bees? and do they give honey twice a day like the cows?" It was Sarah who, when her brother was very anxious to see the pigs on Mr. White's farm, said, "Oh, be quiet, Cobb, dear; it is too late tonight; the pigs must have gone into their holes."

I think poor Cobb and Sarah might have had a pleasant time at the picnic, after all—for my little Alice made friends with them, and Mrs. Sim White's Charlie—had it not been for their mother's obliging them to eat her hygienic biscuits for their luncheons. It was really pitiful to see them looking so wistfully at the cake and pie. I had a feeling of relief that all the rest of us were not obliged to make our repast of hygienic bread. I had a fear lest Mrs. Jameson might try to force us to do so. However, all she did was to wait until we were fairly started upon our meal, and then send around her children with her biscuits, following them herself with the most tender entreaties that we would put aside that unwholesome food and not risk our precious lives. She would not, however, allow us to drink our own coffee—about that she was firm. She insisted upon our making some hygienic coffee which she had brought from the city, and we were obliged to yield, or appear in a very stubborn and ungrateful light. The coffee was really very good, and we did not mind. The other parcel which she had brought contained a health food, to be made into a sort of porridge with hot water, and little cups of that were passed around, Mrs. Jameson's face fairly beaming with benevolence the while, and there was no doubt that she was entirely in earnest.

Still, we were all so disturbed—that is, all of us elder people—that I doubt if anybody enjoyed that luncheon unless it was Grandma Cobb. She did not eat hygienic biscuits, but did eat cake and pie in unlimited quantities. I was really afraid that she would make herself ill with Mrs. Butters' fruit cake. One thing was a great relief, to me at least: Flora Clark did not know the true story of her jumbles until some time afterward. Mrs. White told her that the pail had been upset and they were broken, and we were all so sorry; and she did not suspect. We were glad to avoid a meeting between her and Mrs. Jameson, for none of us felt as if we could endure it then.

I suppose the young folks enjoyed the picnic if we did not, and that was the principal thing to be considered, after all. I know that Harry Liscom and Harriet Jameson enjoyed it, and all the more that it was a sort of stolen pleasure. Just before we went home I was strolling off by myself near the brook, and all of a sudden saw the two young things under a willow tree. I stood back softly, and they never knew that I was there, but they were sitting side by side, and Harry's arm was around the girl's waist, and her head was on his shoulder, and they were looking at each other as if they saw angels, and I thought to myself that, whether it was due to hygienic bread or pie, they were in love—and what would Mrs. H. Boardman Jameson and Caroline Liscom say?

III

MRS. JAMESON IMPROVES US

It was some time before we really understood that we were to be improved. We might have suspected it from the episode of the hygienic biscuits at the picnic, but we did not. We were not fairly aware of it until the Ladies' Sewing Circle met one afternoon with Mrs. Sim White, the president, the first week in July.

It was a very hot afternoon, and I doubt if we should have had the meeting that day had it not been that we were anxious to get off a barrel as soon as possible to a missionary in Minnesota. The missionary had seven children, the youngest only six weeks old, and they were really suffering. Flora Clark did say that if it were as hot in Minnesota as it was in Linnville she would not thank anybody to send her clothes; she would be thankful for the excuse of poverty to go without them. But Mrs. Sim White would not hear to having the meeting put off; she said that a cyclone might come up any minute in Minnesota and cool the air, and then think of all those poor children with nothing to cover them. Flora Clark had the audacity to say that after the cyclone there might not be any children to cover, and a few of the younger members tittered; but we never took Flora's speeches seriously. She always came to the sewing meeting, no matter how much she opposed it, and sewed faster than any of us. She came that afternoon and made three flannel petticoats for three of the children, though she did say that she thought the money would have been better laid out in palm-leaf fans.

We were astonished to see Mrs. H. Boardman Jameson come that very hot afternoon, for we knew that she considered herself delicate, and, besides, we wondered that she should feel interested in our sewing circle. Her daughter Harriet came with her; Madam Cobb, as I afterward learned, went, instead, to Mrs. Ketchum's, and stayed all the afternoon, and kept her from going to the meeting at all.

Caroline Liscom came with her boarders, and I knew, the minute I saw her, that something was wrong. She had a look of desperation and defiance which I had seen on her face before. Thinks I to my-self: "You are all upset over something, but you have made up your mind to hide it, whether or no."

Mrs. Jameson had a book in her hand, and when she first came in she laid it on the table where we cut out our work. Mrs. Liscom went around the room with her, introducing her to the ladies whom she had not met before. I could see that she did not like to do it, and was simply swallowing her objections with hard gulps every time she introduced her.

Harriet walked behind her mother and Mrs. Liscom, and spoke very prettily every time she was addressed.

Harriet Jameson was really an exceedingly pretty girl, with a kind of apologetic sweetness and meekness of manner which won her friends. Her dress that afternoon was pretty, too: a fine white lawn trimmed with very handsome embroidery, and a white satin ribbon at the waist and throat. I understood afterward that Mrs. Jameson did not allow her daughters to wear their best clothes generally to our village festivities, but kept them for occasions in the city, since their fortunes were reduced, thinking that their old finery, though it might be a little the worse for wear, was good enough for our unsophisticated eyes. But that might not have been true; Harriet was very well dressed that afternoon, at all events.

Mrs. Jameson seemed to be really very affable. She spoke cordially to us all, and then asked to have some work given her; but, as it happened, there was nothing cut out except a black dress for the missionary's wife, and she did not like to strain her eyes working on black.

"Let me cut something out," said she in her brisk manner; "I have come here to be useful. What is there needing to be cut out?"

It was Flora Clark who replied, and I always suspected her of a motive in it, for she had heard about her jumbles by that time. She said there was a little pair of gingham trousers needed for the missionary's five-year-old boy, and Mrs. Jameson, without a quiver of hesitation, asked for the gingham and scissors. I believe she would have undertaken a suit for the missionary with the same alacrity.

Mrs. Jameson was given another little pair of trousers, a size smaller than those required, for a pattern, a piece of blue and white gingham and the shears, and she began. We all watched her furtively, but she went slashing away with as much confidence as if she had served an apprenticeship with a tailor in her youth. We began to think that possibly she knew better how to cut out trousers than we did. Mrs. White whispered to me that she had heard that many of those rich city women learned how to do everything in case they lost their money, and she thought it was so sensible.

When Mrs. Jameson had finished cutting out the trousers, which was in a very short space of time, she asked for some thread and a needle, and Flora Clark started to get some, and got thereby an excuse to examine the trousers. She looked at them, and held them up so we all could see, and then she spoke.

"Mrs. Jameson," said she, "these are cut just alike back and front, and they are large enough for a boy of twelve." She spoke very clearly and decisively. Flora Clark never minces matters.

We fairly shivered with terror as to what would come next, and poor Mrs. White clutched my arm hard. "Oh," she whispered, "I am so sorry she spoke so."

But Mrs. Jameson was not so easily put down. She replied very coolly and sweetly, and apparently without the slightest resentment, that she had made them so on purpose, so that the boy would not outgrow them, and she always thought it better to have the back and front cut alike; the trousers could then be worn either way, and would last much longer.

To our horror, Flora Clark spoke again. "I guess you are right about their lasting," said she; "I shouldn't think those trousers would wear out any faster on a five-year-old boy than they would on a pair of tongs. They certainly won't touch him anywhere."

Mrs. Jameson only smiled in her calmly superior way at that, and we concluded that she must be good-tempered. As for Flora, she said nothing more, and we all felt much relieved.

Mrs. Jameson went to sewing on the trousers with the same confidence with which she had cut them out; but I must say we had a little more doubt about her skill. She sewed with incredible swiftness; I did not time her exactly, but it did not seem to me that she was more than an hour in making those trousers. I know the meeting began at two o'clock, and it was not more than half-past three when she announced that they were done.

Flora Clark rose, and Mrs. White clutched her skirt and held her back while she whispered something. However, Flora went across the room to the table, and held up the little trousers that we all might see. Mrs. Jameson had done what many a novice in trousers-making does: sewed one leg over the other and made a bag of them. They were certainly a comical sight. I don't know whether Flora's sense of humor got the better of her wrath, or whether Mrs. White's expostulation influenced her, but she did not say one word, only stood there holding the trousers, her mouth twitching. As for the rest of us, it was all we could do to keep our faces straight. Mrs. Jameson was looking at her book, and did not seem to notice anything; and Harriet was sitting with her back to Flora, of which I was glad. I should have been sorry to have had the child's feelings hurt.

Flora laid the trousers on the table and came back to her seat without a word, and I know that Mrs. White sat up nearly all night ripping them, and cutting them over, and sewing them together again, in season to have them packed in the barrel the next day.

In the mean time, Mrs. Jameson was finding the place in her book; and just as Mrs. Peter Jones had asked Mrs. Butters if it were true that Dora Peckham was going to marry Thomas Wells and had bought her wedding dress, and before Mrs. Butters had a chance to answer her (she lives next door to the Peckhams), she rapped with the scissors on the table.

"Ladies," said she. "Ladies, attention!"

I suppose we all did stiffen up involuntarily; it was so obviously not Mrs. Jameson's place to call us to order and attention. Of course she should have been introduced by our President, who should herself have done the rapping with the scissors. Flora Clark opened her mouth to speak, but Mrs. White clutched her arm and looked at her so beseechingly that she kept quiet.

Mrs. Jameson continued, utterly unconscious of having given any offence. We supposed that she did not once think it possible that we knew what the usages of ladies' societies were. "Ladies," said she, "I am sure that you will all prefer having your minds improved and your spheres enlarged by the study and contemplation of one of the greatest authors of any age, to indulging in narrow village gossip. I will now read to you a selection from Robert Browning."

Mrs. Jameson said Robert Browning with such an impressive and triumphantly introductory air that it was almost impossible for a minute not to feel that Browning was actually there in our sewing circle. She made a little pause, too, which seemed to indicate just that. It was borne upon Mrs. White's mind that she ought to clap, and she made a feeble motion with her two motherly hands which one or two of us echoed.

Mrs. Jameson began to read the selection from Robert Browning. Now, as I have said before, we have a literary society in our village, but we have never attempted to read Browning at our meetings. Some of us read him a little and strive to appreciate him, but we have been quite sure that some other author would interest a larger proportion of the ladies. I don't suppose that more than three of us had ever read or even heard of the selection which Mrs. Jameson read. It was, to my way of thinking, one of the most difficult of them all to be understood by an untrained mind, but we listened politely, and with a semblance, at least, of admiring interest.

I think Harriet Jameson was at first the only seriously disturbed listener, to judge from her expression. The poor child looked so anxious and distressed that I was sorry for her. I heard afterward that she had begged her mother not to take the Browning book, saying that she did not believe the ladies would like it; and Mrs. Jameson had replied that she felt it to be her duty to teach them to like it, and divert their minds from the petty gossip which she had always heard was the distinguishing feature of rural sewing meetings.

Mrs. Jameson read and read; when she had finished the first selection she read another. At half-past four o'clock, Mrs. White, who had been casting distressed glances at me, rose and stole out on tiptoe.

I knew why she did so; Mrs. Bemis' hired girl next door was baking her biscuits for her that she need not heat her house up, and she had brought them in. I heard the kitchen door open.

Presently Mrs. White stole in again and tried to listen politely to the reading, but her expression was so strained to maintain interest that one could see the anxiety underneath. I knew what worried her before she told me, as she did presently. "I have rolled those biscuits up in a cloth," she whispered, "but I am dreadfully afraid that they will be spoiled."

Mrs. Jameson began another selection, and I did pity Mrs. White. She whispered to me again that her table was not set, and the biscuits would certainly be spoiled.

The selection which Mrs. Jameson was then reading was a short one, and I saw Mrs. White begin to brighten as she evidently drew near the end. But her joy was of short duration, as Mrs. Jameson began another selection.

However, Mrs. White laid an imploring hand on Flora Clark's arm when she manifested symptoms of rising and interrupting the reading. Flora was getting angry—I knew by the way her forehead was knitted and by the jerky way she sewed. Poor Harriet Jameson looked more and more distressed. I was sure she saw Mrs. White holding back Flora, and knew just what it meant. Harriet was sitting quite idle with her little hands in her lap; we had set her to hemming a ruffle for the missionary's wife's dress, but her stitches were so hopelessly uneven that I had quietly taken it from her and told her I was out of work and would do it myself. The poor child had blushed when she gave it up. She evidently knew her deficiencies.

Mrs. Jameson read selections from Robert Browning until six 'oclock, and by that time Mrs. White had attained to the calmness of despair. At a quarter of six she whispered to me that the biscuits were spoiled, and then her face settled into an expression of stony peace. When Mrs. Jameson finally closed her book there was a murmur which might have been considered expressive of relief or applause, according to the amount of self-complacency of the reader. Mrs. Jameson evidently considered it applause, for she bowed in a highly gracious manner, and remarked: "I am very glad if I have given you pleasure, ladies, and I shall be more than pleased at some future time to read some other selections even superior to these which I have given, and also to make some remarks upon them."

There was another murmur, which might have been of pleasure at the prospect of the future reading, or the respite from the present one; I was puzzled to know which it did mean.

We always had our supper at our sewing meetings at precisely five o'clock, and now it was an hour later. Mrs. White rose and went out directly, and Flora Clark and I followed her to assist. We began laying the table as fast as we could, while Mrs. White was cutting the cake. The ladies of the society brought the cake and pie, and Mrs. White furnished the bread and tea. However, that night it was so very warm we had decided to have lemonade instead of tea. Mrs. White had put it to vote among the ladies when they first came, and we had all decided in favor of lemonade. There was another reason for Mrs. White not having tea: she has no dining-room, but eats in her kitchen summer and winter. It is a very large room, but of course in such heat as there was that day even a little fire would have made it unendurably warm. So she had planned to have her biscuits baked in Mrs. Bemis' stove and have lemonade.

Our preparations were nearly completed, and we were placing the last things on the table, when my sister-in-law, Louisa Field, came out, and I knew that something was wrong.

"What is the matter?" said I.

Louisa looked at Flora as if she were almost afraid to speak, but finally it came out: Mrs. Jameson must have some hot water to prepare her health food, as she dared not eat our hurtful cake and pie, especially in such heat.

Flora Clark's eyes snapped. She could not be repressed any longer, so she turned on poor Louisa as if she were the offender. "Let her go home, then!" said she. "She sha'n't have any hot water in this house!"

Flora spoke very loud, and Mrs. White was in agony. "Oh, Flora! don't, don't!" said she. But she looked at the cold kitchen stove in dismay.

I suggested boiling the kettle on Mrs. Bemis' stove; but that could not be done, for the hired girl had gone away buggy-riding with her beau after she had brought in the biscuits, and Mrs. Bemis was not at the sewing circle: her mother, in the next town, was ill, and she had gone to see her. So the Bemis house was locked up, and the fire no doubt out. Mrs. White lives on an outlying farm, and there was not another neighbor within a quarter of a mile. If Mrs. Jameson must have that hot water for her hygienic food there was really nothing to do but to make up the fire in the kitchen stove, no matter how uncomfortable we all might be in consequence.

Flora Clark said in a very loud voice, and Mrs. White could not hush her, that she would see Mrs. H. Boardman Jameson in Gibraltar first; and she was so indignant because Mrs. White began to put kindlings into the stove that she stalked off into the other room. Mrs. White begged me to follow her and try to keep her quiet, but I was so indignant myself that I was almost tempted to wish she would speak out her mind. I ran out and filled the tea-kettle, telling Mrs. White that I guessed Flora wouldn't say anything, and we started the fire.

It was a quarter of seven before the water was hot, and we asked the ladies to walk out to supper. Luckily, the gentlemen were not coming that night. It was haying-time, and we had decided, since we held the meeting principally because of the extra work, that we would not have them. We often think that the younger women don't do as much work when the gentlemen are coming; they are upstairs so long curling their hair and prinking.

I wondered if Flora Clark had said anything. I heard afterward that she had not, but I saw at once that she was endeavoring to wreak a little revenge upon Mrs. Jameson. By a series of very skilful and scarcely perceptible manœuvres she gently impelled Mrs. Jameson, without her being aware of it, into the seat directly in front of the stove. I knew it was not befitting my age and Christian character, but I was glad to see her there. The heat that night was something terrific, and the fire in the stove, although we had made no more than we could help, had increased it decidedly. I thought that Mrs. Jameson, between the stove at her back and the hot water in her health food, would have her just deserts. It did seem as if she must be some degrees warmer than any of the rest of us.

However, who thought to inflict just deserts upon her reckoned without Mrs. H. Boardman Jameson. She began stirring the health food, which she had brought, in her cup of hot water; but suddenly she looked around, saw the stove at her back, and sweetly asked Mrs. White if she could not have another seat, as the heat was very apt to affect her head.

It was Harriet, after all, upon whom the punishment for her mother's thoughtlessness fell. She jumped up at once, and eagerly volunteered to change seats with her.

"Indeed, my place is quite cool, mamma," she said. So Mrs. Jameson and her daughter exchanged places; and I did not dare look at Flora Clark.

Though the kitchen was so hot, I think we all felt that we had reason to be thankful that Mrs. Jameson did not beseech us to eat health food as she did at the picnic, and also that the reading was over for that day.

Louisa, when we were going home that night, said she supposed that Mrs. Jameson would try to improve our literary society also; and she was proved to be right in her supposition at the very next meeting. Mrs. Jameson came, and she not only read selections from Browning, but she started us in that mad problem of Shakespeare and Bacon.[3] Most of the ladies in our society had not an intimate acquaintance with either, having had, if the truth were told, their minds too fully occupied with such humble domestic questions of identity as whether Johnny or Tommy stole the sugar.

However, when we were once fairly started there was no end to our interest; we all agonized over it, and poor Mrs. Sim White was so exercised over the probable deception of either Bacon or Shakespeare, in any case, that she told me privately that she was tempted to leave the literary society and confine herself to her Bible.

There was actual animosity between some members of our society in consequence. Mrs. Charles Root and Rebecca Snow did not speak to each other for weeks because Mrs. Root believed that Shakespeare was Bacon, and Rebecca believed he was himself. Rebecca even stayed away from church and the society on that account.

Mrs. Jameson expressed herself as very much edified at our interest, and said she considered it a proof that our spheres were widening.

Louisa and I agreed that if we could only arrive at a satisfactory conclusion in the matter we should feel that ours were wider; and Flora Clark said it did not seem of much use to her, since Shakespeare and Bacon were both dead and gone, and we were too much concerned with those plays which were written anyhow, and no question about it, to bother about anything else. It did not seem to her that the opinion of our literary society would make much difference to either of them, and that possibly we had better spend our time in studying the plays.

At the second meeting of our society which Mrs. Jameson attended she gave us a lecture, which she had written and delivered before her Shakespeare club in the city. It was upon the modern drama, and we thought it must be very instructive, only as few of us ever went to the theatre, or even knew the name of a modern playwright, it was almost like a lecture in an unknown tongue. Mrs. Ketchum went to sleep and snored, and told me on the way home that she did not mean to be ungrateful, but she could not help feeling that it would have been as improving for her to stay at home and read a new Sunday-school book that she was interested in.

Mrs. Jameson did not confine herself in her efforts for our improvement to our diet and our literary tastes. After she had us fairly

started in our bewildering career on the tracks of Bacon and Shakespeare—doing a sort of amateur detective work in the tombs, as it
were—and after she had induced the storekeeper to lay in a supply
of health food—which he finally fed to the chickens—she turned
her attention to our costumes. She begged us to cut off our gowns
at least three inches around the bottoms, for wear when engaged in
domestic pursuits, and she tried to induce mothers to take off the
shoes and stockings of their small children, and let them run barefoot. Children of a larger growth in our village quite generally go
barefoot in the summer, but the little ones are always, as a rule, well
shod. Mrs. Jameson said that it was much better for them also to go
without shoes and stockings, and Louisa and I were inclined to
think she might be right—it does seem to be the natural way of
things. But people rather resented her catching their children on the
street and stripping off their shoes and stockings, and sending the
little things home with them in their hands. However, their mothers
put on the shoes and stockings, and thought she must mean well.
Very few of them said anything to her by way of expostulation; but
the children finally ran when they saw her coming, so they would
not have their shoes and stockings taken off.

All this time, while Mrs. H. Boardman Jameson was striving to
improve us, her daughter Harriet was seemingly devoting all her
energies to the improvement of Harry Liscom, or to the improvement of her own ideal in his heart, whichever it may have been; and
I think she succeeded in each case.

Neither Mrs. Liscom nor Mrs. Jameson seemed aware of it, but
people began to say that Harry Liscom and the eldest Jameson girl
were going together.

I had no doubt of it after what I had seen in the grove; and one
evening during the last of July I had additional evidence. In the cool
of the day I strolled down the road a little way, and finally stopped
at the old Wray house. Nobody lived there then; it had been shut
up for many a year. I thought I would sit down on the old doorstep
and rest, and I had barely settled myself when I heard voices. They
came around the corner from the south piazza, and I could not help
hearing what they said, though I rose and went away as soon as I
had my wits about me and fairly knew that I was eavesdropping.

"You are so far above me," said a boy's voice which I knew was
Harry Liscom's.

Then came the voice of the girl in reply: "Oh, Harry, it is you who are so far above me." Then I was sure that they kissed each other.

I reflected as I stole softly away, lest they should discover me and be ashamed, that, after all, it was only love which could set people upon immeasurable heights in each other's eyes, and stimulate them to real improvement and to live up to each other's ideals.

IV

THEY TAKE A FARM

I had wondered a little, after Mrs. Jameson's frantic appeal to me to secure another boarding-place for her, that she seemed to settle down so contentedly at Caroline Liscom's. She said nothing more about her dissatisfaction, if she felt any. However, I fancy that Mrs. Jameson is one to always conceal her distaste for the inevitable, and she must have known that she could not have secured another boarding-place in Linnville. As for Caroline Liscom, her mouth is always closed upon her own affairs until they have become matters of history. She never said a word to me about the Jamesons until they had ceased to be her boarders, which was during the first week in August. My sister-in-law, Louisa Field, came home one afternoon with the news. She had been over to Mrs. Gregg's to get her receipt for blackberry jam, and had heard it there. Mrs. Gregg always knew about the happenings in our village before they fairly gathered form on the horizon of reality.

"What do you think, Sophia?" said Louisa when she came in— she did not wait to take off her hat before she began—"the Jamesons are going to leave the Liscoms, and they have rented the old Wray place, and are going to run the farm and raise vegetables and eggs. Mr. Jameson is coming on Saturday night, and they are going to move in next Monday."

I was very much astonished; I had never dreamed that the Jamesons had any taste for farming, and then, too, it was so late in the season.

"Old Jonas Martin is planting the garden now," said Louisa. "I saw him as I came past."

"The garden," said I; "why, it is the first of August!"

"Mrs. Jameson thinks that she can raise late peas and corn, and set hens so as to have spring chickens very early in the season," replied Louisa, laughing; "at least, that is what Mrs. Gregg says.

The Jamesons are going to stay here until the last of October, and then Jonas Martin is going to take care of the hens through the winter."

I remembered with a bewildered feeling what Mrs. Jameson had said about not wanting to board with people who kept hens, and here she was going to keep them herself.

Louisa and I wondered what kind of a man Mr. H. Boardman Jameson might be; he had never been to Linnville, being kept in the city by his duties at the custom-house.

"I don't believe that he will have much to say about the farm while Mrs. Jameson has a tongue in her head," said Louisa; and I agreed with her.

When we saw Mr. H. Boardman Jameson at church the next Sunday we were confirmed in our opinion.

He was a small man, much smaller than his wife, with a certain air of defunct style about him. He had quite a fierce bristle of moustache, and a nervous briskness of carriage, yet there was something that was unmistakably conciliatory and subservient in his bearing toward Mrs. Jameson. He stood aside for her to enter the pew, with the attitude of vassalage; he seemed to respond with an echo of deference to every rustle of her silken skirts and every heave of her wide shoulders. Mrs. Jameson was an Episcopalian, and our church is Congregational. Mrs. Jameson did not attempt to kneel when she entered, but bent her head forward upon the back of the pew in front of her. Mr. Jameson waited until she was fairly in position, with observant and anxious eyes upon her, before he did likewise.

This was really the first Sunday on which Mrs. Jameson herself had appeared at church. Ever since she had been in our village the Sundays had been exceptionally warm, or else rainy and disagreeable, and of course Mrs. Jameson was in delicate health. The girls and Cobb had attended faithfully, and always sat in the pew with the Liscoms. To-day Harry and his father sat in the Jones pew to make room for the two elder Jamesons.

There was an unusual number at meeting that morning, partly, no doubt, because it had been reported that Mr. Jameson was to be there, and that made a little mistake of his and his wife's more conspicuous. The minister read that morning the twenty-third Psalm, and after he had finished the first verse Mrs. Jameson promptly responded with the second, as she would have done in her own church, raising her solitary voice with great emphasis. It would not have been so ludicrous had not poor Mr. Jameson, evidently seeing the mistake, and his face blazing, yet afraid to desert his wife's standard, followed her dutifully just a few words in the rear. While Mrs. Jameson was beside the still waters, Mr. Jameson was in the green pastures, and so on. I pitied the Jameson girls. Harriet looked ready to cry with mortification, and Sarah looked so alarmed that I did not know but she would run out of the church. As for Cobb, he kept staring at his mother, and opening his mouth to speak, and swallowing and never saying anything, until it seemed as if he might go into convulsions. People tried not to laugh, but a little repressed titter ran over the congregation, and the minister's voice shook. Mrs. Jameson was the only one who did not appear in the least disturbed; she did not seem to realize that she had done anything unusual.

Caroline Liscom was not at church—indeed, she had not been much since the boarders arrived; she had to stay at home to get the dinner. Louisa and I wondered whether she was relieved or disturbed at losing her boarders, and whether we should ever know which. When we passed the Wray house on our way home, and saw the blinds open, and the fresh mould in the garden, and the new shingles shining on the hen-house roof, we speculated about it.

"Caroline had them about nine weeks, and at fifteen dollars a week she will have one hundred and thirty-five dollars," said Louisa. "That will buy her something extra."

"I know that she has been wanting some portières[4] for her parlor, and a new set for her spare chamber, and maybe that is what she will get," said I. And I said furthermore that I hoped she would feel paid for her hard work and the strain it must have been on her mind.

Louisa and I are not very curious, but the next day we did watch—though rather furtively—the Jamesons moving into the old Wray house.

All day we saw loads of furniture passing, which must have been bought in Grover. So many of the things were sewed up in burlap that we could not tell much about them, which was rather unfortunate. It was partly on this account that we did not discourage Tommy Gregg—who had been hanging, presumably with his mother's connivance, around the old Wray house all day—from reporting to us as we were sitting on the front door-step in the twilight. Mrs. Peter Jones and Amelia Powers had run over, and were sitting there with Louisa and me. Little Alice had gone to bed; we had refused to allow her to go to see what was going on, and yet listened to Tommy Gregg's report, which was not, I suppose, to our credit. I have often thought that punctilious people will use cats'-paws to gratify curiosity when they would scorn to use them for anything else. Still, neither Louisa nor I would have actually beckoned Tommy Gregg up to the door, as Mrs. Jones did, though I suppose we had as much cause to be ashamed, for we certainly listened full as greedily as she.

It seemed to me that Tommy had seen all the furniture unpacked, and much of it set up, by lurking around in the silent, shrinking, bright-eyed fashion that he has. Tommy Gregg is so single-minded in his investigations that I can easily imagine that he might seem as impersonal as an observant ray of sunlight in the window. Anyway, he had evidently seen everything, and nobody had tried to stop him.

"It ain't very handsome," said Tommy Gregg with a kind of disappointment and wonder. "There ain't no carpets in the house except in Grandma Cobb's room, and that's jest straw mattin'; and there's some plain mats without no roses on 'em; and there ain't no stove 'cept in the kitchen; jest old andirons like mother keeps up garret; and there ain't no stuffed furniture at all; and they was eatin' supper without no table-cloth."

Amelia Powers and Mrs. Jones thought that it was very singular that the Jamesons had no stuffed furniture, but Louisa and I did not feel so. We had often wished that we could afford to change the haircloth furniture, which I had had when I was married, for some pretty rattan or plain wood chairs. Louisa and I rather fancied the Jamesons' style of house-furnishing when we called there. It was rather odd, certainly, from our village standpoint, and we were not accustomed to see bare floors if people could possibly buy a carpet; the floors were pretty rough in the old house, too. It did look as if some of the furniture was sliding down-hill, and it was quite a steep descent from the windows to the chimney in all the rooms. Of course, a carpet would have taken off something of that effect. Another thing struck us as odd, and really scandalized the village at large: the Jamesons had taken down every closet and cupboard door in the house. They had hung curtains before the clothes-closets, but the shelves of the pantry which opened out of the dining-room, and the china-closet in the parlor, were quite exposed, and furnished with, to us, a very queer assortment of dishes. The Jamesons had not one complete set, and very few pieces alike. They had simply ransacked the neighborhood for forsaken bits of crockery-ware, the remnants of old wedding-sets which had been long stored away on top shelves, or used for baking or preserving purposes.

I remember Mrs. Gregg laughing, and saying that the Jamesons were tickled to death to get some old blue cups which she had when she was married and did not pay much for then, and had used for fifteen years to put up her currant jelly in; and had paid her enough money for them to make up the amount which she had been trying to earn, by selling eggs, to buy a beautiful new tea-set of a brown-and-white ware. I don't think the Jamesons paid much for any of the dishes which they bought in our village; we are not very shrewd people, and it did not seem right to ask large prices for articles which had been put to such menial uses. I think many things were given them. I myself gave Harriet Jameson an old blue plate and another brown one which I had been using to bake extra pies in when my regular pie-plates gave out. They were very discolored and cracked, but I never saw anybody more pleased than Harriet was.

I suppose the special feature of the Jamesons' household adornments which roused the most comment in the village was the bean-pots. The Jamesons, who did not like baked beans and never cooked them, had bought, or had given them, a number of old bean-pots, and had them sitting about the floor and on the tables with wild flowers in them. People could not believe that at first; they thought they must be some strange kind of vase which they had had sent from New York. They cast sidelong glances of sharpest scrutiny at them when they called. When they discovered that they were actually bean-pots, and not only that, but were sitting on the floor, which had never been considered a proper place for bean-pots in any capacity, they were really surprised. Flora Clark said that for her part her bean-pot went into the oven with beans in it, instead of into the corner with flowers in it, as long as she had her reason. But I must say I did not quite agree with her. I have only one bean-pot, and we eat beans, therefore mine has to be kept sacred to its original mission; and I must say that I thought Mrs. Jameson's with goldenrod in it really looked better than mine with beans. I told Louisa that I could not see why the original states of inanimate things ought to be remembered against them when they were elevated to finer uses any more than those of people, and now that the bean-pot had become a vase in a parlor why its past could not be forgotten. Louisa agreed with me, but I don't doubt that many people never looked at those pots full of goldenrod without seeing beans. It was to my way of thinking more their misfortune than the Jamesons' mistake; and they made enough mistakes which were not to be questioned not to have the benefit of any doubt.

Soon the Jamesons, with their farm, were the standing joke in our village. I had never known there was such a strong sense of humor among us as their proceedings awakened. Mr. H. Boardman Jameson did not remain in Fairville long, as he had to return to his duties at the custom-house. Mrs. Jameson, who seemed to rouse herself suddenly from the languid state which she had assumed at times, managed the farm. She certainly had original ideas and the courage of her convictions.

She stopped at nothing; even Nature herself she had a try at, like some mettlesome horse which does not like to be balked by anything in the shape of a wall.

Old Jonas Martin was a talker, and he talked freely about the people for whom he worked. "Old Deacon Sears had a cow once that would jump everything. Wa'n't a wall could be built that was high enough to stop her," he would say. " 'Tain't no ways clear to my mind that she ain't the identical critter that jumped the moon;— and I swan if Mis' Jameson ain't like her. There ain't nothin' that's goin' to stop her; she ain't goin' to be hendered by any sech little things as times an' seasons an' frost from raisin' corn an' green peas an' flowers in her garden. 'The frost'll be a-nippin' of 'em, marm,' says I, 'as soon as they come up, marm.' 'I wish you to leave that to me, my good man,' says she. Law, she ain't a-goin' to hev any frost a-nippin' her garden unless she's ready for it. And as for the chickens, I wouldn't like to be in their shoes unless they hatch when Mis' Jameson she wants 'em to. They have to do everything else she wants 'em to, and I dunno but they'll come to time on that. They're the fust fowls I ever see that a woman could stop scratchin'."

With that, old Jonas Martin would pause for a long cackle of mirth, and his auditor would usually join him, for Mrs. Jameson's hens were enough to awaken merriment, and no mistake. Louisa and I could never see them without laughing enough to cry; and as for little Alice, who, like most gentle, delicate children, was not often provoked to immoderate laughter, she almost went into hysterics. We rather dreaded to have her catch sight of the Jameson hens. There were twenty of them, great, fat Plymouth Rocks, and every one of them in shoes, which were made of pieces of thick cloth sewed into little bags and tied firmly around the legs of the fowls, and they were effectually prevented thereby from scratching up the garden seeds. The gingerly and hesitating way in which these hens stepped around the Jameson premises was very funny. It was quite a task for old Jonas Martin to keep the hens properly shod, for the cloth buskins had to be often renewed; and distressed squawkings amid loud volleys of aged laughter indicated to us every day what was going on.

The Jamesons kept two Jersey cows, and Mrs. Jameson caused their horns to be wound with strips of cloth terminating in large, soft balls of the same, to prevent their hooking. When the Jamesons first began farming, their difficulty in suiting themselves with cows occasioned much surprise. They had their pick of a number of fine ones, but invariably took them on trial, and promptly returned them with the message that they were not satisfactory. Old Jonas always took back the cows, and it is a question whether or not he knew what the trouble was, and was prolonging the situation for his own enjoyment.

At last it came out. Old Jonas came leading back two fine Jerseys to Sim White's, and he said, with a great chuckle: "Want to know what ails these ere critters, Sim? Well, I'll tell ye: they ain't got no upper teeth. The Jamesons ain't goin' to git took in with no cows without no teeth in their upper jaws, you bet."

That went the rounds of the village. Mrs. White was so sorry for the Jamesons in their dilemma of ignorance of our rural wisdom that she begged Sim to go over and persuade them that cows were created without teeth in their upper jaw, and that the cheating, if cheating there were, was done by Nature, and all men alike were victimized. I suppose Mr. White must have convinced her, for they bought the cows; but it must have been a sore struggle for Mrs. Jameson at least to swallow instruction, for she had the confidence of an old farmer in all matters pertaining to a farm.

She, however, did listen readily to one singular piece of information which brought much ridicule upon them. She chanced to say to Wilson Gregg, who is something of a wag, and had just sold the Jamesons a nice little white pig, that she thought that ham was very nice in alternate streaks of fat and lean, though she never ate it herself, and only bought the pig for the sake of her mother, who had old-fashioned tastes in her eating and would have pork, and she thought that home-raised would be so much healthier.

"Why, bless you, ma'am," said he, "if you want your ham streaky all you have to do is to feed the pig one day and starve him the next."

The Jamesons tried this ingenious plan; then, luckily for the pig, old Jonas, who had chuckled over it for a while, revealed the fraud and put him on regular rations.

I suppose the performance of the Jamesons which amused the village the most was setting their hens on hard-boiled eggs for sanitary reasons. That seemed incredible to me at first, but we had it on good authority—that of Hannah Bell, a farmer's daughter from the West Corners, who worked for the Jamesons. She declared that she told Mrs. Jameson that hens could not set to any purpose on boiled eggs; but Mrs. Jameson had said firmly that they must set upon them or none at all; that she would not have eggs about the premises so long otherwise; she did not consider it sanitary. Finally, when the eggs would not hatch submitted to such treatment, even at her command, she was forced to abandon her position, though even then with conditions of her surrender to Nature. She caused the nests to be well soaked with disinfectants.

The Jamesons shut the house up the last of October and went back to the city, and I think most of us were sorry. I was, and Louisa said that she missed them.

Mrs. Jameson had not been what we call neighborly through the summer, when she lived in the next house. Indeed, I think she never went into any of the village houses in quite a friendly and equal way, as we visit one another. Generally she came either with a view toward improving us—on an errand of mercy as it were, which some resented—or else upon some matter of business. Still we had, after all, a kindly feeling for her, and especially for Grandma Cobb and the girls, and the little meek boy. Grandma Cobb had certainly visited us, and none of us were clever enough to find out whether it was with a patronizing spirit or not. The extreme freedom which she took with our houses, almost seeming to consider them as her own, living in them some days from dawn till late at night, might have indicated either patronage or the utmost democracy. We missed her auburn-wigged head appearing in our doorways at all hours, and there was a feeling all over the village as if company had gone home.

I missed Harriet more than any of them. During the last of the time she had stolen in to see me quite frequently when she was released from her mother's guardianship for a minute. None of our village girls were kept as close as the Jamesons. Louisa and I used to wonder whether Mrs. Jameson kept any closer ward because of Harry Liscom. He certainly never went to the Jameson house. We knew that either Mrs. Jameson had prohibited it, or his own mother. We thought it must be Mrs. Jameson, for Harry had a will of his own, as well as his mother, and was hardly the man to yield to her in a matter of this kind without a struggle.

Though Harry did not go to the Jameson house, I, for one, used to see two suspicious-looking figures steal past the house in the summer evenings; but I said nothing. There was a little grove on the north side of our house, and there was a bench under the trees. Often I used to see a white flutter out there of a moonlight evening, and I knew that Harriet Jameson had a little white cloak. Louisa saw it too, but we said nothing, though we more than suspected that Harriet must steal out of the house after her mother had gone to her room, which we knew was early. Hannah Bell must know if that were the case, but she kept their secret.

Louisa and I speculated as to what was our duty if we were witnessing clandestine meetings, but we could never bring our minds to say anything.

The night before the Jamesons left it was moonlight and there was a hard frost, and I saw those young things stealing down the road for their last stolen meeting, and I pitied them. I was afraid, too, that Harriet would take cold in the sharp air. I thought she had on a thin cloak. Then I did something which I never quite knew whether to blame myself for or not. It did seem to me that, if the girl were a daughter of mine, and would in any case have a clandestine meeting with her lover, I should prefer it to be in a warm house rather than in a grove on a frosty night. So I caught a shawl from the table, and ran out to the front door, and called.

"Harry!" said I, "is that you?" They started, and I suppose poor Harriet was horribly frightened; but I tried to speak naturally, and as if the two being there together were quite a matter of course.

"I wonder if it will be too much for me to ask of you," said I, when Harry had responded quite boldly with a "Good-evening, Aunt Sophia"—he used to call me Aunt when he was a child, and still kept it up—"I wonder if it will be too much to ask if you two will just step in here a minute while I run down to Mrs. Jones'? I want to get a pattern to use the first thing in the morning. Louisa has gone to meeting, and I don't like to leave Alice alone."

They said they would be glad to come in, though, of course, with not as much joy as they felt later, when they saw that I meant to leave them to themselves for a time.

I stayed at Mrs. Jones' until I knew that Louisa would be home if

I waited any longer, and I thought, besides, that the young people had been alone long enough. Then I went home. I suppose that they were sorry to see me so soon, but they looked up at me very gratefully when I bade them good-night and thanked them. I said quite meaningly that it was a cold night and there would be a frost, and Harriet must be careful and not take cold. I thought that would be enough for Harry Liscom, unless being in love had altered him and made him selfish. I did not think he would keep his sweetheart out, even if it were his last chance of seeing her alone for so long, if he thought she would get any harm by it, especially after he had visited her for a reasonable length of time.

I was right in my opinion. They did not turn about directly and go home—I did not expect that, of course—but they walked only to the turn of the road the other way; then I saw them pass the house, and presently poor Harry returned alone.

I did pity Harry Liscom when I met him on the street a few days after the Jamesons had left. I guessed at once that he was missing his sweetheart sorely, and had not yet had a letter from her. He looked pale and downcast, though he smiled as he lifted his hat to me, but he colored a little as if he suspected that I might guess his secret.

I met him the next day, and his face was completely changed, all radiant and glowing with the veritable light of youthful hope upon it. He bowed to me with such a flash of joy in his smile that I felt quite warmed by it, though it was none of mine. I thought, though I said nothing, "Harry Liscom, you have had a letter."

V

THEIR SECOND SUMMER

The Jamesons returned to Linnville the first of June. For some weeks we had seen indications of their coming. All through April and May repairs and improvements had been going on in their house. Some time during the winter the Jamesons had purchased the old Wray place, and we felt that they were to be a permanent feature in our midst.

The old Wray house had always been painted white, with green blinds, as were most of our village houses; now it was painted red, with blinds of a darker shade. When Louisa and I saw its bright walls through the budding trees we were somewhat surprised, but thought it might look rather pretty when we became accustomed to it. Very few of the neighbors agreed with us, however; they had been so used to seeing the walls of their dwellings white that this startled them almost as much as a change of color in their own faces would have done.

"We might as well set up for red Injuns and done with it," said Mrs. Gregg one afternoon at the sewing circle. "What anybody can want anything any prettier than a neat white house with green blinds for, is beyond me."

Every month during the winter a letter had come to our literary society in care of the secretary, who was my sister-in-law, Louisa Field. Louisa was always secretary because she was a schoolteacher and was thought to have her hand in at that sort of work. Mrs. Jameson wrote a very kind, if it was a somewhat patronizing, sort of letter. She extended to us her very best wishes for our improvement and the widening of our spheres, and made numerous suggestions which she judged calculated to advance us in those respects. She recommended selections from Robert Browning to be read at our meetings, and she sent us some copies of explanatory and critical essays to be used in connection with them. She also in March sent us a copy of another lecture about the modern drama which she had herself written and delivered before her current literature club. With that she sent us some works of Ibsen and the Belgian writer, Maeterlinck, with the recommendation that we devote ourselves to the study of them at once, they being eminently calculated for the widening of our spheres.

Flora Clark, who is the president of the society; Mrs. Peter Jones, who is the vice-president; Louisa, and I, who am the treasurer, though there is nothing whatever to treasure, held a council over the books. We all agreed that while we were interested in them ourselves, though they were a strange savor to our mental palates, yet we would not read Mrs. Jameson's letter concerning them to the society, nor advise the study of them.

"I, for one, don't like to take the responsibility of giving the women of this village such reading," said Flora Clark. "It may be improving and widening, and it certainly is interesting, and there are fine things in it, but it does not seem to me that it would be wise to take it into the society when I consider some of the members. I would just as soon think of asking them to tea and giving them nothing but olives and Russian caviare, which, I understand, hardly anybody likes at first. I never tasted them myself. We know what the favorite diet of this village is; and as long as we can eat it ourselves it seems to me it is safer than to try something which we may like and everybody else starve on, and I guess we haven't exhausted some of the older, simpler things, and that there is some nourishment to be gotten out of them yet for all of us. It is better for us all to eat bread and butter and pie than for two or three of us to eat the olives and caviare, and the rest to have to sit gnawing their forks and spoons."

Mrs. Peter Jones, who is sometimes thought of for the president instead of Flora, bridled a little. "I suppose you think that these books are above the ladies of this village," said she.

"I don't know as I think they are so much above as too far to one side," said Flora. "Sometimes it's longitude, and sometimes it's latitude that separates people. I don't know but we are just as far from Ibsen and Maeterlinck as they are from us."

Louisa and I thought Flora might be right. At all events, we did not wish to set ourselves up in opposition to her. We never carried the books into the society, and we never read Mrs. Jameson's letter about them, though we did feel somewhat guilty, especially as we reflected that Flora had never forgotten the affair of the jumbles, and might possibly have allowed her personal feelings to influence her.

"I should feel very sorry," said Louisa to me, "if we were preventing the women of this village from improving themselves."

"Well, we can wait until next summer, and let Mrs. Jameson take the responsibility. I don't want to be the means of breaking up the society, for one," said I.

However, when Mrs. Jameson finally arrived in June, she seemed to be on a slightly different tack, so to speak, of improvement. She was not so active in our literary society and our sewing circle as she had been the summer before, but now, her own sphere having possibly enlarged, she had designs upon the village in the abstract.

Hannah Bell came over from the West Corners to open the house for them, and at five o'clock we saw the Grover stage rattle past with their trunks on top, and Grandma Cobb and the girls and Cobb looking out of the windows. Mrs. Jameson, being delicate, was, of course, leaning back, exhausted with her journey. Jonas Martin, who had been planting the garden, was out at the gate of the Wray house to help the driver carry in the trunks, and Hannah Bell was there too.

Louisa and I had said that it seemed almost too bad not to have some one of the village women go there and welcome them, but we did not know how Mrs. H. Boardman Jameson might take it, and nobody dared go. Mrs. White said that she would have been glad to make some of her cream biscuits and send them over, but she knew that Mrs. Jameson would not eat them, of course, and she did not know whether she would like any of the others to, and might think it a liberty.

So nobody did anything but watch. It was not an hour after the stage coach arrived before we saw Grandma Cobb coming up the road. We did not know whether she was going to Amelia Powers', or Mrs. Jones', or to our house; but she turned in at our gate.

We went to the door to meet her, and I must say she did seem glad to see us, and we were glad to see her. In a very short time we knew all that had happened in the Jameson family since they had left Linnville, and with no urging, and with even some reluctance on our part. It did not seem quite right for us to know how much Mrs. Jameson had paid her dressmaker for making her purple satin, and still less so for us to know that she had not paid for the making of her black lace net and the girls' organdy muslins, though she had been dunned three times. The knowledge was also forced upon us that all these fine new clothes were left in New York, since the shabby old ones must be worn out in the country, and that Harriet had cried because she could not bring some of her pretty gowns with her.

"Her mother does not think that there is any chance of her making a match here, and she had better save them up till next winter. Dress does make so much difference in a girl's prospects, you know," said Grandma Cobb shrewdly.

I thought of poor Harry Liscom, and how sorry his little sweetheart must have felt not to be able to show herself in her pretty dresses to him. However, I was exceedingly glad to hear that she had cried, because it argued well for Harry, and looked as if she had not found another lover more to her mind in New York.

Indeed, Grandma Cobb informed us presently as to that. "Harriet does not seem to find anybody," said she. "I suppose it is because H. Boardman lost his money; young men are so careful nowadays."

Grandma Cobb stayed to tea with us that night; our supper hour came, and of course we asked her.

Grandma Cobb owned with the greatest frankness that she should like to stay. "There isn't a thing to eat at our house but hygienic biscuits and eggs," said she. "My daughter wrote Hannah not to cook anything until we came; Hannah would have made some cake and pie, otherwise. I tell my daughter I have got so far along in life without living on hygienic food, and I am not going to begin. I want to get a little comfort out of the taste of my victuals, and my digestion is as good as hers, in spite of all her fussing. For my part," continued Grandma Cobb, who had at times an almost coarsely humorous method of expressing herself, "I believe in not having your mind on your inwards any more than you can possibly help. I believe the best way to get along with them is to act as if they weren't there."

After Grandma Cobb went home, as late as nine o'clock, I saw a clinging, shadowy couple stroll past our house, and knew it was Harriet Jameson and Harry, as did Louisa, and our consciences began to trouble us again.

"I feel like a traitor to Caroline and to Mrs. Jameson sometimes," said I.

"Well, maybe that is better than to be traitor to true love," said Louisa, which did sound rather sentimental.

The next morning about eleven o'clock Mrs. Jameson came in, and we knew at once that she was, so to speak, fairly rampant in the field of improvement for our good, or rather the good of the village, for, as I said before, she was now resolved upon the welfare of the village at large, and not that of individuals or even societies.

"I consider that my own sphere has been widened this winter," said Mrs. Jameson, and Louisa and I regarded her with something like terror. Flora Clark said, when she heard that remark of Mrs. Jameson's, that she felt, for her part, as if a kicking horse had got out of the pasture, and there was no knowing where he would stop.

We supposed that it must be an evidence of Mrs. Jameson's own advance in improvement that she had adopted such a singular costume, according to our ideas. She was dressed no longer in the rich fabrics which had always aroused our admiration, but, instead, wore a gown of brown cloth cut short enough to expose her ankles, which were, however, covered with brown gaiters made of cloth like her dress. She wore a shirt-waist of brown silk, and a little cutaway jacket. Mrs. Jameson looked as if she were attired for riding the wheel, but that was a form of exercise to which she was by no means partial either for herself or for her daughters. I could never understand just why she was not partial to wheeling. Wheels were not as fashionable then as now, but Mrs. Jameson was always quite up with, if not in advance of, her age.

Neither of us admired her in this costume. Mrs. Jameson was

very stout, and the short skirt was not, to our way of thinking, becoming.

"Don't you think that I have adopted a very sensible and becoming dress for country wear?" said she, and Louisa and I did not know what to say. We did not wish to be untruthful and we disliked to be impolite. Finally, Louisa said faintly that she thought it must be very convenient for wear in muddy weather, and I echoed her.

"Of course, you don't have to hold it up at all," said I.

"It is the only costume for wear in the country," said Mrs. Jameson, "and I hope to have all the women in Linnville wearing it before the summer is over."

Louisa and I glanced at each other in dismay. I think that we both had mental pictures of some of the women whom we knew in that costume. Some of our good, motherly, village faces, with their expressions of homely dignity and Christian decorousness, looking at us from under that jaunty English walking-hat, in lieu of their sober bonnets, presented themselves to our imaginations, and filled us with amusement and consternation.

"Only think how Mrs. Sim White would look," Louisa said after Mrs. Jameson had gone, and we both saw Mrs. White going down the street in that costume indicative of youthful tramps over long stretches of road, and mad spins on wheels, instead of her nice, softly falling black cashmere skirts covering decently her snowy stockings and her cloth congress boots[5]; and we shuddered.

"Of course, she would have to wear gaiters like Mrs. Jameson," said Louisa, "but it would be dreadful."

"Well, there's one comfort," said I; "Mrs. White will never wear it."

"Nor anybody else," said Louisa.

Still we did feel a little nervous about it; there is never any estimating the influence of a reformer. However, we were sure of ourselves. Louisa and I agreed that we never would be seen out in any such costume. Not very many in the village were. There were a few women, who were under the influence of Mrs. Jameson, who did cut off some of their old dresses and make themselves some leggings with hers for a pattern. After their housework was done they started off for long tramps with strides of independence and defiance, but they did not keep it up very long; none of them after Mrs. Jameson went away. To tell the truth, most of the women in our village had so much work to do, since they kept no servants, that they could not take many ten-mile walks, no matter what length skirts they wore. However, many wore the short ones while doing housework, which was very sensible.

During that morning call, Mrs. Jameson, besides the reformed costume, advocated another innovation which fairly took our breaths away. She was going to beautify the village. We had always considered the village beautiful as it was, and we bridled a little at that.

"There is scarcely a house in this village which is overgrown with vines," said she. "I am going to introduce vines."

Louisa ventured to say that she thought vines very pretty, but she knew some people objected to them on the score of spiders, and also thought that they were bad for the paint. We poor, frugal village folk have always to consider whether beauty will trespass on utility, and consequently dollars and cents. There are many innocent slaves to Mammon[6] in our midst.

Mrs. Jameson sniffed in her intensely scornful way. "Spiders and paint!" said she. "I am going to have the houses of this village vine-clad. It is time that the people were educated in beauty."

"People won't like it if she does go to planting vines around their houses without their permission, even if she does mean well," said Louisa after she had gone.

"She never will dare to without their permission," said I; but I wondered while I spoke, and Louisa laughed.

"Don't you be too sure of that," said she—and she was right.

Permission in a few cases Mrs. Jameson asked, and in the rest she assumed. Old Jonas Martin ransacked the woods for vines—clematis and woodbine—then he, with Mrs. Jameson to superintend, set them out around our village houses. The calm insolence of benevolence with which Mrs. Jameson did this was inimitable. People actually did not know whether to be furious or amused at this liberty taken with their property. They saw with wonder Mrs. Jameson, with old Jonas following laden with vines and shovel, also the girls and Cobb, who had been pressed, however unwillingly, into service, tagging behind trailing with woodbine and clematis; they stood by and saw their house-banks dug up and the vines set, and in most cases said never a word. If they did expostulate, Mrs. Jameson only directed Jonas where to put the next vine, and assured the bewildered owner of the premises that he would in time thank her.

However, old Jonas often took the irate individual aside for a consolatory word. "Lord a-massy, don't ye worry," old Jonas would say, with a sly grin; "ye know well enough that there won't a blamed one of the things take root without no sun an' manure; might as well humor her long as she's sot on 't."

Then old Jonas would wink slowly with a wink of ineffable humor. There was no mistaking the fact that old Jonas was getting a deal of solid enjoyment out of the situation. He had had a steady, hard grind of existence, and was for the first time seeing the point of some of those jokes of life for which his natural temperament had given him a relish. He acquired in those days a quizzical cock to his right eyebrow, and a comically confidential quirk to his mouth, which were in themselves enough to provoke a laugh.

Mrs. Jameson, however, did not confine herself, in her efforts for the wholesale decoration of our village, to the planting of vines around our house-walls; and there were, in one or two cases, serious consequences.

When, thinking that corn-cockles and ox-eyed daisies would be a charming combination at the sides of the country road, she caused them to be sowed, and thereby introduced them into Jonas Green's wheat-field, he expostulated in forcible terms, and threatened a suit for damages; and when she caused a small grove of promising young hemlocks to be removed from Eben Betts' woodland and set out in the sandy lot in which the schoolhouse stands, without leave or license, it was generally conceded that she had exceeded her privileges as a public benefactress.

I said at once there would be trouble, when Louisa came home and told me about it.

"The schoolhouse looks as if it were set in a shady grove," said she, "and is ever so pretty. The worst of it is, of course, the trees won't grow in that sand-hill."

"The worst of it is, if she has taken those trees without leave or license, as I suspect, Eben Betts will not take it as a joke," said I; and I was right.

Mr. H. Boardman Jameson had to pay a goodly sum to Eben Betts to hush the matter up; and the trees soon withered, and were cut up for firewood for the schoolhouse. People blamed old Jonas Martin somewhat for his share of this transaction, arguing that he ought not to have yielded to Mrs. Jameson in such a dishonest transaction, even in the name of philanthropy; but he defended himself, saying: "It's easy 'nough to talk, but I'd like to see any of ye stand up agin that woman. When she gits headed, it's either git out from under foot or git knocked over."

Mrs. Jameson not only strove to establish improvements in our midst, but she attacked some of our time-honored institutions, one against which she directed all the force of her benevolent will being our front doors. Louisa and I had always made free with our front door, as had some others; but, generally speaking, people in our village used their front doors only for weddings, funerals, and parties. The side doors were thought to be good enough for ordinary occasions, and we never dreamed, when dropping in for a neighborly call, of approaching any other. Mrs. H. Boardman Jameson resolved to do away with this state of things, and also with our sacred estimate of the best parlors, which were scarcely opened from one year's end to the other, and seemed redolent of past grief and joy, with no dilution by the every-day occurrences of life. Mrs. Jameson completely ignored the side door, marched boldly upon the front one, and compelled the mistress to open it to her resolute knocks. Once inside, she advanced straight upon the sacred precincts of the best parlor, and seated herself in the chilly, best rocking-chair with the air of one who usurps a throne, asking with her manner of sweet authority if the blinds could not be opened and the sun let in, as it felt damp to her, and she was very susceptible to dampness. It was told, on good authority, that in some cases she even threw open the blinds and windows herself while the person who admitted her was calling other members of the family.

It was also reported that she had on several occasions marched straight up to a house which she had no design of entering, thrown open the parlor blinds, and admitted the sunlight, with its fading influence, on the best carpet, and then proceeded down the street with the bearing of triumphant virtue. It was related that in a number of instances the indignant housewife, on entering her best parlor, found that the sun had been streaming in there all day, right on the carpet.

Mrs. Jameson also waged fierce war on another custom dear to the average village heart, and held sacred, as everything should be which is innocently dear to one's kind, by all who did not exactly approve of it.

In many of our village parlors, sometimes in the guest-chambers, when there had been many deaths in the family, hung the framed coffin-plates and faded funeral wreaths of departed dear ones. Now and then there was a wreath of wool flowers, a triumph of domestic art, which encircled the coffin-plate instead of the original funeral garland. Mrs. Jameson set herself to work to abolish this grimly pathetic New England custom with all her might. She did everything but actually tear them from our walls. That, even in her fiery zeal of improvement, she did not quite dare attempt. She made them a constant theme of conversation at sewing circle and during her neighborly calls. She spoke of the custom quite openly as grewsome and barbarous, but I must say without much effect. Mrs. Jameson found certain strongholds of long-established customs among us which were impregnable to open rancor or ridicule—and that was one of them. The coffin-plates and the funeral wreaths continued to hang in the parlors and chambers.

Once Flora Clark told Mrs. Jameson to her face, in the sewing circle, when she had been talking for a good hour about the coffin-plates, declaring them to be grewsome and shocking, that, for her part, she did not care for them, did not have one in her house—though every one of her relations were dead, and she might have her walls covered with them—but she believed in respecting those who did; and it seemed to her that, however much anybody felt called upon to interfere with the ways of the living, the relics of the dead should be left alone. Flora concluded by saying that it seemed to her that if the Linnville folks let Mrs. Jameson's bean-pots alone, she might keep her hands off their coffin-plates.

Mrs. Jameson was quite unmoved even by that. She said that Miss Clark did not realize, as she would do were her sphere wider, the incalculable harm that such a false standard of art might do in a community: that it might even pervert the morals.

"I guess if we don't have anything to hurt our morals any worse than our coffin-plates, we shall do," returned Flora. She said afterward that she felt just like digging up some of her own coffin-plates, and having them framed and hung up, and asking Mrs. Jameson to tea.

All through June and a part of July Louisa and I had seen the clandestine courtship between Harry Liscom and Harriet Jameson going on. We could scarcely help it. We kept wondering why neither Caroline Liscom nor Mrs. Jameson seemed aware of it. Of course, Mrs. Jameson was so occupied with the village welfare that it might account for it in her case, but we were surprised that Caroline was so blinded. We both of us thought that she would be very much averse to the match, from her well-known opinion of the Jamesons; and it proved that she was. Everybody talked so much about Harry and his courtship of Harriet that it seemed incredible that Caroline should not hear of it, even if she did not see anything herself to awaken suspicion. We did not take into consideration the fact that a strong-minded woman like Caroline Liscom has difficulty in believing anything which she does not wish to be true, and that her will stands in her own way.

However, on Wednesday of the second week of July both she and Mrs. Jameson had their eyes opened perforce. It was a beautiful moonlight evening, and Louisa and I were sitting at the windows looking out and chatting peacefully. Little Alice had gone to bed, and we had not lit the lamp, it was so pleasant in the moonlight. Presently, about half-past eight o'clock, two figures strolled by, and we knew who they were.

"It is strange to me that Grandma Cobb does not find it out, if Mrs. Jameson is too wrapped up in her own affairs and with grafting ours into them," said Louisa thoughtfully.

I remarked that I should not be surprised if she did know; and it turned out afterward that it was so. Grandma Cobb had known all the time, and Harriet had gone through her room to get to the back stairs, down which she stole to meet Harry.

The young couple had not been long past when a stout, tall figure went hurriedly by with an angry flirt of skirts—short ones.

"Oh, dear, that is Mrs. Jameson!" cried Louisa.

We waited breathless. Harry and Harriet could have gone no farther than the grove, for in a very short time back they all came, Mrs. Jameson leading—almost pulling—along her daughter, and Harry pressing close at her side, with his arm half extended as if to protect his sweetheart. Mrs. Jameson kept turning and addressing him; we could hear the angry clearness of her voice, though we could not distinguish many words; and finally, when they were almost past we saw poor Harriet also turn to him, and we judged that she, as well as her mother, was begging him to go, for he directly caught her hand, gave it a kiss, said something which we almost caught, to the effect that she must not be afraid—he would take care that all came out right—and was gone.

"Oh, dear," sighed Louisa, and I echoed her. I did pity the poor young things.

To our surprise, and also to our dismay, it was not long before we saw Mrs. Jameson hurrying back, and she turned in at our gate.

Louisa jumped and lighted the lamp, and I set the rocking-chair for Mrs. Jameson.

"No, I can't sit down," said she, waving her hand. "I am too

much disturbed to sit down," but even as she said that she did drop
into the rocking-chair. Louisa said afterward that Mrs. Jameson was
one who always would sit down during all the vicissitudes of life,
no matter how hard she took them.

Mrs. Jameson was very much disturbed; we had never seen her
calm superiority so shaken; it actually seemed as if she realized for
once that she was not quite the peer of circumstances, as Louisa
said.

"I wish to inquire if you have known long of this shameful clandestine love affair of my daughter's?" said she, and Louisa and I
were nonplussed. We did not know what to say. Luckily, Mrs.
Jameson did not wait for an answer; she went on to pour her griev-
ance into our ears, without even stopping to be sure whether they
were sympathizing ones or not.

"My daughter cannot marry into one of these village families,"
said she, without apparently the slightest consideration of the fact
that we were a village family. "My daughter has been very differ-
ently brought up. I have other views for her; it is impossible; it must
be understood at once that I will not have it."

Mrs. Jameson was still talking, and Louisa and I listening with
more of dismay than sympathy, when who should walk in but Caroline Liscom herself.

She did not knock—she never does; she opened the door with no
warning whatsoever, and stood there.

Louisa turned pale, and I know I must have. I could not command my voice, though I tried hard to keep calm.

I said "Good-morning," when it should have been "Good-
evening," and placed Alice's little chair, in which she could not by
any possibility sit, for Caroline.

"No, I don't want to sit down," said Caroline, and she kept her
word better than Mrs. Jameson. She turned directly to the latter. "I
have just been over to your house," said she, "and they told me that
you had come over here. I want to say something to you, and that
is, I don't want my son to marry your daughter, and I will never
give my consent to it, never, never!"

Mrs. Jameson's face was a study. For a minute she had not a word
to say; she only gasped. Finally she spoke. "You can be no more
unwilling to have your son marry my daughter than I am to have
my daughter marry your son," said she.

Then Caroline said something unexpected. "I would like to know what you have against my son, as fine a young man as there is anywhere about, I don't care who he is," said she.

And Mrs. Jameson said something unexpected. "I should like to inquire what you have against my daughter?" said she.

"Well, I'll tell you one thing," returned Caroline; "she doesn't know enough to keep a doll-baby's house, and she ain't neat."

Mrs. Jameson choked; it did not seem as if she could reply in her usual manner to such a plain statement of objections. She and Caroline glared at each other a minute; then to our great relief, for no one wants her house turned into the seat of war, Caroline simply repeated, "I shall never give my consent to have my son marry your daughter," and went out.

Mrs. Jameson did not stay long after that. She rose, saying that her nerves were very much shaken, and that she felt it sad that all her efforts for the welfare and improvement of the village should have ended in this, and bade us a mournful good-evening and left.

Louisa and I had an impression that she held us in some way responsible, and we could not see why, though I did reflect guiltily how I had asked the lovers into my house that October night. Louisa and I agreed that, take it altogether, we had never seen so much mutual love and mutual scorn in two families.

VI

THE CENTENNIAL

The older one grows, the less one wonders at the sudden, inconsequent turns which an apparently reasonable person will make in a line of conduct. Still I must say that I was not prepared for what Mrs. H. Boardman Jameson did in about a week after she had declared that her daughter should never marry Harry Liscom: capitulated entirely, and gave her consent.

It was Grandma Cobb who brought us the news, coming in one morning before we had our breakfast dishes washed.

"My daughter told Harriet last night that she had written to her father and he had no objections, and that she would withdraw hers on further consideration," said Grandma Cobb, with a curious, unconscious imitation of Mrs. Jameson's calm state of manner. Then she at once relapsed into her own. "My daughter says that she is convinced that the young man is worthy, though he is not socially quite what she might desire, and she does not feel it right to part them if they have a true affection for each other," said Grandma Cobb. Then she added, with a shake of her head and a gleam of malicious truth in her blue eyes: "That is not the whole of it; Robert Browning was the means of bringing it about."

"Robert Browning!" I repeated. I was bewildered, and Louisa stared at me in a frightened way. She said afterward that she thought for a minute that Grandma Cobb was out of her head.

But Grandma Cobb went on to explain. "Yes, my daughter seems to look upon Robert Browning as if everything he said was written on tables of stone," said she; "and last night she had a letter from Mrs. Addison Sears, who feels just the same way. My daughter had written her about Harriet's love affair, and this was in answer. Mrs. Sears dwelt a good deal upon Mr. Browning's own happy marriage; and then she quoted passages; and my daughter became convinced that Robert Browning would have been in favor of the match,—and that settled it. My daughter proves things by Browning almost the same way as people do by Scripture, it seems to me sometimes. I am thankful that it has turned out so," Grandma Cobb went on to say, "for I like the young man myself; and as for Harriet, her mind is set on him, and she's something like me: once get her mind set on anybody, that's the end of it. My daughter has got the same trait, but it works the contrary way: when she once gets her mind set against anybody, that's the end of it unless Robert Browning steps in to turn her."

Louisa and I were heartily glad to hear of Mr. Browning's unconscious intercession and its effect upon Mrs. Jameson, but we wondered what Caroline Liscom would say.

"It will take more than passages of poetry to move her," said Louisa when Grandma Cobb had gone.

All we could do was to wait for developments concerning Caroline. Then one day she came in and completely opened her heart to us with that almost alarming frankness which a reserved woman often displays if she does lose her self-restraint.

"I can't have it anyhow," said Caroline Liscom; and I must say I did pity her, though I had a weakness for little Harriet. "I feel as if it would kill me if Harry marries that girl—and I am afraid he will; but it shall never be with my consent, and he shall never bring her to my house while I am in it."

Then Caroline went on to make revelations about Harriet which were actually dire accusations from a New England housewife like her.

"It was perfectly awful the way her room looked while she was at my house," said Caroline; "and she doesn't know how to do one thing about a house. She can't make a loaf of bread to save her life, and she has no more idea how to sweep a room and dust it than a baby. I had it straight from Hannah Bell that she dusted her room and swept it afterward. Think of my boy, brought up the way he has been, everything as neat as wax, if I do say it, and his victuals always cooked nice, and ready when he wanted them, marrying a girl like that. I can't and I won't have it. It's all very well now, he's captivated by a pretty face; but wait a little, and he'll find out there's something else. He'll find out there's comfort to be considered as well as love. And she don't even know how to do plain sewing. Only look at the bottoms of her dresses, with the braid hanging; and I know she never mends her stockings—I had it from the woman who washes them. Only think of my son, who has always had his stockings mended as smooth as satin, either going with holes in them, or else having them gathered up in hard bunches and getting corns. I can't and I won't have it!"

Caroline finished all her remarks with that, setting her mouth hard. It was evident that she was firm in her decision. I suggested mildly that the girl had never been taught, and had always had so much money that she was excusable for not knowing how to do all these little things which the Linnville girls had been forced to do.

"I know all that," said Caroline; "I am not blaming her so much as I am her mother. She had better have stopped reading Browning and improving her own mind and the village, and improved her own daughter, so she could walk in the way Providence has set for a woman without disgracing herself. But I am looking at her as she is, without any question of blame, for the sake of my son. He shall not marry a girl who don't know how to make his home comfortable any better than she does—not if his mother can save him from it."

Louisa asked timidly—we were both of us rather timid, Caroline was so fierce—if she did not think she could teach Harriet.

"I don't know whether I can or not!" said Caroline. "Anyway, I am not going to try. What kind of a plan would it be for me to have her in the house teaching her, where Harry could see her every day, and perhaps after all find out that it would not amount to anything. I'd rather try to cure drink than make a good housewife of a girl who hasn't been brought up to it. How do I know it's in her? And there I would have her right under Harry's nose. She shall never marry him; I can't and I won't have it."

Louisa and I speculated as to whether Caroline would be able to help it, when she had taken her leave after what seemed to us must have been a most unsatisfactory call, with not enough sympathy from us to cheer her.

"Harry Liscom has a will, as well as his mother, and he is a man grown, and running the woollen factory on shares with his father, and able to support a wife. I don't believe he is going to stop, now the girl's mother has consented, because his mother tells him to," said Louisa; and I thought she was right.

That very evening Harry went past to the Jamesons, in his best suit, carrying a cane, which he swung with the assured air of a young man going courting where he is plainly welcome.

"I am glad for one thing," said I, "and that is there is no more secret strolling in my grove, but open sitting up in her mother's parlor."

Louisa looked at me a little uncertainly, and I saw that there was something which she wanted to say and did not quite dare.

"What is it?" said I.

"Well," said Louisa, hesitatingly, "I was thinking that I supposed—I don't know that it would work at all—maybe her mother wouldn't be willing, and maybe she wouldn't be willing herself—but I was thinking that you were as good a housekeeper as Caroline Liscom, and—you might have the girl in here once in a while and teach her."

"I will do it," said I at once,—"if I can, that is."

I found out that I could. The poor child was only too glad to come to my house and take a few lessons in housekeeping. I waylaid her when she was going past one day, and broached the subject delicately. I said it was a good idea for a young girl to learn as much as she could about keeping a house nice before she had one of her own, and Harriet blushed as red as a rose and thanked me, and arranged to come for her first lesson the very next morning. I got a large gingham apron for her, and we began. I gave her a lesson in bread-making that very day, and found her an apt pupil. I told her that she would make a very good housekeeper—I should not wonder if as good as Mrs. Liscom, who was, I considered, the best in the village; and she blushed again and kissed me.

Louisa and I had been a little worried as to what Mrs. Jameson would say; but we need not have been. Mrs. Jameson was strenuously engaged in uprooting poison-ivy vines, which grew thickly along the walls everywhere in the village. I must say it seemed Scriptural to me, and made me think better in one way of Mrs. Jameson, since it did require considerable heroism.

Luckily, old Martin was one of the few who are exempt from the noxious influence of poison-ivy, and he pulled up the roots with impunity, but I must say without the best success. Poison-ivy is a staunch and persistent thing, and more than a match for Mrs. Jameson. She suffered herself somewhat in the conflict, and went about for some time with her face and hands done up in castor-oil, which we consider a sovereign remedy for poison-ivy. Cobb, too, was more or less a victim to his mother's zeal for uprooting noxious weeds.

It was directly after the poison-ivy that Mrs. Jameson made what may be considered her grand attempt of the season. All at once she discovered what none of the rest of us had thought of—I suppose we must have been lacking in public feeling not to have done so— that our village had been settled exactly one hundred years ago that very August.

Mrs. Jameson came into our house with the news on the twenty-seventh day of July. She had just found it out in an old book which had been left behind and forgotten in the garret of the Wray house.

"We must have a centennial, of course," said she magisterially.

Louisa and I stared at her. "A centennial!" said I feebly. I think visions of Philadelphia,[7] and exhibits of the products of the whole world in our fields and cow-pastures, floated through my mind. Centennial had a stupendous sound to me, and Louisa said afterward it had to her.

"How would you make it?" asked Louisa vaguely of Mrs. Jameson, as if a centennial were a loaf of gingerbread.

Mrs. Jameson had formed her plans with the rapidity of a great general on the eve of a forced battle. "We will take the oldest house in town," said she promptly. "I think that it is nearly as old as the village, and we will fit it up as nearly as possible like a house of one hundred years ago, and we will hold our celebration there."

"Let me see, the oldest house is the Shaw house," said I.

"Why, Emily Shaw is living there," said Louisa in wonder.

"We shall make arrangements with her," returned Mrs. Jameson, with confidence. She looked around our sitting-room, and eyed our old-fashioned highboy, of which we are very proud, and an old-fashioned table which becomes a chair when properly manipulated. "Those will be just the things to go in one of the rooms," said she, without so much as asking our leave.

"Emily Shaw's furniture will have to be put somewhere if so many other things are to be moved in," suggested Louisa timidly; but Mrs. Jameson dismissed that consideration with merely a wave of her hand.

"I think that Mrs. Simeon White has a swell-front bureau and an old looking-glass which will do very well for one of the chambers," she went on to say, "and Miss Clark has a mahogany table." Mrs. Jameson went on calmly enumerating articles of old-fashioned furniture which she had seen in our village houses which she considered suitable to be used in the Shaw house for the centennial.

"I don't see how Emily Shaw is going to live there while all this is going on," remarked Louisa in her usual deprecatory tone when addressing Mrs. Jameson.

"I think we may be able to leave her one room," said Mrs. Jameson; and Louisa and I fairly gasped when we reflected that Emily Shaw had not yet heard a word of the plan.

"I don't know but Emily Shaw will put up with it, for she is pretty meek," said Louisa when Mrs. Jameson had gone hurrying down the street to impart her scheme to others; "but it is lucky for Mrs. Jameson that Flora Clark hasn't the oldest house in town."

I said I doubted if Flora would even consent to let her furniture be displayed in the centennial; but she did. Everybody consented to everything. I don't know whether Mrs. H. Boardman Jameson had really any hypnotic influence over us, or whether we had a desire for the celebration, but the whole village marshalled and marched to her orders with the greatest docility. All our cherished pieces of old furniture were loaded into carts and conveyed to the old Shaw house.

The centennial was to be held the tenth day of August, and there was necessarily quick work. The whole village was in an uproar; none of us who had old-fashioned possessions fairly knew where we were living, so many of them were in the Shaw house; we were short of dishes and bureau drawers, and counterpanes and curtains. Mrs. Jameson never asked for any of these things; she simply took them as by right of war, and nobody gainsaid her, not even Flora Clark. However, poor Emily Shaw was the one who displayed the greatest meekness under provocation. The whole affair must have seemed revolutionary to her. She was a quiet, delicate little woman,

no longer young. She did not go out much, not even to the sewing
circle or the literary society, and seemed as fond of her home as an
animal of its shell—as if it were a part of her. Old as her house was,
she had it fitted up in a modern, and, to our village ideas, a very
pretty fashion. Emily was quite well-to-do. There were nice tapestry carpets on all the downstairs floors, lace curtains at the windows, and furniture covered with red velvet in the parlor. She had
also had the old fireplaces covered up and marble slabs set. There
was handsome carved black walnut furniture in the chambers; and
taken altogether, the old Shaw house was regarded as one of the
best furnished in the village. Mrs. Sim White said she didn't know
as she wondered that Emily didn't like to go away from such nice
things.

Now every one of these nice things was hustled out of sight to
make room for the pieces of old-fashioned furniture. The tapestry
carpets were taken up and stowed away in the garrets, the lace curtains were pulled down. In their stead were the old sanded bare
floors and curtains of homespun linen trimmed with hand-knitted
lace. Emily's nice Marseilles counterpanes were laid aside for the
old blue-and-white ones which our grandmothers spun and wove,
and her fine oil paintings gave way to old engravings of Webster
death-bed scenes and portraits of the Presidents, and samplers.
Emily was left one room to herself—a little back chamber over the
kitchen—and she took her meals at Flora Clark's, next door. She
was obliged to do that, for her kitchen range had been taken down,
and there was only the old fireplace furnished with kettles and
crane to cook in.

"I suppose my forefathers used to get all their meals there," said
poor Emily Shaw, who has at all times a gentle, sad way of speaking, and then seemed on the verge of uncomplaining tears, "but I
don't quite feel competent to undertake it now. It looks to me as if
the kettles might be hard to lift." Emily glanced at her hands and
wrists as she spoke. Emily's hands and arms are very small and
bony, as she is in her general construction, though she is tall.

The little chamber which she inhabited during the preparation
for the centennial was very hot in those midsummer days, and her
face was always suffused with a damp pink when she came out of it;
but she uttered no word of complaint, not even when they took
down her marble slabs and exposed the yawning mouths of the old
fireplaces again. All she said was once in a deprecatory whisper to

me, to the effect that she was a little sorry to have strangers see her house looking so, but she supposed it was interesting.

We expected a number of strangers. Mrs. Sim White's brother, who had gone to Boston when he was a young man and turned out so smart, being the head of a large dry-goods firm, was coming, and was to make a speech; and Mr. Elijah M. Mills, whose mother's people came from Linnville, was to be there, as having a hereditary interest in the village. Of course, everybody knows Elijah M. Mills. He was to make a speech. Mrs. Lucy Beers Wright, whose aunt on her father's side, Miss Jane Beers, used to live in Linnville before she died, was to come and read some selections from her own works. Mrs. Lucy Beers Wright writes quite celebrated stories, and reads them almost better than she writes them. She has enormous prices, too, but she promised to come to the centennial and read for nothing; she used to visit her aunt in Linnville when she was a girl, and wrote that she had a sincere love for the dear old place. Mrs. Jameson said that we were very fortunate to get her.

Mrs. Jameson did not stop, however, at celebrities of local traditions; she flew higher still. She wrote the Governor of the State, inviting him to be present, and some of us were never quite certain that she did not invite the President of the United States. However, if she had done so, it seemed incredible that since he was bidden by Mrs. H. Boardman Jameson he neither came nor wrote a letter. The Governor of the State did not come, but he wrote a very handsome letter, expressing the most heartfelt disappointment that he was unable to be present on such an occasion; and we all felt very sorry for him when we heard it read. Mrs. Sim White said that a governor's life must be a hard one, he must have to deny himself many pleasures. Our minister, the Rev. Henry P. Jacobs, wrote a long poem to be read on the occasion; it was in blank verse like Young's "Night Thoughts,"[8] and some thought he had imitated it; but it was generally considered very fine, though we had not the pleasure of hearing it at the centennial—why, I will explain later.

There was to be a grand procession, of course, illustrative of the arts, trades, and professions in our village a hundred years ago and at the present time, and Mrs. Jameson engineered that. I never saw a woman work as she did. Louisa and I agreed that she could not be so very delicate after all. She had a finger in everything except the cooking; that she left mostly to the rest of us, though she did break over in one instance to our sorrow. We made pound-cake, and cupcake, and Indian puddings, and pies, and we baked beans enough for a standing army. Of course, the dinner was to be after the fashion of one of a hundred years ago. The old oven in the Shaw kitchen was to be heated, and Indian puddings and pies baked in it; but that would not hold enough for such a multitude as we expected, so we all baked at home—that is, all except Caroline Liscom. She would not bake a thing because Mrs. Jameson got up the centennial, and she declared that she would not go. However, she changed her mind, which was fortunate enough as matters afterward transpired.

The tenth of August, which was the one hundredth anniversary of the settlement of our village, dawned bright and clear, for which we were thankful, though it was very hot. The exercises were to begin at eleven o'clock in the morning with the procession. We were to assemble at the old Shaw house at half-past twelve; the dinner was to be at half-past one, after an hour of social intercourse which would afford people an opportunity of viewing the house, and a few of us an opportunity of preparing the dinner. After dinner were to be the speeches and readings, which must be concluded in season for the out-of-town celebrities to take the Grover stage-coach to connect with the railroad train.

By eight o'clock people began to arrive from other villages, and to gather on the street corners to view the procession. It was the very first procession ever organized in our village, and we were very proud of it. For the first time Mrs. Jameson began to be regarded with real gratitude and veneration as a local benefactress. We told all the visitors that Mrs. H. Boardman Jameson got up the centennial, and we were proud that she was one of us when we saw her driving past in the procession. We thought it exceedingly appropriate that the Jamesons—Mr. Jameson had come on from New York for the occasion—should ride in the procession with the minister and the lawyer in a barouche[9] from Grover. Barouches seemed that day to be illustrative of extremest progress in carriages, in contrast with the old Linnville and Wardville stage-coaches, and the old chaise and doctor's sulky,[10] all of which had needed to be repaired with infinite care, and were driven with gingerly foresight, lest they fall to pieces on the line of march. We really pitied the village doctor in the aged sulky, for it seemed as if he might have to set a bone for himself by reason of the sudden and total collapse of his vehicle. Mrs. Jameson had decreed that he should ride in it, however, and there was no evading her mandate.

Mrs. Jameson looked very imposing in her barouche, and we

were glad that she wore one of her handsome black silks instead of her sensible short costume. There was a good deal of jet about the waist, and her bonnet was all made of jet, with a beautiful tuft of pink roses on the front, and she glittered resplendently as she rode past, sitting up very straight, as befitted the dignity of the occasion.

"That is Mrs. H. Boardman Jameson," said we, and we mentioned incidentally that the gentleman beside her was Mr. Jameson. We were not as proud of him, since all that he had done which we knew of was to lose all his money and have his friends get him a place in the custom-house; he was merely a satellite of his wife, who had gotten up our centennial.

Words could not express the admiration which we all felt for the procession. It was really accomplished in a masterly manner, especially taking into consideration the shortness of the time for preparation; but that paled beside the wonders of the old Shaw house. I was obliged to be in the kitchen all during that hour of inspection and social intercourse, but I could hear the loud bursts of admiration. The house seemed full of exclamation points. Flora Clark said for her part she could not see why folks could not look at a thing and think it was pretty without screaming; but she was tired, and probably a little vexed at herself for working so hard when Mrs. Jameson had gotten up the centennial. It was very warm in the kitchen, too, for Mrs. Jameson had herself started the hearth fire in order to exemplify to the utmost the old custom. The kettles on the crane were all steaming. Flora Clark said it was nonsense to have a hearth-fire on such a hot day because our grandmothers were obliged to, but she was in the minority. Most of the ladies were inclined to follow Mrs. Jameson's lead unquestionably on that occasion. They even exclaimed admiringly over two chicken pies which she brought, and which I must say had a singular appearance. The pastry looked very hard and of a curious leaden color. Mrs. Jameson said that she made them herself out of whole wheat, without shortening, and she evidently regarded them as triumphs of wholesomeness and culinary skill. She furthermore stated that she had remained up all night to bake them, which we did not doubt, as Hannah Bell, her help, had been employed steadily in the old Shaw house. Mrs. Jameson had cut the pies before bringing them, which Flora Clark whispered was necessary. "I know that she had to cut them with a hatchet and a hammer," whispered she; and really when we came to try them later it did not seem so unlikely. I never saw such pastry, anything like the toughness and cohesiveness of it;

the chicken was not seasoned well, either. We could eat very little; with a few exceptions, we could do no more than taste of it, which was fortunate.

I may as well mention here that the few greedy individuals, who I fancy frequent all social functions with an undercurrent of gastronomical desire for their chief incentive, came to grief by reason of Mrs. Jameson's chicken pies. She baked them without that opening in the upper crust which, as every good housewife knows, is essential, and there were dire reports of sufferings in consequence. The village doctor, after his precarious drive in the ancient sulky, had a night of toil. Caleb—commonly called Kellup—Bates, and his son Thomas, were the principal sufferers, they being notorious eaters and the terrors of sewing-circle suppers. Flora Clark confessed to me that she was relieved when she saw them out again, since she had passed the pies to them three times, thinking that such devourers would stop at nothing and she might as well save the delicacies for the more temperate.

We were so thankful that none of the out-of-town celebrities ate Mrs. Jameson's chicken pies, since they had a rather unfortunate experience as it was. The dinner was a very great success, and Flora Clark said to me that if people a hundred years ago ate those hearty, nourishing victuals as these people did, she didn't wonder that the men had strength to found a Republic, but she did wonder how the women folks who had to cook for them had time and strength to live.

After dinner the speechifying began. The Rev. Henry P. Jacobs made the opening address; we had agreed that he should be invited to do so, since he was the minister. He asked the blessing before we began to eat, and made the opening address afterward. Mr. Jacobs is considered a fine speaker, and he is never at a loss for ideas. We all felt proud of him as he stood up and began to speak of the state of the Linnville church a hundred years ago, and contrasted those days of fireless meeting-houses with the comforts of the sanctuary at the present time. He also had a long list of statistics. I began at last to feel a little uneasy lest he might read his poem, and so rob the guests who were to speak of their quotas of time. Louisa said she thought he was intending to, but she saw Mrs. Jameson whisper to her husband, who immediately tiptoed around to him with a scared and important look, and said something in a low voice. Then the minister, with a somewhat crestfallen air, curtailed his remarks, saying something about his hoping to read a poem a little later on that auspicious occasion, but that he would now introduce Mrs. H. Board-man Jameson, to whom they were all so much indebted.

Mrs. Jameson arose and bowed to the company, and adjusted her eyeglasses. Her jets glittered, her eyes shone with a commanding brightness, and she really looked very imposing. After a few words, which even Flora Clark acknowledged were very well chosen, she read the Governor's letter with great impressiveness. Then she went on to read other letters from people who were noteworthy in some way and had some association with the village. Flora Clark said that she believed that Mrs. Jameson had written to every celebrity whose grandfather ever drove through Linnville. She did have a great many letters from people who we were surprised to hear had ever heard of us, and they were very interesting. Still it did take time to read them; and after she had finished them all, Mrs. Jameson commenced to speak on her own account. She had some notes which she consulted unobtrusively from time to time. She dwelt mainly upon the vast improvement for the better in our condition during the last hundred years. She mentioned in this connection Robert Browning, the benefit of whose teaching was denied our ancestors of a hundred years ago. She also mentioned hygienic bread as a contrast to the heavy, indigestible masses of corn-meal concoctions and the hurtful richness of pound-cake. Mrs. Jameson galloped with mild state all her little hobbies for our delectation, and the time went on. We had sat very long at dinner; it was later than we had planned when the speechifying began. Mrs. Jameson did not seem to be in the least aware of the flight of time as she peacefully proceeded; nor did she see how we were all fidgeting. Still, nobody spoke to her; nobody quite dared, and then we thought every sentence would be her last.

The upshot of it was that the Grover stage-coach arrived, and Mrs. Sim White's brother, Elijah M. Mills, and Mrs. Lucy Beers Wright, besides a number of others of lesser fame, were obliged to leave without raising their voices, or lose their trains, which for such busy people was not to be thought of. There was much subdued indignation and discomfiture among us, and I dare say among the guests themselves. Mrs. Lucy Beers Wright was particularly haughty, even to Mrs. Sim White, who did her best to express her regret without blaming Mrs. Jameson. As for Elijah M. Mills, Louisa said she heard him say something which she would not repeat, when he was putting on his hat. He is a fine speaker, and noted for the witty stories which he tells; we felt that we had missed a great deal. I must say, to do her justice, that Mrs. Jameson seemed somewhat perturbed, and disposed to be conciliating when she bade the guests good-by; she was even apologetic in her calmly superior way.

However, the guests had not been gone long before something happened to put it all out of our minds for the time. The Rev. Henry P. Jacobs had just stood up again, with a somewhat crestfallen air, to read his poem—I suppose he was disappointed to lose the more important part of his audience—when there was a little scream, and poor Harriet Jameson was all in a blaze. She wore a white muslin dress, and somehow it had caught—I suppose from a spark; she had been sitting near the hearth, though we had thought the fire was out. Harry Liscom made one spring for her when he saw what had happened; but he had not been very near her, and a woman was before him. She caught up the braided rug from the floor, and in a second Harriet was borne down under it, and then Harry was there with his coat, and Sim White, and the fire was out. Poor Harriet was not much hurt, only a few trifling burns; but if it had not been for the woman she might easily have gotten her death, and our centennial ended in a tragedy.

It had all been done so quickly that we had not fairly seen who the woman who snatched up the rug was, but when the fire was out we knew: Caroline Liscom. She was somewhat burned herself, too, but she did not seem to mind that at all. She was, to our utter surprise—for we all knew how she had felt about Harry's marrying Harriet—cuddling the girl in her motherly arms, the sleeves of her best black grenadine[11] being all scorched, too, and telling her that she must not be frightened, the fire was all out, and calling her my dear child, and kissing her. I, for one, never knew that Caroline Liscom could display so much warmth of love and pity, and that toward a girl whom she was determined her son should not marry, and before so many. I suppose when she saw the poor child all in a blaze, and thought she would be burned to death, her heart smote her, and she felt that she would do anything in the world if she only lived.

Harry Liscom was as white as a sheet. Once or twice he tried to push his mother away, as if he wished to do the comforting and cuddling himself; but she would not have it. "Poor child! poor child!" she kept repeating; "it's all over, don't be frightened," as if Harriet had been a baby.

Then Mrs. H. Boardman Jameson came close to Caroline Liscom, and tears were running down her cheeks quite openly. She did not even have out her handkerchief, and she threw her arms right around the other woman who had saved her daughter. "God bless you! Oh, God bless you!" she said; then her voice broke and she sobbed out loud. I think a good many of us joined her. As for Caroline Liscom, she sort of pushed Harriet toward her son, and then she threw her poor, scorched arms around Mrs. H. Boardman Jameson and kissed her. "Oh, let us both thank God!" sobbed Caroline.

As soon as we got calm enough we took Harriet upstairs; her pretty muslin was fluttering around her in yellow rags, and the slight burns needed attention; she was also exhausted with the nervous shock, and was trembling like a leaf, her cheeks white and her eyes big with terror. Caroline Liscom and her mother came too, and Caroline concealed her burns until Harriet's were dressed. Luckily, the doctor was there. Then Harriet was induced to lie down on the north chamber bed on the old blue-and-white counterpane that Mrs. Sim White's mother spun and wove.

Rev. Henry P. Jacobs did not read his poem; we were too much perturbed to listen to it, and nobody mentioned it to him. Flora Clark whispered to me that if he began she should go home; for her part, she felt as if she had gone through enough that day without poetry. The poem was delivered by special request at our next sewing circle, but I think the minister was always disappointed, though he strove to bear it with Christian grace. However, within three months he had to console him a larger wedding fee than often falls to a minister in Linnville.

The centennial dissolved soon after the burning accident. There was nothing more to do but to put the Shaw house to rights again and restore the various articles to their owners, which, of course, could not be done that day, nor for many days to come. I think I never worked harder in my life than I did setting things to rights after our centennial; but I had one consolation through it, and that was the happiness of the two young things, who had had indirectly their love tangle smoothed out by it.

Caroline Liscom and Mrs. Jameson were on the very best of terms, and Harriet was running over to Caroline's house to take lessons in housekeeping, instead of to mine, before the week was out.

There was a beautiful wedding the last of October, and young Mrs. Harry Liscom has lived in our midst ever since, being considered one of the most notable housekeepers in the village for her age. She and her husband live with Caroline Liscom, and Louisa says sometimes that she believes Caroline loves the girl better than she does her own son, and that she fairly took her into her heart when she saved her life.

"Some women can't love anybody except their own very much unless they can do something for them," says Louisa; and I don't know but she is right.

The Jamesons are still with us every summer—even Grandma Cobb, who does not seem to grow feeble at all. Sarah is growing to be quite a pretty girl, and there is a rumor that Charlie White is attentive to her, though they are both almost too young to think of such things. Cobb is a very nice boy, and people say they had as soon have him come in and sit a while and talk, as a girl. As for Mrs. Jameson, she still tries to improve us at times, not always with our full concurrence, and her ways are still not altogether our ways, provoking mirth, or calling for charity. Yet I must say we have nowadays a better understanding of her good motives, having had possibly our spheres enlarged a little by her, after all, and having gained broader views from the points of view of people outside our narrow lives. I think we most of us are really fond of Mrs. H. Boardman Jameson, and are very glad that the Jamesons came to our village.

One Good Time

RICHARD STONE WAS nearly seventy-five years old when he died, his wife was over sixty, and his daughter Narcissa past middle age. Narcissa Stone had been very pretty, and would have been pretty still had it not been for those lines, as distinctly garrulous of discontent and worry as any words of mouth, which come so easily in the face of a nervous, delicate-skinned woman. They were around Narcissa's blue eyes, her firmly closed lips, her thin nose; a frown like a crying repetition of some old anxiety and indecision was on her forehead; and she had turned her long neck so much to look over her shoulder for new troubles on her track that the lines of fearful expectation had settled there. Narcissa had yet her beautiful thick hair, which the people in the village had never quite liked because it was red, her cheeks were still pink, and she stooped only a little from her slender height when she walked. Some people said that Narcissa Stone would be quite good-looking now if she had a decent dress and bonnet. Neither she nor her mother had any clothes which were not deemed shabby, even by the humbly attired women in the little mountain village. "Mis' Richard Stone, she 'ain't had a new silk dress since Narcissa was born," they said; "and as for Narcissa, she 'ain't never had anything that looked fit to wear to meeting."

When Richard Stone died, people wondered if his widow and Narcissa would not have something new. Mrs. Nathan Wheat, who was a third cousin to Richard Stone, went, the day before the funeral, a half-mile down the brook road to see Hannah Turbin, the dressmaker. The road was little travelled; she walked through an undergrowth of late autumn flowers, and when she reached the Turbins' house her black thibet gown was gold-powdered and white-flecked to the knees with pollen and winged seeds of passed flowers.

Hannah Turbin's arm, brown and wrinkled like a monkey's, in its woollen sleeve, described arcs of jerky energy past the window, and never ceased when Mrs. Wheat came up the path and entered the house. Hannah herself scarcely raised her seamy brown face from her work.

"Good-afternoon," said Mrs. Wheat.

Hannah nodded. "Good-afternoon," she responded then, as if words were an afterthought.

Mrs. Wheat shook her black skirts vigorously. "I'm all over dust from them yaller weeds," said she. "Well, I don't care about this old thibet." She pulled a rocking-chair forward and seated herself. "Warm for this time of year," said she.

Hannah drew her thread through her work. "Yes, 'tis," she returned, with a certain pucker of scorn, as if the utter foolishness of allusions to obvious conditions of nature struck her. Hannah Turbin was not a favorite in the village, but she was credited with having much common-sense, and people held her in somewhat distant respect.

"Guess it's Injun summer," remarked Mrs. Wheat.

Hannah Turbin said nothing at all to that. Mrs. Wheat cast furtive glances around the room as she swayed in her rocking-chair. Everything was very tidy, and there were few indications of its owner's calling. A number of fashion papers were neatly piled on a bureau in the corner, and some nicely folded breadths of silk lay beside them. There was not a scrap or shred of cloth upon the floor; not a thread, even. Hannah was basting a brown silk basque. Mrs. Wheat could see nowhere the slightest evidence of what she had come to ascertain, so was finally driven to inquiry, still, however, by devious windings.

"Seems sad about Richard," she said.

"Yes," returned Hannah, with a sudden contraction of her brown face, which seemed to flash a light over a recollection in Mrs. Wheat's mind. She remembered that there was a time, years ago, when Richard Stone had paid some attention to Hannah Turbin, and people had thought he might marry her instead of Jane Basset. However, it had happened so long ago that she did not really believe that Hannah dwelt upon it, and it faded immediately from her own mind.

"Well," said she, with a sigh, "it is a happy release, after all, he's been such a sufferer so long. It's better for him, and it's better for Jane and Narcissa. He's left 'em comfortable; they've got the farm, and his life's insured, you know. Besides, I suppose Narcissa 'll marry William Crane now. Most likely they'll rent the farm, and Jane will go and live with Narcissa when she's married. I want to know—"

Hannah Turbin sewed.

"I was wondering," continued Mrs. Wheat, "if Jane and Narcissa wasn't going to have some new black dresses for the funeral. They 'ain't got a thing that's fit to wear, I know. I don't suppose they've got much money on hand now except what little Richard saved up for his funeral expenses. I know he had a little for that because he told me so, but the life-insurance is coming in, and anybody would trust them. There's a nice piece of black cashmere down to the store, a dollar a yard. I didn't know but they'd get dresses off it; but Jane she never tells me anything—anybody 'd think she might, seeing as I was poor Richard's cousin; and as for Narcissa, she's as close as her mother."

Hannah Turbin sewed.

" 'Ain't Jane and Narcissa said anything to you about making them any new black dresses to wear to the funeral?" asked Mrs. Wheat, with desperate directness.

"No, they 'ain't," replied Hannah Turbin.

"Well, then, all I've got to say is they'd ought to be ashamed of themselves. There they've got fourteen if not fifteen hundred dollars coming in from poor Richard's insurance money, and they ain't even going to get decent clothes to wear to his funeral out of it. They 'ain't made any plans for new bonnets, I know. It ain't showing proper respect to the poor man. Don't you say so?"

"I suppose folks are their own best judges," said Hannah Turbin, in her conclusive, half-surly fashion, which intimidated most of her neighbors. Mrs. Wheat did not stay much longer. When she went home through the ghostly weeds and grasses of the country road she was almost as indignant with Hannah Turbin as with Jane Stone and Narcissa. "Never saw anybody so close in my life," said she to herself. "Needn't talk if she don't want to. Dun'no' as thar's any harm in my wanting to know if my own third cousin is going to have mourning wore for him."

Mrs. Wheat, when she reached home, got a black shawl which had belonged to her mother out of the chest, where it had lain in camphor, and hung it on the clothesline to air. She also removed a spray of bright velvet flowers from her bonnet, and sewed in its place a black ostrich feather. She found an old crape veil too, and steamed it into stiffness. "I'm going to go to that funeral looking decent, if his own wife and daughter ain't," she told her husband.

"If I wa'n't along, folks would take you for the widder," said Nathan Wheat, with a chuckle. Nathan Wheat was rather inclined to be facetious with his wife.

However, Mrs. Wheat was not the only person who attended poor Richard Stone's funeral in suitable attire. Hannah Turbin was black from head to foot; the material, it is true, was not of the conventional mourning kind, but the color was. She wore a black silk gown, a black ladies'-cloth mantle, a black velvet bonnet trimmed with black flowers, and a black lace veil.

"Hannah Turbin looked as if she was dressed in second mourning," Mrs. Wheat said to her husband after the funeral. "I should have thought she'd most have worn some color, seeing as some folks might remember she was disappointed about Richard Stone; but, anyway, it was better than to go looking the way Jane and Narcissa did. There was Jane in that old brown dress, and Narcissa in her green, with a blue flower in her bonnet. I think it was dreadful, and poor Richard leaving them all that money through his dying, too."

In truth, all the village was scandalized at the strange attire of the widow and daughter of Richard Stone at his funeral, except William Crane. He could not have told what Mrs. Stone wore, through scarcely admitting her in any guise into his inmost consciousness, and as for Narcissa, he admitted her so fully that he could not see her robes at all in such a dazzlement of vision.

"William Crane never took his eyes off Narcissa Stone all through the funeral; shouldn't be surprised if he married her in a month or six weeks," people said.

William Crane took Jane and Narcissa to the grave in his covered wagon, keeping his old white horse at a decorous jog behind the hearse in the little funeral procession, and people noted that. They wondered if he would go over to the Stones' that evening, and watched, but he did not. He left the mother and daughter to their closer communion of grief that night, but the next the neighbors saw him in his best suit going down the road before dark. "Must have done up his chores early to get started soon as this," they said.

William Crane was about Narcissa's age but he looked older. His gait was shuffling, his hair scanty and gray, and, moreover, he had that expression of patience which comes only from long abiding, both of body and soul. He went through the south yard to the side door of the house, stepping between the rocks. The yard abounded in mossy slopes of half-sunken rocks, as did the entire farm. Folks often remarked of Richard Stone's place, as well as himself, "Stone by name, and stone by nature." Underneath nearly all his fields, cropping plentifully to the surface, were rock ledges. The grass could be mown only by hand. As for this south yard, it required skilful manœuvring to drive a team through it. When William Crane knocked that evening, Narcissa opened the door. "Oh, it's you!" she said. "How do you do?"

"How do you do, Narcissa?" William responded, and walked in. He could have kissed his old love in the gloom of the little entry, but he did not think of that. He looked at her anxiously with his soft, patient eyes. "How are you gettin' on?" he asked.

"Well as can be expected," replied Narcissa.

"How's your mother?"

"She's well as can be expected."

William followed Narcissa, who led the way, not into the parlor, as he had hoped, but into the kitchen. The kitchen's great interior of smoky gloom was very familiar to him, but to-night it looked strange. For one thing, the arm-chair to which Richard Stone had been bound with his rheumatism for the last fifteen years was vacant, and pushed away into a corner. William looked at it, and it seemed to him that he must see the crooked, stern old figure in it, and hear again the peremptory tap of the stick which he kept always at his side to summon assistance. After his first involuntary glance at the dead man's chair, William saw his widow coming forward out of her bedroom with a great quilt over her arm.

"Good-evenin', William," she said, with faint melancholy, then lapsed into feeble weeping.

"Now, mother, you said you wouldn't; you know it don't do any good, and you'll be sick," Narcissa cried out, impatiently.

"I know it, Narcissa, but I can't help it, I can't. I'm dreadful upset! Oh, William, I'm dreadful upset! It ain't his death alone— it's—"

"Mother, I'd rather tell him myself," interrupted Narcissa. She took the quilt from her mother, and drew the rocking-chair towards her. "Do sit down and keep calm, mother," said she.

But it was not easy for the older woman, in her bewilderment of grief and change, to keep calm.

"Oh, William, do you know what we're goin' to do?" she wailed, yet seating herself obediently in the rocking-chair. "We're goin' to New York. Narcissa says so. We're goin' to take the insurance money, when we get it, an' we're goin' to New York. I tell her we hadn't ought to, but she won't listen to it! There's the trunk. Look at there, William! She dragged it down from the garret this forenoon. Look at there, William!"

William's startled eyes followed the direction of Mrs. Stone's wavering index finger, and saw a great ancient trunk lined with blue and white wall-paper, standing open against the opposite wall.

"She dragged it down from the garret this forenoon," continued Mrs. Stone, in the same tone of unfaltering tragedy, while Narcissa, her delicate lips pursed tightly, folded up the bedquilt which her mother had brought. "It bumped so hard on those garret stairs I thought she'd break it, or fall herself, but she wouldn't let me help her. Then she cleaned it, an' made some paste, an' lined it with some of the parlor paper. There ain't any key to it—I never remember none. The trunk was in this house when I come here. Richard had it when he went West before we were married. Narcissa she says she is goin' to tie it up with the clothes-line. William, can't you talk to her? Seems to me I can't go to New York nohow."

William turned then to Narcissa, who was laying the folded bedquilt in the trunk. He looked pale and bewildered, and his voice trembled when he spoke. "This ain't true, is it, Narcissa?" he said.

"Yes, it is," she replied, shortly, still bending over the trunk.

"We ain't goin' for a month," interposed her mother again; "we can't get the insurance money before then, Lawyer Maxham says; but she says she's goin' to have the trunk standin' there, an' put things in when she thinks of it, so she won't forgit nothin'. She says we'd better take one bedquilt with us, in case they don't have 'nough clothes on the bed. We've got to stay to a hotel. Oh, William, can't you say anything to stop her?"

"This ain't true, Narcissa?" William repeated, helplessly.

Narcissa raised herself and faced him. Her cheeks were red, her blue eyes glowing, her hair tossing over her temples in loose waves. She looked as she had when he first courted her. "Yes, it is, William Crane," she cried. "Yes, it is."

William looked at her so strangely and piteously that she softened a little. "I've got my reasons," said she. "Maybe I owe it to you to tell them. I suppose you were expecting something different." She hesitated a minute, looking at her mother, who cried out again:

"Oh, William, say somethin' to stop her! Can't you say somethin' to stop her?"

Then Narcissa motioned to him resolutely. "Come into the parlor, William," said she, and he followed her out across the entry. The parlor was chilly; the chairs stood as they had done at the funeral, primly against the walls glimmering faintly in the dusk with

blue and white paper like the trunk lining. Narcissa stood before
William and talked with feverish haste. "I'm going," said she—"I'm
going to take that money and go with mother to New York, and
you mustn't try to stop me, William. I know what you've been expecting. I know, now father's gone, you think there ain't anything
to hinder our getting married; you think we'll rent this house,
and mother and me will settle down in yours for the rest of our
lives. I know you ain't counting on that insurance money; it ain't
like you."

"The Lord knows it ain't, Narcissa," William broke out with pathetic pride.

"I know that as well as you do. You thought we'd put it in the
bank for a rainy day, in case mother got feeble, or anything, and
that is all you did think. Maybe I'd ought to. I s'pose I had, but I
ain't going to. I 'ain't never done anything my whole life that I
thought I ought not to do, but now I'm going to. I'm going to if it's
wicked. I've made up my mind. I 'ain't never had one good time in
my whole life, and now I'm going to, even if I have to suffer for it
afterwards.

"I 'ain't never had anything like other women. I've never had
any clothes nor gone anywhere. I've just stayed at home here and
drudged. I've done a man's work on the farm. I've milked and made
butter and cheese; I've waited on father; I've got up early and gone
to bed late. I've just drudged, drudged, ever since I can remember. I
don't know anything about the world nor life. I don't know anything but my own old tracks, and—I'm going to get out of them for
a while, whether or no."

"How long are you calculating to stay?"

"I don't know."

"I've been thinking," said William, "I'd have some new gilt paper
on the sitting-room at my house, and a new stove in the kitchen. I
thought—"

"I know what you thought," interrupted Narcissa, still trembling and glowing with nervous fervor. "And you're real good,
William. It ain't many men would have waited for me as you've
done, when father wouldn't let me get married as long as he lived. I
know by good rights I hadn't ought to keep you waiting, but I'm
going to, and it ain't because I don't think enough of you—it
ain't that; I can't help it. If you give up having me at all, if you
think you'd rather marry somebody else, I can't help it; I won't
blame you—"

"Maybe you want me to, Narcissa," said William, with a sad dignity. "If you do, if you want to get rid of me, if that's it—"

Narcissa started. "That ain't it," said she. She hesitated, and added, with formal embarrassment—she had the usual reticence of a New England village woman about expressions of affection, and had never even told her lover in actual words that she loved him— "My feelings towards you are the same as they have always been, William."

It was almost dark in the parlor. They could see only each other's faces gleaming as with pale light. "It would be a blow to me if I thought they wa'n't, Narcissa," William returned, simply.

"They are."

William put his arm around her waist, and they stood close together for a moment. He stroked back her tumbled red hair with clumsy tenderness. "You have had a hard time, Narcissa," he whispered, brokenly. "If you want to go, I ain't going to say anything against it. I ain't going to deny I'm kind of disappointed. I've been living alone so long, and I feel kind of sore sometimes with waitin', but—"

"I shouldn't make you any kind of a wife if I married you now, without waiting," Narcissa said, in a voice at once stern and tender. She stood apart from him, and put up her hand with a sort of involuntary maiden primness to smooth her hair where his had stroked it awry. "If," she went on, "I had to settle down in your house, as I have done in father's, and see the years stretching ahead like a long road without any turn, and nothing but the same old dog-trot of washing and ironing and scrubbing and cooking and sewing and washing dishes till I drop into my grave, I should hate you, William Crane."

"I could fetch an' carry all the water for the washin', Narcissa, and I could wash the dishes," said William, with humble beseeching.

"It ain't that. I know you'd do all you could. It's— Oh, William! I've got to have a break; I've got to have one good time. I—like you, and—I liked father; but love ain't enough sometimes when it ties anybody. Everybody has got their own feet and their own wanting to use 'em, and sometimes when love comes in the way of that, it ain't anything but a dead wall. Once we had a black heifer that would jump all the walls; we had to sell her. She always made me think of myself. I tell you, William, I've got to jump my wall, and I've got to have one good time."

William Crane nodded his gray head in patient acquiescence. His forehead was knitted helplessly; he could not in the least understand what his sweetheart meant; in her present mood she was in altogether a foreign language for him, but still the unintelligible sound of her was sweet as a song to his ears. This poor village lover had at least gained the crown of absolute faith through his weary years of waiting; the woman he loved was still a star, and her rays not yet resolved into human reachings and graspings.

"How long do you calculate to be gone, Narcissa?" he asked again.

"I don't know," she replied. "Fifteen hundred dollars is a good deal of money. I s'pose it'll take us quite a while to spend it, even if we ain't very saving."

"You ain't goin' to spend it all, Narcissa!" William gave a little dismayed gasp in spite of himself.

"Land, no! we couldn't, unless we stayed three years, an' I ain't calculating to be gone as long as that. I'm going to bring home what we don't want, and put it in the bank; but—I shouldn't be surprised if it took 'most a year to spend what I've laid out to."

" 'Most a year!"

"Yes; I've got to buy us both new clothes for one thing. We 'ain't neither of us got anything fit to wear, and 'ain't had for years. We didn't go to the funeral lookin' decent, and I know folks talked. Mother felt bad about it, but I couldn't help it. I wa'n't goin' to lay out money foolish and get things here when I was going to New York and could have others the way they ought to be. I'm going to buy us some jewelry too; I 'ain't never had a good breastpin even; and as for mother, father never even bought her a ring when they were married. I ain't saying anything against him; it wa'n't the fashion so much in those days."

"I was calculatin'—" William stammered, blushing. "I always meant to, Narcissa."

"Yes, I know you have; but you mustn't lay out too much on it, and I don't care anything about a stone ring—just a plain gold one. There's another thing I'm going to have, too, an' that's a gold watch. I've wanted one all my life."

"Mebbe—" began William, painfully.

"No!" cried Narcissa, peremptorily. "I don't want you to buy me one. I 'ain't ever thought of it. I'm going to buy it myself. I'm going to buy mother a real cashmere shawl, too, like the one that New York lady had that came to visit Lawyer Maxham's wife. I've got a list of things written down on paper. I guess I'll have to buy another trunk in New York to put them in."

"Well," said William, with a great sigh, "I guess I'd better be goin'. I hope you'll have as good a time as you're countin' on, Narcissa."

"It's the first good time I ever did count on, and I'd ought to," said Narcissa. "I'm going to take mother to the theatre, too. I don't know but it's wicked, but I'm going to." Narcissa fluttered out of the parlor and William shuffled after her. He would not go into the kitchen again.

"Well, good-night," said Narcissa, and William also said good-night, with another heavy sigh. "Look out for them rocks going out of the yard, an' don't tumble over 'em," she called after him.

"I'm used to 'em," he answered back, sadly, from the darkness.

Narcissa shut and bolted the door. "He don't like it; he feels real bad about it; but I can't help it—I'm going."

Through the next few weeks Narcissa Stone's face looked strange to those who had known her from childhood. While the features were the same, her soul informed them with a new purpose, which overlighted all the old ones of her life, and even the simple village folks saw the effect, though with no understanding. Soon the news that Narcissa and her mother were going to New York was abroad. On the morning they started, in the three-seated open wagon which served as stage to connect the little village with the railroad ten miles away, all the windows were set with furtively peering faces.

"There they go," the women told one another. "Narcissa an' her mother an' the trunk. Wonder if Narcissa's got that money put away safe? They're wearin' the same old clothes. S'pose we sha'n't know 'em when they get back. Heard they was goin' to stay a year. Guess old Mr. Stone would rise up in his grave if he knew it. Lizzy saw William Crane a-helpin' Narcissa h'ist the trunk out ready for the stage. I wouldn't stan' it if I was him. Ten chances to one Narcissa 'll pick up somebody down to New York, with all that money. She's good-lookin', and she looks better since her father died."

Narcissa, riding out of her native village to those unknown fields in which her imagination had laid the scene of the one good time of her life, regarded nothing around her. She sat straight, her slender body resisting stiffly the jolt of the stage. She said not a word, but looked ahead with shining eyes. Her mother wept, a fold of her old shawl before her face. Now and then she lamented aloud, but softly, lest the driver hear. "Goin' away from the place where I was born an' married, an' have lived ever since I knew anything, to stay a year. I can't stan' it, I can't."

"Hush, mother! You'll have a real good time."

"No, I sha'n't, I sha'n't. Goin'—to stay a whole—year. I—can't, nohow."

"S'pose we sha'n't see you back in these parts for some time," the stage-driver said, when he helped them out at the railroad station. He was an old man, and had known Narcissa since her childhood.

"Most likely not," she replied. Her mother's face was quite stiff with repressed emotion when the stage-driver lifted her out. She did not want him to report in the village that she was crying when she started for New York. She had some pride in spite of her distress.

"Well, I'll be on the lookout for ye a year from to-day," said the stage-driver, with a jocular twist of his face. There were no passengers for his village on the in-coming train, so he had to drive home alone through the melancholy autumn woods. The sky hung low with pale, freezing clouds; over everything was that strange hush which prevails before snow. The stage-driver, holding the reins loosely over his tramping team, settled forward with elbows on his knees, and old brows bent with aimless brooding. Over and over again his brain worked the thought, like a peaceful cud of contemplation. "They're goin' to be gone a year. Narcissa Stone an' her mother are goin' to be gone a year, afore I'll drive 'em home."

So little imagination had the routine of his life fostered that he speculated not, even upon the possible weather of that far-off day, or the chances of his living to see it. It was simply, "They're goin' to be gone a year afore I'll drive 'em home."

So fixed was his mind upon that one outcome of the situation that when Narcissa and her mother reappeared in less than one week—in six days—he could not for a moment bring his mind intelligently to bear upon it. The old stage-driver may have grown something like his own horses through his long sojourn in their company, and his intelligence, like theirs, been given to only the halts and gaits of its first breaking.

For a second he had a bewildered feeling that time had flown fast, that a week was a year. Everybody in the village had said the travellers would not return for a year. He hoisted the ancient paper-lined trunk into his stage, then a fine new one, nailed and clamped with shining brass, then a number of packages, all the time with puzzled eyes askant upon Narcissa and her mother. He would scarcely have known them, as far as their dress was concerned. Mrs. Stone wore a fine black satin gown; her perturbed old face looked out of luxurious environments of fur and lace and rich black plumage. As for Narcissa, she was almost regal. The old stage-driver backed and ducked awkwardly, as if she were a stranger, when she approached. Her fine skirts flared imposingly, and rustled with unseen silk; her slender shoulders were made shapely by the graceful spread of rich fur, her red hair shone under a hat fit for a princess, and there was about her a faint perfume of violets which made the stage driver gaze confusedly at the snowy ground under the trees when they had started on the homeward road. "Seems as if I smelt posies, but I know there ain't none hereabouts this time of year," he remarked, finally, in a tone of mild ingratiation, as if more to himself than to his passengers.

"It's some perfumery Narcissa's got on her pocket-handkerchief that she bought in New York," said Mrs. Stone, with a sort of sad pride. She looked worn and bewildered, ready to weep at the sight of familiar things, and yet distinctly superior to all such weakness. As for Narcissa, she looked like a child thrilled with scared triumph at getting its own way, who rejoices even in the midst of correction at its own assertion of freedom.

"That so?" said the stage-driver, admiringly. Then he added, doubtfully, bringing one white-browed eye to bear over his shoulder, "Didn't stay quite so long as you calculated on?"

"No, we didn't," replied Narcissa, calmly. She nudged her mother with a stealthy, firm elbow, and her mother understood well that she was to maintain silence.

"I ain't going to tell a living soul about it but William Crane; I owe it to him," Narcissa had said to her mother before they started on their homeward journey. "The other folks sha'n't know. They can guess and surmise all they want to, but they sha'n't know. I sha'n't tell; and William, he's as close-mouthed as a rock; and as for you, mother, you always did know enough to hold your tongue when you made up your mind to it."

Mrs. Stone had compressed her mouth until it looked like her daughter's. She nodded. "Yes," said she; "I know some things that I 'ain't never told you, Narcissa."

The stage passed William Crane's house. He was shuffling

around to the side-door from the barn, with a milk-pail in each hand, when they reached it.

"Stop a minute," Narcissa said to the driver. She beckoned to William, who stared, standing stock-still, holding his pails. Narcissa beckoned again imperatively. Then William set the pails down on the snowy ground and came to the fence. He looked over it, quite pale, and gaping.

"We've got home," said Narcissa.

William nodded; he could not speak.

"Come over by-and-by," said Narcissa.

William nodded.

"I'm ready to go now," Narcissa said to the stage-driver. "That's all."

That evening, when William Crane reached his sweetheart's house, a bright light shone on the road from the parlor windows. Narcissa opened the door. He stared at her open-mouthed. She wore a gown the like of which he had never seen before—soft lengths of blue silk and lace trailed about her, blue ribbons fluttered.

"How do you do?" said she.

William nodded solemnly.

"Come in."

William followed her into the parlor, with a wary eye upon his feet, lest they trample her trailing draperies. Narcissa settled gracefully into the rocking-chair; William sat opposite and looked at her. Narcissa was a little pale, still her face wore that look of insistent triumph.

"Home quicker 'n you expected," William said, at length.

"Yes," said Narcissa. There was a wonderful twist on her red hair, and she wore a high shell comb. William's dazzled eyes noted something sparkling in the laces at her throat; she moved her hand, and something on that flashed like a point of white flame. William remembered vaguely how, often in the summer-time when he had opened his house-door in the sunny morning, the dewdrops on the grass had flashed in his eyes. He had never seen diamonds.

"What started you home so much sooner than you expected?" he asked, after a little.

"I spent—all the money—"

"All—that money?"

"Yes."

"Fifteen hundred dollars in less 'n a week?"

"I spent more'n that."

"More'n that?" William could scarcely bring out the words. He was very white.

"Yes," said Narcissa. She was paler than when he had entered, but she spoke quite decidedly. "I'm going to tell you all about it, William. I ain't going to make a long story of it. If after you've heard it you think you'd rather not marry me, I sha'n't blame you. I sha'n't have anything to say against it. I'm going to tell you just what I've been doing; then you can make up your mind.

"To-day's Tuesday, and we went away last Thursday. We've been gone just six days. Mother an' me got to New York Thursday night, an' when we got out of the cars the men come round hollering this hotel an' that hotel. I picked out a man that looked as if he didn't drink and would drive straight, an' he took us to an elegant carriage, an' mother an' me got in. Then we waited till he got the trunk an' put it up on the seat with him where he drove. Mother she hollered to him not to let it fall off.

"We went to a beautiful hotel. There was a parlor with a red velvet carpet and red stuffed furniture, and a green sitting-room, and a blue one. The ceilin' had pictures on it. There was a handsome young gentleman down-stairs at a counter in the room where we went first, and mother asked him, before I could stop her, if the folks in the hotel was all honest. She'd been worrying all the way for fear somebody 'd steal the money.

"The gentleman said—he was real polite—if we had any money or valuables, we had better leave them with him, and he would put them in the safe. So we did. Then a young man with brass buttons on his coat took us to the elevator and showed us our rooms. We had a parlor with a velvet carpet an' stuffed furniture and a gilt clock on the mantel-shelf, two bedrooms, and a bath-room. There ain't anything in town equal to it. Lawyer Maxham ain't got anything to come up to it. The young man offered to untie the rope on the trunk, so I let him. He seemed real kind about it.

"Soon's the young man went I says to mother, 'We ain't going down to get any tea to-night.'

" 'Why not?' says she.

" 'I ain't going down a step in this old dress,' says I, 'an' you ain't going in yours.'

"Mother didn't like it very well. She said she was faint to her stomach, and wanted some tea, but I made her eat some gingerbread we'd brought from home, an' get along. The young man with the brass buttons come again after a while an' asked if there was any-thing we wanted, but I thanked him an' told him there wasn't.

"I would have asked him to bring up mother some tea and a hot biscuit, but I didn't know but what it would put 'em out; it was af-ter seven o'clock then. So we got along till morning.

"The next morning mother an' me went out real early, an' went into a bakery an' bought some cookies. We ate 'em as we went down the street, just to stay our stomachs; then we went to buying. I'd taken some of the money in my purse, an' I got mother an' me, first of all, two handsome black silk dresses, and we put 'em on as soon as we got back to the hotel, and went down to breakfast.

"You never see anythin' like the dining-room, and the kinds of things to eat. We couldn't begin to eat 'em all. There were men standin' behind our chairs to wait on us all the time.

"Right after breakfast mother an' me put our rooms to rights; then we went out again and bought things at the stores. Everybody was buying Christmas presents, an' the stores were all trimmed with evergreen—you never see anything like it. Mother an' me never had any Christmas presents, an' I told her we'd begin, an' buy 'em for each other. When the money I'd taken with us was gone, I sent things to the hotel for the gentleman at the counter to pay, the way he'd told me to. That day we bought our breastpins and this ring, an' mother's and my gold watch, an'—I got one for you too, William. Don't you say anything—it's your Christmas present. That afternoon we went to Central Park, an' that evenin' we went to the theatre. The next day we went to the stores again, an' I bought mother a black satin dress, and me a green one. I got this I've got on, too. It's what they call a tea-gown. I always wore it to tea in the hotel after I got it. I got a hat, too, an' mother a bonnet; an' I got a fur cape, and mother a cloak with fur on the neck an' all around it. That evening mother an' me went to the opera; we sat in something they call a box. I wore my new green silk and breastpin, an' mother wore her black satin. We both of us took our bonnets off. The music was splendid; but I wouldn't have young folks go to it much.

"The next day was Sunday. Mother an' me went to meeting in a splendid church, and wore our new black silks. They gave us seats way up in front, an' there was a real good sermon, though mother thought it wa'n't very practical, an' folks got up an' sat down more'n we do. Mother an' me set still, for fear we'd get up an' down in the wrong place. That evening we went to a sacred concert.

Everywhere we went we rode in a carriage. They invited us to at the hotel, an' I s'posed it was free, but it wa'n't, I found out afterwards.

"The next day was Monday—that's yesterday. Mother an' me went out to the stores again. I bought a silk bed-quilt, an' some handsome vases, an' some green an' gilt teacups setting in a tray to match. I've got 'em home without breaking. We got some silk stockings, too, an' some shoes, an' some gold-bowed spectacles for mother, an' two more silk dresses, an' mother a real cashmere shawl. Then we went to see some wax-works, and the pictures and curiosities in the Art Museum; then in the afternoon we went to ride again, and we were goin' to the theatre in the evening; but the gentleman at the counter called out to me when I was going past an' said he wanted to speak to me a minute.

"Then I found out we'd spent all that fifteen hundred dollars, an' more too. We owed 'em 'most ten dollars at the hotel; an' that wa'n't the worst of it—we didn't have enough money to take us home.

"Mother she broke right down an' cried, an' said it was all we had in the world besides the farm, an' it was poor father's insurance money, an' we couldn't get home, an' we'd have to go to prison.

"Folks come crowding round, an' I couldn't stop her. I don't know what I did do myself; I felt kind of dizzy, an' things looked dark. A lady come an' held a smelling-bottle to my nose, an' the gentleman at the counter sent a man with brass buttons for some wine.

"After I felt better an' could talk steady they questioned me up pretty sharp, an' I told 'em the whole story—about father an' his rheumatism, an' everything, just how I was situated, an' I must say they treated us like Christian folks, though, after all, I don't know as we were much beholden to 'em. We never begun to eat all there was on the list, an' we were real careful of the furniture; we didn't really get our money's worth after all was said. But they said the rest of our bill to them was no matter, an' they gave us our tickets to come home."

There was a pause. William looked at Narcissa in her blue gown as if she were a riddle whose answer was lost in his memory. His honest eyes were fairly pitiful from excess of questioning.

"Well," said Narcissa, "I've come back, an' I've spent all that money. I've been wasteful an' extravagant an'— There was a gentleman beautifully dressed who sat at our table, an' he talked real pleasant about the weather, an'—I got to thinking about him a little.

Of course I didn't like him as well as you, William, for what comes first comes last with all our folks, but somehow he seemed to be kind of a part of the good time. I sha'n't never see him again, an' all there was betwixt us was his saying twice it was a pleasant day, an' once it was cold, an' me saying yes; but I'm going to tell you the whole. I've been an' wasted fifteen hundred dollars; I've let my thoughts wander from you; an' that ain't all. I've had a good time, an' I can't say I 'ain't. I've had one good time, an'—I ain't sorry. You can—do just what you think best, William, an'—I won't blame you."

William Crane went over to the window. When he turned round and looked at Narcissa his eyes were full of tears and his wide mouth was trembling. "Do you think you can be contented to—stay on my side of the wall now, Narcissa?" he said, with a sweet and pathetic dignity.

Narcissa in her blue robes went over to him, and put, for the first time of her own accord, an arm around his faithful neck. "I wouldn't go out again if the bars were down," said she.

The Love of Parson Lord

ON MONDAY MORNING Love Lord sat on the side-door step, stitching some fine linen shirt-bands for her father. It was a day in early May, moving from dawn to dark with a rush of strong fresh winds, made almost as palpable as wings by the apple and cherry blossoms which they loosened and bore away from the trees. There was a fine apple-orchard in full bloom in the rear of Parson Reuben Lord's gray-shingled house, three large white-plumed cherry-trees stood in the side yard, but Love would never taste the apples and cherries therefrom, unless perchance some scanty measure of poor fruit could not be readily sold. All of Parson Lord's alabaster boxes of life were sold, and the proceeds devoted to foreign missions. Love had never questioned the wisdom of it; she had never questioned the wisdom of any of the orderings of her life. She regarded them as indirectly ordained by Providence through her father, and not to be cavilled at, except possibly in one instance. Love at twelve years of age had had many lacks of life, but only one active sorrow, and that sense of loss and deprivation after the delight of possession which induces rebellion.

Love had lost her mother when she was scarce more than a baby; she had been brought up by a rigorous widow, a distant relative of her father's, who had trained her according to all letters of law and faith. So inexorable had been her method, so thoroughly had Love been taught to perform her duties, that there had seemed to be danger of their losing the distinction of hand and individual work. Little Love had lived as under the self-regulating motive power of an automaton, her native inclinations, whether towards grace or perversity, being wholly amenable to her instructress, as to a spiritual sun and wind. Cousin Daphne Weatherhead, as the widow was called, was the only person with whom she was brought in close contact through her childhood. Of her father she saw very little except at meals, at family prayers, and on Sabbath days, when she sat for hours, with her solemn innocent eyes intent upon him, as he proclaimed the truths of the Word and the terrors of the law from his beetling pulpit.

Parson Reuben Lord was so closely welded to his faith and his devotion that he seemed to gain therefrom a strange stiffness, almost ossification, of spirit. People, while holding him in utmost respect for his stern consistency of life, yet regarded him with awe which had in it something of terror. His fervent zeal for the cause of missions seemed the ruling passion of his life. His two brothers were still laboring in foreign fields. It had been the sorest trial of his life that delicate health in his youth had kept him at home in narrower and more peaceful tillage. It had also been a sore trial to him that his first-born child had not been a son, whom he could devote, with more certainty of the acceptability of the sacrifice, to the cause of Christ in heathen lands. There was, however, a belief in the village that he had so devoted his first-born daughter, Elizabeth. When the child died, at the early age of seven, after a most wonderful life and precocious maturity of religious experience, afterwards celebrated in a memoir which became a village classic, people were strengthened in this belief. It was also reported, on the authority of Aunt Betsey Ware, who had officiated at both births, that the parson made a similar dedication to the Lord of his second daughter, Love, in spite of the expostulations of his poor wife Mehitable, whose maternal affection overcame her religious ardor.

It was even said that Mehitable Lord had faded away and died because of her preying grief over the loss of her first-born, and the fear lest the second, who was delicate, and had that sensitiveness of disposition which is sometimes thought prophetic of early death, should follow her. However that may have been, Mehitable Lord died when Love was too young to have anything but that vague sense of loss of love in the abstract which, while it changes the whole savor of life, does not rend it with bitterness.

Love had no little mates during her childhood. Cousin Daphne Weatherhead, seemingly with the best of motives, kept her aloof from them. "You are the minister's daughter, and should endeavor to follow in the foot-steps of your sainted sister," Cousin Daphne would remark if the little maid seemed to cast a wistful eye towards the frolics of the young of her kind. Poor little Love used, for she learned to read at an early age, to strive to console and amuse herself with the perusal of the memoir of her sainted sister. Sitting in her little chair, with the book on her small aproned knees, she bent her childish brows over its pious pages, and pondered gravely its every word.

Love's childhood, which might well have been considered somewhat dull and joyless, though so straightly ordered in the paths of righteousness and peace, held, however, but one grief. When she was six years old she had had a doll presented to her by a loving old dame who had brought up a family of fourteen children. The doll had belonged to her youngest daughter, and was a homely, rustic specimen of her race; but Love took it to her heart with a great content and the most credulous admiration. She was guilty of the one act of deception and the one lie of her childhood for the protection of this poor doll which had come to her for motherhood. She hid the fact of its possession from Cousin Daphne, and then she told a falsehood when questioned.

The pleased old grandmother who had given it to her told of it here and there with innocent garrulity, not dreaming it would do harm. But when Cousin Daphne heard the news, home she came, and poor little Love underwent a miniature inquisition, and remained firm under her rack and thumb-screw. "No, Grandma Streeter didn't ever give me any doll," declared she, with blue eyes looking straight into Cousin Daphne's, yet with a recoil glance of horror at her own wickedness. The word of this small sister of a departed saint was pitted against that of an ancient mother in Israel, but Cousin Daphne made diligent search, and discovered the doll hidden away under Love's feather-bed. When she held it before Love, and the child saw the beloved symbolic baby, never of any beauty whatever, and now battered and marred by the caresses and corrections of many mothers, until only a little girl in whom the first strength of maternal imagination can encompass miracles could hold her of any account whatever, she expressed no shame or contrition; she only stretched out her arms with a cry of love and agony: "Give her to me! oh, give her to me! Don't take her away, Cousin Daphne!"

That confirmed matters. Love knelt in prayer with her father and Cousin Daphne, until, out of docility and terror, her soul was melted within her with contrition for her heinous sin. Poor little Love seemed to almost see the lapping of the infernal fires around her, and she could not even hold the doll in her arms for comfort. She did not see the doll again for years. She used often to wonder where it was, what Cousin Daphne had done with it; but she would no more have asked her than she would have taken the name of the Lord in vain. And as for asking her father, she would never forget till her dying day his countenance of stern wretchedness and condemnation when Cousin Daphne had told him of her wickedness, and the almost despairing fervor of his prayer. She would as soon have asked for a little graven image.

Love was twelve years old when Cousin Daphne was found one afternoon sitting stiffly in her chair, with her knitting-work in her motionless hands. She did not come to prayers, and when Love went to call her, Cousin Daphne's face looked at her unseeingly out of the gathering dusk. After Cousin Daphne's death she lived alone with her father, it being held that with her fine training she was able to keep his house at the age of twelve. Love knelt with her father an hour every morning and evening, and listened to his reading of the Scriptures and prayers. She prepared his frugal meals, and sat timidly and respectfully opposite him at table. The rest of the time he remained alone in his study, walled in, as it were, with the thoughts of dead divines and fathers of the Church in mummy-cases of old calf-skin, and was in sore labor over his many-headed sermons.

Love kept his house, as she had been taught, as if it were her own soul; she cleaned it as she would have cleaned her heart of sin; she made all the poor furnishings shine as if they had been the trappings of the Temple, and acquitted herself like a housewife of twice her age, to the approbation of all the village matrons. This morning, although it was still early, the house was neatly set in order from garret to cellar, and there were two hours for the fine stitching before dinner. She sat there, hearing the soft rush of the spring wind and breathing in the flurrying sweetness of the cherry blossoms, but with no consciousness thereof. She set the beautiful stitches, like a little row of pearls, with the precision of a machine, her fingers working with no aid from her mind, which was intent upon a dream she had the night before about her lost doll.

As Love sat there the dream was to her what the perfume was to the cherry blossom, and would have been as evident to a sense made for its perception. Love had dreamed, the night before, that she was up in the garret of her father's house, when she heard a little wail, like that of a young baby. She started and looked around, and it came again, seemingly from the vicinity of an old hair trunk which her father had carried to college in his youth. An experience which she had had at church that day had possibly, by some obscure system of suggestion, induced the dream. That Sunday Love had seen for the first time the squire's new wife. The squire had lately married for the second time, a woman from the city, elderly, but very beautiful and stately. She had brought her orphan grandson to live with her. This grandson, Richard Pierce, was a boy of fourteen, large for his age and forward of understanding. He was nearly fitted to enter Harvard College. That Sunday, young Richard, sitting in the squire's pew, looked across at Love, sitting all alone in the parson's pew. Love was slim and tall, but with a pretty roundness under her little drab spencer cape, with apple curves of pink cheeks under her scooping bonnet, tied under her sweet chin with a sober-colored ribbon like her cape. Not a bright tint was there about Love, except in her face and hair. Young Master Richard looked at her with the half-indifferent, half-earnest gaze of an intellectual boy whose mind is devoted to matters in his estimation more important than the faces of girls, and yet has at times, in his own despite, his heart stirred faintly with the instincts and imaginations of his kind. At last Love, compelled perhaps by his gaze, looked at him, though it was in the midst of a fiery appeal from the pulpit. She gazed at the boy with an utter calmness and unconsciousness of scrutiny, as if he were something inanimate. Indeed, to this young Love, with her perfect innocence of ignorance and the long training of her mind on spiritual lines, a boy did not mean as much as a girl, nor much more than a rose-bush or an apple-tree. Richard, as if something in himself, of which he had not known, was discovered by her gaze, looked away with a great blush, and then Love turned her eyes from him towards his grandmother. They were suddenly alert, full of the most timid yet ardent admiration. The one love with which the child had any acquaintance, and for which she had as yet any yearning, was in the face of that elderly dame. It shone plain to her sight when she glanced at the grandson by her side, and it beamed forth, like a light in the windows of a home, when she saw little Love gazing at her in such timidly beseeching and admiring wise. Love cast down her eyes before the sweet mother-look of the squire's lady, her heart leaped, her mouth quivered as if she would weep. She thought that never, never since her own mother, whose caresses she remembered better than her face, had there been any one as beautiful as this woman. That morning Love heard no more of her father's discourse. She was conscious of nothing except that mother-presence, which seemed to pervade the whole church. The inexorable fatherhood of God, as set forth in the parson's sermon, was not as evident to the hungry little heart in His sanctuary as the motherhood of the squire's lady. She continued to gaze at her at intervals, with softly furtive eyes of adoration, as if the lady were the Blessed Mary, and she a little papist; and when she sometimes received a tenderly benignant glance in return, she scarcely knew where her body was, such was the elation of her spirit. When, after meeting, she was going down the aisle, and came abreast of the wonderful lady, and the soft sweep of her velvet cloak brushed her face like a wing, she could not help an involuntary nestle against her side, as if she were a baby. Then the squire's lady bent down, her beautiful old face framed in gray curls, and smiled, and lifted her hand, and patted Love gently on the smooth curve of her cheek. Love could have gone down at her feet. Nobody since her mother's death had ever caressed her to that extent. She gave a quick look up at the lady with something between a sob and a smile, then shrank back, followed her out of church, and watched her drive away with the squire and Master Richard, though she did not see them at all.

Somehow this encounter with the squire's lady set Love to thinking, more strenuously than usual, of the lost doll of her childhood, and that night she dreamed that she went over to the old trunk, and suddenly her doll peeped at her from behind it. It wore the same muslin frock sprigged with green which she remembered well, and the same bonnet made of pasteboard covered with green satin; but the little face, which looked up at her with the lips parted in a wail, was, curiously enough, that of the squire's lady, gray curls and all, with the tiny cheeks crumpled delicately in pink and white, like an old rose-bud. When Love awoke, she could scarcely believe that the dream was not true, being one of those for whom dreams are separated from the real by insensible shadings rather than sharp divisions.

Love pondered over it all the morning, and that afternoon, her father being away, she stole guiltily up to the garret, and stood listening, breathless, in the midst of the great stretch of space, with the rafters converging over her head. There was only one small window, and the afternoon was growing old. On either side of the garret, under the eaves, lay long shadows of dark mystery, which to the child's excited fancy seemed often stirring to arise. The garret, like the rest of the house, was very clean and sparse. All the small store of discarded household furnishings was stowed away neatly against the eaves, and the middle space was bare. Love could see the great arc of an old tow-wheel which had not been used for many a year, and near it a cedar chest which contained her mother's meagre wardrobe, two barrels full of old sermons, and the little hair trunk. There was not much besides, except a surtout which had belonged to her grandfather, which hung on a nail over the trunk.

Love stood listening, she scarcely knew for what, but the influence of her dream was strong upon her. She was like a little statue of fearful attention, in her straight blue gown, her hands clutching nervously at her sides, her eyes dilating to the dusk and her own fears. Finally Love went over to the trunk and peered behind it. There was no doll there, at once to her disappointment and her relief. She opened the trunk, and it was full of old letters. Love straightened herself, and in so doing jostled her grandfather's surtout. One sleeve swung out and hit her cheek with a curious impetus for anything so presumably soft and light. Love started back; a sense of the uncanny thrilled her; then she caught hold of the sleeve eagerly, and there was her doll. Cousin Daphne had been a subtle concealer; people had seldom found out anything which she wished to keep secret. She had doubtless many curious hiding-places in empty habits and meaningless forms for the privacies of her own character, and she was at no loss, working from within out to practical illustrations, to find a concealment for poor Love's doll.

Love slipped up the sleeve, and looked irresolutely at the clumsy rag feet; she looked at the pantalets edged with knitted lace, and the hem of the green-sprigged muslin skirt. Love removed the doll and looked at it tremblingly. It was the same old doll. Love went over to the front window and sat down on the floor, clasping it closely. She felt unutterably guilty, still there was a sweet comfort from the feeling of the doll in her arms which she could not help realizing, in spite of her conviction of sin. There was in her consciousness a savor, faint and diluted, of the joy of a mother united to a long-lost child. She gazed at its poor old rag face, its wide mouth painted grotesquely with pokeberry juice, its staring eyes outlined in circles of India ink. She stroked lovingly the scanty locks made from a ravelled brown silk stocking. She knew that the doll was miserably ugly, but, by a sort of underknowledge of love, she also knew she was fair. She pressed her closely to her childish bosom, throbbing with a sense of shame and guilt, and yet with defiant joy. She kissed her as she had never kissed any living thing.

That night Parson Lord's supper was an hour late. He, working by candle-light in his study, felt that vague uneasiness which results from the interruption of a habit upon which no especial stress of mind has been laid, although it may have continued through a lifetime. Through his surfeit of spiritual food, he had scarcely ever been conscious of any desire for that of the flesh. He had never looked forward impatiently to his supper hour, and it was doubtful if he had ever partaken of the meal with a full perception of its quality or quantity, being always more or less abstracted from all material things. Tonight he fidgeted over his sixthly without knowing why. He did not even know, when his daughter came trembling to his study door, that the meal was late, but followed her without a word, and took his place at the table, and bowed his head for the solemnly muttered blessing. The meal was frugal, as all meals were at Parson Lord's—just a brown loaf, a pitcher of milk, and tea made of steeped sage leaves. Genuine tea was not to be thought of, with foreign missions in such sore need.

That night Parson Lord ate his supper with a curious mechanical gusto, as if his body, through its long fast, might be asserting itself without the knowledge or connivance of his mind. He did not notice that his daughter ate nothing, nor her disturbed face. After he had done he bowed his head reverently again, gave thanks to the Lord for His mercies in a lengthy list, and returned to his study.

An hour afterwards, when Love had washed and put away the supper dishes and set the bread to rising, she knocked at the study door, twice and thrice before her father heard her. At last he bade her enter, and looked up absently when the door opened, expecting to see some brother or sister in quest of spiritual aid, as was often the case. Instead, there stood his own daughter, pale and trembling piteously, holding the old doll in her arms. Parson Lord stared at her, took off his spectacles, wiped them, and stared again. "What do you want, my child?" he inquired.

Before he had finished speaking, Love came to his side and stood there in an agony of contrition, displaying the doll. "I found her where Cousin Daphne hid her," she said, in a strained, quick way; then she sobbed; all her staidness and propriety of demeanor had failed her.

The parson stared at her, his thin lips parted, his high forehead knitted. He had entirely forgotten the episode of the doll. Poor Love had to repeat the whole story. A light of understanding came into the parson's eyes as he listened. "And you found it, you say, this afternoon?" he said, in a curious voice.

"Yes, father," replied Love. Then she cried, with a great sob of appeal, "Oh, father, may I keep her now?"

Parson Lord's face quivered a little as he looked at her, then settled again into its usual lines of ascetic sternness and gravity. None but his Maker knew if it cost him a struggle, but he refused the child; he bade her carry the doll back where she had found it. Love obeyed without a demur. She took a candle, went slowly up the steep garret stairs, stole tremblingly through the dark flickering stretch of shadows to the old surtout hanging with an awful semblance of life from the nail in the rafters, gave the poor doll one last fervent caress, and thrust it back in the sleeve, pinning it therein as before. That night Reuben Lord knelt long with his daughter in earnest prayer; her old sins of disobedience and deception were rekindled to their full enormity, until they shone before her as in characters of fire. That night Love slept little, being kept awake by the war between her innocent members and her fierce New England conscience. Many a time, as she lay there, it seemed to her that she must arise, steal up-stairs, rescue the doll from the darkness and loneliness, and hold it through the rest of the night close in her arms.

The next day was the Sabbath, and Love, sitting alone in the parson's pew, was much paler and soberer of countenance than usual. Once in a while, though she strove to keep her mind upon the sermon, her mouth quivered when she thought of the doll. Perhaps it was that which led the squire's lady to favor her with such special and gracious notice at the close of the services. That beautiful and stately lady, when she reached Love lingering at the door of the pew, actually put caressingly about her an arm draped with silk shimmering with purples like the breast of a dove, and bade her a "Good-morning, my dear child." Love never knew whether she answered her or not. She went home in a sort of ecstasy, as of first love.

The squire's lady was in reality her first love. However fond she might be again of others, the affection would go forth in a worn channel. The girl heard that tender voice multiplying into infinite cadences of love and comfort in' all the voices of the spring day. Love's cheeks were so flushed and her eyes so strange with happiness that even her father noticed it when she sat opposite him at the dinner-table.

His mind had been intent upon his afternoon discourse, when suddenly he looked up as if at a touch upon the shoulder. His daughter sat before him just as usual, dressed in her little homely gown of a dull drab-color, with never a ribbon bow to brighten it. Her pretty, fair hair, braided so smoothly and tightly that the very color seemed compressed, was crossed in the usual flat mat at the back of her head, and brought over her ears in two satin-like folds, with high lights of polish at the sides. Her father saw nothing unusual in her except that blue shining of eyes which seemed almost wild, and that flush of cheeks which seemed almost fever, and an involuntary curving of lips into smiles which seemed almost levity.

First the parson inquired of his daughter if she were ailing, and then if she were in a state of mind befitting the day. To both inquiries Love replied dutifully, her color deepening, to the former with a respectful negative, to the latter with a modest hesitancy of hope that she might be, which was reassuring. However, her father continued to gaze at her now and then in the same curious and anxious way. He looked not only at her face, but at her dress and her hair, as if he saw them for the first time. He continued to gaze at her in the same fashion later on when they walked to the meeting-house for the afternoon service. He seemed to see the patient, sober young figure at his side with ever-recurring surprise. He scanned again and again the homely dun-colored gown, falling in scanty folds to the clumsy little shoes, the poor bonnet tied with dull ribbon. Then he looked from her to some gayer figures moving along the road with flutters of bright streamers and flounces.

Love would have been disturbed by this unwonted notice of her father had not her whole mind been intent upon the squire's lady, who was not there, indeed, but whose presence seemed more vital to her than that of any who sat under the parson's preaching. Until the sermon began she watched anxiously for the object of her adoration to enter, and when she became certain that she was not coming, she felt a pang at heart the like of which she had never known before. She could have wept when she saw Master Richard Pierce coming up the aisle alone. She could not bear to look at the squire's pew; once when young Richard's persistent gaze of admiration forced her unwilling attention, she almost scowled at him, so sad and impatient was she, and jealous of her own self for the sake of the squire's lady. However, after a while she became in a manner reconciled to her disappointment, and fell to musing tenderly over past joy, and building air-castles for the future.

Love's face then took on such an expression that the boy in the squire's pew gazed at her as if fascinated, seeing for the first time the dream of love in a young girl's face. Richard that day managed to be at the door of the parson's pew when Love emerged; he cast a keen though somewhat shamefaced glance at her, but she did not see him at all. "I don't think that girl is very pretty, come to see her close to," he reflected, on his way home. He resolved not to take the trouble to look at her again, with the unconfessed masculine assurance of her annoyance in that case.

Love would not at that time have known whether he looked or not, having eyes for his grandmother only; and the next day but one something happened to distract her still further. Upon that day Love had the first great and beautiful surprise of her life. She had been alone since morning, as she had been the day before. On Monday and Tuesday of every week the parson travelled to neighboring towns, where they had not the benefit of regular Sabbath services in a church of his own denomination, and gave them a week-day rendering of his Lord's day sermon. On Tuesday afternoon Love grew weary of her needle work, and thought that she would have a change of task by way of harmless recreation. So thinking, she went up to her chamber to get a sampler which she was working. When Love had crossed the threshold of her chamber she stopped short with a gasp. There in her little chair sat a doll, not the old rag doll, but a new, resplendent creature—a very ideal of dollhood. No unskilled hands had ever fashioned this radiant thing of blooming wax and real flaxen ringlets, of sweetest smiles of baby candor and innocence, of blue eyes intently beaming at the whole world of child-women without a special glance of favor for one, of pink satins and ribbons, of fine linens and laces. Love stood looking, her eyes dilated, her breath coming short and quick. At length she gained courage, and went nearer and knelt down before the wonderful thing. Her face was rapt. It was long before she dared to touch the doll, to do anything but drink in its beauty with her eyes and embrace it with her soul. Finally she rose, with a great sigh of delicious terror, took up the doll, and seated herself. As she sat there, with the little flaxen head on her shoulder, fingering with gentle, reverent fingers the delicate mysteries of the fine apparel, she was, for the first time in her life, in a state of actual bliss. She had experienced ecstasy at the caressing touch of the squire's lady and her loving words, but this was fruition and realization of the vague sweet promise of that touch and word. Love did not doubt for one minute that the doll came from the bountiful hand of the squire's lady. She reasoned away easily enough all difficulties in the way of its having been brought secretly to the house and deposited in her chamber. Love had that order of mind which springs to conviction, and afterwards proves the route to it by a facile imagination. Old Aunt Betsey Ware was then living at the squire's.

"Aunt Betsey," reasoned Love, conclusively, "is well acquainted with this house; she knows well where my chamber is, and I have been at work in the kitchen, where I could not have heard any one enter, had they stepped softly." Moreover, that very forenoon Love had seen Aunt Betsey hurrying down the road, with head averted, as if she did not wish to be noticed. Love *knew* that the squire's lady had given her the doll. When she heard her father open the door she rose without a second's hesitation, and still clasping the doll, followed him into the study before he had seated himself at his desk.

When the parson turned at the sound of the opening door and saw his daughter standing there, with the great doll in her arms, a strange expression which she had never seen came over his face. But Love did not heed that, neither did she fairly know the matter of her father's answer to her quivering statement concerning the doll, and her pitiful petition that she be allowed to keep it. In truth, it was a long and somewhat stilted speech which Parson Lord made to his trembling daughter, and it was not singular that Love, in her agitation, should grasp only the gist of it—that she might keep the doll. Love, with her New England shamefacedness as to all demonstration, only dropped a prim little courtesy, said "Thank you, sir," and went out, with the doll's pink face looking over her shoulder; but there might well have been a perceptible darkening of the room, so much joy went with her.

Love that night was fairly possessed with affection and gratitude; she loved her father as she had never loved him before, and he seemed nearer to her. She had not mentioned her belief that the squire's lady was the donor of the precious gift. She thought, jumping at that conclusion as she had done at the other, that her father must know it as well as she. Who but the squire's lady could have given her the doll?

Love then entered at once upon a new epoch in her life. It seemed a strange thing that the possession of a plaything of childhood should all at once transform her character from that of a child to that of a woman, but such was apparently the case. Love never played, in the strictest sense of the word, with her doll; she never tended it with that sweet make-believe of motherhood in dressing and nursing; but the doll surely sent her heart into blossom, being perhaps the little stimulus of love needed for that end. At this time there came into the girl's face that expression of sweet intelligence and gentle comprehension, instead of the mere innocent outlook of childhood. People meeting Love in those days used to look at her carelessly, as one looks at any wonted object, then look again and again with growing wonder, as at a change which they could not define. Some, after meeting her so, said she had grown tall, some that she had grown pretty, some that she grew to look more like her mother, or father, or Cousin Daphne. Whatever they said, people noticed her more. A few weeks after she had come into the possession of her doll, the squire's lady, one morning, sent over Aunt Betsey Ware with a formally worded message.

"Mrs. Squire Hawkes desires her compliments to Miss Love Lord, and would be pleased to have her company at tea this afternoon," said Aunt Betsey, with a fine and consequential pucker, and Love could only courtesy in unquestioning gratitude and acquiescence, like one who is bidden to an audience with a queen.

That very morning Master Richard Pierce had departed for college, and his grandmother, feeling sad and lonely, had bethought herself of the parson's sweet little daughter whom she had noticed so often in meeting, that it would be a comfort to have another young face at her tea table that night.

Love had never been in the squire's house since the advent of this second wife. This was to institute a new order of things. She sat at the dainty tea-table opposite the squire's lady—the squire himself was confined to his room with rheumatism—ate gingerly and delicately of the cream biscuits, the quince-sauce, and the poundcake. She sipped her tea from the blue china cup, with timid lifts, over the rim, of blue eyes at the kind and gracious face opposite; she spoke modestly when she was spoken to, and if she volunteered a remark, did so with a sweet deference which was pretty to behold. The squire's lady was even more pleased with the child than she had thought to be.

"She is a dear child," she told the squire when Love had gone, and she was in his chamber mixing the sleeping-cup for which she had a dainty hand. "She is a dear child. I mean to have her often to tea. 'Tis a treat to her, too. I hear the good parson keeps her close and is over-strict with her."

"Did she tell you so?" asked the squire, beginning to sip his spiced and comforting drink from his silver cup.

"No; she said nothing; she never would, unless I mistake her greatly," replied his wife. "I had it from Aunt Betsey, who formerly lived there." The squire's lady, beautiful and gracious though she was, still got some savor to life from a little harmless gossip.

"Well, 'tis true enough," said the squire, "true enough. The parson has driven her with a mighty tight rein, and taught her to shy at the first scent of the devil." The squire had been in his day, and was still, a great lover of horse-flesh. "Why, bless you, my dear," said the squire, "I don't suppose that child ever had anything but the drippings of the contribution-box to eat or wear or make merry with. Every cent that the parson can save goes to foreign missions. Why, he sells every apple in his orchard—all except the windfalls— and sends the proceeds to India's burning strand; never one left for that poor child to have a bite of, fine apples too, a rare kind, brought from overseas by his grandfather. I've tried to graft from 'em, and couldn't. I don't suppose that child ever has a lollypop or a sweet-cake unless it's given her, and I don't know but her father would make her sell it then and drop in the penny next Sabbath day. Never a ribbon flying, or a frill setting her off. I've noticed her myself. I used to know her mother; used to think sometimes—I was perfectly satisfied with my own wife, you know, my dear—but I used to think that if I had been a young man, and my wife had married somebody else, I would have known how to look out for her better than the man who had her—one of the prettiest girls anywhere about. I wonder if the parson intends to send his daughter to Burmah or the Fiji Islands? Well, he is a good man, and he has stepped along in his path of duty without a kick or a shy, and I suppose he is sure of finding his heavenly pasture at last. I wish some other people were as sure." The squire finished his cup as he spoke, and handed it to his wife for replenishment.

"It would be a cruel thing for him to send that little wild rose of a girl to any of those deadly climates; she looks as if she might have inherited delicacy from her mother too. I can't believe he will," said she, tilting the china pitcher carefully. "I shall invite her to tea again next week. I think the poor child will be benefited by it."

So it came to pass that every Wednesday afternoon Love went to take tea at the squire's house. Her father gave his consent, Love could not help thinking, with a certain constraint of pleasure at the invitation. "The squire's wife is a godly woman, and, I hear, a notable housekeeper; her example may profit you in some things, as your mother's would have done," the parson said.

Love thought that her father seemed pleased when some fresh

gifts, which she attributed, like the others, to the bounty of the squire's lady, arrived. A few days after her first tea-drinking at the squire's, on a warm night in early May, there was a loud knock at the front door, and when Love answered it, no one was there, but a dainty package was swinging by a cord to the latch.

Love, after opening it in the sitting-room, carried it to her father, who sat over his sermon in the study, and displayed, with rapture and terror at what he might say, the fine India muslin for a gown, the beautiful blue ribbon to tie around her waist, and the little morocco shoes. Her father, much to her astonishment, did not withhold his permission for her to keep the gifts, yet he spoke almost sternly regarding them, and impressed upon her her duty in not placing undue importance upon such frivolities, in view of the serious life work before her.

Love went clad in her new finery to take tea with the squire's lady, and her heart was in such a flutter of gratitude she made no expression of it, except by an eloquent look at her friend when she praised the beauty of her gown.

"Why, my dear, what have we here, a little white rose instead of a little Quaker lady?" the squire's wife asked, smiling at Love, fluttering before her in her muslin frills; and Love only smiled back at her, and blushed with modest pride and affection.

Love had a delicacy, perhaps exaggerated and misplaced, about returning open thanks for surreptitious benefits. She said never a word to the squire's wife about the gifts. Indeed, a number of times Mrs. Squire Abner Hawkes gave the child presents with no pretence of secrecy; there were three old gowns of her own among them—one, the pride of Love's heart, of a blue figured satin. Love altered these gowns to fit her slender shape, and wore them to the admiration and somewhat to the wonder of all beholders. They thought it strange that Parson Lord should allow his daughter to go dressed so gayly, especially to the house of God. Love, who was henceforth always a bird of fine plumage, never talked much about these showers of surreptitious benefits to her father. She never mentioned the squire's lady in that connection, except now and then to remark upon her kindness, once especially when she wore for the first time the remodelled gown of blue figured satin. It was on a Wednesday, when she was going to take tea at the squire's, and it was four years after her first visit there. The squire's wife was a faithful friend, and Love a faithful admirer.

Parson Lord might have pleaded, with truth, the strength of the temptation, had he felt some purely temporal pride in the appearance of his daughter as she stood before him in that gown, shimmering with blue lights from shoulder to heel, and her lovely head shining with a golden crown of braids. In fact, a smile of that utter weakness and fondness which would have better suited her mother's face came over her father's, to Love's wonder. But he enjoined her as sternly as ever not to allow her heart to dwell upon such vanities, but to remember that it was only her poor dying body which was so adorned, then turned again with his usual grave dignity to his sermon.

Mr. Richard Pierce was to be at the tea-drinking that afternoon, and Love did not anticipate the occasion with quite as much pleasure as usual. Now, she thought, it would be good-bye to her pleasant sittings and her confidential talks with the squire's lady. She had confessed as much to her friend, who had only patted her cheek fondly and smiled. Love was afterwards afraid that she had been rude and forgetful of the claims upon her gratitude and deference. There, she had actually as good as told her that she was sorry her grandson was coming home, when she had not seen him for so long. Mr. Richard Pierce, having developed within himself an amazing spirit of independence, had been away the greater part of his vacations, earning money as tutor, and possibly in other capacities. There were those who claimed to have seen Mr. Richard Pierce, the squire's step-grandson, following the plough on a farm twenty miles away like any farmer's son. During his last vacation he had been in the old country with two boys whom he was fitting for college; the one before that, when he had been home for a few weeks, Love had been housed with a quinsy sore throat, and had not seen him. Indeed, with the exception of a few chance encounters with him at his grandmother's, when he had just arrived or was just leaving, the girl had not seen him at all.

When she reached the squire's house, and entered the stately old sitting-room, hung, as to its walls, with dim old oil-paintings and blurred engravings in heavy frames, furnished with old mahogany pieces reflecting the light, as in little pools, from their polished surfaces, it was at first so dark to her, coming out of the afternoon sunlight, that she could see nobody. The shutters were nearly closed, because the squire's wife had a headache. Love saw her friend's face smiling dimly out of the gloom, heard her voice greeting her fondly, and felt her soft lips on her cheek; then she was presented formally to Mr. Richard Pierce, and courtesied vaguely before a bowing shadow. After Love had removed her worked muslin cape and her bonnet, she seated herself and took out her needle-work—a fine handkerchief which she was hem-stitching for her father, having coveted a little daintiness for him as well as herself. She worked industriously, answering modestly and prettily the squire's wife when she spoke to her, and frequently giving her fond glances; but she looked very seldom at Mr. Richard, and replied in gentle but cool monosyllables when he ventured to address her.

The young man could scarcely take his eyes from her, though he strove hard not to stare rudely. It seemed to him that he had never in his whole life seen anything quite so fair and wonderful as this girl, who seemed to sit in a sort of blue radiance, with a shaft of sunlight from the open upper half of the shutter gilding her head. All the courtly ease of manner for which he had been quite famed among his associates deserted him. He heard his voice tremble when he addressed this unresponsive girl; he knew that his remarks were boyish commonplaces. It seemed to him that his grandmother's fair guest was in a mood not of maiden shyness only, but of decided aversion towards himself. He wondered in what way he could have offended her so soon. He wondered if she simply objected to him on the score of his personal appearance. It had always been considered fair beyond the average, but it might easily not be so regarded by her. Richard was not a large man; he considered that fact uneasily. He straightened himself to his fullest height when he crossed the room to open a shutter. However, his pains were thrown away; Love did not look at him at all. Still, although she was apparently oblivious of his presence, she was, in reality, fully aware of it.

The moment Love had entered the room, she had been conscious of a strange and pungent odor. She did not know what it was, but Mr. Richard smoked tobacco, and the scent of it was in his clothes. Love did not find it disagreeable, but she perceived it with every breath she drew, and it gave her a strange impulse of maiden rebellion, quite out of proportion to the cause, as if this man were fairly forcing his presence upon her, making it a part of her, whether she would or not.

Love, with a little impatient air foreign to her, removed the lid from a potpourri jar on a stand near her, and bent her face over it. The scent of rose leaves, lavender, and spices seemed like a reassertion of the flavor of her own maiden individuality, which this man in his tobacco-scented garments, with his glances of hitherto un-known masculine pleading, was striving to overcome.

"It is too pleasant an afternoon for you to sit here in this dark room with your needle-work," said the squire's lady, presently. "Put it away, my dear, and Richard will take you out for a stroll in the garden."

Love started. "Thank you," she faltered, "I would rather remain here with you, if you please."

"Do as I bid you, my dear," repeated the squire's wife, with her air of gentle authority which no one ever gainsaid.

Love, with no further demur, folded her needle-work and put it in her bead bag, and went with Mr. Richard into the garden at the back of the house.

Up and down the long box-bordered paths they paced. Love kept her eyes downcast, and face turned, so that only the pink curve of it was visible to her companion. She answered in soft monosylla-bles, a yes, sir, or a no, sir, when he addressed her with anxious def-erence. It spoke well for her charms that this young man, who had been heretofore treated very kindly by her sex, should have had a relish for this strolling in his grandmother's garden with one so sparing of responsive words and smiles. But Mr. Richard Pierce, far from appearing bored or dull, wore a look of rapture, as he paced the tortuous garden paths, Love's blue flounces rustling against him, no matter how far she shrank away, the pungent odor of the rank box, which was waist-high in places, in his nostrils, and now and then, like the melody triumphing over the swell of the bass, a breath of lavender from Love's garments.

They threaded the green maze of the garden, Richard more ador-ing at every step; he held Love's parasol jealously between her face and the sun. It would have pleased him, doubtless, had the snap-dragons in the garden beds been real ones, that he might have slain them in her defence. He ventured to pick a nosegay and offer it to her. She accepted it with courtesy, and when they returned to the house, gave it to his grandmother.

The tea-drinking that afternoon was a sore embarrassment and trial to Love. The squire was away, and his lady's headache had waxed so severe that she had been obliged to retire to her room and leave her guest to sup alone with her grandson.

So she and Mr. Richard sat alone at the table, Love behind the tea-tray with its silver cream-jug and sugar-bowl and blue cups and saucers. She poured out the tea, tilting the silver pot with a dainty turn of her round elbow, and inquired politely as to the number of lumps of sugar, but volunteered scarcely a word beside.

She sipped her tea delicately, and made a pretence at her biscuit and a glass of syllabub and a square of sponge-cake, but was all the time anxiously furtive as to Richard's progress, that she might rise from the table.

Even after tea Love was not as soon quit of her admirer as she had expected, for he must needs walk home with her to guard her from the deadly perils of the village street at dusk. She began to fear that she would not be rid of him at her house door, knowing that it would be incumbent upon her, unless she violated her sense of courtesy and hospitality, to invite him to enter. However, the young man, desirous as he might have been to accept the invitation, had the wisdom to refuse.

When Mr. Richard Pierce returned to Boston, some six weeks later, to take up the study of the law, Love had smiled in his face a few times, she had addressed him of her own accord upon as many occasions as he could count on his fingers, and twice when returning in his company from tea-drinkings at his grandmother's, she had strolled with him a half-mile past her house. Once, coming on some errand for his grandmother, and having met with no response to his knocks, he had peered around the house and caught a glimpse of something blue through the trees in the apple orchard. He had followed up that glimpse of blue, and found Love seated with her needle-work in a natural arbor made by the growth of a wild grapevine over an old apple-tree, and had ventured to throw himself on the grass at her feet. Love cast a startled glance at him, half rose as if to run away, then settled herself and resumed her needle-work. Love's eyes were so intent upon this work that presently the young man dared still further. He gently laid hold of the hem of her blue muslin gown and kissed it fervently.

Love was on her feet in a flash, and her work—a lace tucker which she was embroidering—her scissors, her emery, her thread were on the ground. "I will never come here again, never, never," said she, in a voice between anger and tears, and then was gone, flying like a blue-clad nymph through the green distance to the house.

There was a certain shrewdness about Richard Pierce, although he seemed such a humble lover. He doubtless was abashed and conscience-stricken before Love's indignation, but he argued hopefully from her declaration that she would never visit the arbor again. "She must have thought of the possibility of my meeting her here," reasoned Richard Pierce.

Richard was to leave for Boston the next day but one. The following afternoon he repaired full of hope to the grape-arbor, reaching it by a circuitous way across the fields, lest Love spy him from her window, and so not be able to excuse her coming to herself.

Richard waited long, but Love did not come; finally he repaired boldly to the house and knocked; but no one opened the door. The parson was away; and as for Love, she had been weeping so bitterly that not for the whole world would she have faced Richard Pierce with her red eyes.

Richard came again that evening, and then the parson admitted him, and ushered him into the study, concluding, as a matter of course, that the young man was there upon some errand connected with his soul's salvation.

Richard, after a period of solemn waiting, on the parson's part, for the unburdening of his spirit, inquired somewhat awkwardly if Miss Love were at home. The parson directly inferred that he had come on some errand for his grandmother, and replied that his daughter had retired to her room, suffering with a severe headache, but that he would deliver the message in the morning.

Richard, for very shame before this man so unconscious of his selfish designs, must needs plunge himself still further into deceit and invent a message, and thereby also accomplish a purpose of his own. He took out of his pocket a neat little parcel in silver-paper, and stated wickedly that his grandmother desired her compliments to Miss Love, and here was a little gift which she begged her to accept, the said gift being a most exquisite and dainty tucker of wrought lace, and a pair of embroidery-scissors, and an emery of painted velvet in an ivory case, for all of which treasures he had ridden hard that morning to the next market-town.

Love, up in her chamber, knew perfectly well who was downstairs; she heard him come and heard him go; and although she would not go down to see him and bid him good-bye, she wept because she would not.

The next morning, when her father gave her the parcel, she knew at once from whom it had come, in spite of that deceptive message. She colored so hotly that her father looked at her in a puzzled way, and she never thanked Madam Diantha (she had come to call the squire's lady by that name), though here was a fine chance with such an openly presented gift.

That night in his prayer the parson betrayed the fact that, however oblivious he had seemed, he had possibly conceived suspicions. He prayed fervently to the effect that his beloved child might ever be mindful of the daily fulfilment of her duty to the Lord. He quoted Saint Paul in terms rendered somewhat covert by sacred imagery; he declared the blessedness of going into the world and preaching the gospel to every living creature in preference to the joys of this life. He petitioned that she might not forget the example of her sainted sister, that pattern of early piety, and might have strength to follow in that path which she would perchance have trod had her life been spared.

When Love rose from her knees she was very pale. Up in her own chamber, she took the lace tucker and the ivory case, folded them carefully in the silver-paper, and put them in a box of painted satinwood which had belonged to her mother. Then she folded the blue muslin gown, whose hem Richard had kissed, daintily in a linen towel, and packed it away with the satinwood box in the very bottom of her chest.

Love did not sleep that night, and looked wan and pale the next morning. Even her father's prayer, which was a sort of triumphant homily upon the joys which await them who overcome, did not seem to raise her flagging spirits. Sometimes that prospect of pearly gate and golden street, of eternal chorals of triumphant praise, seem all too splendid to a little humble soul who would fain have offered to itself a smaller reward for sacrifice.

If, instead of the sea of jasper and those pavements of gold, Love had had pictured some little door of home, and her mother standing in it with outstretched arms of welcome, it might have filled her with a deeper sense of comfort.

When Richard had been gone a week, he wrote a letter to Love in which he humbly begged her pardon for his boldness the afternoon before he left, and craved the honor of a correspondence.

Love had debated long as to whether her duty demanded that she show this letter to her father and ask his advice in the matter. Finally, being led to a decision largely by the reasoning that her duty it must be since it was such a sore trial, she took the letter to his study, and stood waiting at his elbow, a patient, downcast young figure, while he read it.

The candle-light flickered over the parson's long, pale, heavily corrugated face as he read. It was a face expressive of all the stern resignation and persistency in sacrifice, and of none of its triumphant self-consciousness. Most truly did Parson Lord serve his Maker through pure obedience to His will, and never for the sake of his own. Finally the parson folded the letter, and stated his mind to his daughter, with his usual circumlocution of scriptural imagery. When he had finished, Love courtesied, took her letter, and went back to her chamber.

Poor Richard Pierce received no answer from his divinity, but, instead, a lengthy epistle from her father, assuring him of the receipt of his distinguished favor, which had been submitted to his inspection by his daughter, for whom he had, he begged leave to say, views connected with her spiritual welfare and her true duty in life which rendered it inadvisable, according to his poor judgment, for her to engage in a correspondence of the nature proposed, which might perchance cause her to waste precious time and strength which should be devoted to higher aims, and possibly in the end divert her mind from the favorable contemplation of the one true and acceptable sacrifice of her life. The parson concluded with a few words of pious exhortation to his young friend.

It was quite possible that Richard felt some irritation at that very sweet docility, which he would have so admired if directed towards himself, which led Love to show his letter to her father and allow him to answer it. He did not again subject himself to a similar rebuff, nor endeavor to see Love until the following summer.

Then, at the first sight of the girl, grown far prettier, and with a helpless blush and tremor before his eyes, he felt his resentment vanish, and his admiration and love revive. However, he progressed not at all in his wooing. If he went to call upon Love, he was entertained by her father with a relentless persistency of pious conversation, and he went many a time to the grape-arbor in the hope that Love might be there with her needle-work, but she never was. During the three weeks he was at home she came only once to take tea with his grandmother, and then her father came for her, and himself escorted her home.

Richard could not but feel that he was avoided, and finally went back to Boston, resolved that he would waste no more thought upon a girl who so persistently flouted him.

After Richard had gone, Love grew thin and pale. The subtle inconsistency of reasoning power of her sex was strongly marked in her. Underneath all her keeping to the letter of the law she had a feeling of wonder and grief and injury that her lover should so take her at her word. She would have had him come when he was told not. She would have had him force her to a *tête-à-tête* in that grape-arbor, and make it out of her power to say him nay. She would have had him correspond with her when such correspondence had been forbidden, and somehow ease her conscience of any blame. She would have had him take her love all the more, since she withheld it. She told herself that he did not care now; he had seen a fairer face in Boston; she would sternly put him from her mind, and strive to gain sufficient earthly bliss in the hope of that of heaven. Now and then she talked to her father of her uncles in Burmah and India, how old were their wives when they accompanied them, how old was it necessary for a female missionary to be before the American Board[1] would think it judicious to send her to those far-off lands? Reuben Lord had not always that expression of quick sympathy and joy with which he might have been expected to hear remarks so evidently tending towards the accomplishment of his cherished wish. Instead, he looked at his daughter with a sternly anxious knitting of brows, and replied that it was not so much a matter of years which was in question, as preparation and fitness of spirit and body to perform such work with acceptance to the Lord.

Love reflected humbly that her father considered that she was not spiritually fit for so great a trust; of her bodily state she thought not at all. She wondered why the squire's lady looked at her with such wistful intentness; she wondered why she always insisted upon her drinking a glass of port-wine when she first arrived at her house.

In those days more mysterious gifts than ever were showered upon the girl—a warm fur tippet for her delicate throat, a great muff wherein to nestle her little hands, a warmly wadded cloak, a hood of blue silk edged with swan's-down, and many luxuries to tempt her appetite—oranges and pineapples, and often a plump partridge or quail.

Love's gratitude to the squire's lady seemed to warm her whole heart. She often speculated as to the advisability of thanking her friend for her anonymous gifts, and once she consulted her father. "Do you think it advisable to thank a person for a gift who has given it secretly, sir?" she asked. And her father stared a little, and replied:

"No, daughter; no, certainly it is not advisable," and was again intent upon Doddridge.[2]

All winter, when the stage-coach came in with the mail, Love had a forlorn hope that it might bring a letter from Richard, but it

never did. Sometimes the squire's lady used to read extracts from
her grandson's letters to Love, both to her delight and her fear. Always her heart was beating loud in her ears with the fear lest
Richard had written of some beautiful Boston lady who had won
his heart. It was in such wise that she betrayed herself one afternoon in late June.

It being a fine day, she and Madam Diantha were walking in the
garden when the squire came with the mail, and there was a letter
from Richard.

The squire was a fine, handsome old gentleman, red-cheeked and
clear-eyed, with a silver fleece of hair. Though he limped somewhat
on account of his rheumatic joints, yet he advanced with an almost
boyish impetuosity. He was of rather smaller stature than his wife,
who moved with slow state between the roses, in a wide inflores-
cence of lavender flounces and softly floating laps and frills of lace.

"Open the letter at once, my dear," cried the squire, "and let us
hear if the boy is coming, or if some fair Boston lady has him at her
silk apron strings."

Love had moved aside in the garden path to make room for the
squire, and Madam Diantha saw the girl's face go white and red.

"Read it aloud, my dear, if you please," repeated the squire, eagerly.

His wife began to read in her soft voice.

The box in that place was as high as Love's waist, and some
branches of roses were hooping over it. She turned her face away
and smelled of a rose as she listened.

The letter was short. Richard could not come just yet, not until
next month, possibly not until August. He was very much occupied; the weather was very warm. He had been to dine at Mr.
Solomon Purdy's house the week before, and was to go there to a
party to-morrow. Mr. Purdy had two daughters, most amiable
young ladies, and a son whom he found a most desirable companion—

" 'Tis one of the most amiable young ladies!" interrupted the
squire, with a loud laugh. "An amiable young lady and a pretty little apron, and Mr. Richard Pierce stumbling at the length of the
strings. I knew it. She has him fast. Well, 'tis hard lines for us when
we thought to see the lad's face at the table a month ago, and now—
Why, Diantha, my dear, what is the matter with the child?" For
Love was half hanging over the green wall of box, like a broken rose
branch.

"Why, my dear, what is the matter? Are you ill?" cried Madam Diantha, and put her arm around the girl, supporting her tenderly on her broad, motherly bosom. Love was gasping faintly, and her lips were white.

"What do you think is the matter?" asked the squire, anxiously: he was very fond of Love.

"It is nothing, I think," said his wife; "she is not very strong, and the sun is hot. Will you please go to the house and get the camphor-bottle on my dressing-table?"

The squire's lady put her mouth close to the girl's ear when her husband had gone. "My precious child," she whispered, but said no more of comfort; she dared not, since she knew not but the squire's surmise was correct. So she only kissed and patted and soothed as best she could, and repeated that the sun was hot, and she not strong, and no wonder that she was faint.

Poor Love would have given the world to run home and hide herself, but she responded, with a proud impulse towards conceal-ment, to her friend's subterfuge. She owned that she had felt the heat of the sun; she submitted to all that was done for her, and re-mained to tea as usual, eating obediently as much as she was able of a little bird which the squire had ordered to be specially prepared.

"What ailed the child?" the squire asked his wife, after Love had gone home. "No, don't say the sun, my dear, unless you spell it with an o," and the squire laughed with boyish glee at his own joke.

"Hush, my dear, we have no reason—" his wife began; but he nodded obstinately.

"The poor little soul was distressed at the mention of the am-iable Purdy," said he; "but I hope you told her that it was nothing particular."

"Oh, but, my dear, it may be!" said his wife.

"I don't believe a word of it," declared the squire, stoutly. "Well, if the boy should want her, and she him, I would venture ten to one that the parson would try to separate them with the contribution-box."

The next week Love forced herself to go to the squire's, lest they suspect the reason if she stayed away, but after that she did not go any more. Then July came and passed, and August was there, and Richard returned.

Love saw him first as she was walking down the street. He was out driving with his grandmother and the squire. He had come un-expectedly the night before. When Love first lifted her eyes at the roll of wheels and saw Richard, she went so white that Madam Diantha gave an involuntary start as if she would go to her. She thought for a second that the girl would fall. But Love recovered herself quickly, and courtesied prettily, and they had passed.

Richard's grandmother glanced covertly at him, but he looked quite unconcerned, and her heart sank. However, Richard had seen, and the image of Miss Catharine Purdy, which he had rather urged upon his heart of late, faded.

Love wore that day a white muslin gown—one of her mysterious gifts—a little white cape, and a hat with a white ribbon; she looked for all the world like a flying white flower as she came down the street, her white draperies blown in the wind.

The squire had been shrewdly observant. "The parson's daughter looks more like an angel than a thing of flesh and blood," he remarked, presently, "and I fear she'll be one in earnest if they don't look out for her."

Richard stared at the landscape. "Is she out of health?" he inquired, in a somewhat constrained tone.

"She was always delicate, dear," his grandmother replied, evasively.

"Not like this," maintained the squire.

That evening, when he and Richard were sitting together after supper, he turned suddenly upon the young man with a motion of defiance, as if he were throwing secrecy and prudence to the winds. "Well, my boy, your grandmother would have me say nothing, but I am going to get to the bottom of this. Our little Love Lord fainted away when your grandmother read a letter of yours in which you spoke of the Misses Purdy something particularly, and we knew— Now, sir, if you have trifled—"

"Trifled, sir!" cried Richard, staring. "Why, sir, she will have none of me. She has shown me so plainly that there is no mistaking it."

"Then it's the parson," said the squire, reflectively.

"No; it is she herself."

"Go there and see her, and you will find out that I am right, my boy," said the squire.

"I go not the second time where I have as good as had the door in my face, though it was heaven, and an angel shutting it," replied Richard, and was true to his resolution for some little time.

Poor Love stayed close at home, and always, when the weather was fine, repaired of an afternoon to the grape-arbor, and sat there until tea-time, with an eye of wistful hope for a young man coming across the field; but he never came.

But one afternoon, during the last of August, Love went into her father's study, bringing a letter in which Mr. Richard Pierce begged her to be in the grape-arbor at eight o'clock, for the purpose of conversation upon a matter pertaining to them both. He concluded by stating that he would consider her failure to be there as final, and would henceforth obtrude himself no further upon her, whose obedient servant he would ever be.

Parson Reuben Lord read the letter, while his daughter looked at him with that same expression with which she had pleaded for the doll.

"Daughter, you know what my will has been for you from your youth up," said the parson, solemnly.

Love went out without a word; her father heard her sob on the stairs. She ate no supper, though a little crock of honey had mysteriously come for her late that afternoon. She went up to her room at half-past seven o'clock.

Parson Lord stood listening at the foot of the stairs leading to his daughter's chamber; now and then he heard a stifled sob. He put foot on the stair, as if to ascend, then drew back; at every sob his own face was convulsed. At last he took his hat and went out, shutting the front door softly.

That night the sky was overcast and the dusk was early. When Richard, at eight o'clock, crossed the fields, all the trees were forgathering in shadows, and all white flower bushes and white house walls in the distance seemed luminous. Long before he reached the arbor he saw something white shining therein, and his heart leaped for joy, he thinking it was surely Love's white gown and she had come. But when he went in, it was only a soft lavender-scented mass of silken shawl.

"She has been here and gone," thought Richard, in a great turmoil of grief and wrath. "She has been here and not waited. I will have no more of her. If she loves me not, I will not follow her any longer; and if she loves me, she has no spirit which is worthy of the love. The clock has not yet struck eight, and she did not wait—"

Then, just as Richard spoke, the town-clock struck the half-hour after eight. And here it may be said that the next day, when the Boston stage-coach came in, there was great amazement all over the village to find that the town-clock was a half-hour fast.

But Richard Pierce, that night when he heard the half-hour strike, went straight to the parson's house and let fall the knocker with a bold clang, and when the parson came, demanded to see his daughter.

"She has retired, I fear," replied the parson, who was strangely pale, and whose voice quivered convulsively. "Will you walk into my study, sir?"

But Richard would not come in, and would see his daughter at the door.

Love did not know the voice in which her father called; she asked, tremblingly, who had spoken.

"Come down, daughter," said her father, still in that strange voice. "There is some one at the door who is desirous of speaking with you." Then he went into his study and shut the door.

Love went down, and Richard's face shone white framed in the doorway against a background of night gloom. He flung an arm around her and drew her outside.

"We have had enough of this, dear," he said, shortly. "If you love me, tell me so now, for God's sake!"

"Oh, it is not right! I fear it is not right!" Love gasped, and trembled in his arms.

"Let the right alone. Tell me!"

"I must not!"

"Let the must not alone. Tell me!"

"Yes," said Love, with a sigh, and then tried with a faint assertion of maiden dignity to ward off Richard's kisses. "It can be no more than—this," she whispered, brokenly. "We cannot be—married, Richard."

"Why not?" demanded Richard. "Why not, sweetheart?"

"Father—father has vowed— He does not wish me to marry, Richard."

"Well, marry you will, nevertheless, sweetheart."

"Never without his consent. I cannot, Richard."

"With or without, you shall marry me, Love; but he will consent."

"Oh, he will not, unless—" Love looked with sudden courage in his face. "Oh," she whispered—"oh, Richard, if you would only be a missionary!"

Richard Pierce laughed so loud that the gay ring of it penetrated to the parson in the study. "I will not be a missionary, and yet marry me you shall, now I know that you love me, sweetheart," said he; then, before Love knew it, they were standing before her father.

"Sir," said Richard, speaking with a fine manly air, "I should have come to you before and asked for your daughter's hand had she not been so desirous of following your wishes instead of her own, and concealed her feelings from me so well that I judged it to be useless. Now we know that we love each other, and I beg that you will give me your daughter for my wife."

"My daughter has long known that my plans for her were otherwise than the married estate," said Parson Lord, looking past them and speaking with stiff lips.

"Is the soul of your daughter yours to command in a matter like this, sir?" inquired the young man, hotly, and yet with some show of deference.

"I cannot give my consent," Parson Lord said, and turned to his sermon.

"Cannot you reconsider this, sir?"

"I cannot give my consent," repeated the parson. "It is final."

"Then," said Richard, drawing Love's arm firmly through his own, "marry without your consent we must, sir, for marry her I will, now I know that she loves me."

The next Sunday the banns between Richard Pierce, Esquire, and Love Lord, spinster, were published—not proclaimed from the pulpit, but copied neatly on a fair sheet, and hung in the frame used for that purpose beside the meeting-house door, where all who entered might read. The parson might have discerned a greater spirit of astonishment and gossip in the faces of his audience than of pious attention to the precepts of the gospel, had he been interested to decipher it.

His plans for his daughter were well known, and here were her banns published. Had the parson yielded unto the pleading of earthly affection, or was this without his knowledge or approval? Public opinion rather inclined to the latter view, although far from sure that the banns could be set up, even with the squire to manage matters, without the parson's knowledge. Love was not at meeting, but Richard Pierce was sitting between his grandmother and the squire, and holding up his head with a gallant air, looking straight at the parson, as if he were weighing every word of the discourse.

The banns were published three Sundays, and on Monday following the third, the squire, the squire's lady, and Mr. Richard

Pierce drove in the coach to Parson Reuben Lord's house. When they entered the study, having been ushered therein by the parson with a grave dignity, Richard looked around anxiously, but Love was not there. He glanced imploringly at his grandmother. "Where is Love, sir?" she asked the parson, in her sweetly imperative voice.

"In her chamber," he replied. When he was dead, Parson Lord would be no whiter.

"I will call her," said Madam Diantha, and called "Love! Love, dear child!" And when the girl did not come for the calling, she went up-stairs, and found her weeping and moaning that she could not wed without her father's consent, and he would never give it, and if he would, he would fly in the face of his own conscience, and bring a curse upon himself for breaking his solemn promise to the Lord.

Thus the poor child, in her bewilderment of love and conscience, until the squire's lady would hear no more, but bathed her eyes and led her down-stairs to Richard, who took her hand with an air as if he challenged the whole world.

Then Squire Hawkes spoke to the parson. "Sir," he said, "my grandson loves your daughter, and she returns his love. The banns have been published for the requisite length of time, as you are aware, and they stand before you humbly beseeching that you give them your blessing and unite them in matrimony."

"I cannot do so, sir," replied Parson Lord, in a set, sad voice. "I cannot, sir."

"May I inquire why not, sir?"

"When my child was born, I solemnly dedicated her to God. I vowed that she should be set apart for the service of the Lord, should she be spared to me," replied the Parson. "I can break my vow no more than Jephthah of old."

"Damn Jephthah!" shouted the squire, who had an uncompromising tongue when aroused. "You are mad, sir."

The parson remained silent.

"Will you, or will you not, marry them?" demanded the squire.

"I cannot."

"Will you give your consent, then?"

"I cannot."

Love was clinging weakly to her lover's arm. The squire faced them suddenly. " 'Tis the rankest folly," he cried, "and the cruelest! What are you, Reuben Lord, to dispose of your daughter, heart and soul, as you propose? How dare you come thrusting your damned covenant like a wedge between two young things who love each other in the fear of the Lord, and refusing to make them happy, because you are afraid you will go to hell for it? How dare you tamper with the holiest feeling of the human heart? Here is your daughter, an angel if ever there was one, loving this young man, and ready and willing to honor and obey him all the days of her life, comfort him in sorrow, and nurse him in sickness, are you not, sweetheart?"

Love nodded, sobbing.

"And here is my grandson, with all his heart set upon loving, cherishing, and protecting her in sickness or health, and cleaving to her for better or worse, are you not, Richard?"

"Yes, sir, I am," replied Richard, with a start of amazement.

"Then," said the squire, his voice changing suddenly from a tone of easy interrogation to one of solemn proclamation, "in virtue of the authority vested in me as justice of the peace of this township, I pronounce you man and wife."

The squire gave a loud laugh of triumph, which he checked suddenly as he saw Parson Reuben Lord's face. It was shocked beyond words, and with a strange expression of guilt.

"Before the Lord, sir," cried Squire Hawkes, "neither your daughter nor my grandson nor my wife was a party to this, nor I myself, until the fancy struck me. I saw in a flash 'twas the only way; unless she had been trapped thus, she would never have brought herself to wed without your consent."

Parson Lord went over to his daughter, kissed her solemnly on her forehead, said "God bless you, my daughter! May you and the husband you have chosen dwell together in the love of the Lord, and may the day be sanctified to you!" and went out.

A crowd which had gathered outside, gaping silently out of the shadows, stood back in a very hush of wonder when the bridal party emerged from the parson's house, got into the coach, and were driven away. "She's coming! She's married to him!" said one exclaiming voice, and then no more.

For days the village was thrilled to its fullest capacity for excitement by the wedding of the squire's grandson and the parson's daughter; but no one ever knew the full particulars, for principals and witnesses kept them to themselves.

Everybody agreed that the parson aged fast after his daughter's marriage, and that his whole character seemed strangely changed. Whereas he had moved among his people, discharging his religious duties towards them with a stern rigidity of faithfulness, he now bore himself with a meek lovingness which caused folk to turn and stare at him as at a stranger. Moreover, his sermons lost their directness of application concerning the justice and righteous judgments of the Lord, and some feared lest he might be falling off in the doctrines.

Aunt Betsey Ware, who kept house for him, said never was such a change in mortal man before, and when a sour-apple tree begun to bear sweetings, 'twas a sure sign that it would blossom next spring in another world. She was right in that case, for Parson Reuben Lord died very suddenly the spring after his daughter's marriage.

Love was sent for, and came with her husband, and mourned for her father, though in somewhat unwonted fashion. It was as if she grieved more sorely for that father whom she had never had than for him whom she had lost.

Then, a few days after the funeral, she found among his papers his journal, which she read, and had therefrom a revelation. When her husband came in she ran and clung to him, weeping and trembling in a passion of remorseful love and pity.

"Oh," she cried—"oh, Richard! it was father—it was father!"

"What do you mean, sweetheart?"

"It was father who gave me the doll, and not Madam Diantha. It was father who gave me the pretty gowns and the bonnets and the ribbons. It was father who gave me everything! Oh, Richard, it was poor father! Look at this—look!"

Richard took the parson's journal and read, here and there, where she indicated:

March 6.—I have purchased the doll. Alas! I am weak and selfish, and under the sway of my natural affection. The price of the toy should have gone elsewhere; but the heart of the child is sore, and I cannot have it. Oh, her face as she stood there holding the old treasure of her childhood, which she had found, and which I could not let her keep for very consistency in discipline! Daphne was too hard upon such a tender heart of such a little girl.

God forgive me if I have erred through too great love for my child! Methinks I could have been burned at the stake in Thy cause, I could have been broken upon the wheel, but this martyrdom of pain in the heart of the child of my love I cannot bear.

March 7.—She looks as I have never seen her; the joy in her face causes my heart to leap. I have given her the toy in a manner secretly, hoping that she will not confound me with her innocent delight and thanks, which would convey to me such reproaches; and she was delicately mindful of my wish. She is wise beyond her years. How can I crave forgiveness when I do not truly repent, remembering the child's face and the joy in it? Right or wrong, I would do it over again. Oh, my poor heart!

July 8.—Have purchased a gown of white muslin for my daughter. The ornament of a meek and quiet spirit should have been sufficient for her, but she was not attired as others of her age, and it perchance has tried her: the heart of a maid is a tender and unknown thing. Oh, my weak and degenerate nature! May it not foster in her too great love of dress and the pleasures of the world; for myself it matters not, so she be innocently glad.

September 6.—She is grieving because of that youth to whom her heart has turned, as I have known for some time, to my great sadness. What will become of that tender heart, yielding so helplessly and so guilelessly unto the great call of life? I cannot give my consent; I dare not break my vow unto the Lord. Herein, at least, I must stand firm. She has no appetite. I have purchased delicacies for her. It may be that I do wrong, when the heathen starve for the milk of the word; but she is my only child.

January 9.—She is very poor in health. She shivers in the cold meeting-house. I have purchased a fur tippet for her, and a large muff, and a wadded cloak at a price which would have done incalculable good in purchasing spiritual raiment for the needy in foreign fields. The child does not put me to shame with her openly expressed gratitude, but takes her gift, as usual, with her sweet docility and meek grace.

March 18.—I have to-day purchased a new gown of fine texture and a pretty color. She still pines and grieves, and I strive to render her content with these little gewgaws, which, I have understood, sweeten the greater lacks of life to the feminine heart. May God forgive me for yielding to this so great weakness, and striving to temper the sorrow which may be ordained for her good to my daughter, and even perchance awakening thereby a love for vanity in her heart!

July 26.—The youth upon whom she has fixed her affections is in the village; she is watching for him and he does not come. Can I keep to my resolution and see her unhappy?

August 27.—All is over. I have yielded to the strength of my paternal love. They have met and plighted their vows, and by my means. I myself, in spite of everything, have brought about a meeting between them, and that by methods which bring me to shame. I resorted to subterfuge, even to deception. I cannot recall even to myself the means which I used, involving, as they did, deception and trickery, without the deepest mortification and the most painful prickings of conscience, and yet I acknowledge, to my still deeper humiliation, that I do not regret the result which was brought about by such means, and I confess that I am sure, in the depths of my guilty and self-betraying heart, that, for the sake of her happiness, I would repeat, as long as I drew the breath of life, my folly and my fault.

September 30.—My daughter is wedded to the man of her choice. The letter of my vow I kept, yet broke it undeniably in the spirit. I humbly confess to my Maker my joy and exceeding happiness that the vow be not fulfilled, sinful though it may be. In spite of my backsliding, my lack of steadfastness, and my weakness of the flesh, I have upon me a deep peace and certainty of good to come which will not be gainsaid by any self-blame. I marvel greatly if I perchance have rightfully estimated the love of God towards us, which may—and I be not led astray by my evil imagination—acknowledge as its own offspring all the natural affections of the human heart, and the human weakness therefrom be thus forgiven by the divine love.

The Parrot

THE PARROT WAS A SUPERB BIRD—a vociferous symmetry of green
and gold and ruby red, with eyes like jewels, with their identical irresponsibility of fire, with a cling, not of loving dependence, but of
ruthless insistence, to his mistress's hand, or the wires of his cage,
and a beak of such a fine curve of cruelty as was never excelled.

The parrot's mistress was a New England woman, with the influence of a stern training strong upon her, and yet with a rampant
force of individuality constantly at war with it. She lived alone, except for the parrot, in a sharply angled village house, looking out at
the world with a clean, repellent glare of windows and white broadside of wall, in a yard whose grass seemed as if combed always by
one wind, so evenly slanted was it. There was a decorously trimmed
rosebush on either side of the front door, and one elm-tree at the
gate which leaned decidedly to the south with all its green sweep of
branches, and always in consequence gave the woman a vague and
unreasoning sense of immorality.

Inside, the house showed stiff parallelograms of white curtains,
and dull carpets threadbare with cleanliness, and little pools of reflected light from the polished surfaces of old tables and desks, and
one glass-doored bookcase filled with works on divinity bound
uniformly in rusty black.

The woman's father had been a Congregational clergyman, and
this was his old library. She had read every book over and over with
a painful concentration, and afterwards admitted her crime of light-
mindedness, and prayed to be forgiven, and have her soul so
wrought upon by grace that she might truthfully enjoy these godly
publications. She had never read a novel; she looked upon cards as
wiles of the devil; once, and once only, had she been to a concert
of strictly secular music in the town-hall, and had felt thereby con-
taminated for days, having a temperament which was strangely
wrought upon by music, and yet a total ignorance of it. She felt
guilty under the influence of all harmonies which did not, through
being linked to spiritual words, turn her soul to thoughts of heaven;
and yet sometimes, to her sore bewilderment, the tunes which she

heard in church did not so sway her wayward fancy; and then she accused herself of being perverted in her comprehension of good through the influence of that worldly concert.

This woman went nowhere except to church, to prayer-meeting, to the village store, and once a month to the missionary sewing-circle, and to the supper and sociable in the evening. She dressed always in black, her face was delicately spare, her lips were a compressed line of red, and yet she was pretty, with a prettiness almost of youth, from that undiminished fire of the spirit which dwelt within her, as securely caged by her training and narrowness of life as was the parrot by the strong wires of his house.

The parrot was the one bright thing in the woman's life; he was the link with that which was outside her, and yet with that which was of her truest inwardness of self. This tropical thing, screaming and laughing, and shrieking out dissonant words, and oftentimes speeches, with a seemingly diabolical comprehension of the situation, was the one note of utter freedom and irresponsibility in her life. She adored him, but always with a sense of guilt upon her. Often she said to herself that some judgment would come upon her for so loving such a bird, for there was in truth about him as much utter gracelessness as can be conceived of in one of the lower creation. He swore such oaths that his mistress would fairly fly out of the door with hands to her ears. Always, when she saw a caller coming, she would remove his cage to a distant room and shut all the doors between. She felt that if any one heard him sending forth those profane shrieks, possibly to his spiritual contamination, she might be driven by her sense of duty to have the bird put to death. She knew, as she believed, that she risked her own soul by listening and yet loving, but that she had no courage to forego.

As for the parrot, he loved his mistress, if he loved anything. He would extend an ingratiating but deceitful claw towards her between his cage wires whenever she approached. If ever she had a torn finger in consequence, she made light of it, like any wound of love. He would take morsels of food from between her thin lips.

When she talked to him with that language of love which every soul knows by instinct, and which is intelligible to all who are not too deadened and deafened with self, he would cock his glittering head and look at her with that inscrutable jewel-eye of his. Then he would thrust out a claw towards her with that insistence which was ruthless, and yet not more ruthless than the insistence of love, and often say something which confounded her with its apparent wisdom of sequence, and then the doubt and the conviction which at once tormented and enraptured her would seize upon her.

She tried to conceal it from herself, she held it as the rankest atheism, she thought vaguely of the idols of wood and stone in the hymn-book, of Baal,[1] and the golden calf,[2] and the witch of Endor,[3] and every forbidden thing which is the antithesis of holiness, and yet she could not be sure that her parrot had not a soul. Sometimes she wondered if she ought to speak of her state of mind to the minister, and ask his advice, but she shrank from doing that, both because of her natural reserve and because he was unmarried, and she knew that people had coupled his name with hers. He was of suitable age, and it was urged that a match for him with the solitary daughter of the former minister would be eminently appropriate.

The woman had never considered the possibility of such a thing, although she had heard of the plan of the parish from many a female friend. She had had her stifled dreams in her early youth, but she had not been one to attract lovers, being perchance bound as to her true graces somewhat too much after the fashion of her father's old divinity books. No man in her whole life had ever looked at her with a look of love, and she had never heard the involuntary break of it in his voice. Sometimes on summer evenings, she, sitting by her open window, saw village lovers going past with covert arms of affection around slim, girlish waists. One night she saw, half shrinking from the sight, a fond pair standing in the shadow of the elm-tree at her gate, and clasped in each other's arms, and saw the girl's face raised to the young man's for his eager kisses, the while a murmur of love, like a song in an unknown tongue, came to her ears.

It was a warm night, and the parrot's cage was slung for coolness on a peg over the window, and he shrieked out, with his seemingly unholy apprehension of things, "What is that? What is that? Do you know what that is, Martha?" Then ended his query with such a wild clamor of laughter that the lovers at the gate fled, and his mistress, Martha, rose and took the bird in.

She set him on the sitting-room table along with the Bible and the Concordance, and a neat little pile of religious papers, while she lighted a lamp. Then she looked half affrightedly, half with loving admiration, at the gorgeous thing, swinging himself frantically on the ring in his cage.

Then, swifter than lightning, down on his perch he dropped, cast a knowing eye like a golden spark at the solitary woman, and shrieked out again:

"What was that? What was that, Martha? Martha, Martha, Martha, Martha. Polly don't want a cracker; Polly don't want a cracker; Polly will be damned if she eats a cracker. You don't want a cracker, do you, Martha? Martha, Martha, Martha, want a cracker? What was that, Martha? Martha, want a cracker? Martha will be damned if she eat a cracker. Martha, Martha, Martha!"

Then the bird was off in such another explosion of laughs, thrusting a claw through his wires at his mistress, that the house rang with them. Martha took the extended claw tenderly; she put her pretty, delicate, faded face to that treacherous beak; she murmured fond words. Then ceased suddenly as she heard a step on the walk, and the parrot cried out, with a cry of sharpest and most sardonic exultation:

"He's coming, he's coming, Martha!"

Then, to Martha's utter horror, before she had time to remove the bird, a knock came on her front door, which stood open, and there was the minister.

He had called upon her before, in accordance with his pastoral duty, but seldom, and always with his mother, who kept his house with him. This time he was alone, and there was something new in his manner.

He was a handsome man, no younger than she, but looking younger, with a dash of manner which many considered unministerial. He would not allow Martha to remove the parrot, though she strove tremblingly to do so, and laughed with a loud peal like a boy when the parrot shrieked, to his mistress's sore discomfiture:

"He's come, Martha, damned if he ain't. Martha, Martha, where in hell is that old cracker?"

Martha felt as if her hour of retribution had come, and she was vaguely and guiltily pleased and relieved when the minister not only did not seem shocked with the free speaking of her bird, but was apparently amused.

She watched him touch the parrot caressingly, and heard him talk persuasively, coaxing him to further speech, and for the first time in her life a complete sense of human comradeship came to her.

After a while the parrot resolved himself into a gorgeous plumy ball of slumber on his perch, then his mistress sat an hour in the moonlight with the minister.

She had put out the lamp at his request, timidly, and yet with a conviction that such a course must be strictly proper, since it was proposed by the minister.

The two sat near each other at the open window, and the soft sweetness of the summer night came in, and the influence of the moonlight was over them both. The lovers continued to stroll past the gate, and a rule of sequence holds good in all things. Presently, for the first time in her life, this solitary woman felt a man's hand clasping her own little slender one in her black cashmere lap. The minister made no declaration of love in words, but the tones of his voice were enough.

When he spoke of exchanging with a neighboring clergyman in two weeks, the speech was set to the melody of a love-song, and there was no cheating ears which were attuned to it, no matter if it had been long in coming.

When the minister took his leave, and Martha lighted her lamp again, the parrot stirred and woke, and brought that round golden eye of his to bear upon her face flushed like a girl's, and cried out:

"Why, Martha! why, Martha! what is the matter?"

Then Martha dropped on her knees beside the cage, and touched the bird's head with a finger of tenderest caressing.

"Oh, you darling, you darling, you precious!" she murmured, and began to weep. And the parrot did not laugh, but continued to eye her.

"He has come, hasn't he, Martha?" said he.

Then Martha was more than ever inclined to think that the bird had a soul; still she doubted, because of the unorthodoxy of it, and the remembrance of man and man alone being made in God's own image.

Still, through having no friend in whom to confide her new hope and happiness, the parrot became doubly dear to her. Curiously enough, in the succeeding weeks he was not so boisterous, he did not swear so much, but would sit watching his mistress as she sat dreaming, and now and then he said something which seemed inconceivable to her simple mind, unless he had a full understanding of the situation.

The minister came oftener and oftener; he stayed longer. He

came home on Sunday nights with her after meeting. He kissed her at the door. He always held her little hand, which yielded to his with an indescribably gentle and innocent maidenliness, while he talked about the mission work in foreign lands, and always his lightest speech was set to that love-melody.

Martha began to expect to marry him. She overlooked her supply of linen. Visions of a new silk for a wedding-dress, brown instead of black, flashed before her eyes. She talked more than usual to the parrot in those days, using the words and tone which she might have used towards the minister, had not the restraints of her New England birth and training enclosed her like the wires of a cage, and the parrot eyed her with wise attentiveness which grew upon him, only now and then uttering one of his favorite oaths.

Then suddenly the disillusion of the poor soul as to her first gospel of love came. She went to the sewing-circle one Wednesday in early spring, after the minister had been to see her for nearly a year, and she wore her best black silk, thinking he would be there, and she had crimped her hair and looked as radiant as a girl when she entered the low vestry filled with the discordant gabble of sewing-women.

Then she heard the news. It was told her with some protest and friendly preparation, for everybody had thought that the match between herself and the minister was as good as made. There was a whispered discussion among groups of women, with sly eyes upon her face; then one, who was a leader among them, a woman of affectionate glibness, approached her, after Martha had heard a feminine voice lingering in the outskirts of a sudden hush say:

"And she's got on her best silk, too, poor thing."

Martha now looked up, and her radiant face paled slowly as the woman began to talk to her. The news seemed to smite her like some hammer of fate, her brain reeled, and her ears rang with it.

The minister was engaged, and had, in fact, gone to be married. He would bring his bride home the next week; another minister was to occupy his pulpit the next Sunday. He was to marry a woman to whom he had been attached for years, but the marriage had been delayed.

Martha listened, then suddenly the color flashed back into her white cheeks—she had stanch blood in her.

"Well, I am glad to hear it," she said, and lied with no compunction for the first time in her life, and never repented it. "I have always thought it was much better for a minister to be married," she said. "I have always thought that his usefulness would be much enhanced. Father used to say so." Then she took out her needle and thread and went to work with the others.

The women eyed her furtively, but she made no sign of noticing it. When one said to her that she had kind of thought that maybe the minister was shining up to her, she only laughed, and said gently that they were very good friends, but there had never been a word of anything else between them.

She overheard one woman whisper to another that, "if Martha was cut up, she would deceive the very elect," and the other reply, "that maybe he had told Martha all about the woman he was going to marry."

Martha stayed as usual to the supper and the entertainment. A young couple sat on a settee in front of her while some singing was going on, and at a tender passage she saw the boy furtively press the girl's hand, and she set her lips hard.

But at last she was free to go home, and when she had unlocked the door and entered her lonely house, down upon the floor in her sitting-room she flung herself, with all the floodgates of her New England nature open at last. She wept and wailed her grief and anger aloud like a Southern woman.

Then in the midst of it all came a wild wailing cry from the parrot, a cry of uncanny sympathy and pain and tenderness outside the pale of humanity.

"Why, Martha! why, Martha! what's the matter?"

Then the woman rose and went to the cage, her delicate face and lips so swollen with grief that she was appalling; she had even trailed her best black silk in the mud on her way home. She was past the bounds of decency in her frenzy of misery. She opened the cage door, and the parrot flew out and to her slender shoulder, and she sobbed out her grief to him amid his protesting cries.

"Poor Martha, why, poor Martha," he said, and she felt almost certain that he had a soul, and she no longer felt so shocked by her leaning towards that belief, but was comforted.

But all of a sudden the parrot on her shoulder gave a tweak at her hair, and shrieked out:

"That was a damned cracker, Martha," and her belief wavered.

She put him back in his cage and locked up her house for the night, and put out her lamp and went to bed, but she could not go to sleep, for the loss of her old dream of love gave the whole world and all life such a hollowness and emptiness that it was like thunder in her ears, and forced its waking realization upon her.

All during the next week, if it had not been for the parrot, she felt that she would have gone mad. She went out in her small daily tracks to the village store, and the prayer-meetings, and on Sunday to church, her agony of concern being that no one should know that she was fretting over the minister's desertion of her.

She talked about the engagement and marriage with her gentle stateliness of manner, which never failed her, but when she got home to her parrot, and the healing solitariness of her own house, she felt like one who had a cooling lotion applied to a burn.

And she wondered more and more if the parrot had not verily a soul, and could not approach her with a sympathy which was better than any human sympathy, since it was so beyond all human laws, but she was not fully convinced of it until the minister brought his new wife to call upon her a few weeks after his marriage.

She had wondered vaguely if he would do it, if he could do it, but he came in with all his dashing grace of manner, and his bride was smiling at his side, in her wedding silks, and Martha greeted them with no disturbance of her New England calm and stiffness, but inwardly her very soul stormed and protested; and as they were sitting in the parlor there came of a sudden from the next room, where he had been at large, the parrot, like a very whirlwind of feathered rage, and, with a wild shriek, he dashed upon the bridal bonnet, plucking furiously at roses and plumes.

Then there was a frightened and flurried exit, with confusion and apologies, and screams of baffled wrath, and rueful smoothing of torn finery.

And after the minister and his bride had gone, Martha looked at her parrot, and his golden eyes met hers, and she recognized in the fierce bird a comradeship and an equality, for he had given vent to an emotion of her own nature, and she knew forevermore that the parrot had a soul.

The Lost Ghost

MRS. JOHN EMERSON, sitting with her needlework beside the window, looked out and saw Mrs. Rhoda Meserve coming down the street, and knew at once by the trend of her steps and the cant of her head that she meditated turning in at her gate. She also knew by a certain something about her general carriage—a thrusting forward of the neck, a bustling hitch of the shoulders—that she had important news. Rhoda Meserve always had the news as soon as the news was in being, and generally Mrs. John Emerson was the first to whom she imparted it. The two women had been friends ever since Mrs. Meserve had married Simon Meserve and come to the village to live.

Mrs. Meserve was a pretty woman, moving with graceful flirts of ruffling skirts; her clearcut, nervous face, as delicately tinted as a shell, looked brightly from the plumy brim of a black hat at Mrs. Emerson in the window. Mrs. Emerson was glad to see her coming. She returned the greeting with enthusiasm, then rose hurriedly, ran into the cold parlour and brought out one of the best rocking-chairs. She was just in time, after drawing it up beside the opposite window, to greet her friend at the door.

"Good-afternoon," said she. "I declare, I'm real glad to see you. I've been alone all day. John went to the city this morning. I thought of coming over to your house this afternoon, but I couldn't bring my sewing very well. I am putting the ruffles on my new black dress skirt."

"Well, I didn't have a thing on hand except my crochet work," responded Mrs. Meserve, "and I thought I'd just run over a few minutes."

"I'm real glad you did," repeated Mrs. Emerson. "Take your things right off. Here, I'll put them on my bed in the bedroom. Take the rocking-chair."

Mrs. Meserve settled herself in the parlour rocking-chair, while Mrs. Emerson carried her shawl and hat into the little adjoining bedroom. When she returned Mrs. Meserve was rocking peacefully and was already at work hooking blue wool in and out.

"That's real pretty," said Mrs. Emerson.

"Yes, I think it's pretty," replied Mrs. Meserve.

"I suppose it's for the church fair?"

"Yes. I don't suppose it'll bring enough to pay for the worsted, let alone the work, but I suppose I've got to make something."

"How much did that one you made for the fair last year bring?"

"Twenty-five cents."

"It's wicked, ain't it?"

"I rather guess it is. It takes me a week every minute I can get to make one. I wish those that bought such things for twenty-five cents had to make them. Guess they'd sing another song. Well, I suppose I oughtn't to complain as long as it is for the Lord, but sometimes it does seem as if the Lord didn't get much out of it."

"Well, it's pretty work," said Mrs. Emerson, sitting down at the opposite window and taking up her dress skirt.

"Yes, it is real pretty work. I just *love* to crochet."

The two women rocked and sewed and crocheted in silence for two or three minutes. They were both waiting. Mrs. Meserve waited for the other's curiosity to develop in order that her news might have, as it were, a befitting stage entrance. Mrs. Emerson waited for the news. Finally she could wait no longer.

"Well, what's the news?" said she.

"Well, I don't know as there's anything very particular," hedged the other woman, prolonging the situation.

"Yes, there is; you can't cheat me," replied Mrs. Emerson.

"Now, how do you know?"

"By the way you look."

Mrs. Meserve laughed consciously and rather vainly.

"Well, Simon says my face is so expressive I can't hide anything more than five minutes no matter how hard I try," said she. "Well, there is some news. Simon came home with it this noon. He heard it in South Dayton. He had some business over there this morning. The old Sargent place is let."

Mrs. Emerson dropped her sewing and stared.

"You don't say so!"

"Yes, it is."

"Who to?"

"Why, some folks from Boston that moved to South Dayton last year. They haven't been satisfied with the house they had there—it wasn't large enough. The man has got considerable property and can afford to live pretty well. He's got a wife and his unmarried sister in the family. The sister's got money, too. He does business in

Boston and it's just as easy to get to Boston from here as from South Dayton, and so they're coming here. You know the old Sargent house is a splendid place."

"Yes, it's the handsomest house in town, but——"

"Oh, Simon said they told him about that and he just laughed. Said he wasn't afraid and neither was his wife and sister. Said he'd risk ghosts rather than little tucked-up sleeping-rooms without any sun, like they've had in the Dayton house. Said he'd rather risk *seeing* ghosts, than risk being ghosts themselves. Simon said they said he was a great hand to joke."

"Oh, well," said Mrs. Emerson, "it is a beautiful house, and maybe there isn't anything in those stories. It never seemed to me they came very straight anyway. I never took much stock in them. All I thought was—if his wife was nervous."

"Nothing in creation would hire me to go into a house that I'd ever heard a word against of that kind," declared Mrs. Meserve with emphasis. "I wouldn't go into that house if they would give me the rent. I've seen enough of haunted houses to last me as long as I live."

Mrs. Emerson's face acquired the expression of a hunting hound.

"Have you?" she asked in an intense whisper.

"Yes, I have. I don't want any more of it."

"Before you came here?"

"Yes; before I was married—when I was quite a girl."

Mrs. Meserve had not married young. Mrs. Emerson had mental calculations when she heard that.

"Did you really live in a house that was——" she whispered fearfully.

Mrs. Meserve nodded solemnly.

"Did you really ever—see—anything——"

Mrs. Meserve nodded.

"You didn't see anything that did you any harm?"

"No, I didn't see anything that did me harm looking at it in one way, but it don't do anybody in this world any good to see things that haven't any business to be seen in it. You never get over it."

There was a moment's silence. Mrs. Emerson's features seemed to sharpen.

"Well, of course I don't want to urge you," said she, "if you don't feel like talking about it; but maybe it might do you good to tell it out, if it's on your mind, worrying you."

"I try to put it out of my mind," said Mrs. Meserve.

"Well, it's just as you feel."

"I never told anybody but Simon," said Mrs. Meserve. "I never felt as if it was wise perhaps. I didn't know what folks might think. So many don't believe in anything they can't understand, that they might think my mind wasn't right. Simon advised me not to talk about it. He said he didn't believe it was anything supernatural, but he had to own up that he couldn't give any explanation for it to save his life. He had to own up that he didn't believe anybody could. Then he said he wouldn't talk about it. He said lots of folks would sooner tell folks my head wasn't right than to own up they couldn't see through it."

"I'm sure I wouldn't say so," returned Mrs. Emerson reproachfully. "You know better than that, I hope."

"Yes, I do," replied Mrs. Meserve. "I know you wouldn't say so."

"And I wouldn't tell it to a soul if you didn't want me to."

"Well, I'd rather you wouldn't."

"I won't speak of it even to Mr. Emerson."

"I'd rather you wouldn't even to him."

"I won't."

Mrs. Emerson took up her dress skirt again; Mrs. Meserve hooked up another loop of blue wool. Then she begun:

"Of course," said she, "I ain't going to say positively that I believe or disbelieve in ghosts, but all I tell you is what I saw. I can't explain it. I don't pretend I can, for I can't. If you can, well and good; I shall be glad, for it will stop tormenting me as it has done and always will otherwise. There hasn't been a day nor a night since it happened that I haven't thought of it, and always I have felt the shivers go down my back when I did."

"That's an awful feeling," Mrs. Emerson said.

"Ain't it? Well, it happened before I was married, when I was a girl and lived in East Wilmington. It was the first year I lived there. You know my family all died five years before that. I told you."

Mrs. Emerson nodded.

"Well, I went there to teach school, and I went to board with a Mrs. Amelia Dennison and her sister, Mrs. Bird. Abby, her name was—Abby Bird. She was a widow; she had never had any children. She had a little money—Mrs. Dennison didn't have any—and she had come to East Wilmington and bought the house they lived in. It was a real pretty house, though it was very old and run down. It had cost Mrs. Bird a good deal to put it in order. I guess that was the reason they took me to board. I guess they thought it would help along a little. I guess what I paid for my board about kept us all in victuals. Mrs. Bird had enough to live on if they were careful, but she had spent so much fixing up the old house that they must have been a little pinched for awhile.

"Anyhow, they took me to board, and I thought I was pretty lucky to get in there. I had a nice room, big and sunny and furnished pretty, the paper and paint all new, and everything as neat as wax. Mrs. Dennison was one of the best cooks I ever saw, and I had a little stove in my room, and there was always a nice fire there when I got home from school. I thought I hadn't been in such a nice place since I lost my own home, until I had been there about three weeks.

"I had been there about three weeks before I found it out, though I guess it had been going on ever since they had been in the house, and that was most four months. They hadn't said anything about it, and I didn't wonder, for there they had just bought the house and been to so much expense and trouble fixing it up.

"Well, I went there in September. I begun my school the first Monday. I remember it was a real cold fall, there was a frost the middle of September, and I had to put on my winter coat. I remember when I came home that night (let me see, I began school on a Monday, and that was two weeks from the next Thursday), I took off my coat downstairs and laid it on the table in the front entry. It was a real nice coat—heavy black broadcloth trimmed with fur; I had had it the winter before. Mrs. Bird called after me as I went upstairs that I ought not to leave it in the front entry for fear somebody might come in and take it, but I only laughed and called back to her that I wasn't afraid. I never was much afraid of burglars.

"Well, though it was hardly the middle of September, it was a real cold night. I remember my room faced west, and the sun was getting low, and the sky was a pale yellow and purple, just as you see it sometimes in the winter when there is going to be a cold snap. I rather think that was the night the frost came the first time. I know Mrs. Dennison covered up some flowers she had in the front yard, anyhow. I remember looking out and seeing an old green plaid shawl of hers over the verbena bed. There was a fire in my little wood-stove. Mrs. Bird made it, I know. She was a real motherly sort of woman; she always seemed to be the happiest when she was doing something to make other folks happy and comfortable. Mrs. Dennison told me she had always been so. She said she had coddled her husband within an inch of his life. 'It's lucky Abby never had any children,' she said, 'for she would have spoilt them.'

"Well, that night I sat down beside my nice little fire and ate an apple. There was a plate of nice apples on my table. Mrs. Bird put them there. I was always very fond of apples. Well, I sat down and ate an apple, and was having a beautiful time, and thinking how lucky I was to have got board in such a place with such nice folks, when I heard a queer little sound at my door. It was such a little hesitating sort of sound that it sounded more like a fumble than a knock, as if some one very timid, with very little hands, was feeling along the door, not quite daring to knock. For a minute I thought it was a mouse. But I waited and it came again, and then I made up my mind it was a knock, but a very little scared one, so I said, 'Come in.'

"But nobody came in, and then presently I heard the knock again. Then I got up and opened the door, thinking it was very queer, and I had a frightened feeling without knowing why.

"Well, I opened the door, and the first thing I noticed was a draught of cold air, as if the front door downstairs was open, but there was a strange close smell about the cold draught. It smelled more like a cellar that had been shut up for years, than out-of-doors. Then I saw something. I saw my coat first. The thing that held it was so small that I couldn't see much of anything else. Then I saw a little white face with eyes so scared and wishful that they seemed as if they might eat a hole in anybody's heart. It was a dreadful little face, with something about it which made it different from any other face on earth, but it was so pitiful that somehow it did away a good deal with the dreadfulness. And there were two little hands spotted purple with the cold, holding up my winter coat, and a strange little far-away voice said: 'I can't find my mother.'

" 'For Heaven's sake,' I said, 'who are you?'

"Then the little voice said again: 'I can't find my mother.'

"All the time I could smell the cold and I saw that it was about the child; that cold was clinging to her as if she had come out of some deadly cold place. Well, I took my coat, I did not know what else to do, and the cold was clinging to that. It was as cold as if it had come off ice. When I had the coat I could see the child more plainly. She was dressed in one little white garment made very simply. It was a nightgown, only very long, quite covering her feet, and I could see dimly through it her little thin body mottled purple with the cold. Her face did not look so cold; that was a clear waxen white. Her hair was dark, but it looked as if it might be dark only because it was so damp, almost wet, and might really be light hair. It clung very close to her forehead, which was round and white. She would have been very beautiful if she had not been so dreadful.

" 'Who are you?' says I again, looking at her.

"She looked at me with her terrible pleading eyes and did not say anything.

" 'What are you?' says I. Then she went away. She did not seem to run or walk like other children. She flitted, like one of those little filmy white butterflies, that don't seem like real ones they are so light, and move as if they had no weight. But she looked back from the head of the stairs. 'I can't find my mother,' said she, and I never heard such a voice.

" 'Who is your mother?' says I, but she was gone.

"Well, I thought for a moment I should faint away. The room got dark and I heard a singing in my ears. Then I flung my coat onto the bed. My hands were as cold as ice from holding it, and I stood in my door, and called first Mrs. Bird and then Mrs. Dennison. I didn't dare go down over the stairs where that had gone. It seemed to me I should go mad if I didn't see somebody or something like other folks on the face of the earth. I thought I should never make anybody hear, but I could hear them stepping about downstairs, and I could smell biscuits baking for supper. Somehow the smell of those biscuits seemed the only natural thing left to keep me in my right mind. I didn't dare go over those stairs. I just stood there and called, and finally I heard the entry door open and Mrs. Bird called back:

" 'What is it? Did you call, Miss Arms?'

" 'Come up here; come up here as quick as you can, both of you,' I screamed out; 'quick, quick, quick!'

"I heard Mrs. Bird tell Mrs. Dennison: 'Come quick, Amelia, something is the matter in Miss Arms' room.' It struck me even then that she expressed herself rather queerly, and it struck me as very queer, indeed, when they both got upstairs and I saw that they knew what had happened, or that they knew of what nature the happening was.

" 'What is it, dear?' asked Mrs. Bird, and her pretty, loving voice had a strained sound. I saw her look at Mrs. Dennison and I saw Mrs. Dennison look back at her.

" 'For God's sake,' says I, and I never spoke so before—'for God's sake, what was it brought my coat upstairs?'

" 'What was it like?' asked Mrs. Dennison in a sort of failing voice, and she looked at her sister again and her sister looked back at her.

" 'It was a child I have never seen here before. It looked like a child,' says I, 'but I never saw a child so dreadful, and it had on a nightgown, and said she couldn't find her mother. Who was it? What was it?'

"I thought for a minute Mrs. Dennison was going to faint, but Mrs. Bird hung onto her and rubbed her hands, and whispered in her ear (she had the cooingest kind of voice), and I ran and got her a glass of cold water. I tell you it took considerable courage to go downstairs alone, but they had set a lamp on the entry table so I could see. I don't believe I could have spunked up enough to have gone downstairs in the dark, thinking every second that child might be close to me. The lamp and the smell of the biscuits baking seemed to sort of keep my courage up, but I tell you I didn't waste much time going down those stairs and out into the kitchen for a glass of water. I pumped as if the house was afire, and I grabbed the first thing I came across in the shape of a tumbler: it was a painted one that Mrs. Dennison's Sunday school class gave her, and it was meant for a flower vase.

"Well, I filled it and then ran upstairs. I felt every minute as if something would catch my feet, and I held the glass to Mrs. Dennison's lips, while Mrs. Bird held her head up, and she took a good long swallow, then she looked hard at the tumbler.

" 'Yes,' says I, 'I know I got this one, but I took the first I came across, and it isn't hurt a mite.'

" 'Don't get the painted flowers wet,' says Mrs. Dennison very feebly, 'they'll wash off if you do.'

" 'I'll be real careful,' says I. I knew she set a sight by that painted tumbler.

"The water seemed to do Mrs. Dennison good, for presently she pushed Mrs. Bird away and sat up. She had been laying down on my bed.

" 'I'm all over it now,' says she, but she was terribly white, and her eyes looked as if they saw something outside things. Mrs. Bird wasn't much better, but she always had a sort of settled sweet, good look that nothing could disturb to any great extent. I knew I looked dreadful, for I caught a glimpse of myself in the glass, and I would hardly have known who it was.

"Mrs. Dennison, she slid off the bed and walked sort of tottery to a chair. 'I was silly to give way so,' says she.

" 'No, you wasn't silly, sister,' says Mrs. Bird. 'I don't know what this means any more than you do, but whatever it is, no one ought to be called silly for being overcome by anything so different from other things which we have known all our lives.'

"Mrs. Dennison looked at her sister, then she looked at me, then back at her sister again, and Mrs. Bird spoke as if she had been asked a question.

" 'Yes,' says she, 'I do think Miss Arms ought to be told—that is, I think she ought to be told all we know ourselves.'

" 'That isn't much,' said Mrs. Dennison with a dying-away sort of sigh. She looked as if she might faint away again any minute. She was a real delicate-looking woman, but it turned out she was a good deal stronger than poor Mrs. Bird.

" 'No, there isn't much we do know,' says Mrs. Bird, 'but what little there is she ought to know. I felt as if she ought to when she first came here.'

" 'Well, I didn't feel quite right about it,' said Mrs. Dennison, 'but I kept hoping it might stop, and any way, that it might never trouble her, and you had put so much in the house, and we needed the money, and I didn't know but she might be nervous and think she couldn't come, and I didn't want to take a man boarder.'

" 'And aside from the money, we were very anxious to have you come, my dear,' says Mrs. Bird.

" 'Yes,' says Mrs. Dennison, 'we wanted the young company in the house; we were lonesome, and we both of us took a great liking to you the minute we set eyes on you.'

"And I guess they meant what they said, both of them. They were beautiful women, and nobody could be any kinder to me than they were, and I never blamed them for not telling me before, and, as they said, there wasn't really much to tell.

"They hadn't any sooner fairly bought the house, and moved into it, than they began to see and hear things. Mrs. Bird said they were sitting together in the sitting-room one evening when they heard it the first time. She said her sister was knitting lace (Mrs. Dennison made beautiful knitted lace) and she was reading the *Missionary Herald*[1] (Mrs. Bird was very much interested in mission

work), when all of a sudden they heard something. She heard it first
and she laid down her *Missionary Herald* and listened, and then
Mrs. Dennison she saw her listening and she drops her lace. 'What
is it you are listening to, Abby?' says she. Then it came again and
they both heard, and the cold shivers went down their backs to hear
it, though they didn't know why. 'It's the cat, isn't it?' says Mrs.
Bird.

" 'It isn't any cat,' says Mrs. Dennison.

" 'Oh, I guess it *must* be the cat; maybe she's got a mouse,' says
Mrs. Bird, real cheerful, to calm down Mrs. Dennison, for she saw
she was 'most scared to death, and she was always afraid of her
fainting away. Then she opens the door and calls, 'Kitty, kitty,
kitty!' They had brought their cat with them in a basket when they
came to East Wilmington to live. It was a real handsome tiger cat, a
tommy, and he knew a lot.

"Well, she called 'Kitty, kitty, kitty!' and sure enough the kitty
came, and when he came in the door he gave a big yawl that didn't
sound unlike what they had heard.

" 'There, sister, here he is; you see it was the cat,' says Mrs. Bird.
'Poor kitty!'

"But Mrs. Dennison she eyed the cat, and she give a great
screech.

" 'What's that? What's that?' says she.

" 'What's what?' says Mrs. Bird, pretending to herself that she
didn't see what her sister meant.

" 'Somethin's got hold of that cat's tail,' says Mrs. Dennison.
'Somethin's got hold of his tail. It's pulled straight out, an' he can't
get away. Just hear him yawl!'

" 'It isn't anything,' says Mrs. Bird, but even as she said that she
could see a little hand holding fast to that cat's tail, and then the
child seemed to sort of clear out of the dimness behind the hand,
and the child was sort of laughing then, instead of looking sad, and
she said that was a great deal worse. She said that laugh was the
most awful and the saddest thing she ever heard.

"Well, she was so dumfounded that she didn't know what to do,
and she couldn't sense at first that it was anything supernatural. She
thought it must be one of the neighbour's children who had run
away and was making free of their house, and was teasing their cat,
and that they must be just nervous to feel so upset by it. So she
speaks up sort of sharp.

" 'Don't you know that you mustn't pull the kitty's tail?' says she. 'Don't you know you hurt the poor kitty, and she'll scratch you if you don't take care. Poor kitty, you mustn't hurt her.'

"And with that she said the child stopped pulling that cat's tail and went to stroking her just as soft and pitiful, and the cat put his back up and rubbed and purred as if he liked it. The cat never seemed a mite afraid, and that seemed queer, for I had always heard that animals were dreadfully afraid of ghosts; but then, that was a pretty harmless little sort of ghost.

"Well, Mrs. Bird said the child stroked that cat, while she and Mrs. Dennison stood watching it, and holding onto each other, for, no matter how hard they tried to think it was all right, it didn't look right. Finally Mrs. Dennison she spoke.

" 'What's your name, little girl?' says she.

"Then the child looks up and stops stroking the cat, and says she can't find her mother, just the way she said it to me. Then Mrs. Dennison she gave such a gasp that Mrs. Bird thought she was going to faint away, but she didn't. 'Well, who is your mother?' says she. But the child just says again 'I can't find my mother—I can't find my mother.'

" 'Where do you live, dear?' says Mrs. Bird.

" 'I can't find my mother,' says the child.

"Well, that was the way it was. Nothing happened. Those two women stood there hanging onto each other, and the child stood in front of them, and they asked her questions, and everything she would say was: 'I can't find my mother.'

"Then Mrs. Bird tried to catch hold of the child, for she thought in spite of what she saw that perhaps she was nervous and it was a real child, only perhaps not quite right in its head, that had run away in her little nightgown after she had been put to bed.

"She tried to catch the child. She had an idea of putting a shawl around it and going out—she was such a little thing she could have carried her easy enough—and trying to find out to which of the neighbours she belonged. But the minute she moved toward the child there wasn't any child there; there was only that little voice seeming to come from nothing, saying 'I can't find my mother,' and presently that died away.

"Well, that same thing kept happening, or something very much the same. Once in awhile Mrs. Bird would be washing dishes, and all at once the child would be standing beside her with the dishtowel, wiping them. Of course, that was terrible. Mrs. Bird would

wash the dishes all over. Sometimes she didn't tell Mrs. Dennison, it
made her so nervous. Sometimes when they were making cake they
would find the raisins all picked over, and sometimes little sticks of
kindling-wood would be found laying beside the kitchen stove.
They never knew when they would come across that child, and always she kept saying over and over that she couldn't find her
mother. They never tried talking to her, except once in awhile Mrs.
Bird would get desperate and ask her something, but the child never
seemed to hear it; she always kept right on saying that she couldn't
find her mother.

"After they had told me all they had to tell about their experience with the child, they told me about the house and the people
that had lived there before they did. It seemed something dreadful
had happened in that house. And the land agent had never let on to
them. I don't think they would have bought it if he had, no matter
how cheap it was, for even if folks aren't really afraid of anything,
they don't want to live in houses where such dreadful things have
happened that you keep thinking about them. I know after they
told me I should never have stayed there another night, if I hadn't
thought so much of them, no matter how comfortable I was made;
and I never was nervous, either. But I stayed. Of course, it didn't
happen in my room. If it had I could not have stayed."

"What was it?" asked Mrs. Emerson in an awed voice.

"It was an awful thing. That child had lived in the house with her
father and mother two years before. They had come—or the father
had—from a real good family. He had a good situation: he was a
drummer for a big leather house in the city, and they lived real
pretty, with plenty to do with. But the mother was a real wicked
woman. She was as handsome as a picture, and they said she came
from good sort of people enough in Boston, but she was bad clean
through, though she was real pretty spoken and most everybody
liked her. She used to dress out and make a great show, and she
never seemed to take much interest in the child, and folks began to
say she wasn't treated right.

"The woman had a hard time keeping a girl. For some reason one
wouldn't stay. They would leave and then talk about her awfully,
telling all kinds of things. People didn't believe it at first; then they
began to. They said that the woman made that little thing, though
she wasn't much over five years old, and small and babyish for her
age, do most of the work, what there was done; they said the house
used to look like a pig-sty when she didn't have help. They said the

little thing used to stand on a chair and wash dishes, and they'd seen her carrying in sticks of wood most as big as she was many a time, and they'd heard her mother scolding her. The woman was a fine singer, and had a voice like a screech-owl when she scolded.

"The father was away most of the time, and when that happened he had been away out West for some weeks. There had been a married man hanging about the mother for some time, and folks had talked some; but they weren't sure there was anything wrong, and he was a man very high up, with money, so they kept pretty still for fear he would hear of it and make trouble for them, and of course nobody was sure, though folks did say afterward that the father of the child had ought to have been told.

"But that was very easy to say; it wouldn't have been so easy to find anybody who would have been willing to tell him such a thing as that, especially when they weren't any too sure. He set his eyes by his wife, too. They said all he seemed to think of was to earn money to buy things to deck her out in. And he about worshiped the child, too. They said he was a real nice man. The men that are treated so bad mostly are real nice men. I've always noticed that.

"Well, one morning that man that there had been whispers about was missing. He had been gone quite a while, though, before they really knew that he was missing, because he had gone away and told his wife that he had to go to New York on business and might be gone a week, and not to worry if he didn't get home, and not to worry if he didn't write, because he should be thinking from day to day that he might take the next train home and there would be no use in writing. So the wife waited, and she tried not to worry until it was two days over the week, then she run into a neighbour's and fainted dead away on the floor; and then they made inquiries and found out that he had skipped—with some money that didn't belong to him, too.

"Then folks began to ask where was that woman, and they found out by comparing notes that nobody had seen her since the man went away; but three or four women remembered that she had told them that she thought of taking the child and going to Boston to visit her folks, so when they hadn't seen her around, and the house shut, they jumped to the conclusion that was where she was. They were the neighbours that lived right around her, but they didn't have much to do with her, and she'd gone out of her way to tell them about her Boston plan, and they didn't make much reply when she did.

"Well, there was this house shut up, and the man and woman missing and the child. Then all of a sudden one of the women that lived the nearest remembered something. She remembered that she had waked up three nights running, thinking she heard a child crying somewhere, and once she waked up her husband, but he said it must be the Bisbees' little girl, and she thought it must be. The child wasn't well and was always crying. It used to have colic spells, especially at night. So she didn't think any more about it until this came up, then all of a sudden she did think of it. She told what she had heard, and finally folks began to think they had better enter that house and see if there was anything wrong.

"Well, they did enter it, and they found that child dead, locked in one of the rooms. (Mrs. Dennison and Mrs. Bird never used that room; it was a back bedroom on the second floor.)

"Yes, they found that poor child there, starved to death, and frozen, though they weren't sure she had frozen to death, for she was in bed with clothes enough to keep her pretty warm when she was alive. But she had been there a week, and she was nothing but skin and bone. It looked as if the mother had locked her into the house when she went away, and told her not to make any noise for fear the neighbours would hear her and find out that she herself had gone.

"Mrs. Dennison said she couldn't really believe that the woman had meant to have her own child starved to death. Probably she thought the little thing would raise somebody, or folks would try to get in the house and find her. Well, whatever she thought, there the child was, dead.

"But that wasn't all. The father came home, right in the midst of it; the child was just buried, and he was beside himself. And—he went on the track of his wife, and he found her, and he shot her dead; it was in all the papers at the time; then he disappeared. Nothing had been seen of him since. Mrs. Dennison said that she thought he had either made way with himself or got out of the country, nobody knew, but they did know there was something wrong with the house.

" 'I knew folks acted queer when they asked me how I liked it when we first came here,' says Mrs. Dennison, 'but I never dreamed why till we saw the child that night.' "

"I never heard anything like it in my life," said Mrs. Emerson, staring at the other woman with awestruck eyes.

"I thought you'd say so," said Mrs. Meserve. "You don't wonder that I ain't disposed to speak light when I hear there is anything queer about a house, do you?"

"No, I don't, after that," Mrs. Emerson said.

"But that ain't all," said Mrs. Meserve.

"Did you see it again?" Mrs. Emerson asked.

"Yes, I saw it a number of times before the last time. It was lucky I wasn't nervous, or I never could have stayed there, much as I liked the place and much as I thought of those two women; they were beautiful women, and no mistake. I loved those women. I hope Mrs. Dennison will come and see me sometime.

"Well, I stayed, and I never knew when I'd see that child. I got so I was very careful to bring everything of mine upstairs, and not leave any little thing in my room that needed doing, for fear she would come lugging up my coat or hat or gloves or I'd find things done when there'd been no live being in the room to do them. I can't tell you how I dreaded seeing her; and worse than the seeing her was the hearing her say, 'I can't find my mother.' It was enough to make your blood run cold. I never heard a living child cry for its mother that was anything so pitiful as that dead one. It was enough to break your heart.

"She used to come and say that to Mrs. Bird oftener than to any one else. Once I heard Mrs. Bird say she wondered if it was possible that the poor little thing couldn't really find her mother in the other world, she had been such a wicked woman.

"But Mrs. Dennison told her she didn't think she ought to speak so nor even think so, and Mrs. Bird said she shouldn't wonder if she was right. Mrs. Bird was always very easy to put in the wrong. She was a good woman, and one that couldn't do things enough for other folks. It seemed as if that was what she lived on. I don't think she was ever so scared by that poor little ghost, as much as she pitied it, and she was 'most heartbroken because she couldn't do anything for it, as she could have done for a live child.

" 'It seems to me sometimes as if I should die if I can't get that awful little white robe off that child and get her in some clothes and feed her and stop her looking for her mother,' I heard her say once, and she was in earnest. She cried when she said it. That wasn't long before she died.

"Now I am coming to the strangest part of it all. Mrs. Bird died very sudden. One morning—it was Saturday, and there wasn't any school—I went downstairs to breakfast, and Mrs. Bird wasn't there;

there was nobody but Mrs. Dennison. She was pouring out the coffee when I came in. 'Why, where's Mrs. Bird?' says I.

" 'Abby ain't feeling very well this morning,' says she; 'there isn't much the matter, I guess, but she didn't sleep very well, and her head aches, and she's sort of chilly, and I told her I thought she'd better stay in bed till the house gets warm.' It was a very cold morning.

" 'Maybe she's got cold,' says I.

" 'Yes, I guess she has,' says Mrs. Dennison. 'I guess she's got cold. She'll be up before long. Abby ain't one to stay in bed a minute longer than she can help.'

"Well, we went on eating our breakfast, and all at once a shadow flickered across one wall of the room and over the ceiling the way a shadow will sometimes when somebody passes the window outside. Mrs. Dennison and I both looked up, then out of the window; then Mrs. Dennison she gives a scream.

" 'Why, Abby's crazy!' says she. 'There she is out this bitter cold morning, and—and——' She didn't finish, but she meant the child. For we were both looking out, and we saw, as plain as we ever saw anything in our lives, Mrs. Abby Bird walking off over the white snow-path with that child holding fast to her hand, nestling close to her as if she had found her own mother.

" 'She's dead,' says Mrs. Dennison, clutching hold of me hard. 'She's dead; my sister is dead!'

"She was. We hurried upstairs as fast as we could go, and she was dead in her bed, and smiling as if she was dreaming, and one arm and hand was stretched out as if something had hold of it; and it couldn't be straightened even at the last—it lay out over her casket at the funeral."

"Was the child ever seen again?" asked Mrs. Emerson in a shaking voice.

"No," replied Mrs. Meserve; "that child was never seen again after she went out of the yard with Mrs. Bird."

Old Woman Magoun

THE HAMLET OF BARRY'S FORD is situated in a sort of high valley among the mountains. Below it the hills lie in moveless curves like a petrified ocean; above it they rise in green-cresting waves which never break. It is *Barry's* Ford because at one time the Barry family was the most important in the place; and *Ford* because just at the beginning of the hamlet the little turbulent Barry River is fordable. There is, however, now a rude bridge across the river.

Old Woman Magoun was largely instrumental in bringing the bridge to pass. She haunted the miserable little grocery, wherein whiskey and hands of tobacco were the most salient features of the stock in trade, and she talked much. She would elbow herself into the midst of a knot of idlers and talk.

"That bridge ought to be built this very summer," said Old Woman Magoun. She spread her strong arms like wings, and sent the loafers, half laughing, half angry, flying in every direction. "If I were a *man*," said she, "I'd go out this very minute and lay the fust log. If I were a passel of lazy men layin' round, I'd start up for once in my life, I would." The men cowered visibly—all except Nelson Barry; he swore under his breath and strode over to the counter.

Old Woman Magoun looked after him majestically. "You can cuss all you want to, Nelson Barry," said she; "I ain't afraid of you. I don't expect you to lay ary log of the bridge, but I'm goin' to have it built this very summer." She did. The weakness of the masculine element in Barry's Ford was laid low before such strenuous feminine assertion.

Old Woman Magoun and some other women planned a treat—two sucking pigs, and pies, and sweet cake—for a reward after the bridge should be finished. They even viewed leniently the increased consumption of ardent spirits.

"It seems queer to me," Old Woman Magoun said to Sally Jinks, "that men can't do nothin' without havin' to drink and chew to keep their sperits up. Lord! I've worked all my life and never done nuther."

"Men is different," said Sally Jinks.

"Yes, they be," assented Old Woman Magoun, with open contempt.

The two women sat on a bench in front of Old Woman Magoun's house, and little Lily Barry, her granddaughter, sat holding her doll on a small mossy stone near by. From where they sat they could see the men at work on the new bridge. It was the last day of the work.

Lily clasped her doll—a poor old rag thing—close to her childish bosom, like a little mother, and her face, round which curled her long yellow hair, was fixed upon the men at work. Little Lily had never been allowed to run with the other children of Barry's Ford. Her grandmother had taught her everything she knew—which was not much, but tending at least to a certain measure of spiritual growth—for she, as it were, poured the goodness of her own soul into this little receptive vase of another. Lily was firmly grounded in her knowledge that it was wrong to lie or steal or disobey her grandmother. She had also learned that one should be very industrious. It was seldom that Lily sat idly holding her doll-baby, but this was a holiday because of the bridge. She looked only a child, although she was nearly fourteen; her mother had been married at sixteen. That is, Old Woman Magoun said that her daughter, Lily's mother, had married at sixteen; there had been rumors, but no one had dared openly gainsay the old woman. She said that her daughter had married Nelson Barry, and he had deserted her. She had lived in her mother's house, and Lily had been born there, and she had died when the baby was only a week old. Lily's father, Nelson Barry, was the fairly dangerous degenerate of a good old family. Nelson's father before him had been bad. He was now the last of the family, with the exception of a sister of feeble intellect, with whom he lived in the old Barry house. He was a middle-aged man, still handsome. The shiftless population of Barry's Ford looked up to him as to an evil deity. They wondered how Old Woman Magoun dared brave him as she did. But Old Woman Magoun had within her a mighty sense of reliance upon herself as being on the right track in the midst of a maze of evil, which gave her courage. Nelson Barry had manifested no interest whatever in his daughter. Lily seldom saw her father. She did not often go to the store which was his favorite haunt. Her grandmother took care that she should not do so.

However, that afternoon she departed from her usual custom and sent Lily to the store.

She came in from the kitchen, whither she had been to baste the roasting pig. "There's no use talkin'," said she, "I've got to have some more salt. I've jest used the very last I had to dredge over that pig. I've got to go to the store."

Sally Jinks looked at Lily. "Why don't you send her?" she asked.

Old Woman Magoun gazed irresolutely at the girl. She was herself very tired. It did not seem to her that she could drag herself up the dusty hill to the store. She glanced with covert resentment at Sally Jinks. She thought that she might offer to go. But Sally Jinks said again, "Why don't you let her go?" and looked with a languid eye at Lily holding her doll on the stone.

Lily was watching the men at work on the bridge, with her childish delight in a spectacle of any kind, when her grandmother addressed her.

"Guess I'll let you go down to the store an' git some salt, Lily," said she.

The girl turned uncomprehending eyes upon her grandmother at the sound of her voice. She had been filled with one of the innocent reveries of childhood. Lily had in her the making of an artist or a poet. Her prolonged childhood went to prove it, and also her retrospective eyes, as clear and blue as blue light itself, which seemed to see past all that she looked upon. She had not come of the old Barry family for nothing. The best of the strain was in her, along with the splendid stanchness in humble lines which she had acquired from her grandmother.

"Put on your hat," said Old Woman Magoun; "the sun is hot, and you might git a headache." She called the girl to her, and put back the shower of fair curls under the rubber band which confined the hat. She gave Lily some money, and watched her knot it into a corner of her little cotton handkerchief. "Be careful you don't lose it," said she, "and don't stop to talk to anybody, for I am in a hurry for that salt. Of course, if anybody speaks to you answer them polite, and then come right along."

Lily started, her pocket-handkerchief weighted with the small silver dangling from one hand, and her rag doll carried over her shoulder like a baby. The absurd travesty of a face peeped forth from Lily's yellow curls. Sally Jinks looked after her with a sniff.

"She ain't goin' to carry that rag doll to the store?" said she.

"She likes to," replied Old Woman Magoun, in a half-shamed yet defiantly extenuating voice.

"Some girls at her age is thinkin' about beaux instead of rag dolls," said Sally Jinks.

The grandmother bristled, "Lily ain't big nor old for her age," said she. "I ain't in any hurry to have her git married. She ain't none too strong."

"She's got a good color," said Sally Jinks. She was crocheting white cotton lace, making her thick fingers fly. She really knew how to do scarcely anything except to crochet that coarse lace; somehow her heavy brain or her fingers had mastered that.

"I know she's got a beautiful color," replied Old Woman Magoun, with an odd mixture of pride and anxiety, "but it comes an' goes."

"I've heard that was a bad sign," remarked Sally Jinks, loosening some thread from her spool.

"Yes, it is," said the grandmother. "She's nothin' but a baby, though she's quicker than most to learn."

Lily Barry went on her way to the store. She was clad in a scanty short frock of blue cotton; her hat was tipped back, forming an oval frame for her innocent face. She was very small, and walked like a child, with the clapclap of little feet of babyhood. She might have been considered, from her looks, under ten.

Presently she heard footsteps behind her; she turned around a little timidly to see who was coming. When she saw a handsome, well-dressed man, she felt reassured. The man came alongside and glanced down carelessly at first, then his look deepened. He smiled, and Lily saw he was very handsome indeed, and that his smile was not only reassuring but wonderfully sweet and compelling.

"Well, little one," said the man, "where are you bound, you and your dolly?"

"I am going to the store to buy some salt for grandma," replied Lily, in her sweet treble. She looked up in the man's face, and he fairly started at the revelation of its innocent beauty. He regulated his pace by hers, and the two went on together. The man did not speak again at once. Lily kept glancing timidly up at him, and every time that she did so the man smiled and her confidence increased. Presently when the man's hand grasped her little childish one hanging by her side, she felt a complete trust in him. Then she smiled up at him. She felt glad that this nice man had come along, for just here the road was lonely.

After a while the man spoke. "What is your name, little one?" he asked, caressingly.

"Lily Barry."

The man started. "What is your father's name?"

"Nelson Barry," replied Lily.

The man whistled. "Is your mother dead?"

"Yes, sir."

"How old are you, my dear?"

"Fourteen," replied Lily.

The man looked at her with surprise. "As old as that?"

Lily suddenly shrank from the man. She could not have told why. She pulled her little hand from his, and he let it go with no remonstrance. She clasped both her arms around her rag doll, in order that her hand should not be free for him to grasp again.

She walked a little farther away from the man, and he looked amused.

"You still play with your doll?" he said, in a soft voice.

"Yes, sir," replied Lily. She quickened her pace and reached the store.

When Lily entered the store, Hiram Gates, the owner, was behind the counter. The only man besides in the store was Nelson Barry. He sat tipping his chair back against the wall; he was half asleep, and his handsome face was bristling with a beard of several days' growth and darkly flushed. He opened his eyes when Lily entered, the strange man following. He brought his chair down on all fours, and he looked at the man—not noticing Lily at all—with a look compounded of defiance and uneasiness.

"Hullo, Jim!" he said.

"Hullo, old man!" returned the stranger.

Lily went over to the counter and asked for the salt, in her pretty little voice. When she had paid for it and was crossing the store, Nelson Barry was on his feet.

"Well, how are you, Lily? It is Lily, isn't it?" he said.

"Yes, sir," replied Lily, faintly.

Her father bent down and, for the first time in her life, kissed her, and the whiskey odor of his breath came into her face.

Lily involuntarily started, and shrank away from him. Then she rubbed her mouth violently with her little cotton handkerchief, which she held gathered up with the rag doll.

"Damn it all! I believe she is afraid of me," said Nelson Barry, in a thick voice.

"Looks a little like it," said the other man, laughing.

"It's that damned old woman," said Nelson Barry. Then he

smiled again at Lily. "I didn't know what a pretty little daughter I was blessed with," said he, and he softly stroked Lily's pink cheek under her hat.

Now Lily did not shrink from him. Hereditary instincts and nature itself were asserting themselves in the child's innocent, receptive breast.

Nelson Barry looked curiously at Lily. "How old are you, anyway, child?" he asked.

"I'll be fourteen in September," replied Lily.

"But you still play with your doll?" said Barry, laughing kindly down at her.

Lily hugged her doll more tightly, in spite of her father's kind voice. "Yes, sir," she replied.

Nelson glanced across at some glass jars filled with sticks of candy. "See here, little Lily, do you like candy?" said he.

"Yes, sir."

"Wait a minute."

Lily waited while her father went over to the counter. Soon he returned with a package of the candy.

"I don't see how you are going to carry so much," he said, smiling. "Suppose you throw away your doll?"

Lily gazed at her father and hugged the doll tightly, and there was all at once in the child's expression something mature. It became the reproach of a woman. Nelson's face sobered.

"Oh, it's all right, Lily," he said; "keep your doll. Here, I guess you can carry this candy under your arm."

Lily could not resist the candy. She obeyed Nelson's instructions for carrying it, and left the store laden. The two men also left, and walked in the opposite direction, talking busily.

When Lily reached home, her grandmother, who was watching for her, spied at once the package of candy.

"What's that?" she asked, sharply.

"My father gave it to me," answered Lily, in a faltering voice. Sally regarded her with something like alertness.

"Your father?"

"Yes, ma'am."

"Where did you see him?"

"In the store."

"He gave you this candy?"

"Yes, ma'am."

"What did he say?"

"He asked me how old I was, and—"

"And what?"

"I don't know," replied Lily; and it really seemed to her that she did not know, she was so frightened and bewildered by it all, and, more than anything else, by her grandmother's face as she questioned her.

Old Woman Magoun's face was that of one upon whom a long-anticipated blow had fallen. Sally Jinks gazed at her with a sort of stupid alarm.

Old Woman Magoun continued to gaze at her grandchild with that look of terrible solicitude, as if she saw the girl in the clutch of a tiger. "You can't remember what else he said?" she asked, fiercely, and the child began to whimper softly.

"No, ma'am," she sobbed. "I—don't know, and—"

"And what? Answer me."

"There was another man there. A real handsome man."

"Did he speak to you?" asked Old Woman Magoun.

"Yes, ma'am; he walked along with me a piece," confessed Lily, with a sob of terror and bewilderment.

"What did *he* say to you?" asked Old Woman Magoun, with a sort of despair.

Lily told, in her little, faltering, frightened voice, all of the conversation which she could recall. It sounded harmless enough, but the look of the realization of a long-expected blow never left her grandmother's face.

The sun was getting low, and the bridge was nearing completion. Soon the workmen would be crowding into the cabin for their promised supper. There became visible in the distance, far up the road, the heavily plodding figure of another woman who had agreed to come and help. Old Woman Magoun turned again to Lily.

"You go right up-stairs to your own chamber now," said she.

"Good land! ain't you goin' to let that poor child stay up and see the fun?" said Sally Jinks.

"You jest mind your own business," said Old Woman Magoun, forcibly, and Sally Jinks shrank. "You go right up there now, Lily," said the grandmother, in a softer tone, "and grandma will bring you up a nice plate of supper."

"When be you goin' to let that girl grow up?" asked Sally Jinks, when Lily had disappeared.

"She'll grow up in the Lord's good time," replied Old Woman

Magoun, and there was in her voice something both sad and threatening. Sally Jinks again shrank a little.

Soon the workmen came flocking noisily into the house. Old Woman Magoun and her two helpers served the bountiful supper. Most of the men had drunk as much as, and more than, was good for them, and Old Woman Magoun had stipulated that there was to be no drinking of anything except coffee during supper.

"I'll git you as good a meal as I know how," she said, "but if I see ary one of you drinkin' a drop, I'll run you all out. If you want anything to drink, you can go up to the store afterward. That's the place for you to go to, if you've got to make hogs of yourselves. I ain't goin' to have no hogs in my house."

Old Woman Magoun was implicitly obeyed. She had a curious authority over most people when she chose to exercise it. When the supper was in full swing, she quietly stole up-stairs and carried some food to Lily. She found the girl, with the rag doll in her arms, crouching by the window in her little rocking-chair—a relic of her infancy, which she still used.

"What a noise they are makin', grandma!" she said, in a terrified whisper, as her grandmother placed the plate before her on a chair.

"They've 'most all of 'em been drinkin'. They air a passel of hogs," replied the old woman.

"Is the man that was with—with my father down there?" asked Lily, in a timid fashion. Then she fairly cowered before the look in her grandmother's eyes.

"No, he ain't; and what's more, he never will be down there if I can help it," said Old Woman Magoun, in a fierce whisper. "I know who he is. They can't cheat me. He's one of them Willises—that family the Barrys married into. They're worse than the Barrys, ef they *have* got money. Eat your supper, and put him out of your mind, child."

It was after Lily was asleep, when Old Woman Magoun was alone, clearing away her supper dishes, that Lily's father came. The door was closed, and he knocked, and the old woman knew at once who was there. The sound of that knock meant as much to her as the whir of a bomb to the defender of a fortress. She opened the door, and Nelson Barry stood there.

"Good-evening, Mrs. Magoun," he said.

Old Woman Magoun stood before him, filling up the doorway with her firm bulk.

"Good-evening, Mrs. Magoun," said Nelson Barry again.

"I ain't got no time to waste," replied the old woman, harshly. "I've got my supper dishes to clean up after them men."

She stood there and looked at him as she might have looked at a rebellious animal which she was trying to tame. The man laughed.

"It's no use," said he. "You know me of old. No human being can turn me from my way when I am once started in it. You may as well let me come in."

Old Woman Magoun entered the house, and Barry followed her.

Barry began without any preface. "Where is the child?" asked he.

"Up-stairs. She has gone to bed."

"She goes to bed early."

"Children ought to," returned the old woman, polishing a plate.

Barry laughed. "You are keeping her a child a long while," he remarked, in a soft voice which had a sting in it.

"She *is* a child," returned the old woman, defiantly.

"Her mother was only three years older when Lily was born."

The old woman made a sudden motion toward the man which seemed fairly menacing. Then she turned again to her dish-washing.

"I want her," said Barry.

"You can't have her," replied the old woman, in a still stern voice.

"I don't see how you can help yourself. You have always acknowledged that she was my child."

The old woman continued her task, but her strong back heaved. Barry regarded her with an entirely pitiless expression.

"I am going to have the girl, that is the long and short of it," he said, "and it is for her best good, too. You are a fool, or you would see it."

"Her best good?" muttered the old woman.

"Yes, her best good. What are you going to do with her, anyway? The girl is a beauty, and almost a woman grown, although you try to make out that she is a baby. You can't live forever."

"The Lord will take care of her," replied the old woman, and again she turned and faced him, and her expression was that of a prophetess.

"Very well, let Him," said Barry, easily. "All the same I'm going to have her, and I tell you it is for her best good. Jim Willis saw her this afternoon, and—"

Old Woman Magoun looked at him. "Jim Willis!" she fairly shrieked.

"Well, what of it?"

"One of them Willises!" repeated the old woman, and this time her voice was thick. It seemed almost as if she were stricken with paralysis. She did not enunciate clearly.

The man shrank a little. "Now what is the need of your making such a fuss?" he said. "I will take her, and Isabel will look out for her."

"Your half-witted sister?" said Old Woman Magoun.

"Yes, my half-witted sister. She knows more than you think."

"More wickedness."

"Perhaps. Well, a knowledge of evil is a useful thing. How are you going to avoid evil if you don't know what it is like? My sister and I will take care of my daughter."

The old woman continued to look at the man, but his eyes never fell. Suddenly her gaze grew inconceivably keen. It was as if she saw through all externals.

"I know what it is!" she cried. "You have been playing cards and you lost, and this is the way you will pay him."

Then the man's face reddened, and he swore under his breath.

"Oh, my God!" said the old woman; and she really spoke with her eyes aloft as if addressing something outside of them both. Then she turned again to her dish-washing.

The man cast a dogged look at her back. "Well, there is no use talking. I have made up my mind," said he, "and you know me and what that means. I am going to have the girl."

"When?" said the old woman, without turning around.

"Well, I am willing to give you a week. Put her clothes in good order before she comes."

The old woman made no reply. She continued washing dishes. She even handled them so carefully that they did not rattle.

"You understand," said Barry. "Have her ready a week from to-day."

"Yes," said Old Woman Magoun, "I understand."

Nelson Barry, going up the mountain road, reflected that Old Woman Magoun had a strong character, that she understood much better than her sex in general the futility of withstanding the inevitable.

"Well," he said to Jim Willis when he reached home, "the old woman did not make such a fuss as I expected."

"Are you going to have the girl?"

"Yes; a week from to-day. Look here, Jim; you've got to stick to your promise."

"All right," said Willis. "Go you one better."

The two were playing at cards in the old parlor, once magnificent, now squalid, of the Barry house. Isabel, the half-witted sister, entered, bringing some glasses on a tray. She had learned with her feeble intellect some tricks, like a dog. One of them was the mixing of sundry drinks. She set the tray on a little stand near the two men, and watched them with her silly simper.

"Clear out now and go to bed," her brother said to her, and she obeyed.

Early the next morning Old Woman Magoun went up to Lily's little sleeping-chamber, and watched her a second as she lay asleep, with her yellow locks spread over the pillow. Then she spoke. "Lily," said she—"Lily, wake up. I am going to Greenham across the new bridge, and you can go with me."

Lily immediately sat up in bed and smiled at her grandmother. Her eyes were still misty, but the light of awakening was in them.

"Get right up," said the old woman. "You can wear your new dress if you want to."

Lily gurgled with pleasure like a baby. "And my new hat?" asked she.

"I don't care."

Old Woman Magoun and Lily started for Greenham before Barry Ford, which kept late hours, was fairly awake. It was three miles to Greenham. The old woman said that, since the horse was a little lame, they would walk. It was a beautiful morning, with a diamond radiance of dew over everything. Her grandmother had curled Lily's hair more punctiliously than usual. The little face peeped like a rose out of two rows of golden spirals. Lily wore her new muslin dress with a pink sash, and her best hat of a fine white straw trimmed with a wreath of rosebuds; also the neatest black open-work stockings and pretty shoes. She even had white cotton gloves. When they set out, the old, heavily stepping woman, in her black gown and cape and bonnet, looked down at the little pink fluttering figure. Her face was full of the tenderest love and admiration, and yet there was something terrible about it. They crossed the new bridge—a primitive structure built of logs in a slovenly fashion. Old Woman Magoun pointed to a gap.

"Jest see that," said she. "That's the way men work."

"Men ain't very nice, be they?" said Lily, in her sweet little voice.

"No, they ain't, take them all together," replied her grandmother.

"That man that walked to the store with me was nicer than some, I guess," Lily said, in a wishful fashion. Her grandmother reached down and took the child's hand in its small cotton glove. "You hurt me, holding my hand so tight," Lily said presently, in a deprecatory little voice.

The old woman loosened her grasp. "Grandma didn't know how tight she was holding your hand," said she. "She wouldn't hurt you for nothin', except it was to save your life, or somethin' like that." She spoke with an undertone of tremendous meaning which the girl was too childish to grasp. They walked along the country road. Just before they reached Greenham they passed a stone wall overgrown with blackberry-vines, and, an unsual thing in that vicinity, a lusty spread of deadly nightshade full of berries.

"Those berries look good to eat, grandma," Lily said.

At that instant the old woman's face became something terrible to see. "You can't have any now," she said, and hurried Lily along.

"They look real nice," said Lily.

When they reached Greenham, Old Woman Magoun took her way straight to the most pretentious house there, the residence of the lawyer, whose name was Mason. Old Woman Magoun bade Lily wait in the yard for a few moments, and Lily ventured to seat herself on a bench beneath an oak-tree; then she watched with some wonder her grandmother enter the lawyer's office door at the right of the house. Presently the lawyer's wife came out and spoke to Lily under the tree. She had in her hand a little tray containing a plate of cake, a glass of milk, and an early apple. She spoke very kindly to Lily; she even kissed her, and offered her the tray of refreshments, which Lily accepted gratefully. She sat eating, with Mrs. Mason watching her, when Old Woman Magoun came out of the lawyer's office with a ghastly face.

"What are you eatin'?" she asked Lily, sharply. "Is that a sour apple?"

"I thought she might be hungry," said the lawyer's wife, with loving, melancholy eyes upon the girl.

Lily had almost finished the apple. "It's real sour, but I like it; it's real nice, grandma," she said.

"You ain't been drinkin' milk with a sour apple?"

"It was real nice milk, grandma."

"You ought never to have drunk milk and eat a sour apple," said her grandmother. "Your stomach was all out of order this mornin', an' sour apples and milk is always apt to hurt anybody."

"I don't know but they are," Mrs. Mason said, apologetically, as she stood on the green lawn with her lavender muslin sweeping around her. "I am real sorry, Mrs. Magoun. I ought to have thought. Let me get some soda for her."

"Soda never agrees with her," replied the old woman, in a harsh voice. "Come," she said to Lily, "it's time we were goin' home."

After Lily and her grandmother had disappeared down the road, Lawyer Mason came out of his office and joined his wife, who had seated herself on the bench beneath the tree. She was idle, and her face wore the expression of those who review joys forever past. She had lost a little girl, her only child, years ago, and her husband always knew when she was thinking about her. Lawyer Mason looked older than his wife; he had a dry, shrewd, slightly one-sided face.

"What do you think, Maria?" he said. "That old woman came to me with the most pressing entreaty to adopt that little girl."

"She is a beautiful little girl," said Mrs. Mason, in a slightly husky voice.

"Yes, she is a pretty child," assented the lawyer, looking pityingly at his wife; "but it is out of the question, my dear. Adopting a child is a serious measure, and in this case a child who comes from Barry's Ford."

"But the grandmother seems a very good woman," said Mrs. Mason.

"I rather think she is. I never heard a word against her. But the father! No, Maria, we cannot take a child with Barry blood in her veins. The stock has run out; it is vitiated physically and morally. It won't do, my dear."

"Her grandmother had her dressed up as pretty as a little girl could be," said Mrs. Mason, and this time the tears welled into her faithful, wistful eyes.

"Well, we can't help that," said the lawyer, as he went back to his office.

Old Woman Magoun and Lily returned, going slowly along the road to Barry's Ford. When they came to the stone wall where the blackberry-vines and the deadly nightshade grew, Lily said she was tired, and asked if she could not sit down for a few minutes. The strange look on her grandmother's face had deepened. Now and then Lily glanced at her and had a feeling as if she were looking at a stranger.

"Yes, you can set down if you want to," said Old Woman Magoun, deeply and harshly.

Lily started and looked at her, as if to make sure that it was her grandmother who spoke. Then she sat down on a stone which was comparatively free of the vines.

"Ain't you goin' to set down, grandma?" Lily asked, timidly.

"No; I don't want to get into that mess," replied her grandmother. "I ain't tired. I'll stand here."

Lily sat still; her delicate little face was flushed with heat. She extended her tiny feet in her best shoes and gazed at them. "My shoes are all over dust," said she.

"It will brush off," said her grandmother, still in that strange voice.

Lily looked around. An elm-tree in the field behind her cast a spray of branches over her head; a little cool puff of wind came on her face. She gazed at the low mountains on the horizon, in the midst of which she lived, and she sighed, for no reason that she knew. She began idly picking at the blackberry-vines; there were no berries on them; then she put her little fingers on the berries of the deadly nightshade. "These look like nice berries," she said.

Old Woman Magoun, standing stiff and straight in the road, said nothing.

"They look good to eat," said Lily.

Old Woman Magoun still said nothing, but she looked up into the ineffable blue of the sky, over which spread at intervals great white clouds shaped like wings.

Lily picked some of the deadly nightshade berries and ate them. "Why, they are real sweet," said she. "They are nice." She picked some more and ate them.

Presently her grandmother spoke. "Come," she said, "it is time we were going. I guess you have set long enough."

Lily was still eating the berries when she slipped down from the wall and followed her grandmother obediently up the road.

Before they reached home, Lily complained of being very thirsty. She stopped and made a little cup of a leaf and drank long at a mountain brook. "I am dreadful dry, but it hurts me to swallow," she said to her grandmother when she stopped drinking and joined the old woman waiting for her in the road. Her grandmother's face seemed strangely dim to her. She took hold of Lily's hand as they went on. "My stomach burns," said Lily, presently. "I want some more water."

"There is another brook a little farther on," said Old Woman Magoun, in a dull voice.

When they reached that brook, Lily stopped and drank again, but she whimpered a little over her difficulty in swallowing. "My stomach burns, too," she said, walking on, "and my throat is so dry, grandma." Old Woman Magoun held Lily's hand more tightly. "You hurt me holding my hand so tight, grandma," said Lily, looking up at her grandmother, whose face she seemed to see through a mist, and the old woman loosened her grasp.

When at last they reached home, Lily was very ill. Old Woman Magoun put her on her own bed in the little bedroom out of the kitchen. Lily lay there and moaned, and Sally Jinks came in.

"Why, what ails her?" she asked. "She looks feverish."

Lily unexpectedly answered for herself. "I ate some sour apples and drank some milk," she moaned.

"Sour apples and milk are dreadful apt to hurt anybody," said Sally Jinks. She told several people on her way home that Old Woman Magoun was dreadful careless to let Lily eat such things.

Meanwhile Lily grew worse. She suffered cruelly from the burning in her stomach, the vertigo, and the deadly nausea. "I am so sick, I am so sick, grandma," she kept moaning. She could no longer see her grandmother as she bent over her, but she could hear her talk.

Old Woman Magoun talked as Lily had never heard her talk before, as nobody had ever heard her talk before. She spoke from the depths of her soul; her voice was as tender as the coo of a dove, and it was grand and exalted. "You'll feel better very soon, little Lily," said she.

"I am so sick, grandma."

"You will feel better very soon, and then—"

"I am sick."

"You shall go to a beautiful place."

Lily moaned.

"You shall go to a beautiful place," the old woman went on.

"Where?" asked Lily, groping feebly with her cold little hands. Then she moaned again.

"A beautiful place, where the flowers grow tall."

"What color? Oh, grandma, I am so sick."

"A blue color," replied the old woman. Blue was Lily's favorite color. "A beautiful blue color, and as tall as your knees, and the flowers always stay there, and they never fade."

"Not if you pick them, grandma? Oh!"

"No, not if you pick them; they never fade, and they are so sweet you can smell them a mile off; and there are birds that sing, and all the roads have gold stones in them, and the stone walls are made of gold."

"Like the ring grandpa gave you? I am so sick, grandma."

"Yes, gold like that. And all the houses are built of silver and gold, and the people all have wings, so when they get tired walking they can fly, and—"

"I am so sick, grandma."

"And all the dolls are alive," said Old Woman Magoun. "Dolls like yours can run, and talk, and love you back again."

Lily had her poor old rag doll in bed with her, clasped close to her agonized little heart. She tried very hard with her eyes, whose pupils were so dilated that they looked black, to see her grandmother's face when she said that, but she could not. "It is dark," she moaned, feebly.

"There where you are going it is always light," said the grandmother, "and the commonest things shine like that breastpin Mrs. Lawyer Mason had on to-day."

Lily moaned pitifully, and said something incoherent. Delirium was commencing. Presently she sat straight up in bed and raved; but even then her grandmother's wonderful compelling voice had an influence over her.

"You will come to a gate with all the colors of the rainbow," said her grandmother; "and it will open, and you will go right in and walk up the gold street, and cross the field where the blue flowers come up to your knees, until you find your mother, and she will take you home where you are going to live. She has a little white room all ready for you, white curtains at the windows, and a little white looking-glass, and when you look in it you will see—"

"What will I see? I am so sick, grandma."

"You will see a face like yours, only it's an angel's; and there will be a little white bed, and you can lay down an' rest."

"Won't I be sick, grandma?" asked Lily. Then she moaned and babbled wildly, although she seemed to understand through it all what her grandmother said.

"No, you will never be sick anymore. Talkin' about sickness won't mean anything to you."

It continued. Lily talked on wildly, and her grandmother's great voice of soothing never ceased, until the child fell into a deep sleep, or what resembled sleep; but she lay stiffly in that sleep, and a candle flashed before her eyes made no impression on them.

Then it was that Nelson Barry came. Jim Willis waited outside the door. When Nelson entered he found Old Woman Magoun on her knees beside the bed, weeping with dry eyes and a might of agony which fairly shook Nelson Barry, the degenerate of a fine old race.

"Is she sick?" he asked, in a hushed voice.

Old Woman Magoun gave another terrible sob, which sounded like the gasp of one dying.

"Sally Jinks said that Lily was sick from eating milk and sour apples," said Barry, in a tremulous voice. "I remember that her mother was very sick once from eating them."

Lily lay still, and her grandmother on her knees shook with her terrible sobs.

Suddenly Nelson Barry started. "I guess I had better go to Greenham for a doctor if she's as bad as that," he said. He went close to the bed and looked at the sick child. He gave a great start. Then he felt of her hands and reached down under the bedclothes for her little feet. "Her hands and feet are like ice," he cried out. "Good God! why didn't you send for some one—for me—before? Why, she's dying; she's almost gone!"

Barry rushed out and spoke to Jim Willis, who turned pale and came in and stood by the bedside.

"She's almost gone," he said, in a hushed whisper.

"There's no use going for the doctor; she'd be dead before he got here," said Nelson, and he stood regarding the passing child with a strange, sad face—unutterably sad, because of his incapability of the truest sadness.

"Poor little thing, she's past suffering, anyhow," said the other man, and his own face also was sad with a puzzled, mystified sadness.

Lily died that night. There was quite a commotion in Barry's Ford until after the funeral, it was all so sudden, and then everything went on as usual. Old Woman Magoun continued to live as she had done before. She supported herself by the produce of her tiny farm; she was very industrious, but people said that she was a trifle touched, since every time she went over the log bridge with her eggs or her garden vegetables to sell in Greenham, she carried with her, as one might have carried an infant, Lily's old rag doll.

The Winning Lady

MRS. ADELINE WYATT stood before her long mirror. She held a silver-framed hand-glass, and she surveyed her head crowned with a pretty toque at every possible angle. Adeline was always conscious of exercising stern heroism when she stood before her mirror. She spared herself nothing. She looked unflinchingly at every crease in her chin, every crow's-foot about her eyes, every hollow in her cheeks, also the little sprays of marks, as if made by some tiny besom of time, beneath her ears. She faced the worst, and as far as possible, without the use of arts which she despised, she remedied defects. She practised before her mirror exactly the carriage of head and arrangement of hair which were most becoming. When her gloves were adjusted she was complete, as perfect a figure of a middle-aged woman as one could find. She wore a charming gown of prune color. Her toque was of prune-colored velvet trimmed with a knot of violets, in the midst of which nestled a pink rose. After Ellen had helped her on with her coat she practised holding up her long skirt, for she was to walk to Mrs. Charles Lennox's, where the Whist Club met that afternoon. The Wyatts kept no carriage, and Adeline never hired one from the livery-stable when she could possibly avoid it. Her husband, Thomas Wyatt, was a comparatively rich man, but very parsimonious. Adeline had nothing to spend upon her own personal expenses except the tiny income derived from her inheritance from her father. That was uncertain. She never quite reached two hundred a year at the most, but Thomas Wyatt thought that a very large sum for a woman to spend upon herself. He thought she ought to save some of it. He allowed her ten dollars per week for household expenses, and considered himself very generous. There were only four in the family, including Ellen, the maid. Thomas Wyatt's nephew, Walter Wyatt, had lived with his uncle ever since his parents' death when he was a child, and Thomas loved him as his own son. Walter had opened a tiny law office on the main street of the village, and was struggling hard to succeed and enable himself to marry Violet Ames and support her comfortably.

Thomas Wyatt in one respect was not parsimonious. He had

never dreamed of charging young Walter a penny for his board. Adeline, although she would have been distressed had her husband proposed such a measure, was sometimes surprised and occasionally she did consider, when she saw Walter taking flowers to Violet and smoking cigars, how many things she needed in her home—that is, aesthetic things. All the essentials were hers. She was what is called "a splendid manager." How Adeline Wyatt contrived to dress and set her table upon her income would have puzzled a financier. She might have made the matter plainer had she told of her sleepless hours of planning, and her supervision of every item purchased, and her countless schemes for saving. The prune-colored gown which she wore the day of the whist party was seven years old. It had been daintily wrapped in tissue-paper and laid away until the wheel of fashion turned. Adeline did not believe in spending money upon remodelling. Now long, tight sleeves had come into vogue again, and everybody would think the gown new. When she was on the street she held it up carefully, almost too carefully, and two little girls playing on the sidewalk stared at her display of black stocking, and giggled delightedly.

Adeline was one of the last to reach the Lennox house. After she had entered the large room and taken a seat, she regarded many of the other ladies with a somewhat pharisaical feeling. She noticed that a hook gaped on the collar of a lady at another table, also that Mrs. John Sears' lace waist bloused much more than the style allowed, and that the sleeves were short, and Mrs. Sears' arms very thin to be displayed. She gave the slightest glance of sweet complacency at her own nice prune-colored sleeves, with their very much up-to-date ornament of fringe which she had made herself. Then Mrs. Ames, Violet's mother, who was her partner, noticed the glance, and also viewed the prune-colored gown admiringly.

"If you will allow me to say so, what a perfectly charming gown you have," she said.

"Thank you, dear," replied Adeline, sitting very straight, and conscious in every nerve of her body of her prune-colored daintiness.

"You always have such lovely clothes," Mrs. Ames went on.

"You have pretty clothes yourself," said Adeline.

Mrs. Ames gave a slightly self-conscious glance at her own sleeves, which her dressmaker had just remodelled. "*I* always wear black, and that is the reason why people cannot tell when my gown is old," replied Mrs. Ames. "But you wear different colors."

Adeline smiled. She did not state that she wore only two colors—gray and prune. She was a subtle woman, and that choice of two colors had been subtle. She could be as economical and more so in her two colors than Mrs. Ames in her invariable black, and nobody would suspect her of economy. She felt quite superior to Mrs. Ames, although she was fond of her for her own sake, and especially as Walter's prospective mother-in-law. Mrs. Ames' daughter Violet was there that afternoon, but she was not playing. Violet Ames was one of the sweet, unselfish young girls who immolate themselves for the sake of their elders. Violet, with her periwinkle-blue eyes, exactly matched by her little blue-satin gown and her blue feather in her hat, flitted from one table to another, passed the bonbon-dishes, and made herself generally useful. There was more excitement this afternoon than usual, for there were prizes. Generally bridge was played without prizes, because of a covert fear among the ladies that bridge was a wicked gambling game. But Mrs. Charles Lennox had come out openly with prizes, and such prizes! Mrs. Ames had called Adeline's attention to them at the first. "My dear," she said, "have you seen the prizes?" She had touched upon a childish weakness of the other woman's which had survived the passage of time. In most people there are childish weaknesses, or traits, which survive time, and are unconquerable by it. In Mrs. Adeline Wyatt a love for presents and prizes which had been strong during her childhood endured in full force. If she had worn amid her smooth grayish elderly tresses one round shining curl of babyhood, it could not have been more marked than that trait in her soul.

She turned eyes of a child upon the prizes, which were displayed upon a table between the front windows, then she gasped. "You don't mean," said she, "that—?"

"Yes," said Mrs. Ames. "That cut-glass punch-bowl is the first prize, and the second prize is that set of Shakespeare. It does seem to me rather funny that Mrs. Lennox should think Shakespeare beneficial to people who play bridge badly." Mrs. Ames had a fine sense of humor. Adeline Wyatt had none whatever. She took everything very seriously.

"That is, a beautiful set of Shakespeare," said she, "but that *punch-bowl!*" she gasped.

"Yes," assented the other woman. "It's a beauty, and it must be good cut-glass, too, if Alice Lennox bought it."

Adeline Wyatt sighed. The charming facets of the glass punch-bowl looked to her admiring eyes like those of a diamond. It stood in a window in full sunlight, and beautiful rose tints gleamed here and there from its convexities. Adeline Wyatt's eyes had a strange expression. All her life she had been good and honest, never consumed by unholy longings, for her childish delight in presents and prizes could not be called unholy. It was simply primitive and naïve. Now, however, it took a different phase. Positive lust for that punch-bowl gleamed in Adeline's eyes. It happened to be the one treasure of all treasures which she immediately coveted. She wished to give soon a reception in honor of her dear Walter and his Violet, and fruit punch was of course a necessity at such a function. Everybody in Rawson had fruit punch at receptions. Adeline had heretofore borrowed Mrs. Frank Jennings' punch-bowl, but upon the last occasion of her doing so she had resolved that it was too much of a sacrifice to her pride. Either Mrs. Jennings had said something disagreeable, or had been reported so to have said, and Adeline had made up her mind not to borrow her punch-bowl again. She had thought of borrowing one belonging to Mrs. Lennox, but that was supposed to represent such enormous value that she was afraid. Mrs. John Sears owned a punch-bowl. Mrs. Sears' daughter Jessie had earned it by scouring Rawson and neighboring towns for subscribers for a certain brand of soap. Mrs. Sears esteemed the bowl highly, but Adeline had doubts. It was decorated crockery, and its origin was so widely known that it was not in much request. Nobody could say positively of a glass bowl that it did not belong to the giver of a tea, but Mrs. Sears' treasure, with its decoration of splashy roses in crude hues, was unmistakable.

Adeline had not seen her way clear toward giving a tea on account of the lack of a punch-bowl. "I ought to give an afternoon tea for Violet, now everybody knows that she and Walter are engaged," she had remarked, tentatively, to her husband.

"Well, why don't you?" he had replied.

"There are various reasons," said Adeline. "There are some things I ought to own to give such an affair properly."

"Why don't you get them?" asked Thomas.

"I need a punch-bowl, and a really good one *costs.*"

"Oh, get a good one while you are about it," said Thomas, and he spoke with such entire unconsciousness that Adeline gave a responsive murmur and said no more. She dared not ask Thomas to buy a punch-bowl. He had such entire faith in the inexhaustibility of her small resources that he had infected her own line of thought.

She really wondered if she might not have money enough to buy the bowl. She had endeavored to retrench in various ways, but had not been successful. She had had a hard struggle to keep Ellen from leaving, because when she worried about the size of the butter bill, Ellen had imagined that her mistress suspected her of taking it home to her married sister.

It seemed now to Adeline Wyatt (although she shuddered a little at the possible sacrilege of the fancy) that Providence had interposed. There stood the punch-bowl, radiating colors like a diamond. She had only to—play for it. Adeline set her mouth hard, a furrow which she usually suppressed came between her eyes, and she played. The worst of it was, she was neither a good player nor did she hold high cards. As for trumps, she had not even the advantage of chicane. When the first rubber was finished, Adeline had held exactly one honor in trumps, and that a ten-spot, and her partner had not fared much better.

Mrs. Ames, who was optimistic, and did not care about a punch-bowl, who had, in fact, on several occasions given teas, and set out a little table with cups already filled, and a pressed glass pitcher of punch to refill them (she was economizing for Violet's trousseau), only laughed gayly when the two winning ladies passed on to a higher table, and left her and Adeline seated in ignominy. "Small chance we have of that punch-bowl," she remarked, and laughed again.

Adeline did not laugh. "No human being can win with the cards we have held," she returned.

"My last hand was not very bad," said Mrs. Ames. "I think I made a mistake in leading clubs."

As she spoke she changed her place, and Miss Judith Armstead came to play with Adeline, and Mrs. Austin Freer against her. Adeline tried to speak pleasantly to Judith, who was elderly, always wore her thin hair the same way, and played bridge about as successfully as she could have flown. She knew there was no chance for her as far as her partner was concerned. Judith had acquired bridge too late in life. She was of abnormal conservatism, and might have carried off all honors at checkers played in her teens, but at bridge she was a dismal object.

However, she sat up very straight, showed all her cards to Mrs. Freer, who had a sly, sidewise glance for them, and, it being her deal, passed a no-trump hand of four aces to Adeline. Poor Adeline had one heart and four spades, ten high, and she made it spades, and

Mrs. Freer doubled; she had a long heart suit and a guarded king in clubs. When it was over, Adeline glared at Judith.

"Why didn't you make it no trumps—you had four aces?" she demanded.

"I had no side cards," replied Judith, undisturbed. It was easy for her to be undisturbed. She boarded, and had no need for a punch-bowl. But although a truism, fate is ironic. All that afternoon Judith Armstead, who did not know how to play, held the cards. Adeline, sometimes winning, glanced frequently at Judith's score. It was assuming phenomenal proportions. Violet Ames, moving from one table to another, also kept watch of Judith's score. Each lady had her own score, with a little colored ribbon and pencil attached. The ladies said among themselves that Judith Armstead was sure to win the prize. Adeline, after a little, kept her score hidden, tucked in the lace of her bodice. Her delicate, well-preserved face wore an expression which was almost like a mask. Often the other ladies would glance at her wonderingly and not know why they did so. Adeline had her mouth fixed in a smile; her eyes were always intent, crafty. She played as she had never done before, and her luck was better, but always at the end of a rubber Judith waved her little blue score-card with a fatuous, irritating smile. Judith began to grow excited. Every time she gathered in a trick she chuckled offensively. She antagonized even the ladies who did not care so much about winning the bowl. Adeline, even if she were at another table, never once lost sight of that blue score. She never failed to hear Judith's latest record proclaimed in her high, cackling tone of triumph, and always she evaded a direct answer to inquiries respecting her own, and always she kept the score hidden in her bodice lace. The time drew near for the close of the play. The last rubber had begun, and now Adeline was playing with the worst player in the club, Mrs. Leonidas Bennett, who did not approve of bridge, and felt a qualm of conscience every time she put down a card. Mrs. Bennett had a firmly fixed conviction that she must always play second hand high, and that she was a great sinner even while doing that, and the results were, even with good hands, disastrous. Adeline had for opponents Judith Armstead, flushed with victory, her long score dangling ostentatiously from her passementerie trimming, and Mrs. Austin Freer, who knew how to play. Adeline was lucky enough to secure the deal, but her hand was hopeless, and she knew if she passed it to her partner it would be worse, so she made it spades in her own hand, and Mrs. Freer doubled. Adeline's smile never relaxed, but a deadly animosity shot through her at the sound of Mrs. Freer's quiet card-voice saying that she would double spades.

There was a nervous tension all over the room. The gambling atmosphere reigned. These village women were playing for high stakes, and traits of roystering ancestors who had slumbered for generations awoke. Mild, middle-aged eyes gleamed, red spots appeared upon cheeks, sweet middle-aged mouths grew stern, but Adeline Wyatt wore the face of the true warrior of fate. No red spots upon cheeks betrayed her inward excitement, her mouth never relaxed from its smile, her eyes never lost their expression of sly, calm watchfulness. Toward the last of the rubber Adeline and her partner held such extraordinarily good cards that even stupid play prevailed. Adeline held repeatedly four aces. She always made no trumps on her own and every past make, and doubled her opponent's. She by this last sunset glow of victory made her attempt at deception successful. Yes, poor Adeline Wyatt, who had been all her life a virtuous and God-fearing woman, now fell for the first time before the snare of a glass punch-bowl. It was only a very, very little thing which she did—merely the changing of the numeral six to eight. It required only one little curving stroke of her pencil. It was not exactly a perfect eight, but it could not be mistaken for anything else, and it raised her score to an amount sufficient to overbalance Judith Armstead's.

Mrs. Lennox came around to collect the scores then, and Violet Ames and Mrs. Lennox's maid and a niece of Judith Armstead spread the tables with nice little embroidered cloths, and served ice-cream and cake and coffee. Afterward there was a hush, and Mrs. Lennox's slightly affected although pleasant voice arose.

She announced that Mrs. Thomas Wyatt, as the winning lady, had a claim to the first prize, and Miss Judith Armstead to the second. There was a booby prize, a book on bridge, which Mrs. Leonidas Bennett won, and there was a subdued titter as her name was read. Adeline did not titter. She had her mind intent upon the figures of the scores as read by Mrs. Lennox. Judith Armstead, after all her boasting, had either been misunderstood by her, or those last no-trumpers had counted for more than she had reckoned. Adeline had cheated at cards. She had added to her score, and for no purpose. She would have won in any case. Judith's score would not have equalled hers by many points. When the great glass bowl was brought and set carefully on the table before Adeline, she rose and bowed vaguely in response to the murmur of congratulation. Judith

Armstead was also rising and bowing. Adeline heard her remark that she had always wanted to own a set of Shakespeare, but she heard her as through a mist, and she saw her new punch-bowl as through a mist. She began to realize what she had done, now that the excitement of the deed was over. She had not only done a dishonest deed, but she had done it without need. She would have been the winner in any case. It was bad enough to have fallen from her standard of self-respect, but to have fallen without any reason! Adeline realized that she was not only a sinner, but a fool, and her realization brought her agony. When she had entered Mrs. Lennox's house that afternoon she had been a good, handsome, happy, self-satisfied, within-the-limits-of-virtue woman. She would leave it a fool and a sinner; that she was becomingly clad in prune-color would make not a whit of difference. Adeline lost all sight of her external self; she saw only her miserable naked soul, which had sold itself for a miserable glass bowl that it could have owned without perjury.

Ever afterward Adeline's memory of that terrible afternoon seemed to stare her in her mental eyes like a concentrated light. She could never forget the smallest detail. No matter what came to her afterward of joy or sorrow, the dinning memory of that time sounded always within her consciousness. She remembered exactly what this one said, what that one said, the various expressions of the various faces regarding her and her dishonestly acquired bowl. She remembered how Judith Armstead looked with her set of Shakespeare. Mrs. Lennox sent Adeline and Judith home with their prizes in her carriage, drawn by a sleek bay horse and a sleek gray, and driven by a coachman in green livery. The bowl and the set of Shakespeare were upon the seat opposite the two ladies. Neither talked much; indeed, it was only a short drive to Adeline's home. Judith lived farther. All that either woman said was to exchange remarks upon the pleasantness of the occasion. Neither said a word about her prize. When Adeline reached home she saw her husband looking out of a sitting-room window and beckoned, and he came out at once to the carriage.

"Will you please take this in?" said Adeline, in a strained voice.

Thomas stared. "Did you stop at the store on your way home?" he inquired.

"No," replied Adeline. "This is—a prize."

Thomas reached in and lifted out the bowl. He glanced at the books. "Did you win these too?" he inquired of his wife, after speaking to the other woman.

"No," said Adeline. "Miss Armstead won those."

"Oh!" said Thomas.

When he and Adeline were in the house, and he had set the bowl on the table, he looked rather wonderingly at his wife. "I thought you women never played for prizes," he observed.

"We don't, generally," said Adeline, "but Mrs. Lennox had prizes this afternoon."

"I don't see why you didn't buy a punch-bowl if you wanted one, instead of getting one after this fashion," said Thomas, examining the prize. "I don't think much of this, anyway; don't believe it cost more than three dollars and ninety-eight cents. You ought to have paid at least five dollars and got something worth while."

"Thomas Wyatt!" gasped Adeline. "You don't suppose Mrs. Charles Lennox would give a bowl that cost only three dollars and ninety-eight cents for a prize!"

"I don't believe it cost a cent more," said Thomas, stoutly. "It is always the people with most means who buy the cheapest things." Then he settled down to his newspaper, while Adeline went up-stairs to take off her things, with her mind dwelling upon this new contingency. She knew absolutely nothing about cut glass. Could it be possible that she had bartered away her honor and self-respect for three dollars and ninety-eight cents? An old bit of pious doggerel of her childhood came into her mind:

> *It is a sin to steal a pin,*
> *Much more to steal a greater thing.*

Had she stolen the pin?

When Walter Wyatt came home he examined the bowl, and he differed with his uncle. He thought the bowl had cost more than three dollars and ninety-eight cents. "She may have paid five dollars for it," he said, examining it critically. Adeline, who knew what good cut glass was worth, shivered.

After supper Walter went out as usual to call upon Violet Ames. He came home in a short time. He had not been gone half an hour when he entered the house, slammed the front door after him, and rushed heavily up-stairs to his room.

"What is the matter?" said Thomas.

"I am sure I don't know," replied Adeline, uneasily. She had no reason for her surmise, but somehow she connected this unusual circumstance with the bowl.

"Maybe they have had a falling out," said Thomas. "Well, they will get over it." Then he resumed reading and smoking.

Adeline was doing some fancy-work. The bowl had been put away in the parlor, but always she saw it, every point in the rosettes and whorls gleaming out with their colored lights. She worried about Walter. After a while she went up-stairs, and Walter opened his door and spoke to her. He was pale, and his hair was ruffled wretchedly with his despairing fingers.

"Violet has broken our engagement, Aunt Adeline," he said, in a choking voice—"that is, she has made a condition which I can't agree to for years to come, and it isn't fair to her to make her wait. I never was cut out to be a dog in the manger."

Adeline was as pale as he. "What is the condition?" she asked.

"She says she will not come here to live, as we have planned. She is as set as can be about it. And I can't keep her decently for years unless she does. I won't take a girl like her to live in any old place, though she did say she didn't care where she lived as long as it wasn't here, and I won't be taken into her house to live, either."

Adeline listened, standing very stiff.

"Did she give you any reason?" she said.

Walter shook his head angrily. "No; she was as obstinate as a mule. A girl is the very dickens when she gets anything into her head."

"If I were you I would go to bed, and try and keep calm to-night and get some sleep," said Adeline. "Maybe she will think better of it."

"Oh, Aunt Adeline, will you see her, and try to make her listen to reason? She has always thought everything of you."

"Yes, I will," replied Adeline.

The next morning Adeline sent Ellen with a note to Violet, and soon the young girl came, walking wearily. Adeline was at the front door to greet her.

"Good-morning," she said, in a curious, scared voice.

"Good-morning, Mrs. Wyatt," replied Violet. Her young face was pale and wan. She evidently endeavored to speak with dignity, but succeeded only in speaking piteously. Adeline knew that Violet knew.

"Come up-stairs to my room, please," said she.

The sitting-room door stood open, and Adeline saw the young girl glance in as she passed, and she knew what she feared to see there. When they were in her room she closed the door, and she and Violet stood looking at each other. It was strange, but the innocent eyes fell before the guilty ones, fell with a sort of horror and shame at what she saw.

Adeline was very pale, but she spoke firmly. "Did you tell Walter that you would not come here to live on account of *me?*" she asked.

"Yes," replied Violet, in a dull voice; but as she spoke the crimson, flooded her soft young cheeks. "Yes, I was standing behind you."

"And you saw?"

Violet nodded.

"And you don't feel as if you could bear to come here and live, and must break with Walter?"

Violet nodded, her lips quivered, but she did not weep.

"I don't blame you," said Adeline, "but I have to live with myself. I can't help it."

"Oh, what made—" began the girl, in a piteous voice.

"I don't know— What makes any one do wrong? The devil, perhaps."

Suddenly Violet threw her arms around the older woman's neck and clung to her. "Oh!" she moaned, "it is awful. Poor Walter! He looked so, but it did seem as if I couldn't."

Adeline looked at the fluffy head upon her shoulder, and stood very stiff and straight. "You would not need to see much of me," she said. "I think Thomas would finish off another kitchen. You know this is a large house."

"Oh, say you are sorry."

"Sorry!" echoed the older woman. "You don't doubt that! Why, I would gladly die this minute to undo it. But how can I?"

Violet sobbed.

"I lay awake all night thinking how I could make amends," said Adeline. "God knows I am perfectly willing as far as I am concerned to tell Thomas, and then to tell the whole club, and give that awful bowl up. But how can I? It would kill Thomas. I am not afraid of his anger, but I am afraid of making him miserable all the rest of his life. It must be my punishment that I can't tell. There is only one thing I can think of to make amends—that is, partial amends."

"What is it?" sobbed Violet. "Oh, dear Aunt Adeline, I know you didn't mean to do it!"

"Yes, I did. Don't excuse me that way, my dear. The minute I saw that bowl I meant to have it by hook or crook. I never felt so in all my life before. Now I know how people who break laws and do wrong feel. I shall never be hard on anybody again."

"But you are sorry?"

"Sorry!" said Adeline, and her voice was almost scornful. "Sorry is a poor word for what I feel. If I do the one thing I thought of that I can do, I doubt if it will make any difference."

"What is that?"

"I can tell Judith Armstead and give her the bowl."

"But you would have been ahead, anyway."

"That makes no difference. My intention to rob her was the same."

After Violet went away, Adeline put on her black serge gown and her bonnet and coat, and went to see Judith Armstead. Judith saw her coming. She boarded with her niece at Mrs. Sarah Love's. Mrs. Love kept an exclusive boarding-house wherein were stranded many feminine bits of home-wreckage. Judith ran down-stairs and opened the door. She had much the same scared expression that Adeline had worn at the sight of Violet.

"Oh, it is you, Mrs. Wyatt," she said, in a whisper. "Come up to my room."

Judith had two rooms: one was a bedroom, the other was a sitting-room with a divan bed. Adeline glanced involuntarily at the table, and Judith noticed it.

"No, you won't see them there," she said, in a voice quite hoarse with repressed emotion. "I have put them away. I couldn't stand it. I was coming over to see you."

"I came to tell you that the bowl is yours by good rights," said Adeline, jerking out her words. "I cheated yesterday. I changed a figure six to eight."

To Adeline's surprise, Judith nodded.

"Yes, I knew," said she; "that has been all the comfort I have had—that you cheated too."

Adeline was mystified. "As it turned out, I found that I would have won, after all," she said. "I had a better score, though I didn't know it, but what I did was just as bad. I meant to cheat."

"You didn't have a better score," said Judith. "You would have lost if *I* hadn't cheated too, even if you *hadn't* changed that six to eight."

Adeline stared at her.

"I didn't want that great punch-bowl," said Judith. "What could I do with such a thing? But I have wanted a nice set of Shakespeare ever since I can remember, so I didn't add to my score when I saw I would get the bowl if I did. We both cheated, Adeline Wyatt. There is no getting around it."

The two poor women, convicted of actual sin for the first time in their gentle lives, stared at each other in a sort of duet of horror.

"What can we do?" stammered Adeline.

"I don't see anything to do, except to keep still and bear it," said Judith. "I wish I were free to tell it from the housetops, but I am not. I must think of my poor niece. It would kill her."

"And I have to think of Thomas," said Adeline.

"That will have to be our punishment—keeping still," said Judith; "but there is one comfort."

"What?" asked Adeline, hopelessly.

"We can forgive each other."

Adeline brightened a little. "Do you forgive me for wanting to cheat you?"

"I rather think I do; and do you forgive me?"

"Of course I do, but I didn't want that great big punch-bowl, anyway."

"And I didn't want the Shakespeare."

"But we meant to cheat, just the same, and we did," said Judith, solemnly, "and we forgive each other, and I don't see but that is about the only comfort we can get out of it."

The two women wept a little, and when Adeline left she and Judith kissed each other. The two broken reeds clung to each other for support, the two foolish sinners for strength to bear their sin.

When Adeline reached home she went into the parlor and gazed at the great bowl, which would prick her with its facets all her life. She would have liked to take the hammer to it. She hated it. She determined that she, like Mrs. Ames, would use a pitcher for her fruit punch, and then the door opened, and Mrs. Charles Lennox entered. Adeline had not heard the bell ring, and Ellen admitted her with no ceremony. Mrs. Charles Lennox, who was rather magnificently arrayed in a long mink coat, cast an embarrassed glance at the bowl.

"Good-morning, Mrs. Wyatt," she said. Then she plunged directly into her subject. "I am glad I caught you looking at that miserable bowl," said she, "for I have been feeling very uneasy ever since you won the prize yesterday. I knew you thought it was a cut-glass bowl, and—well, it isn't. It is just imitation, and I got it at a sale in the city for one dollar and ninety-eight cents; and the Shakespeare Judith Armstead got was a bargain, too. The set is not complete. There is no *Hamlet*, and there are two *As You Like Its*. I got that for a dollar and forty-nine cents. I can't tell you how mean I have been feeling. I got the prizes as a sort of joke, anyway. You know we have objected to having prizes, but I happened to come across the bowl and Shakespeare, and got them. Then when I realized that you and Judith had gone off thinking you had real cut glass and a beautiful set of Shakespeare, I knew I would have to make a clean breast of it. Can you ever forgive me, Mrs. Wyatt?"

Adeline sighed a queer little relieved sigh. She was thankful, after all, that it was a pin, and not the greater thing. "I would much rather have this than a real cut-glass bowl," she said. "I sha'n't have to worry about its being broken."

After Mrs. Charles Lennox had gone, Adeline even laughed a little as she looked at the bowl. It might, in the nature of things, not endure forever to torment her with visible proof of her false dealing.

Then Violet came running in, and threw her arms around her, and kissed her. "I came back," said Violet, "to tell you that I remembered, after I went home, how I stole—yes, stole—when I was a little girl, one of my sister Jennie's hair ribbons, and I never told her, because *I* knew that I should never take another as long as I lived, but *she* could not know; and we all live in glass houses, and I have sent a note to poor dear Walter, and asked him to come tonight, and I hope he will forgive me."

"Of course he will. He was about heartbroken last night," said Adeline. Then she added, wistfully: "You will not mind living in the same house with me, after all?"

Violet laughed. "Didn't I just say we all lived in glass houses?" said she. "Yes, we will live together in our glass house and never throw stones." Violet was looking sharply at the bowl. "If Mrs. Charles Lennox had not bought that," said she, "I should say I saw one exactly like it at Jackson's in the city last week for one dollar and ninety-eight cents."

Adeline said nothing. She gazed soberly at the bowl; but the sunlight reflected from its sides cast over her face a rosy glow, as of the joy which comes after sinning and repentance.

Dear Annie

ANNIE HEMPSTEAD LIVED on a large family canvas, being the eldest of six children. There was only one boy. The mother was long since dead. If one can imagine the Hempstead family, the head of which was the Reverend Silas, pastor of the Orthodox Church in Lynn Corners, as being the subject of a mild study in village history, the high light would probably fall upon Imogen, the youngest daughter. As for Annie, she would apparently supply only a part of the background.

This afternoon in late July, Annie was out in the front yard of the parsonage, assisting her brother Benny to rake hay. Benny had not cut it. Annie had hired a man, although the Hempsteads could not afford to hire a man, but she had said to Benny, "Benny, you can rake the hay and get it into the barn if Jim Mullins cuts it, can't you?" And Benny had smiled and nodded acquiescence. Benny Hempstead always smiled and nodded acquiescence, but there was in him the strange persistency of a willow bough, the persistency of pliability, which is the most unconquerable of all. Benny swayed gracefully in response to all the wishes of others, but always he remained in his own inadequate attitude toward life.

Now he was raking to as little purpose as he could and rake at all. The clover-tops, the timothy grass, and the buttercups moved before his rake in a faint foam of gold and green and rose, but his sister Annie raised whirlwinds with hers. The Hempstead yard was large and deep, and had two great squares given over to wild growths on either side of the gravel walk, which was bordered with shrubs, flowering in their turn, like a class of children at school saying their lessons. The spring shrubs had all spelled out their floral recitations, of course, but great clumps of peonies were spreading wide skirts of gigantic bloom, like dancers courtesying low on the stage of summer, and shafts of green-white Yucca lilies and Japan lilies and clove-pinks still remained in their school of bloom.

Benny often stood still, wiped his forehead, leaned on his rake, and inhaled the bouquet of sweet scents, but Annie raked with never-ceasing energy. Annie was small and slender and wiry, and moved with angular grace, her thin, peaked elbows showing be-

neath the sleeves of her pink gingham dress, her thin knees outlin-
ing beneath the scanty folds of the skirt. Her neck was long, her
shoulder-blades troubled the back of her blouse at every movement. She was a creature full of ostentatious joints, but the joints
were delicate and rhythmical and charming. Annie had a charming
face, too. It was thin and sunburnt, but still charming, with a sweet,
eager, intent-to-please outlook upon life. This last was the real attitude of Annie's mind; it was, in fact, Annie. She was intent to please
from her toes to the crown of her brown head. She radiated good
will and loving-kindness as fervently as a lily in the border radiated
perfume.

It was very warm, and the northwest sky had a threatening
mountain of clouds. Occasionally Annie glanced at it and raked the
faster, and thought complacently of the water-proof covers in the
little barn. This hay was valuable for the Reverend Silas's horse.

Two of the front windows of the house were filled with girls'
heads, and the regular swaying movement of white-clad arms
sewing. The girls sat in the house because it was so sunny on the piazza in the afternoon. There were four girls in the sitting-room, all
making finery for themselves. On the other side of the front door
one of the two windows was blank; in the other was visible a nodding gray head, that of Annie's father taking his afternoon nap.

Everything was still except the girls' tongues, an occasional burst
of laughter, and the crackling shrill of locusts. Nothing had passed
on the dusty road since Benny and Annie had begun their work.
Lynn Corners was nothing more than a hamlet. It was even seldom
that an automobile got astray there, being diverted from the little
city of Anderson, six miles away, by turning to the left instead of
the right.

Benny stopped again and wiped his forehead, all pink and
beaded with sweat. He was a pretty young man—as pretty as a girl,
although large. He glanced furtively at Annie, then he went with a
soft, padding glide, like a big cat, to the piazza and settled down.
He leaned his head against a post, closed his eyes, and inhaled the
sweetness of flowers alive and dying, of new-mown hay. Annie
glanced at him and an angelic look came over her face. At that moment the sweetness of her nature seemed actually visible.

"He is tired, poor boy!" she thought. She also thought that
probably Benny felt the heat more because he was stout. Then she
raked faster and faster. She fairly flew over the yard, raking the severed grass and flowers into heaps. The air grew more sultry. The

sun was not yet clouded, but the northwest was darker and rumbled ominously.

The girls in the sitting-room continued to chatter and sew. One of them might have come out to help this little sister toiling alone, but Annie did not think of that. She raked with the uncomplaining sweetness of an angel until the storm burst. The rain came down in solid drops, and the sky was a sheet of clamoring flame. Annie made one motion toward the barn, but there was no use. The hay was not half cocked. There was no sense in running for covers. Benny was up and lumbering into the house, and her sisters were shutting windows and crying out to her. Annie deserted her post and fled before the wind, her pink skirts lashing her heels, her hair dripping.

When she entered the sitting-room her sisters, Imogen, Eliza, Jane, and Susan, were all there; also her father, Silas, tall and gaunt and gray. To the Hempsteads a thunder-storm partook of the nature of a religious ceremony. The family gathered together, and it was understood that they were all offering prayer and recognizing God as present on the wings of the tempest. In reality they were all very nervous in thunder-storms, with the exception of Annie. She always sent up a little silent petition that her sisters and brother and father, and the horse and dog and cat, might escape danger, although she had never been quite sure that she was not wicked in including the dog and cat. She was surer about the horse because he was the means by which her father made pastoral calls upon his distant sheep. Then afterward she just sat with the others and waited until the storm was over and it was time to open windows and see if the roof had leaked. Today, however, she was intent upon the hay. In a lull of the tempest she spoke.

"It is a pity," she said, "that I was not able to get the hay cocked and the covers on."

Then Imogen turned large, sarcastic blue eyes upon her. Imogen was considered a beauty, pink and white, golden-haired, and dimpled, with a curious calculating hardness of character and a sharp tongue, so at variance with her appearance that people doubted the evidence of their senses.

"If," said Imogen, "you had only made Benny work instead of encouraging him to dawdle and finally to stop altogether, and if you had gone out directly after dinner, the hay would have been all raked up and covered."

Nothing could have exceeded the calm and instructive superiority of Imogen's tone. A mass of soft white fabric lay upon her lap, although she had removed scissors and needle and thimble to a safe distance. She tilted her chin with a royal air. When the storm lulled she had stopped praying.

Imogen's sisters echoed her and joined in the attack upon Annie.

"Yes," said Jane, "if you had only started earlier, Annie. I told Eliza when you went out in the yard that it looked like a shower."

Eliza nodded energetically.

"It was foolish to start so late," said Susan, with a calm air of wisdom only a shade less exasperating than Imogen's.

"And you always encourage Benny so in being lazy," said Eliza.

Then the Reverend Silas joined in. "You should have more sense of responsibility toward your brother, your only brother, Annie," he said, in his deep pulpit voice.

"It was after two o'clock when you went out," said Imogen.

"And all you had to do was the dinner-dishes, and there were very few to-day," said Jane.

Then Annie turned with a quick, cat-like motion. Her eyes blazed under her brown toss of hair. She gesticulated with her little, nervous hands. Her voice was as sweet and intense as a reed, and withal piercing with anger.

"It was not half past one when I went out," said she, "and there was a whole sinkful of dishes."

"It was after two. I looked at the clock," said Imogen.

"It was not."

"And there were very few dishes," said Jane.

"A whole sinkful," said Annie, tense with wrath.

"You always are rather late about starting," said Susan.

"I am not! I was not! I washed the dishes, and swept the kitchen, and blacked the stove, and cleaned the silver."

"I swept the kitchen," said Imogen, severely. "Annie, I am surprised at you."

"And you know I cleaned the silver yesterday," said Jane.

Annie gave a gasp and looked from one to the other.

"You know you did not sweep the kitchen," said Imogen.

Annie's father gazed at her severely. "My dear," he said, "how long must I try to correct you of this habit of making false statements?"

"Dear Annie does not realize that they are false statements, father," said Jane. Jane was not pretty but she gave the effect of a long, sweet stanza of some fine poetess. She was very tall and slender and large-eyed, and wore always a serious smile. She was attired in a purple muslin gown, cut V-shaped at the throat, and, as always, a black velvet ribbon with a little gold locket attached. The locket contained a coil of hair. Jane had been engaged to a young minister, now dead three years, and he had given her the locket.

Jane no doubt had mourned for her lover, but she had a covert pleasure in the romance of her situation. She was a year younger than Annie, and she had loved and lost, and so had achieved a sentimental distinction. Imogen always had admirers. Eliza had been courted at intervals half-heartedly by a widower, and Susan had had a few fleeting chances. But Jane was the only one who had been really definite in her heart affairs. As for Annie, nobody ever thought of her in such a connection. It was supposed that Annie had no thought of marriage, that she was foreordained to remain unwed and keep house for her father and Benny.

When Jane said that dear Annie did not realize that she made false statements, she voiced an opinion of the family before which Annie was always absolutely helpless. Defense meant counter-accusation. Annie could not accuse her family. She glanced from one to the other. In her blue eyes were still sparks of wrath, but she said nothing. She felt, as always, speechless, when affairs reached such a juncture. She began, in spite of her good sense, to feel guiltily responsible for everything—for the spoiling of the hay, even for the thunder-storm. What was more, she even wished to feel guiltily responsible. Anything was better than to be sure her sisters were not speaking the truth, that her father was blaming her unjustly.

Benny, who sat hunched upon himself with the effect of one set of bones and muscles leaning upon others for support, was the only one who spoke for her, and even he spoke to little purpose.

"One of you other girls," said he, in a thick, sweet voice, "might have come out and helped Annie; then she could have got the hay in."

They all turned on him.

"It is all very well for you to talk," said Imogen. "I saw you myself quit raking hay and sit down on the piazza."

"Yes," assented Jane, nodding violently, "I saw you, too."

"You have no sense of your responsibility, Benjamin, and your sister Annie abets you in evading it," said Silas Hempstead with dignity.

"Benny feels the heat," said Annie.

"Father is entirely right," said Eliza. "Benjamin has no sense of responsibility, and it is mainly owing to Annie."

"But dear Annie does not realize it," said Jane.

Benny got up lumberingly and left the room. He loved his sister Annie, but he hated the mild simmer of feminine rancor to which even his father's presence failed to add a masculine flavor. Benny was always leaving the room and allowing his sisters "to fight it out."

Just after he left there was a tremendous peal of thunder and a blue flash, and they all prayed again, except Annie, who was occupied with her own perplexities of life, and not at all afraid. She wondered, as she had wondered many times before, if she could possibly be in the wrong, if she were spoiling Benny, if she said and did things without knowing that she did so, or the contrary. Then suddenly she tightened her mouth. She knew. This sweet-tempered, anxious-to-please Annie was entirely sane, she had unusual self-poise. She *knew* that she knew what she did and said, and what she did not do or say, and a strange comprehension of her family overwhelmed her. Her sisters were truthful; she would not admit anything else, even to herself; but they confused desires and impulses with accomplishment. They had done so all their lives, some of them from intense egotism, some possibly from slight twists in their mental organisms. As for her father, he had simply rather a weak character, and was swayed by the majority. Annie, as she sat there among the praying group, made the same excuse for her sisters that they made for her. "They don't realize it," she said to herself.

When the storm finally ceased she hurried up-stairs and opened the windows, letting in the rain-fresh air. Then she got supper, while her sisters resumed their needlework. A curious conviction seized her, as she was hurrying about the kitchen, that in all probability some, if not all, of her sisters considered that they were getting the supper. Possibly Jane had reflected that she ought to get supper, then she had taken another stitch in her work and had not known fairly that her impulse of duty had not been carried out. Imogen, presumably, was sewing with the serene consciousness that, since she was herself, it followed as a matter of course that she was performing all the tasks of the house.

While Annie was making an omelet Benny came out into the kitchen and stood regarding her, hands in pockets, making, as usual, one set of muscles rest upon another. His face was full of the utmost good nature, but it also convicted him of too much sloth to obey its commands.

"Say, Annie, what on earth makes them all pick on you so?" he observed.

"Hush, Benny! They don't mean to. They don't know it."

"But say, Annie, you must know that they tell whoppers. You *did* sweep the kitchen."

"Hush, Benny! Imogen really thinks she swept it."

"Imogen always thinks she has done everything she ought to do, whether she has done it or not," said Benny, with unusual astuteness. "Why don't you up and tell her she lies, Annie?"

"She doesn't really lie," said Annie.

"She does lie, even if she doesn't know it," said Benny; "and what is more, she ought to be made to know it. Say, Annie, it strikes me that you are doing the same by the girls that they accuse you of doing by me. Aren't you encouraging them in evil ways?"

Annie started, and turned and stared at him.

Benny nodded. "I can't see any difference," he said. "There isn't a day but one of the girls thinks she has done something you have done, or hasn't done something you ought to have done, and they blame you all the time, when you don't deserve it, and you let them, and they don't know it, and I don't think myself that they know they tell whoppers; but they ought to know. Strikes me you are just spoiling the whole lot, father thrown in, Annie. You are a dear, just as they say, but you are too much of a dear to be good for them."

Annie stared.

"You are letting that omelet burn," said Benny. "Say, Annie, I will go out and turn that hay in the morning. I know I don't amount to much, but I ain't a girl, anyhow, and I haven't got a cross-eyed soul. That's what ails a lot of girls. They mean all right, but their souls have been cross-eyed ever since they came into the world, and it's just such girls as you who ought to get them straightened out. You know what has happened to-day. Well, here's what happened yesterday. I don't tell tales, but you ought to know this, for I believe Tom Reed has his eye on you, in spite of Imogen's being such a beauty, and Susan's having manners like silk, and Eliza's giving everybody the impression that she is too good for this earth, and Jane's trying to make everybody think she is a sweet martyr, without a thought for mortal man, when that is only her way of trying to catch one. You know Tom Reed was here last evening?"

Annie nodded. Her face turned scarlet, then pathetically pale. She bent over her omelet, carefully lifting it around the edges.

"Well," Benny went on, "I know he came to see you, and Imogen went to the door and ushered him into the parlor, and I was out on the piazza, and she didn't know it, but I heard her tell him that she thought you had gone out. She hinted, too, that George Wells had taken you to the concert in the town hall. He did ask you, didn't he?"

"Yes."

"Well, Imogen spoke in this way." Benny lowered his voice and imitated Imogen to the life. " 'Yes, we are all well, thank you. Father is busy, of course; Jane has run over to Mrs. Jacobs's for a pattern; Eliza is writing letters; and Susan is somewhere about the house. Annie—well, Annie—George Wells asked her to go to the concert— I rather—' Then," said Benny, in his natural voice, "Imogen stopped, and she could say truthfully that she didn't lie, but anybody would have thought from what she said that you had gone to the concert with George Wells."

"Did Tom inquire for me?" asked Annie, in a low voice.

"Didn't have a chance. Imogen got ahead of him."

"Oh, well, then it doesn't matter. I dare say he did come to see Imogen."

"He didn't," said Benny, stoutly. "And that isn't all. Say, Annie—"

"What?"

"Are you going to marry George Wells? It is none of my business, but are you?"

Annie laughed a little, although her face was still pale. She had folded the omelet and was carefully watching it.

"You need not worry about that, Benny dear," she said.

"Then what right have the girls to tell so many people the nice things they hear you say about him?"

Annie removed the omelet skilfully from the pan to a hot plate, which she set on the range shelf, and turned to her brother.

"What nice things do they hear me say?"

"That he is so handsome; that he has such a good position; that he is the very best young man in the place; that you should think every girl would be head over heels in love with him; that every word he speaks is so bright and clever."

Annie looked at her brother.

"I don't believe you ever said one of those things," remarked Benny.

Annie continued to look at him.

"Did you?"

"Benny dear, I am not going to tell you."

"You won't say you never did, because that would be putting your sisters in the wrong and admitting that they tell lies. Annie, you are a dear, but I do think you are doing wrong and spoiling them as much as they say you are spoiling me."

"Perhaps I am," said Annie. There was a strange, tragic expression on her keen, pretty little face. She looked as if her mind was contemplating strenuous action which was changing her very features. She had covered the finished omelet and was now cooking another.

"I wish you would see if everybody is in the house and ready, Benny," said she. "When this omelet is done they must come right away, or nothing will be fit to eat. And, Benny dear, if you don't mind, please get the butter and the cream-pitcher out of the ice-chest. I have everything else on the table."

"There is another thing," said Benny. "I don't go about telling tales, but I do think it is time you knew. The girls tell everybody that you like to do the housework so much that they don't dare interfere. And it isn't so. They may have taught themselves to think it is so, but it isn't. You would like a little time for fancy-work and reading as well as they do."

"Please get the cream and butter, and see if they are all in the house," said Annie. She spoke as usual, but the strange expression remained in her face. It was still there when the family were all gathered at the table and she was serving the puffy omelet. Jane noticed it first.

"What makes you look so odd, Annie?" said she.

"I don't know how I look odd," replied Annie.

They all gazed at her then, her father with some anxiety. "You don't look yourself," he said. "You are feeling well, aren't you, Annie?"

"Quite well, thank you, father."

But after the omelet was served and the tea poured Annie rose.

"Where are you going, Annie?" asked Imogen, in her sarcastic voice.

"To my room, or perhaps out in the orchard."

"It will be sopping wet out there after the shower," said Eliza. "Are you crazy, Annie?"

"I have on my black skirt, and I will wear rubbers," said Annie, quietly. "I want some fresh air."

"I should think you had enough fresh air. You were outdoors all the afternoon, while we were cooped up in the house," said Jane.

"Don't you feel well, Annie?" her father asked again, a golden bit of omelet poised on his fork, as she was leaving the room.

"Quite well, father dear."

"But you are eating no supper."

"I have always heard that people who cook don't need so much to eat," said Imogen. "They say the essence of the food soaks in through the pores."

"I am quite well," Annie repeated, and the door closed behind her.

"Dear Annie! She is always doing odd things like this," remarked Jane.

"Yes, she is, things that one cannot account for, but Annie is a dear," said Susan.

"I hope she is well," said Annie's father.

"Oh, she is well enough. Don't worry, father," said Imogen. "Dear Annie is always doing the unexpected. She looks very well."

"Yes, dear Annie is quite stout, for her," said Jane.

"I think she is thinner than I have ever seen her, and the rest of you look like stuffed geese," said Benny, rudely.

Imogen turned upon him in dignified wrath. "Benny, you insult your sisters," said she. "Father, you should really tell Benny that he should bridle his tongue a little."

"You ought to bridle yours, every one of you," retorted Benny. "You girls nag poor Annie every single minute. You let her do all the work, then you pick at her for it."

There was a chorus of treble voices. "We nag dear Annie! We pick at dear Annie! We make her do everything! Father, you should remonstrate with Benjamin. You know how we all love dear Annie!"

"Benjamin," began Silas Hempstead, but Benny, with a smothered exclamation, was up and out of the room.

Benny quite frankly disliked his sisters, with the exception of Annie. For his father he had a sort of respectful tolerance. He could not see why he should have anything else. His father had never done anything for him except to admonish him. His scanty revenue

for his support and college expenses came from his maternal grandmother, who had been a woman of parts and who had openly
scorned her son-in-law.

Grandmother Loomis had left a will which occasioned much
comment. By its terms she had provided sparsely but adequately for
Benjamin's education and living until he should graduate; and her
house, with all her personal property, and the bulk of the sum from
which she had derived her own income, fell to her granddaughter
Annie. Annie had always been her grandmother's favorite. There
had been covert dismay when the contents of the will were made
known, then one and all had congratulated the beneficiary, and said
abroad that they were glad dear Annie was so well provided for. It
was intimated by Imogen and Eliza that probably dear Annie
would not marry, and in that case Grandmother Loomis's bequest
was so fortunate. She had probably taken that into consideration.
Grandmother Loomis had now been dead four years, and her deserted home had been for rent, furnished, but it had remained
vacant.

Annie soon came back from the orchard, and after she had
cleared away the supper-table and washed the dishes she went up to
her room, carefully rearranged her hair, and changed her dress.
Then she sat down beside a window and waited and watched, her
pointed chin in a cup of one little thin hand, her soft muslin skirts
circling around her, and the scent of queer old sachet emanating
from a flowered ribbon of her grandmother's which she had tied
around her waist. The ancient scent always clung to the ribbon,
suggesting faintly as a dream the musk and roses and violets of
some old summer-time.

Annie sat there and gazed out on the front yard, which was sil-
vered over with moonlight. Annie's four sisters all sat out there.
They had spread a rug over the damp grass and brought out chairs.
There were five chairs, although there were only four girls. Annie
gazed over the yard and down the street. She heard the chatter of
the girls, which was inconsequent and absent, as if their minds were
on other things than their conversation. Then suddenly she saw a
small red gleam far down the street, evidently that of a cigar, and
also a dark, moving figure. Then there ensued a subdued wrangle in
the yard. Imogen insisted that her sisters should go into the house.
They all resisted, Eliza the most vehemently. Imogen was arrogant
and compelling. Finally she drove them all into the house except
Eliza, who wavered upon the threshold of yielding. Imogen was

obliged to speak very softly lest the approaching man hear, but Annie, in the window above her, heard every word.

"You know he is coming to see me," said Imogen, passionately. "You know—you know, Eliza, and yet every single time he comes, here are you girls, spying and listening."

"He comes to see Annie, I believe," said Eliza, in her stubborn voice, which yet had indecision in it.

"He never asks for her."

"He never has a chance. We all tell him, the minute he comes in, that she is out. But now I am going to stay, anyway."

"Stay if you want to. You are all a jealous lot. If you girls can't have a beau yourselves, you begrudge one to me. I never saw such a house as this for a man to come courting in."

"I will stay," said Eliza, and this time her voice was wholly firm. "There is no use in my going, anyway, for the others are coming back."

It was true. Back flitted Jane and Susan, and by that time Tom Reed had reached the gate, and his cigar was going out in a shower of sparks on the gravel walk, and all four sisters were greeting him and urging upon his acceptance the fifth chair. Annie, watching, saw that the young man seemed to hesitate. Then her heart leaped and she heard him speak quite plainly, with a note of defiance and irritation, albeit with embarrassment.

"Is Miss Annie in?" asked Tom Reed.

Imogen answered first, and her harsh voice was honey-sweet.

"I fear dear Annie is out," she said. "She will be so sorry to miss you."

Annie, at her window, made a sudden passionate motion, then she sat still and listened. She argued fiercely that she was right in so doing. She felt that the time had come when she must know, for the sake of her own individuality, just what she had to deal with in the natures of her own kith and kin. Dear Annie had turned in her groove of sweetness and gentle yielding, as all must turn who have any strength of character underneath the sweetness and gentleness. Therefore Annie, at her window above, listened.

At first she heard little that bore upon herself, for the conversation was desultory, about the weather and general village topics. Then Annie heard her own name. She was "dear Annie," as usual. She listened, fairly faint with amazement. What she heard from that quartette of treble voices down there in the moonlight seemed almost like a fairy-tale. The sisters did not violently incriminate her.

They were too astute for that. They told half-truths. They told truths which were as shadows of the real facts, and yet not to be contradicted. They built up between them a story marvelously consistent, unless prearranged, and that Annie did not think possible. George Wells figured in the tale, and there were various hints and pauses concerning herself and her own character in daily life, and not one item could be flatly denied, even if the girl could have gone down there and, standing in the midst of that moonlit group, given her sisters the lie.

Everything which they told, the whole structure of falsehood, had beams and rafters of truth. Annie felt helpless before it all. To her fancy, her sisters and Tom Reed seemed actually sitting in a fairy building whose substance was utter falsehood, and yet which could not be utterly denied. An awful sense of isolation possessed her. So these were her own sisters, the sisters whom she had loved as a matter of the simplest nature, whom she had admired, whom she had served.

She made no allowance, since she herself was perfectly normal, for the motive which underlay it all. She could not comprehend the strife of the women over the one man. Tom Reed was in reality the one desirable match in the village. Annie knew, or thought she knew, that Tom Reed had it in mind to love her, and she innocently had it in mind to love him. She thought of a home of her own and his with delight. She thought of it as she thought of the roses coming into bloom in June, and she thought of it as she thought of the every-day happenings of life—cooking, setting rooms in order, washing dishes. However, there was something else to reckon with, and that Annie instinctively knew. She had been long-suffering, and her long-suffering was now regarded as endless. She had cast her pearls, and they had been trampled. She had turned her other cheek, and it had been promptly slapped. It was entirely true that Annie's sisters were not quite worthy of her, that they had taken advantage of her kindness and gentleness, and had mistaken them for weakness, to be despised. She did not understand them, nor they her. They were, on the whole, better than she thought, but with her there was a stern limit of endurance. Something whiter and hotter than mere wrath was in the girl's soul as she sat there and listened to the building of that structure of essential falsehood about herself.

She waited until Tom Reed had gone. He did not stay long. Then she went down-stairs with flying feet, and stood among them in the moonlight. Her father had come out of the study, and Benny had just been entering the gate as Tom Reed left. Then dear Annie spoke. She really spoke for the first time in her life, and there was something dreadful about it all. A sweet nature is always rather dreadful when it turns and strikes, and Annie struck with the whole force of a nature with a foundation of steel. She left nothing unsaid. She defended herself and she accused her sisters as if before a judge. Then came her ultimatum.

"To-morrow morning I am going over to Grandmother Loomis's house, and I am going to live there a whole year," she declared, in a slow, steady voice. "As you know, I have enough to live on, and—in order that no word of mine can be garbled and twisted as it has been to-night, I speak not at all. Everything which I have to communicate shall be written in black and white, and signed with my own name, and black and white cannot lie."

It was Jane who spoke first. "What will people say?" she whimpered, feebly.

"From what I have heard you all say to-night, whatever you make them," retorted Annie—the Annie who had turned.

Jane gasped. Silas Hempstead stood staring, quite dumb before the sudden problem. Imogen alone seemed to have any command whatever of the situation.

"May I inquire what the butcher and grocer are going to think, no matter what your own sisters think and say, when you give your orders in writing?" she inquired, achieving a jolt from tragedy to the commonplace.

"That is my concern," replied Annie, yet she recognized the difficulty of that phase of the situation. It is just such trifling matters which detract from the dignity of extreme attitudes toward existence. Annie had taken an extreme attitude, yet here were the butcher and the grocer to reckon with. How could she communicate with them in writing without appearing absurd to the verge of insanity? Yet even that difficulty had a solution.

Annie thought it out after she had gone to bed that night. She had been imperturbable with her sisters, who had finally come in a body to make entreaties, although not apologies or retractions. There was a stiff-necked strain in the Hempstead family, and apologies and retractions were bitterer cuds for them to chew than for most. She had been imperturbable with her father, who had quoted Scripture and prayed at her during family worship. She had been imperturbable even with Benny, who had whispered to her: "Say, Annie, I don't blame you, but it will be a hell of a time without you. Can't you stick it out?"

But she had had a struggle before her own vision of the butcher and the grocer, and their amazement when she ceased to speak to them. Then she settled that with a sudden leap of inspiration. It sounded too apropos to be life, but there was a little deaf-and-dumb girl, a far-away relative of the Hempsteads, who lived with her aunt Felicia in Anderson. She was a great trial to her aunt Felicia, who was a widow and well-to-do, and liked the elegancies and normalities of life. This unfortunate little Effie Hempstead could not be placed in a charitable institution on account of the name she bore. Aunt Felicia considered it her worldly duty to care for her, but it was a trial.

Annie would take Effie off Aunt Felicia's hands, and no comment would be excited by a deaf-and-dumb girl carrying written messages to the tradesmen, since she obviously could not give them orally. The only comment would be on Annie's conduct in holding herself aloof from her family and the village people generally.

The next morning, when Annie went away, there was an excited conclave among the sisters.

"She means to do it," said Susan, and she wept.

Imogen's handsome face looked hard and set. "Let her, if she wants to," said she.

"Only think what people will say!" wailed Jane.

Imogen tossed her head. "I shall have something to say myself," she returned. "I shall say how much we all regret that dear Annie has such a difficult disposition that she felt she could not live with her own family and must be alone."

"But," said Jane, blunt in her distress, "will they believe it?"

"Why will they not believe it, pray?"

"Why, I am afraid people have the impression that dear Annie has—" Jane hesitated.

"What?" asked Imogen, coldly. She looked very handsome that morning. Not a waved golden hair was out of place on her carefully brushed head. She wore the neatest of blue linen skirts and blouses, with a linen collar and white tie. There was something hard but compelling about her blond beauty.

"I am afraid," said Jane, "that people have a sort of general impression that dear Annie has perhaps as sweet a disposition as any of us, perhaps sweeter."

"Nobody says that dear Annie has not a sweet disposition," said Imogen, taking a careful stitch in her embroidery. "But a sweet disposition is very often extremely difficult for other people. It constantly puts them in the wrong. I am well aware of the fact that dear Annie does a great deal for all of us, but it is sometimes irritating. Of course it is quite certain that she must have a feeling of superiority because of it, and she should not have it."

Sometimes Eliza made illuminating speeches. "I suppose it follows, then," said she, with slight irony, "that only an angel can have a very sweet disposition without offending others."

But Imogen was not in the least nonplussed. She finished her line of thought. "And with all her sweet disposition," said she, "nobody can deny that dear Annie is peculiar, and peculiarity always makes people difficult for other people. Of course it is horribly peculiar what she is proposing to do now. That in itself will be enough to convince people that dear Annie must be difficult. Only a difficult person could do such a strange thing."

"Who is going to get up and get breakfast in the morning, and wash the dishes?" inquired Jane, irrelevantly.

"All I ever want for breakfast is a bit of fruit, a roll, and an egg, besides my coffee," said Imogen, with her imperious air.

"Somebody has to prepare it."

"That is a mere nothing," said Imogen, and she took another stitch.

After a little, Jane and Eliza went by themselves and discussed the problem.

"It is quite evident that Imogen means to do nothing," said Jane.

"And also that she will justify herself by the theory that there is nothing to be done," said Eliza.

"Oh, well," said Jane, "I will get up and get breakfast, of course. I once contemplated the prospect of doing it the rest of my life."

Eliza assented. "I can understand that it will not be so hard for you," she said, "and although I myself always aspired to higher things than preparing breakfasts, still, you did not, and it is true that you would probably have had it to do if poor Henry had lived, for he was not one to ever have a very large salary."

"There are better things than large salaries," said Jane, and her face looked sadly reminiscent. After all, the distinction of being the only one who had been on the brink of preparing matrimonial breakfasts was much. She felt that it would make early rising and early work endurable to her, although she was not an active young woman.

"I will get a dish-mop and wash the dishes," said Eliza. "I can manage to have an instructive book propped open on the kitchen table, and keep my mind upon higher things as I do such menial tasks."

Then Susan stood in the doorway, a tall figure gracefully swaying sidewise, long-throated and prominent-eyed. She was the least attractive-looking of any of the sisters, but her manners were so charming, and she was so perfectly the lady, that it made up for any lack of beauty.

"I will dust," said Susan, in a lovely voice, and as she spoke she involuntarily bent and swirled her limp muslins in such a way that she fairly suggested a moral duster. There was the making of an actress in Susan. Nobody had ever been able to decide what her true individual self was. Quite unconsciously, like a chameleon, she took upon herself the characteristics of even inanimate things. Just now she was a duster, and a wonderfully creditable duster.

"Who," said Jane, "is going to sweep? Dear Annie has always done that."

"I am not strong enough to sweep. I am very sorry," said Susan, who remained a duster, and did not become a broom.

"If we have system," said Eliza, vaguely, "the work ought not to be so very hard."

"Of course not," said Imogen. She had come in and seated herself. Her three sisters eyed her, but she embroidered imperturbably. The same thought was in the minds of all. Obviously Imogen was the very one to take the task of sweeping upon herself. That hard, compact, young body of hers suggested strenuous household work. Embroidery did not seem to be her rôle at all.

But Imogen had no intention of sweeping. Indeed, the very imagining of such tasks in connection with herself was beyond her. She did not even dream that her sisters expected it of her.

"I suppose," said Jane, "that we might be able to engage Mrs. Moss to come in once a week and do the sweeping."

"It would cost considerable," said Susan.

"But it has to be done."

"I should think it might be managed, with system, if you did not hire anybody," said Imogen, calmly.

"You talk of system as if it were a suction cleaner," said Eliza, with a dash of asperity. Sometimes she reflected how she would have hated Imogen had she not been her sister.

"System is invaluable," said Imogen. She looked away from her embroidery to the white stretch of country road, arched over with elms, and her beautiful eyes had an expression as if they sighted system, the justified settler of all problems.

Meantime, Annie Hempstead was traveling to Anderson in the jolting trolley-car, and trying to settle her emotions and her outlook upon life, which jolted worse than the car upon a strange new track. She had not the slightest intention of giving up her plan, but she realized within herself the sensations of a revolutionist. Who in her family, for generations and generations, had ever taken the course which she was taking? She was not exactly frightened—Annie had splendid courage when once her blood was up—but she was conscious of a tumult and grind of adjustment to a new level which made her nervous.

She reached the end of the car line, then walked about half a mile to her Aunt Felicia Hempstead's house. It was a handsome house, after the standard of nearly half a century ago. It had an opulent air, with its swelling breasts of bay windows, through which showed fine lace curtains; its dormer-windows, each with its carefully draped curtains; its black-walnut front door, whose side-lights were screened with medallioned lace. The house sat high on three terraces of velvet-like grass, and was surmounted by stone steps in three instalments, each of which was flanked by stone lions.

Annie mounted the three tiers of steps between the stone lions and rang the front-door bell, which was polished so brightly that it winked at her like a brazen eye. Almost directly the door was opened by an immaculate, white-capped and white-aproned maid, and Annie was ushered into the parlor. When Annie had been a little thing she had been enamoured of and impressed by the splendor of this parlor. Now she had doubts of it, in spite of the long, magnificent sweep of lace curtains, the sheen of carefully kept upholstery, the gleam of alabaster statuettes, and the even piles of gilt-edged books upon the polished tables.

Soon Mrs. Felicia Hempstead entered, a tall, well-set-up woman, with a handsome face and keen eyes. She wore her usual morning costume—a breakfast sacque of black silk profusely trimmed with lace, and a black silk skirt. She kissed Annie, with a slight peck of closely set lips, for she liked her. Then she sat down opposite her and regarded her with as much of a smile as her sternly set mouth could manage, and inquired politely regarding her health and that of the family. When Annie broached the subject of her call, the set calm of her face relaxed, and she nodded.

"I know what your sisters are. You need not explain to me," she said.

"But," returned Annie, "I do not think they realize. It is only because I—"

"Of course," said Felicia Hempstead. "It is because they need a dose of bitter medicine, and you hope they will be the better for it. I understand you, my dear. You have spirit enough, but you don't get it up often. That is where they make their mistake. Often the meek are meek from choice, and they are the ones to beware of. I don't blame you for trying it. And you can have Effie and welcome. I warn you that she is a little wearing. Of course she can't help her affliction, poor child, but it is dreadful. I have had her taught. She can read and write very well now, poor child, and she is not lacking, and I have kept her well dressed. I take her out to drive with me every day, and am not ashamed to have her seen with me. If she had all her faculties she would not be a bad-looking little girl. Now, of course, she has something of a vacant expression. That comes, I suppose, from her not being able to hear. She has learned to speak a few words, but I don't encourage her doing that before people. It is too evident that there is something wrong. She never gets off one tone. But I will let her speak to you. She will be glad to go with you. She likes you, and I dare say you can put up with her. A woman when she is alone will make a companion of a brazen image. You can manage all right for everything except her clothes and lessons. I will pay for them."

"Can't I give her lessons?"

"Well, you can try, but I am afraid you will need to have Mr. Freer come over once a week. It seems to me to be quite a knack to teach the deaf and dumb. You can see. I will have Effie come in and tell her about the plan. I wanted to go to Europe this summer, and did not know how to manage about Effie. It will be a godsend to me, this arrangement, and of course after the year is up she can come back."

With that Felicia touched a bell, the maid appeared with automatic readiness, and presently a tall little girl entered. She was very well dressed. Her linen frock was hand-embroidered, and her shoes were ultra. Her pretty shock of fair hair was tied with French ribbon in a fetching bow, and she made a courtesy which would have befitted a little princess. Poor Effie's courtesy was the one feature in which Felicia Hempstead took pride. After making it the child always glanced at her for approval, and her face lighted up with pleasure at the faint smile which her little performance evoked. Effie would have been a pretty little girl had it not been for that vacant, bewildered expression of which Felicia had spoken. It was the expression of one shut up with the darkest silence of life, that of her own self, and beauty was incompatible with it.

Felicia placed her stiff forefinger upon her own lips and nodded, and the child's face became transfigured. She spoke in a level, awful voice, utterly devoid of inflection, and full of fright. Her voice was as the first attempt of a skater upon ice. However, it was intelligible. "Good morning," said she. "I hope you are well." Then she courtesied again. That little speech and one other, "Thank you, I am very well," were all she had mastered. Effie's instruction had begun rather late, and her teacher was not remarkably skilful.

When Annie's lips moved in response, Effie's face fairly glowed with delight and affection. The little girl loved Annie. Then her questioning eyes sought Felicia, who beckoned, and drew from the pocket of her rustling silk skirt a tiny pad and pencil. Effie crossed the room and stood at attention while Felicia wrote. When she had read the words on the pad she gave one look at Annie, then another at Felicia, who nodded.

Effie courtesied before Annie like a fairy dancer. "Good morning. I hope you are well," she said. Then she courtesied again and said, "Thank you, I am very well." Her pretty little face was quite eager with love and pleasure, and yet there was an effect as of a veil before the happy emotion in it. The contrast between the awful, level voice and the grace of motion and evident delight at once shocked and compelled pity. Annie put her arms around Effie and kissed her.

"You dear little thing," she said, quite forgetting that Effie could not hear.

Felicia Hempstead got speedily to work, and soon Effie's effects were packed and ready for transportation upon the first express to Lynn Corners, and Annie and the little girl had boarded the trolley thither.

Annie Hempstead had the sensation of one who takes a cold plunge—half pain and fright, half exhilaration and triumph—when she had fairly taken possession of her grandmother's house. There was genuine girlish pleasure in looking over the stock of old china and linen and ancient mahoganies, in starting a fire in the kitchen stove, and preparing a meal, the written order for which Effie had taken to the grocer and butcher. There was genuine delight in sit-

ting down with Effie at her very own table, spread with her grandmother's old damask and pretty dishes, and eating, without hearing
a word of unfavorable comment upon the cookery. But there was a
certain pain and terror in trampling upon that which it was difficult
to define, either her conscience or sense of the divine right of the
conventional.

But that night after Effie had gone to bed, and the house was set
to rights, and she in her cool muslin was sitting on the front-door
step, under the hooded trellis covered with wistaria, she was conscious of entire emancipation. She fairly gloated over her new
estate.

"To-night one of the others will really have to get the supper,
and wash the dishes, and not be able to say she did it and I didn't,
when I did," Annie thought with unholy joy. She knew perfectly
well that her viewpoint was not sanctified, but she felt that she must
allow her soul to have its little witch-caper or she could not answer
for the consequences. There might result spiritual atrophy, which
would be much more disastrous than sin and repentance. It was either the continuance of her old life in her father's house, which was
the ignominious and harmful one of the scapegoat, or this. She at
last reveled in this. Here she was mistress. Here what she did, she
did, and what she did not do remained undone. Here her silence
was her invincible weapon. Here she was free.

The soft summer night enveloped her. The air was sweet with
flowers and the grass which lay still unraked in her father's yard. A
momentary feeling of impatience seized her; then she dismissed it,
and peace came. What had she to do with that hay? Her father
would be obliged to buy hay if it were not raked over and dried, but
what of that? She had nothing to do with it.

She heard voices and soft laughter. A dark shadow passed along
the street. Her heart quickened its beat. The shadow turned in at
her father's gate. There was a babel of welcoming voices, of which
Annie could not distinguish one articulate word. She sat leaning
forward, her eyes intent upon the road. Then she heard the click of
her father's gate and the dark, shadowy figure reappeared in the
road. Annie knew who it was; she knew that Tom Reed was coming
to see her. For a second, rapture seized her, then dismay. How well
she knew her sisters—how very well! Not one of them would have
given him the slightest inkling of the true situation. They would
have told him, by the sweetest of insinuations, rather than by
straight statements, that she had left her father's roof and come over

here, but not one word would have been told him concerning her vow of silence. They would leave that for him to discover, to his amazement and anger.

Annie rose and fled. She closed the door, turned the key softly, and ran up-stairs in the dark. Kneeling before a window on the farther side from her old home, she watched with eager eyes the young man open the gate and come up the path between the old-fashioned shrubs. The clove-like fragrance of the pinks in the border came in her face. Annie watched Tom Reed disappear beneath the trellised hood of the door; then the bell tinkled through the house. It seemed to Annie that she heard it as she had never heard anything before. Every nerve in her body seemed urging her to rise and go downstairs and admit this young man whom she loved. But her will, turned upon itself, kept her back. She could not rise and go down; something stronger than her own wish restrained her. She suffered horribly, but she remained. The bell tinkled again. There was a pause, then it sounded for the third time.

Annie leaned against the window, faint and trembling. It was rather horrible to continue such a fight between will and inclination, but she held out. She would not have been herself had she not done so. Then she saw Tom Reed's figure emerge from under the shadow of the door, pass down the path between the sweet-flowering shrubs, seeming to stir up the odor of the pinks as he did so. He started to go down the road; then Annie heard a loud, silvery call, with a harsh inflection, from her father's house. "Imogen is calling him back," she thought.

Annie was out of the room, and, slipping softly down-stairs and out into the yard, crouched close to the fence overgrown with sweetbrier, its foundation hidden in the mallow, and there she listened. She wanted to know what Imogen and her other sisters were about to say to Tom Reed, and she meant to know. She heard every word. The distance was not great, and her sisters' voices carried far, in spite of their honeyed tones and efforts toward secrecy. By the time Tom had reached the gate of the parsonage they had all crowded down there, a fluttering assembly in their snowy summer muslins, like white doves. Annie heard Imogen first. Imogen was always the ringleader.

"Couldn't you find her?" asked Imogen.

"No. Rang three times," replied Tom. He had a boyish voice, and his chagrin showed plainly in it. Annie knew just how he looked, how dear and big and foolish, with his handsome, bewildered face, blurting out to her sisters his disappointment, with innocent faith in their sympathy.

Then Annie heard Eliza speak in a small, sweet voice, which yet, to one who understood her, carried in it a sting of malice. "How very strange!" said Eliza.

Jane spoke next. She echoed Eliza, but her voice was more emphatic and seemed multiple, as echoes do. "Yes, very strange indeed," said Jane.

"Dear Annie is really very singular lately. It has distressed us all, especially father," said Susan, but deprecatingly.

Then Imogen spoke, and to the point. "Annie must be in that house," said she. "She went in there, and she could not have gone out without our seeing her."

Annie could fairly see the toss of Imogen's head as she spoke.

"What in thunder do you all mean?" asked Tom Reed, and there was a bluntness, almost a brutality, in his voice which was refreshing.

"I do not think such forcible language is becoming, especially at the parsonage," said Jane.

Annie distinctly heard Tom Reed snort. "Hang it if I care whether it is becoming or not," said he.

"You seem to forget that you are addressing ladies, sir," said Jane.

"Don't forget it for a blessed minute," returned Tom Reed. "Wish I could. You make it too evident that you are—ladies, with every word you speak, and all your beating about the bush. A man would blurt it out, and then I would know where I am at. Hang it if I know now. You all say that your sister is singular and that she distresses your father, and you"—addressing Imogen—"say that she must be in that house. You are the only one who does make a dab at speaking out; I will say that much for you. Now, if she is in that house, what in thunder is the matter?"

"I really cannot stay here and listen to such profane language," said Jane, and she flitted up the path to the house like an enraged white moth. She had a fleecy white shawl over her head, and her pale outline was triangular.

"If she calls that profane, I pity her," said Tom Reed. He had known the girls since they were children, and had never liked Jane. He continued, still addressing Imogen. "For Heaven's sake, if she is in that house, what is the matter?" said he. "Doesn't the bell ring? Yes, it does ring, though it is as cracked as the devil. I heard it. Has

Annie gone deaf? Is she sick? Is she asleep? It is only eight o'clock. I don't believe she is asleep. Doesn't she want to see me? Is that the trouble? What have I done? Is she angry with me?"

Eliza spoke, smoothly and sweetly. "Dear Annie is singular," said she.

"What the dickens do you mean by singular? I have known Annie ever since she was that high. It never struck me that she was any more singular than other girls, except she stood an awful lot of nagging without making a kick. Here you all say she is singular, as if you meant she was"—Tom hesitated a second—"crazy," said he. "Now, I know that Annie is saner than any girl around here, and that simply does not go down. What do you all mean by singular?"

"Dear Annie may not be singular, but her actions are sometimes singular," said Susan. "We all feel badly about this."

"You mean her going over to her grandmother's house to live? I don't know whether I think that is anything but horse-sense. I have eyes in my head, and I have used them. Annie has worked like a dog here; I suppose she needed a rest."

"We all do our share of the work," said Eliza, calmly, "but we do it in a different way from dear Annie. She makes very hard work of work. She has not as much system as we could wish. She tires herself unnecessarily."

"Yes, that is quite true," assented Imogen. "Dear Annie gets very tired over the slightest tasks, whereas if she went a little more slowly and used more system the work would be accomplished well and with no fatigue. There are five of us to do the work here, and the house is very convenient."

There was a silence. Tom Reed was bewildered. "But—doesn't she want to see me?" he asked, finally.

"Dear Annie takes very singular notions sometimes," said Eliza, softly.

"If she took a notion not to go to the door when she heard the bell ring, she simply wouldn't," said Imogen, whose bluntness of speech was, after all, a relief.

"Then you mean that you think she took a notion not to go to the door?" asked Tom, in a desperate tone.

"Dear Annie is very singular," said Eliza, with such softness and deliberation that it was like a minor chord of music.

"Do you know of anything she has against me?" asked Tom of Imogen; but Eliza answered for her.

"Dear Annie is not in the habit of making confidantes of her sisters," said she, "but we do know that she sometimes takes unwarranted dislikes."

"Which time generally cures," said Susan.

"Oh yes," assented Eliza, "which time generally cures. She can have no reason whatever for avoiding you. You have always treated her well."

"I have always meant to," said Tom, so miserably and helplessly that Annie, listening, felt her heart go out to this young man, badgered by females, and she formed a sudden resolution.

"You have not seen very much of her, anyway," said Imogen.

"I have always asked for her, but I understood she was busy," said Tom, "and that was the reason why I saw her so seldom."

"Oh," said Eliza, "busy!" She said it with an indescribable tone.

"If," supplemented Imogen, "there was system, there would be no need of any one of us being too busy to see our friends."

"Then she has not been busy? She has not wanted to see me?" said Tom. "I think I understand at last. I have been a fool not to before. You girls have broken it to me as well as you could. Much obliged, I am sure. Good night."

"Won't you come in?" asked Imogen.

"We might have some music," said Eliza.

"And there is an orange cake, and I will make coffee," said Susan.

Annie reflected rapidly how she herself had made that orange cake, and what queer coffee Susan would be apt to concoct.

"No, thank you," said Tom Reed, briskly. "I will drop in another evening. Think I must go home now. I have some important letters. Good night, all."

Annie made a soft rush to the gate, crouching low that her sisters might not see her. They flocked into the house with irascible murmurings, like scolding birds, while Annie stole across the grass, which had begun to glisten with silver wheels of dew. She held her skirts closely wrapped around her, and stepped through a gap in the shrubs beside the walk, then sped swiftly to the gate. She reached it just as Tom Reed was passing with a quick stride.

"Tom," said Annie, and the young man stopped short.

He looked in her direction, but she stood close to a great snowball-bush, and her dress was green muslin, and he did not see her. Thinking that he had been mistaken, he started on, when she called again, and this time she stepped apart from the bush and her voice sounded clear as a flute.

"Tom," she said. "Stop a minute, please."

Tom stopped and came close to her. In the dim light she could see that his face was all aglow, like a child's with delight and surprise.

"Is that you, Annie?" he said.

"Yes. I want to speak to you, please."

"I have been here before, and I rang the bell three times. Then you were out, although your sisters thought not."

"No, I was in the house."

"You did not hear the bell?"

"Yes, I heard it every time."

"Then why—?"

"Come into the house with me and I will tell you; at least I will tell you all I can."

Annie led the way and the young man followed. He stood in the dark entry while Annie lit the parlor lamp. The room was on the farther side of the house from the parsonage.

"Come in and sit down," said Annie. Then the young man stepped into a room which was pretty in spite of itself. There was an old Brussels carpet with an enormous rose pattern. The haircloth furniture gave out gleams like black diamonds under the light of the lamp. In a corner stood a what-not piled with branches of white coral and shells. Annie's grandfather had been a sea-captain, and many of his spoils were in the house. Possibly Annie's own occupation of it was due to an adventurous strain inherited from him. Perhaps the same impulse which led him to voyage to foreign shores had led her to voyage across a green yard to the next house.

Tom Reed sat down on the sofa. Annie sat in a rocking-chair near by. At her side was a Chinese teapoy, a nest of lacquer tables, and on it stood a small, squat idol. Annie's grandmother had been taken to task by her son-in-law, the Reverend Silas, for harboring a heathen idol, but she had only laughed.

"Guess as long as I don't keep heathen to bow down before him, he can't do much harm," she had said.

Now the grotesque face of the thing seemed to stare at the two Occidental lovers with the strange, calm sarcasm of the Orient, but they had no eyes or thought for it.

"Why didn't you come to the door if you heard the bell ring?" asked Tom Reed, gazing at Annie, slender as a blade of grass in her clinging green gown.

"Because I was not able to break my will then. I had to break it to go out in the yard and ask you to come in, but when the bell rang I hadn't got to the point where I could break it."

"What on earth do you mean, Annie?"

Annie laughed. "I don't wonder you ask," she said, "and the worst of it is I can't half answer you. I wonder how much, or rather how little explanation will content you?"

Tom Reed gazed at her with the eyes of a man who might love a woman and have infinite patience with her, relegating his lack of understanding of her woman's nature to the background, as a thing of no consequence.

"Mighty little will do for me," he said, "mighty little, Annie dear, if you will only tell a fellow you love him."

Annie looked at him, and her thin, sweet face seemed to have a luminous quality, like a crescent moon. Her look was enough.

"Then you do?" said Tom Reed.

"You have never needed to ask," said Annie. "You knew."

"I haven't been so sure as you think," said Tom. "Suppose you come over here and sit beside me. You look miles away."

Annie laughed and blushed, but she obeyed. She sat beside Tom and let him put his arm around her. She sat up straight, by force of her instinctive maidenliness, but she kissed him back when he kissed her.

"I haven't been so sure," repeated Tom. "Annie darling, why have I been unable to see more of you? I have fairly haunted your house, and seen the whole lot of your sisters, especially Imogen, but somehow or other you have been as slippery as an eel. I have always asked for you, but you were always out or busy."

"I have been very busy," said Annie, evasively. She loved this young man with all her heart, but she had an enduring loyalty to her own flesh and blood.

Tom was very literal. "Say, Annie," he blurted out, "I begin to think you have had to do most of the work over there. Now, haven't you? Own up."

Annie laughed sweetly. She was so happy that no sense of injury could possibly rankle within her. "Oh, well," she said, lightly. "Perhaps. I don't know. I guess housekeeping comes rather easier to me than to the others. I like it, you know, and work is always easier when one likes it. The other girls don't take to it so naturally, and they get very tired, and it has seemed often that I was the one who could hurry the work through and not mind."

"I wonder if you will stick up for me the way you do for your sisters when you are my wife?" said Tom, with a burst of love and admiration. Then he added: "Of course you are going to be my wife, Annie? You know what this means?"

"If you think I will make you as good a wife as you can find," said Annie.

"As good a wife! Annie, do you really know what you are?"

"Just an ordinary girl, with no special talent for anything."

"You are the most wonderful girl that ever walked the earth," exclaimed Tom. "And as for talent, you have the best talent in the whole world; you can love people who are not worthy to tie your shoestrings, and think you are looking up when in reality you are looking down. That is what I call the best talent in the whole world for a woman." Tom Reed was becoming almost subtle.

Annie only laughed happily again. "Well, you will have to wait and find out," said she.

"I suppose," said Tom, "that you came over here because you were tired out, this hot weather. I think you were sensible, but I don't think you ought to be here alone."

"I am not alone," replied Annie. "I have poor little Effie Hempstead with me."

"That deaf-and-dumb child? I should think this heathen god would be about as much company."

"Why, Tom, she is human, if she is deaf and dumb."

Tom eyed her shrewdly. "What did you mean when you said you had broken your will?" he inquired.

"My will not to speak for a while," said Annie, faintly.

"Not to speak—to any one?"

Annie nodded.

"Then you have broken your resolution by speaking to me?"

Annie nodded again.

"But why shouldn't you speak? I don't understand."

"I wondered how little I could say, and have you satisfied," Annie replied, sadly.

Tom tightened his arm around her. "You precious little soul," he said. "I am satisfied. I know you have some good reason for not wanting to, speak, but I am plaguey glad you spoke to me, for I should have been pretty well cast down if you hadn't, and to-morrow I have to go away."

Annie leaned toward him. "Go away!"

"Yes; I have to go to California about that confounded Ames

will case. And I don't know exactly where, on the Pacific coast, the parties I have to interview may be, and I may have to be away weeks, possibly months. Annie darling, it did seem to me a cruel state of things to have to go so far, and leave you here, living in such a queer fashion, and not know how you felt. Lord! but I'm glad you had sense enough to call me, Annie."

"I couldn't let you go by, when it came to it, and Tom—"

"What, dear?"

"I did an awful mean thing: something I never was guilty of before. I—listened."

"Well, I don't see what harm it did. You didn't hear much to your or your sisters' disadvantage, that I can remember. They kept calling you 'dear.' "

"Yes," said Annie, quickly. Again, such was her love and thankfulness that a great wave of love and forgiveness for her sisters swept over her. Annie had a nature compounded of depths of sweetness; nobody could be mistaken with regard to that. What they did mistake was the possibility of even sweetness being at bay at times, and remaining there.

"You don't mean to speak to anybody else?" asked Tom.

"Not for a year, if I can avoid it without making comment which might hurt father."

"Why, dear?"

"That is what I cannot tell you," replied Annie, looking into his face with a troubled smile.

Tom looked at her in a puzzled way, then he kissed her.

"Oh, well, dear," he said, "it is all right. I know perfectly well you would do nothing in which you were not justified, and you have spoken to me, anyway, and that is the main thing. I think if I had been obliged to start to-morrow without a word from you I shouldn't have cared a hang whether I ever came back or not. You are the only soul to hold me here; you know that, darling."

"Yes," replied Annie.

"You are the only one," repeated Tom, "but it seems to me this minute as if you were a whole host, you dear little soul. But I don't quite like to leave you here living alone, except for Effie."

"Oh, I am within a stone's-throw of father's," said Annie, lightly.

"I admit that. Still, you are alone. Annie, when are you going to marry me?"

Annie regarded him with a clear, innocent look. She had lived such a busy life that her mind was unfilmed by dreams. "Whenever you like, after you come home," said she.

"It can't be too soon for me. I want my wife and I want my home. What will you do while I am gone, dear?"

Annie laughed. "Oh, I shall do what I have seen other girls do— get ready to be married."

"That means sewing, lots of hemming and tucking and stitching, doesn't it?"

"Of course."

"Girls are so funny," said Tom. "Now imagine a man sitting right down and sewing like mad on his collars and neckties and shirts the minute a girl said she'd marry him!"

"Girls like it."

"Well, I suppose they do," said Tom, and he looked down at Annie from a tender height of masculinity, and at the same time seemed to look up from the valley of one who cannot understand the subtle and poetical details in a woman's soul.

He did not stay long after that, for it was late. As he passed through the gate, after a tender farewell, Annie watched him with shining eyes. She was now to be all alone, but two things she had, her freedom and her love, and they would suffice.

The next morning Silas Hempstead, urged by his daughters, walked solemnly over to the next house, but he derived little satisfaction. Annie did not absolutely refuse to speak. She had begun to realize that carrying out her resolution to the extreme letter was impossible. But she said as little as she could.

"I have come over here to live for the present. I am of age, and have a right to consult my own wishes. My decision is unalterable." Having said this much, Annie closed her mouth and said no more. Silas argued and pleaded. Annie sat placidly sewing beside one front window of the sunny sitting-room. Effie, with a bit of fancy-work, sat at another. Finally Silas went home defeated, with a last word, half condemnatory, half placative. Silas was not the sort to stand firm against such feminine strength as his daughter Annie's. However, he secretly held her dearer than all his other children.

After her father had gone, Annie sat taking even stitch after even stitch, but a few tears ran over her cheeks and fell upon the soft mass of muslin. Effie watched with shrewd, speculative silence, like a pet cat. Then suddenly she rose and went close to Annie, with her little arms around her neck, and the poor dumb mouth repeating her little speeches: "Thank you, I am very well, thank you, I am very well," over and over.

Annie kissed her fondly, and was aware of a sense of comfort and of love for this poor little Effie. Still, after being nearly two months with the child, she was relieved when Felicia Hempstead came, the first of September, and wished to take Effie home with her. She had not gone to Europe, after all, but to the mountains, and upon her return had missed the little girl.

Effie went willingly enough, but Annie discovered that she too missed her. Now loneliness had her fairly in its grip. She had a telephone installed, and gave her orders over that. Sometimes the sound of a human voice made her emotional to tears. Besides the voices over the telephone, Annie had nobody, for Benny returned to college soon after Effie left. Benny had been in the habit of coming in to see Annie, and she had not had the heart to check him. She talked to him very little, and knew that he was no telltale as far as she was concerned, although he waxed most communicative with regard to the others. A few days before he left he came over and begged her to return.

"I know the girls have nagged you till you are fairly worn out," he said. "I know they don't tell things straight, but I don't believe they know it, and I don't see why you can't come home, and insist upon your rights, and not work so hard."

"If I come home now it will be as it was before," said Annie.

"Can't you stand up for yourself and not have it the same?"

Annie shook her head.

"Seems as if you could," said Benny. "I always thought a girl knew how to manage other girls. It is rather awful the way things go now over there. Father must be uncomfortable enough trying to eat the stuff they set before him and living in such a dirty house."

Annie winced. "Is it so very dirty?"

Benny whistled.

"Is the food so bad?"

Benny whistled again.

"You advised me—or it amounted to the same thing—to take this stand," said Annie.

"I know I did, but I didn't know how bad it would be. Guess I didn't half appreciate you myself, Annie. Well, you must do as you think best, but if you could look in over there your heart would ache."

"My heart aches as it is," said Annie, sadly.

Benny put an arm around her. "Poor girl!" he said. "It is a shame, but you are going to marry Tom. You ought not to have the heartache."

"Marriage isn't everything," said Annie, "and my heart does ache, but—I can't go back there, unless—I can't make it clear to you, Benny, but it seems to me as if I couldn't go back there until the year is up, or I shouldn't be myself, and it seems, too, as if I should not be doing right by the girls. There are things more important even than doing work for others. I have got it through my head that I can be dreadfully selfish being unselfish."

"Well, I suppose you are right," admitted Benny with a sigh.

Then he kissed Annie and went away, and the blackness of loneliness settled down upon her. She had wondered at first that none of the village people came to see her, although she did not wish to talk to them; then she no longer wondered. She heard, without hearing, just what her sisters had said about her.

That was a long winter for Annie Hempstead. Letters did not come very regularly from Tom Reed, for it was a season of heavy snowfalls and the mails were often delayed. The letters were all that she had for comfort and company. She had bought a canary-bird, adopted a stray kitten, and filled her sunny windows with plants. She sat beside them and sewed, and tried to be happy and content, but all the time there was a frightful uncertainty deep down within her heart as to whether or not she was doing right. She knew that her sisters were unworthy, and yet her love and longing for them waxed greater and greater. As for her father, she loved him as she had never loved him before. The struggle grew terrible. Many a time she dressed herself in outdoor array and started to go home, but something always held her back. It was a strange conflict that endured through the winter months, the conflict of a loving, self-effacing heart with its own instincts.

Toward the last of February her father came over at dusk. Annie ran to the door, and he entered. He looked unkempt and dejected. He did not say much, but sat down and looked about him with a half-angry, half-discouraged air. Annie went out into the kitchen and broiled some beefsteak, and creamed some potatoes, and made tea and toast. Then she called him into the sitting-room, and he ate like one famished.

"Your sister Susan does the best she can," he said, when he had finished, "and lately Jane has been trying, but they don't seem to have the knack. I don't want to urge you, Annie, but—"

"You know when I am married you will have to get on without me," Annie said, in a low voice.

"Yes, but in the mean time you might, if you were home, show Susan and Jane."

"Father," said Annie, "you know if I came home now it would be just the same as it was before. You know if I give in and break my word with myself to stay away a year what they will think and do."

"I suppose they might take advantage," admitted Silas, heavily. "I fear you have always given in to them too much for their own good."

"Then I shall not give in now," said Annie, and she shut her mouth tightly.

There came a peal of the cracked door-bell, and Silas started with a curious, guilty look. Annie regarded him sharply. "Who is it, father?"

"Well, I heard Imogen say to Eliza that she thought it was very foolish for them all to stay over there and have the extra care and expense, when you were here."

"You mean that the girls—?"

"I think they did have a little idea that they might come here and make you a little visit—"

Annie was at the front door with a bound. The key turned in the lock and a bolt shot into place. Then she returned to her father, and her face was very white.

"You did not lock your door against your own sisters?" he gasped.

"God forgive me, I did."

The bell pealed again. Annie stood still, her mouth quivering in a strange, rigid fashion. The curtains in the dining-room windows were not drawn. Suddenly one window showed full of her sisters' faces. It was Susan who spoke.

"Annie, you can't mean to lock us out?" Susan's face looked strange and wild, peering in out of the dark. Imogen's handsome face towered over her shoulder.

"We think it advisable to close our house and make you a visit," she said, quite distinctly through the glass.

Then Jane said, with an inaudible sob, "Dear Annie, you can't mean to keep us out!"

Annie looked at them and said not a word. Their half-commanding, half-imploring voices continued a while. Then the faces disappeared.

Annie turned to her father. "God knows if I have done right," she said, "but I am doing what you have taken me to account for not doing."

"Yes, I know," said Silas. He sat for a while silent. Then he rose, kissed Annie—something he had seldom done—and went home. After he had gone Annie sat down and cried. She did not go to bed that night. The cat jumped up in her lap, and she was glad of that soft, purring comfort. It seemed to her as if she had committed a great crime, and as if she had suffered martyrdom. She loved her father and her sisters with such intensity that her heart groaned with the weight of pure love. For the time it seemed to her that she loved them more than the man whom she was to marry. She sat there and held herself, as with chains of agony, from rushing out into the night, home to them all, and breaking her vow.

It was never quite so bad after that night, for Annie compromised. She baked bread and cake and pies, and carried them over after nightfall and left them at her father's door. She even, later on, made a pot of coffee, and hurried over with it in the dawn-light, always watching behind a corner of a curtain until she saw an arm reached out for it. All this comforted Annie, and, moreover, the time was drawing near when she could go home.

Tom Reed had been delayed much longer than he expected. He would not be home before early fall. They would not be married until November, and she would have several months at home first.

At last the day came. Out in Silas Hempstead's front yard the grass waved tall, dotted with disks of clover. Benny was home, and he had been over to see Annie every day since his return. That morning when Annie looked out of her window the first thing she saw was Benny waving a scythe in awkward sweep among the grass and clover. An immense pity seized her at the sight. She realized that he was doing this for her, conquering his indolence. She almost sobbed.

"Dear, dear boy, he will cut himself," she thought. Then she conquered her own love and pity, even as her brother was conquering his sloth. She understood clearly that it was better for Benny to go on with his task even if he did cut himself.

The grass was laid low when she went home, and Benny stood, a conqueror in a battle-field of summer, leaning on his scythe.

"Only look, Annie," he cried out, like a child. "I have cut all the grass."

Annie wanted to hug him. Instead she laughed. "It was time to cut it," she said. Her tone was cool, but her eyes were adoring.

Benny laid down his scythe, took her by the arm, and led her into the house. Silas and his other daughters were in the sitting-room, and the room was so orderly it was painful. The ornaments on the mantel-shelf stood as regularly as soldiers on parade, and it was the same with the chairs. Even the cushions on the sofa were arranged with one corner overlapping another. The curtains were drawn at exactly the same height from the sill. The carpet looked as if swept threadbare.

Annie's first feeling was of worried astonishment; then her eye caught a glimpse of Susan's kitchen apron tucked under a sofa pillow, and of layers of dust on the table, and she felt relieved. After all, what she had done had not completely changed the sisters, whom she loved, faults and all. Annie realized how horrible it would have been to find her loved ones completely changed, even for the better. They would have seemed like strange, aloof angels to her.

They all welcomed her with a slight stiffness, yet with cordiality. Then Silas made a little speech.

"Your father and your sisters are glad to welcome you home, dear Annie," he said, "and your sisters wish me to say for them that they realize that possibly they may have underestimated your tasks and overestimated their own. In short, they may not have been—"

Silas hesitated, and Benny finished. "What the girls want you to know, Annie, is that they have found out they have been a parcel of pigs."

"We fear we have been selfish without realizing it," said Jane, and she kissed Annie, as did Susan and Eliza. Imogen, looking very handsome in her blue linen, with her embroidery in her hands, did not kiss her sister. She was not given to demonstrations, but she smiled complacently at her.

"We are all very glad to have dear Annie back, I am sure," said she, "and now that it is all over, we all feel that it has been for the best, although it has seemed very singular, and made, I fear, considerable talk. But, of course, when one person in a family insists upon taking everything upon herself, it must result in making the others selfish."

Annie did not hear one word that Imogen said. She was crying on Susan's shoulder.

"Oh, I am so glad to be home," she sobbed.

And they all stood gathered about her, rejoicing and fond of her, but she was the one lover among them all who had been capable of hurting them and hurting herself for love's sake.

The Amethyst Comb

MISS JANE CAREW was at the railroad station waiting for the New York train. She was about to visit her friend, Mrs. Viola Longstreet. With Miss Carew was her maid, Margaret, a middle-aged New England woman, attired in the stiffest and most correct of maid-uniforms. She carried an old, large sole-leather bag, and also a rather large sole-leather jewel-case. The jewel-case, carried openly, was rather an unusual sight at a New England railroad station, but few knew what it was. They concluded it to be Margaret's special handbag. Margaret was a very tall, thin woman, unbending as to carriage and expression. The one thing out of absolute plumb about Margaret was her little black bonnet. That was askew. Time had bereft the woman of so much hair that she could fasten no head-gear with security, especially when the wind blew, and that morning there was a stiff gale. Margaret's bonnet was cocked over one eye. Miss Carew noticed it.

"Margaret, your bonnet is crooked," she said.

Margaret straightened her bonnet, but immediately the bonnet veered again to the side, weighted by a stiff jet aigrette. Miss Carew observed the careen of the bonnet, realized that it was inevitable, and did not mention it again. Inwardly she resolved upon the removal of the jet aigrette later on. Miss Carew was slightly older than Margaret, and dressed in a style somewhat beyond her age. Jane Carew had been alert upon the situation of departing youth. She had eschewed gay colors and extreme cuts, and had her bonnets made to order, because there were no longer anything but hats in the millinery shop. The milliner in Wheaton, where Miss Carew lived, had objected, for Jane Carew inspired reverence.

"A bonnet is too old for you, Miss Carew," she said. "Women much older than you wear hats."

"I trust that I know what is becoming to a woman of my years, thank you, Miss Waters," Jane had replied, and the milliner had meekly taken her order.

After Miss Carew had left, the milliner told her girls that she had never seen a woman so perfectly crazy to look her age as Miss Carew. "And she a pretty woman, too," said the milliner; "as

286

straight as an arrer, and slim, and with all that hair, scarcely turned at all."

Miss Carew, with all her haste to assume years, remained a pretty woman, softly slim, with an abundance of dark hair, showing little gray. Sometimes Jane reflected, uneasily, that it ought at her time of life to be entirely gray. She hoped nobody would suspect her of dyeing it. She wore it parted in the middle, folded back smoothly, and braided in a compact mass on the top of her head. The style of her clothes was slightly behind the fashion, just enough to suggest conservatism and age. She carried a little silver-bound bag in one nicely gloved hand; with the other she held daintily out of the dust of the platform her dress-skirt. A glimpse of a silk frilled petticoat, of slender feet, and ankles delicately slim, was visible before the onslaught of the wind. Jane Carew made no futile effort to keep her skirts down before the wind-gusts. She was so much of the gentlewoman that she could be gravely oblivious to the exposure of her ankles. She looked as if she had never heard of ankles when her black silk skirts lashed about them. She rose superbly above the situation. For some abstruse reason Margaret's skirts were not affected by the wind. They might have been weighted with buckram, although it was no longer in general use. She stood, except for her veering bonnet, as stiffly immovable as a wooden doll.

Miss Carew seldom left Wheaton. This visit to New York was an innovation. Quite a crowd gathered about Jane's sole-leather trunk when it was dumped on the platform by the local expressman. "Miss Carew is going to New York," one said to another, with much the same tone as if he had said, "The great elm on the common is going to move into Dr. Jones's front yard."

When the train arrived, Miss Carew, followed by Margaret, stepped aboard with a majestic disregard of ankles. She sat beside a window, and Margaret placed the bag on the floor and held the jewel-case in her lap. The case contained the Carew jewels. They were not especially valuable, although they were rather numerous. There were cameos in brooches and heavy gold bracelets; corals which Miss Carew had not worn since her young girlhood. There were a set of garnets, some badly cut diamonds in ear-rings and rings, some seed-pearl ornaments, and a really beautiful set of amethysts. There were a necklace, two brooches—a bar and a circle—earrings, a ring, and a comb. Each piece was charming, set in filigree gold with seed-pearls, but perhaps of them all the comb was the best. It was a very large comb. There was one great amethyst in the center of the top; on either side was an intricate pattern of plums in small amethysts, and seed-pearl grapes, with leaves and stems of gold. Margaret in charge of the jewel-case was imposing. When they arrived in New York she confronted everybody whom she met with a stony stare, which was almost accusative and convictive of guilt, in spite of entire innocence on the part of the person stared at. It was inconceivable that any mortal would have dared lay violent hands upon that jewel-case under that stare. It would have seemed to partake of the nature of grand larceny from Providence.

When the two reached the up-town residence of Viola Longstreet, Viola gave a little scream at the sight of the case.

"My dear Jane Carew, here you are with Margaret carrying that jewel-case out in plain sight. How dare you do such a thing? I really wonder you have not been held up a dozen times."

Miss Carew smiled her gentle but almost stern smile—the Carew smile, which consisted in a widening and slightly upward curving of tightly closed lips.

"I do not think," said she, "that anybody would be apt to interfere with Margaret."

Viola Longstreet laughed, the ringing peal of a child, although she was as old as Miss Carew. "I think you are right, Jane," said she. "I don't believe a crook in New York would dare face that maid of yours. He would as soon encounter Plymouth Rock. I am glad you have brought your delightful old jewels, although you never wear anything except those lovely old pearl sprays and dull diamonds."

"Now," stated Jane, with a little toss of pride, "I have Aunt Felicia's amethysts."

"Oh, sure enough! I remember you did write me last summer that she had died and you had the amethysts at last. She must have been very old."

"Ninety-one."

"She might have given you the amethysts before. You, of course, will wear them; and I—am going to borrow the corals!"

Jane Carew gasped.

"You do not object, do you, dear? I have a new dinner-gown which clamors for corals, and my bank-account is strained, and I could buy none equal to those of yours, anyway."

"Oh, I do not object," said Jane Carew; still she looked aghast.

Viola Longstreet shrieked with laughter. "Oh, I know. You think the corals too young for me. You have not worn them since you left off dotted muslin. My dear, you insisted upon growing old—I insisted upon remaining young. I had two new dotted muslins last summer. As for corals, I would wear them in the face of an opposing army! Do not judge me by yourself, dear. You laid hold of Age and held him, although you had your complexion and your shape and hair. As for me, I had my complexion and kept it. I also had my hair and kept it. My shape has been a struggle, but it was worth while. I, my dear, have held Youth so tight that he has almost choked to death, but held him I have. You cannot deny it. Look at me, Jane Carew, and tell me if, judging by my looks, you can reasonably state that I have no longer the right to wear corals."

Jane Carew looked. She smiled the Carew smile. "You *do* look very young, Viola," said Jane, "but you are not."

"Jane Carew," said Viola, "I am young. May I wear your corals at my dinner to-morrow night?"

"Why, of course, if you think—"

"If I think them suitable. My dear, if there were on this earth ornaments more suitable to extreme youth than corals, I would borrow them if you owned them, but, failing that, the corals will answer. Wait until you see me in that taupe dinner-gown and the corals!"

Jane waited. She visited with Viola, whom she loved, although they had little in common, partly because of leading widely different lives, partly because of constitutional variations. She was dressed for dinner fully an hour before it was necessary, and she sat in the library reading when Viola swept in.

Viola was really entrancing. It was a pity that Jane Carew had such an unswerving eye for the essential truth that it could not be appeased by actual effect. Viola had doubtless, as she had said, struggled to keep her slim shape, but she had kept it, and, what was more, kept it without evidence of struggle. If she was in the least hampered by tight lacing and length of undergarment, she gave no evidence of it as she curled herself up in a big chair and (Jane wondered how she could bring herself to do it) crossed her legs, revealing one delicate foot and ankle, silk-stockinged with taupe, and shod with a coral satin slipper with a silver heel and a great silver buckle. On Viola's fair round neck the Carew corals lay bloomingly; her beautiful arms were clasped with them; a great coral brooch with wonderful carving confined a graceful fold of the taupe over one hip, a coral comb surmounted the shining waves of Viola's hair. Viola was an ash-blonde, her complexion was as roses, and the corals were ideal for her. As Jane regarded her friend's beauty, however, the fact that Viola was not young, that she was as old as herself, hid it and overshadowed it.

"Well, Jane, don't you think I look well in the corals, after all?" asked Viola, and there was something pitiful in her voice.

When a man or a woman holds fast to youth, even if success-fully, there is something of the pitiful and the tragic involved. It is the everlasting struggle of the soul to retain the joy of earth, whose fleeting distinguishes it from heaven, and whose retention is not ac-complished without an inner knowledge of its futility.

"I suppose you do, Viola," replied Jane Carew, with the inflexi-bility of fate, "but I really think that only very young girls ought to wear corals."

Viola laughed, but the laugh had a minor cadence. "But I *am* a young girl, Jane," she said. "I *must* be a young girl. I never had any girlhood when I should have had. You know that."

Viola had married, when very young, a man old enough to be her father, and her wedded life had been a sad affair, to which, however, she seldom alluded. Viola had much pride with regard to the in-evitable past.

"Yes," agreed Jane. Then she added, feeling that more might be expected, "Of course I suppose that marrying so very young does make a difference."

"Yes," said Viola, "it does. In fact, it makes of one's girlhood an anti-climax, of which many dispute the wisdom, as you do. But have it I will. Jane, your amethysts are beautiful."

Jane regarded the clear purple gleam of a stone on her arm. "Yes," she agreed, "Aunt Felicia's amethysts have always been con-sidered very beautiful."

"And such a full set," said Viola.

"Yes," said Jane. She colored a little, but Viola did not know why. At the last moment Jane had decided not to wear the amethyst comb, because it seemed to her altogether too decorative for a woman of her age, and she was afraid to mention it to Viola. She was sure that Viola would laugh at her and insist upon her wear-ing it.

"The ear-rings are lovely," said Viola. "My dear, I don't see how you ever consented to have your ears pierced."

"I was very young, and my mother wished me to," replied Jane, blushing.

The door-bell rang. Viola had been covertly listening for it all the time. Soon a very beautiful young man came with a curious dancing step into the room. Harold Lind always gave the effect of dancing when he walked. He always, moreover, gave the effect of extreme youth and of the utmost joy and mirth in life itself. He regarded everything and everybody with a smile as of humorous appreciation, and yet the appreciation was so good-natured that it offended nobody.

"Look at me—I am absurd and happy; look at yourself, also absurd and happy; look at everybody else likewise; look at life—a jest so delicious that it is quite worth one's while dying to be made acquainted with it." That is what Harold Lind seemed to say. Viola Longstreet became even more youthful under his gaze; even Jane Carew regretted that she had not worn her amethyst comb and began to doubt its unsuitability. Viola very soon called the young man's attention to Jane's amethysts, and Jane always wondered why she did not then mention the comb. She removed a brooch and a bracelet for him to inspect.

"They are really wonderful," he declared. "I have never seen greater depth of color in amethysts."

"Mr. Lind is an authority on jewels," declared Viola. The young man shot a curious glance at her, which Jane remembered long afterward. It was one of those glances which are as keystones to situations.

Harold looked at the purple stones with the expression of a child with a toy. There was much of the child in the young man's whole appearance, but of a mischievous and beautiful child, of whom his mother might observe, with adoration and ill-concealed boastfulness, "I can never tell what that child will do next!"

Harold returned the bracelet and brooch to Jane, and smiled at her as if amethysts were a lovely purple joke between her and himself, uniting them by a peculiar bond of fine understanding. "Exquisite, Miss Carew," he said. Then he looked at Viola. "Those corals suit you wonderfully, Mrs. Longstreet," he observed, "but amethysts would also suit you."

"Not with this gown," replied Viola, rather pitifully. There was something in the young man's gaze and tone which she did not understand, but which she vaguely quivered before.

Harold certainly thought the corals were too young for Viola. Jane understood, and felt an unworthy triumph. Harold, who was young enough in actual years to be Viola's son, and was younger still by reason of his disposition, was amused by the sight of her in corals, although he did not intend to betray his amusement. He considered Viola in corals as too rude a jest to share with her. Had poor Viola once grasped Harold Lind's estimation of her she would have as soon gazed upon herself in her coffin. Harold's comprehension of the essentials was beyond Jane Carew's. It was fairly ghastly, partaking of the nature of X-rays, but it never disturbed Harold Lind. He went along his dance-track undisturbed, his blue eyes never losing their high lights of glee, his lips never losing their inscrutable smile at some happy understanding between life and himself. Harold had fair hair, which was very smooth and glossy. His skin was like a girl's. He was so beautiful that he showed cleverness in an affectation of carelessness in dress. He did not like to wear evening clothes, because they had necessarily to be immaculate. That evening Jane regarded him with an inward criticism that he was too handsome for a man. She told Viola so when the dinner was over and he and the other guests had gone.

"He is very handsome," she said, "but I never like to see a man quite so handsome."

"You will change your mind when you see him in tweeds," returned Viola. "He loathes evening clothes."

Jane regarded her anxiously. There was something in Viola's tone which disturbed and shocked her. It was inconceivable that Viola should be in love with that youth, and yet— "He looks very young," said Jane in a prim voice.

"He *is* young," admitted Viola; "still, not quite so young as he looks. Sometimes I tell him he will look like a boy if he lives to be eighty."

"Well, he must be very young," persisted Jane.

"Yes," said Viola, but she did not say how young. Viola herself, now that the excitement was over, did not look so young as at the beginning of the evening. She removed the corals, and Jane considered that she looked much better without them.

"Thank you for your corals, dear," said Viola. "Where is Margaret?"

Margaret answered for herself by a tap on the door. She and Viola's maid, Louisa, had been sitting on an upper landing, out of sight, watching the guests down-stairs. Margaret took the corals and placed them in their nest in the jewel-case, also the amethysts, after Viola had gone. The jewel-case was a curious old affair with many compartments. The amethysts required two. The comb was so large that it had one for itself. That was the reason why Margaret did not discover that evening that it was gone. Nobody discovered it for three days, when Viola had a little card-party. There was a whist-table for Jane, who had never given up the reserved and stately game. There were six tables in Viola's pretty living-room, with a little conservatory at one end and a leaping hearth fire at the other. Jane's partner was a stout old gentleman whose wife was shrieking with merriment at an auction-bridge table. The other whist-players were a stupid, very small young man who was aimlessly willing to play anything, and an amiable young woman who believed in self-denial. Jane played conscientiously. She returned trump leads, and played second hand low, and third high, and it was not until the third rubber was over that she saw. It had been in full evidence from the first. Jane would have seen it before the guests arrived, but Viola had not put it in her hair until the last moment. Viola was wild with delight, yet shamefaced and a trifle uneasy. In a soft, white gown, with violets at her waist, she was playing with Harold Lind, and in her ash-blond hair was Jane Carew's amethyst comb. Jane gasped and paled. The amiable young woman who was her opponent stared at her. Finally she spoke in a low voice.

"Aren't you well, Miss Carew?" she asked.

The men, in their turn, stared. The stout one rose fussily. "Let me get a glass of water," he said. The stupid small man stood up and waved his hands with nervousness.

"Aren't you well?" asked the amiable young lady again.

Then Jane Carew recovered her poise. It was seldom that she lost it. "I am quite well, thank you, Miss Murdock," she replied. "I believe diamonds are trumps."

They all settled again to the play, but the young lady and the two men continued glancing at Miss Carew. She had recovered her dignity of manner, but not her color. Moreover, she had a bewildered expression. Resolutely she abstained from glancing again at her amethyst comb in Viola Longstreet's ash-blond hair, and gradually, by a course of subconscious reasoning as she carefully played her cards, she arrived at a conclusion which caused her color to return and the bewildered expression to disappear. When refreshments were served, the amiable young lady said, kindly:

"You look quite yourself, now, dear Miss Carew, but at one time while we were playing I was really alarmed. You were very pale."

"I did not feel in the least ill," replied Jane Carew. She smiled her Carew smile at the young lady. Jane had settled it with herself that of course Viola had borrowed that amethyst comb, appealing to Margaret. Viola ought not to have done that; she should have asked her, Miss Carew; and Jane wondered, because Viola was very well bred; but of course that was what had happened. Jane had come down before Viola, leaving Margaret in her room, and Viola had asked her. Jane did not then remember that Viola had not even been told that there was an amethyst comb in existence. She remembered when Margaret, whose face was as pale and bewildered as her own, mentioned it, when she was brushing her hair.

"I saw it, first thing, Miss Jane," said Margaret. "Louisa and I were on the landing, and I looked down and saw your amethyst comb in Mrs. Longstreet's hair."

"She had asked you for it, because I had gone down-stairs?" asked Jane, feebly.

"No, Miss Jane. I had not seen her. I went out right after you did. Louisa had finished Mrs. Longstreet, and she and I went down to the mailbox to post a letter, and then we sat on the landing, and—I saw your comb."

"Have you," asked Jane, "looked in the jewel-case?"

"Yes, Miss Jane."

"And it is not there?"

"It is not there, Miss Jane." Margaret spoke with a sort of solemn intoning. She recognized what the situation implied, and she, who fitted squarely and entirely into her humble state, was aghast before a hitherto unimagined occurrence. She could not, even with the evidence of her senses against a lady and her mistress's old friend, believe in them. Had Jane told her firmly that she had not seen that comb in that ash-blond hair she might have been hypnotized into agreement. But Jane simply stared at her, and the Carew dignity was more shaken than she had ever seen it.

"Bring the jewel-case here, Margaret," ordered Jane in a gasp.

Margaret brought the jewel-case, and everything was taken out; all the compartments were opened, but the amethyst comb was not there. Jane could not sleep that night. At dawn she herself doubted the evidence of her senses. The jewel-case was thoroughly overlooked again, and still Jane was incredulous that she would ever see her comb in Viola's hair again. But that evening, although there were no guests except Harold Lind, who dined at the house, Viola appeared in a pink-tinted gown, with a knot of violets at her waist, and—she wore the amethyst comb. She said not one word concerning it; nobody did. Harold Lind was in wild spirits. The conviction grew upon Jane that the irresponsible, beautiful youth was covertly amusing himself at her, at Viola's, at everybody's expense. Perhaps he included himself. He talked incessantly, not in reality brilliantly, but with an effect of sparkling effervescence which was fairly dazzling. Viola's servants restrained with difficulty their laughter at his sallies. Viola regarded Harold with ill-concealed tenderness and admiration. She herself looked even younger than usual, as if the innate youth in her leaped to meet this charming comrade.

Jane felt sickened by it all. She could not understand her friend. Not for one minute did she dream that there could be any serious outcome of the situation; that Viola would marry this mad youth, who, she knew, was making such covert fun at her expense; but she was bewildered and indignant. She wished that she had not come. That evening when she went to her room she directed Margaret to pack, as she intended to return home the next day. Margaret began folding gowns with alacrity. She was as conservative as her mistress and she severely disapproved of many things. However, the matter of the amethyst comb was uppermost in her mind. She was wild with curiosity. She hardly dared inquire, but finally she did.

"About the amethyst comb, ma'am?" she said, with a delicate cough.

"What about it, Margaret?" returned Jane, severely.

"I thought perhaps Mrs. Longstreet had told you how she happened to have it."

Poor Jane Carew had nobody in whom to confide. For once she spoke her mind to her maid. "She has not said one word. And, oh, Margaret, I don't know what to think of it."

Margaret pursed her lips.

"What do *you* think, Margaret?"

"I don't know, Miss Jane."

"I don't."

"I did not mention it to Louisa," said Margaret.

"Oh, I hope not!" cried Jane.

"But she did to me," said Margaret. "She asked had I seen Miss Viola's new comb, and then she laughed, and I thought from the way she acted that—" Margaret hesitated.

"That what?"

"That she meant Mr. Lind had given Miss Viola the comb."

Jane started violently. "Absolutely impossible!" she cried. "That, of course, is nonsense. There must be some explanation. Probably Mrs. Longstreet will explain before we go."

Mrs. Longstreet did not explain. She wondered and expostulated when Jane announced her firm determination to leave, but she seemed utterly at a loss for the reason. She did not mention the comb.

When Jane Carew took leave of her old friend she was entirely sure in her own mind that she would never visit her again—might never even see her again.

Jane was unutterably thankful to be back in her own peaceful home, over which no shadow of absurd mystery brooded; only a calm afternoon light of life, which disclosed gently but did not conceal or betray. Jane settled back into her pleasant life, and the days passed, and the weeks, and the months, and the years. She heard nothing whatever from or about Viola Longstreet for three years. Then, one day, Margaret returned from the city, and she had met Viola's old maid Louisa in a department store, and she had news. Jane wished for strength to refuse to listen, but she could not muster it. She listened while Margaret brushed her hair.

"Louisa has not been with Miss Viola for a long time," said Margaret. "She is living with somebody else. Miss Viola lost her money, and had to give up her house and her servants, and Louisa said she cried when she said good-by."

Jane made an effort. "What became of—" she began.

Margaret answered the unfinished sentence. She was excited by gossip as by a stimulant. Her thin cheeks burned, her eyes blazed. "Mr. Lind," said Margaret, "Louisa told me, had turned out to be real bad. He got into some money trouble, and then"—Margaret lowered her voice—"he was arrested for taking a lot of money which didn't belong to him. Louisa said he had been in some business where he handled a lot of other folks' money, and he cheated the men who were in the business with him, and he was tried, and Miss Viola, Louisa thinks, hid away somewhere so they wouldn't call her to testify, and then he had to go to prison; but—" Margaret hesitated.

"What is it?" asked Jane.

"Louisa thinks he died about a year and a half ago. She heard the lady where she lives now talking about it. The lady used to know Miss Viola, and she heard the lady say Mr. Lind had died in prison, that he couldn't stand the hard life, and that Miss Viola had lost all her money through him, and then"—Margaret hesitated again, and her mistress prodded sharply—"Louisa said that she heard the lady say that she had thought Miss Viola would marry him, but she hadn't, and she had more sense than she had thought."

"Mrs. Longstreet would never for one moment have entertained the thought of marrying Mr. Lind; he was young enough to be her grandson," said Jane, severely.

"Yes, ma'am," said Margaret.

It so happened that Jane went to New York that day week, and at a jewelry counter in one of the shops she discovered the amethyst comb. There were on sale a number of bits of antique jewelry, the precious flotsam and jetsam of old and wealthy families which had drifted, nobody knew before what currents of adversity, into that harbor of sale for all the world to see. Jane made no inquiries; the saleswoman volunteered simply the information that the comb was a real antique, and the stones were real amethysts and pearls, and the setting was solid gold, and the price was thirty dollars; and Jane bought it. She carried her old amethyst comb home, but she did not show it to anybody. She replaced it in its old compartment in her jewel-case and thought of it with wonder, with a hint of joy at regaining it, and with much sadness. She was still fond of Viola Longstreet. Jane did not easily part with her loves. She did not know where Viola was. Margaret had inquired of Louisa, who did not know. Poor Viola had probably drifted into some obscure harbor of life wherein she was hiding until life was over.

And then Jane met Viola one spring day on Fifth Avenue.

"It is a very long time since I have seen you," said Jane with a reproachful accent, but her eyes were tenderly inquiring.

"Yes," agreed Viola. Then she added, "I have seen nobody. Do you know what a change has come in my life?" she asked.

"Yes, dear," replied Jane, gently. "My Margaret met Louisa once and she told her."

"Oh yes—Louisa," said Viola. "I had to discharge her. My money is about gone. I have only just enough to keep the wolf from entering the door of a hall bedroom in a respectable boarding-house. However, I often hear him howl, but I do not mind at all. In fact, the howling has become company for me. I rather like it. It is queer what things one can learn to like. There are a few left yet, like the awful heat in summer, and the food, which I do not fancy, but that is simply a matter of time."

Viola's laugh was like a bird's song—a part of her—and nothing except death could silence it for long.

"Then," said Jane, "you stay in New York all summer?"

Viola laughed again. "My dear," she replied, "of course. It is all very simple. If I left New York, and paid board anywhere, I would never have enough money to buy my return fare, and certainly not to keep that wolf from my hall-bedroom door."

"Then," said Jane, "you are going home with me."

"I cannot consent to accept charity, Jane," said Viola. "Don't ask me."

Then, for the first time in her life, Viola Longstreet saw Jane Carew's eyes blaze with anger. "You dare to call it charity coming from me to you?" she said, and Viola gave in.

When Jane saw the little room where Viola lived, she marveled, with the exceedingly great marveling of a woman to whom love of a man has never come, at a woman who could give so much and with no return.

Little enough to pack had Viola. Jane understood with a shudder of horror that it was almost destitution, not poverty, to which her old friend was reduced.

"You shall have that northeast room which you always liked," she told Viola when they were on the train.

"The one with the old-fashioned peacock paper, and the pine-tree growing close to one window?" said Viola, happily.

Jane and Viola settled down to life together, and Viola, despite the tragedy which she had known, realized a peace and happiness beyond her imagination. In reality, although she still looked so youthful, she was old enough to enjoy the pleasures of later life. Enjoy them she did to the utmost. She and Jane made calls together, entertained friends at small and stately dinners, and gave little teas. They drove about in the old Carew carriage. Viola had some new clothes. She played very well on Jane's old piano. She embroidered, she gardened. She lived the sweet, placid life of an older lady in a little village, and loved it. She never mentioned Harold Lind.

Not among the vicious of the earth was poor Harold Lind; rather among those of such beauty and charm that the earth spoils them, making them, in their own estimation, free guests at all its tables of bounty. Moreover, the young man had, deeply rooted in his character, the traits of a mischievous child, rejoicing in his mischief more from a sense of humor so keen that it verged on cruelty than from any intention to harm others. Over that affair of the amethyst comb, for instance, his irresponsible, selfish, childish soul had fairly reveled in glee. He had not been fond of Viola, but he liked her fondness for himself. He had made sport of her, but only for his own entertainment—never for the entertainment of others. He was a beautiful creature, seeking out paths of pleasure and folly for himself alone, which ended as do all paths of earthly pleasure and folly. Harold had admired Viola, but from the same point of view as Jane Carew's. Viola had, when she looked her youngest and best, always seemed so old as to be venerable to him. He had at times compunctions, as if he were making a jest of his grandmother. Viola never knew the truth about the amethyst comb. He had considered that one of the best frolics of his life. He had simply purloined it and presented it to Viola, and merrily left matters to settle themselves.

Viola and Jane had lived together a month before the comb was mentioned. Then one day Viola was in Jane's room and the jewel-case was out, and she began examining its contents. When she found the amethyst comb she gave a little cry. Jane, who had been seated at her desk and had not seen what was going on, turned around.

Viola stood holding the comb, and her cheeks were burning. She fondled the trinket as if it had been a baby. Jane watched her. She began to understand the bare facts of the mystery of the disappearance of her amethyst comb, but the subtlety of it was forever beyond her. Had the other woman explained what was in her mind, in her heart—how that reckless young man whom she had loved had given her the treasure because he had heard her admire Jane's amethysts, and she, all unconscious of any wrong-doing, had ever regarded it as the one evidence of his thoughtful tenderness, it being the one gift she had ever received from him; how she parted with it, as she had parted with her other jewels, in order to obtain money to purchase comforts for him while he was in prison—Jane could not have understood. The fact of an older woman being fond of a young man, almost a boy, was beyond her mental grasp. She had no imagination with which to comprehend that innocent, pathetic, almost terrible love of one who has trodden the earth long for one who has just set dancing feet upon it. It was noble of Jane Carew that, lacking all such imagination, she acted as she did: that, although she did not, could not, formulate it to herself, she would no more have deprived the other woman and the dead man of that one little unscathed bond of tender goodness than she would have robbed his grave of flowers.

Viola looked at her. "I cannot tell you all about it; you would laugh at me," she whispered; "but this was mine once."

"It is yours now, dear," said Jane.

A Retreat to the Goal

HE TRAMPED SLOWLY yet sturdily. He had set for himself exactly the sort of pace which a shrewd mind had ordained that his well-worn bones and muscles could keep up for a tramp of many miles. He kept to the pace.

He was a prodigal of a new variety. He had been on the verge of success. The least said about the quality of that success the better; yet success it would have been. And at the very threshold the man had turned himself about and beat that most ignominious and most glorious retreat of humanity, the retreat of the sinner from the strongholds and fleshpots of sin.

John Dunn could not have told why he had turned about. It was as if some power outside himself, yet projected by himself, had exerted a compelling force before which he was helpless. The day before he had not even dreamed of taking this course. He had been with comrades, enjoying to the full that glimpse of the verge of ill-wrought success.

The man had risen before dawn with his new resolve upon him. He had risen and set forth. He had the clothes he wore, and a little money in his pocket. Secure as he had been of the golden shower, he had lost recklessly at cards the night before. His clothes were unbefitting his manner of return. As soon as the shops were opened he stopped and made a purchase and sale. He emerged from the shop clad in the rough garb of a countryman, with not so much money in his pocket.

He was hardly past middle age; but he looked old with the keen light of the spring morning in his face.

Suddenly he was aware of a soft, padding movement behind him. He glanced over his shoulder and saw a small mongrel dog, brown and thin, with hide glistening in the sun. The dog looked up at him as if he were a god. He was so pathetically humble and beseeching and worshipful that the man started. His own unworthiness of anything like that, even in the understanding of a poor little mongrel dog, smote him fully for the first time. In the eyes of the dog he saw himself, and was shamed to the core.

The dog lay down and rolled in the spring grass, four little paws waving imploringly. The man spoke kindly, and the dog rose. He leaped to the man's caressing hand. John remembered a dog of his childhood, and he immediately named this stranger. "Hullo, Rover!" said he. The dog acted as if he had always followed the call of love and mastery by that name.

John Dunn's face was happier as he walked on with the dog at heel. He thought of the superstition of his boyhood—"It is good luck to have a dog follow one."

The man and the dog progressed until high noon. Then they stopped in a place of sheer beauty. The man, gazing about, had a dazed feeling that it was unreal. The man and the dog sat beside a clear brook flowing, with breaks to the light like facets of brown jewels, over a bed of smooth pebbles. The brook flowed through a meadowland, and its banks were blue with violets.

John Dunn had stopped at a country grocery and bought crackers and cheese. He divided with the dog. Then both ate, the dog with nose buried in violets. Then the man hollowed a hand and drank of the brook, which was sweet and cold. The dog crept close to the gently flowing water and lapped, too. Then the man lay back among the violets, the dog snuggled close, and both slept.

After an hour they woke and resumed their march. High purpose had so strengthened in the soul of the man that he felt almost intoxicated by it. Every now and then he broke from his even pace and almost leaped along. At such times the dog would scurry ahead and return with lithe bounds, barking.

They went on until near sunset. It was true country now, a rolling farming land, with small villages pricked out by white church-spires, then farm-houses on the outskirts. John Dunn began to think about a place for the night. As with all wayfarers, his mind turned instinctively to a barn or a haystack. He had not enough money to pay for a lodging. He began to scrutinize the wayside. He saw no straw-stacks. He approached a large, white farm-house, with well-kept outbuildings. He decided that this could be no place for him. It had too prosperous a look.

As he passed the cow-barn a man with milk-pails crossed the yard to the house. He had closed the doors upon the rows of switching tails of sleek Jerseys and Holsteins. Everything was being made snug for the peaceful night.

John Dunn, as he came opposite the gate in the trim white fence which inclosed the front yard of the farm-house, was arrested by a woman's voice, shrill, tense, yet sweet.

"Good evening," came the words, as if addressed to a well-known neighbor.

A tall, thin, elderly woman, with a strange, unquenchable youth in her eager blue eyes, was standing at the gate.

John Dunn lifted his hat. "Good evening, madam," he returned.

The woman seemed greatly flattered. Never in all her life had she been dubbed "madam." She smiled tightly with her thin lips. She opened the gate. "Goin' far?" she inquired, with almost fierce friendliness.

John Dunn heard a spit of hostility, and saw a large Maltese cat, back up and tail enormous, waving like a battle-flag, with great eyes of fear and hatred upon his dog. The dog got behind him, tail between its legs. The woman picked up a stick and shooed the cat, which fled like a gray shadow close to the ground, then clawed up a tree.

"He'll stay up there all night," remarked the woman. "He always does when he sees a dog. It won't hurt him. It ain't cold. We don't keep no dog, and the cat is awful scared of one. I like dogs. I'd have a dog, but Pa don't like dogs. I'd like a dog, as this place is rather lonesome, and tramps come along. You don't look like a tramp."

The woman ended her statement with a faint, apologetic note of interrogation, and John Dunn looked at her perplexedly. He wondered if he were a tramp.

The woman continued hastily. "I'm sorry I spoke so," said she. "Of course I kin see you ain't no tramp. Do come right in. Where did you say you was goin'?"

"To Bixby Corners," replied John Dunn.

"Why, you don't say so!" cried the woman. "Why, I've got folks there! I was there two months ago. But that's over fifty miles away. You don't mean to walk there?"

John said something feebly about taking his time. The woman nodded knowingly and laughed.

"Oh, I see," said she. "You're one of them over-stout folks tryin' to walk it off. But you can't git to Bixby Corners to-night. You come right in. Pa and me and Billy have had our supper, but it ain't no trouble at all to git you something."

"If," said John, "you could let me sleep in the barn——"

The woman tossed her head affrontedly. "Me and my husband don't ask folks to sleep in no barn," said she, "when we've got two nice, clean spare chambers. You walk right in." She pushed the gate open.

John Dunn walked in, with his dog following. The woman led the way around the house to the side-door. She opened it and entered. John hesitated. He looked doubtfully at the poor little cringing dog.

"Oh, land sake! let the dog come in, too," said the woman. "He can go out in the kitchen, and Abby will give him some supper. Billy has just brought in the milk, too, and he will like some of that. He's a dreadful thin dog. What's his name?"

"Rover."

"Rover, Rover, Rover," called the woman. The dog came at her call, shaking his lean hind quarters and wagging violently.

"He acts like a real nice dog," said the woman, "and Abby and Billy set a lot by dogs."

She opened a door at her left. "Abby," said she, "here's a dog that belongs to this gentleman. Give him plenty of supper, and the gentleman 'ain't had no supper, either. Jest mix up a few more flapjacks, while I set a plate for him in the dinin'-room. Come right in, mister."

John followed the woman into a room where a very large old man sat, quite filling up a great rocking-chair.

"Here, Pa. I've brought you company," said the woman. "I stopped this gentleman from goin' to the Elm House at Wayne. He's goin' to stay here."

"How do you find yourself?" came a gruff voice from the chair. John saw a rather vague face, fringed with a white beard and smiling. Pa was always ready with his smile.

John said something indistinctly about kindness and hesitating to accept so much hospitality.

"Ma is tickled to death to hev comp'ny," said he. "She's sort of lonesome, 'specially since our daughter Laury married an' went away. Billy is a good boy, but he ain't no talker, and Ma likes to hev talkin'. I wa'n't never no talker myself, an' Billy takes arter me, I reckon. Laury was a real lively talker. Set down."

John Dunn sat down. He had never been so absolutely embarrassed in his life as he was before these simple people and their simple hospitality.

The woman ran in and lit a lamp. "Here's a lamp, and you kin see enough to talk," said she. "Supper will be ready before long. Your dog was 'most starved."

The old man stirred uneasily. "Dog?" said he.

"Now, Pa," said the woman, "don't you git excited. It's a real nice, safe little dog; and your cat's up the apple-tree, and thar ain't no call for you to worry."

The woman flew out, her cotton skirts swishing. John Dunn looked about him. A sudden memory smote him with a pang. He might have been in his old boyhood home.

He sat silent, while the old man at the window nodded approvingly at him. "I see you ain't much more of a talker than I be," he said. "Wall, that's right. Let the wimmen folks talk. Men ain't so much given that way. Natur' is natur'."

Then the woman came in with a joyful stir and announced supper, and John followed her into the dining-room, and again history repeated itself, almost to his undoing. Oh, how many suppers like that he had eaten before his wild blood had leaped barriers and his feet had gone astray!

It required all the man's resolution to overmaster that uncanny sense of having eaten recently this identical meal, but he was equal to it. He was, in reality, hungry, and his boyhood relish for boyhood food came back in a flood. He ate, and the woman watched, in the homely rapture of her kind, the feeding of a male creature.

Billy, the son, came in, and she said, simply, "This is my son; Billy, this is the gentleman who is goin' to stay here to-night."

"Glad to see ye," said the man. He was an old-young man who looked like his mother and spoke like his father.

Suddenly John Dunn remembered that these kindly people did not know his name. He also remembered in a flash that the woman had said she knew people in Bixby Corners. He had lied many times in his life, but never had a lie come so hard as the lie he now told.

"You don't even know my name," said he.

Mother and son nodded, and looked interrogatively at him.

"My name," said John Dunn, "is David Mann."

The door opened, and a woman of about the same age as his hostess entered. She was tightly trussed in starched calico.

"Abby, this gentleman is Mr. Mann," said the other woman.

"Abby is some relation to me on my mother's side," said the woman. "She lives with me, and we do the work together. I ain't able to do it alone, and it is so much nicer than keepin' a hired girl." She regarded Abby affectionately. The shadow of a smile flickered over Abby's face.

John Dunn finished his supper. Then he returned to the sitting-room and remained there in absolute silence with the old man and Billy, listening to the faint click of the supper-dishes being washed.

Then the woman and Abby entered and seated themselves, and a very strange thing happened. John Dunn, sitting there, heard the story of his own life, up to a certain point, from the woman. He listened, and realized a queer torture, as from viewing himself in some awful mirror of absolute truth.

The woman talked, with no intermission. She discoursed of the village of Bixby Corners, where John Dunn had been born. Her daughter Laura had married and gone there to live; and she had had an uncle who had lived there during a long life, and brought up a large family. John remembered them.

The woman discoursed upon the family into which her daughter had married, the Upton family, and John remembered them. Then the woman gave a summary of the whole village. She had often visited there in her youth. John began to have a vague impression of having seen her there. She knew about everything, either first-hand or from hearsay, that had happened in Bixby Corners for half a century.

And—she knew about John Dunn! He sat there and listened, with that sensation of strange torture, when she got to that.

"Old Gorham Dunn keeps the store in Bixby Corners," said she. "He's so old he can't do much now, but he gits there every morning and sets. His son Frank tends mostly to the business now, but they say he 'ain't got no business head, though he's as stiddy as a clock an' means real well. Laury says the business is all runnin' behind. Laury said she pitied old Mis' Dunn an' old Mr. Dunn, an' Minnie, too; thar's a daughter. They had a real nice place, a big house with a tower and two bay-windows in front; an' it 'ain't been painted for years, an' the roof leaks. They had a son named John, an' they give him every advantage. They sent him to college, an' had him l'arn a profession—had to mortgage the place to git the money.

"And Laury says folks don't think they've been keepin' up with the interest, an' them poor old folks will lose their home. It is real pitiful, Laury says, but that good-for-nothin' boy's ma don't never speak of him. It's been years sense he run wild and went off, and they never heard any good of him till they begun to hear nothin' at all. They don't know whether he's alive or dead, but Laury says that folks say that his ma has kep' his room up for him—had that papered and the plaster mended when the paper an' plaster was droppin' off every other room in the house. I guess there ain't no doubt them poor old folks is jest livin' in the hopes that that miserable poor tool will come back an' be petted jest the way the one was in the Bible."

The woman paused for breath, and Abby unexpectedly spoke.

"I never took no stock at all in that prodigal son," said she. "Eatin' a fatted calf, an' bein' dressed up. Hm! He'd been better wuth while if he'd hustled 'round an' put on overalls, an' done the chores, an' sold that calf an' made his pa and ma buy somethin' they'd been doin' without on account of his foolishness."

"Scripter is Scripter," said Abby's mistress, "and what don't seem sense to us is jest because we don't understand. It don't make much odds, nohow, I guess. I reckon that scalawag ain't never goin' to go back, nor let his poor old pa and ma pass away easy, nohow."

The old man snored explosively in his chair. John welcomed the guttural snort. The woman ceased talking about Bixby Corners. She sprang up.

"It's past Pa's bedtime; an' the gentleman must be all tuckered out, too," she said.

Pa woke up. "I 'ain't been asleep," he said. "I heard every word ye've said. Ye've talked a real stiddy streak, Ma, but you don't often git such a chance."

"I don't see much company," agreed the woman. "I'd like it if somebody would drop in this way oftener."

In a few moments John Dunn found himself in what was evidently the very best guest-room in the house. It duplicated the best guest-room in his father's house—but not his own room. He had had that fitted up, after he went to college, in a fashion that aroused both admiration and alarm among Bixby Corners people.

John heard the house astir at an early hour, and he rose. That morning his determination was so tense that it almost seemed evident. After breakfast he bade the people good-by, with shamed gratitude, and took again to the highway with his dog.

That night he and the dog slept in a barn. They reached Bixby Corners two days later, in the afternoon. John walked straight to the store, the queer store of such nondescript merchandise as to be almost incredible. Over the door of the long frame building was the sign:

GORHAM DUNN.
GROCERIES AND DRYGOODS.
Hay and Feed.   Brooms.   Tin and Wooden Ware.

John had often laughed at the sign, designed by his poor father to be comprehensive of what was almost incomprehensible. He did not laugh now. He saw a child's gaily trimmed hat in one of the windows, beside tomato-cans, a bolt of calico, and a stack of brooms and gardening utensils, and his stern mouth did not relax. He even remembered how a discarded pulpit from the Congregational church had been kept in the back of the store, without the slightest reversion to the old mirth.

The day was quite warm. The store door stood open. Two men sat on a settee on the sloping piazza. One sat on a keg beside the door.

John advanced and looked blankly at the old man, who looked blankly at him. Then John saw his own father also in the door, seated farther back in an arm-chair. Gorham Dunn's old head lopped over on his breast. He was napping.

"Hullo!" said the other old man, and Gorham roused himself. He looked at his own son with absolute lack of recognition.

"Hullo, Frank!" he called, rather feebly.

John Dunn's brother Frank, lean and lank and homely, with an expression of patience that was almost forcible, came forward. He did not know his brother. He gave the usual interrogative grunt of the country merchant to an unknown customer.

John spoke. "I don't want to buy anythin'," said he, instinctively adopting the dialect. "I want a job in the store."

His father straightened up and looked at him. The other old man stopped chewing and stared at him with dim blue eyes. The men on the settee rose and came forward. Frank Dunn and his father looked at each other.

"Ask him if he knows anythin' about keepin' store," said the old man. His mouth trembled a little and his eyes twitched. Frank asked.

"Orter," replied David Mann, who had been John Dunn. "Brung up in the business. My own father kep' a store like enough to this to be its own brother."

"Ask him ef he used to tend store fur his father," said Gorham Dunn. Frank asked.

"Hed to when I was a young man," replied David Mann. "Got a whalin' ef I didn't."

"Ask him ef he's kep' on tendin' store," said the old man. Frank asked.

"Been in business for myself in town," replied David. "Pardner wasn't no good. He lit out, and I've come huntin' a job, when I'm gittin' over bein' young, too."

The loafers laughed at the feeble joke.

Gorham Dunn and his son Frank talked apart. The old man had risen from his arm-chair and the two had withdrawn to the back of the store. The old man's voice was heard, quite strong and shrill. "Ask him what he wants fur pay."

Frank shambled forward and asked.

"Gosh-a-mighty! 'Most anythin' that 'll keep me from starvin'," replied David. The little dog, snuggled close to him, wagged propitiatingly, as if he understood every word.

Finally David Mann, otherwise John Dunn, was engaged to work in his father's store.

Gorham Dunn was a bit distrustful. He wished to keep this stranger under his own roof. It was arranged that David was to occupy an attic room, unfinished but comfortable enough, which he remembered well. The hired man used to occupy it; but the days of hired men for the Dunn family were over.

Gorham and Frank had discussed putting David in one of the spare rooms, but had met with strenuous objection.

"Ef," said David, "you ain't got some sort of hole under the ruff where you can stow me away, me and my dog will light out. Room up in the garret was plenty good enough for the man that tended my father's store when I was a boy, an' I guess it's good enough for me."

David took off his coat. A wagon laden with bags of seed-corn had drawn up in front of the store. He helped his brother and the farmer who brought the corn to unload; then he and his brother stowed it away, and he assisted in selling the farmer some groceries. He was secretly elated at his own handiness. He was also surprised, but he need not have been. It was that very versatility, that power of adaptation to all situations, which had been largely instrumental in the wreck of his life. It was not at all wonderful that the same agency which had wrecked might build.

When David went home with his father that night he was conscious of an almost childish fear. Suppose his mother should recognize him? Suppose his sister Minnie should? He had learned that Minnie was still at home, unmarried. Old Man Dunn was garrulous.

"Minnie was keepin' company with a real likely young man when she was a girl," he told his new assistant. "Then somethin' come up. Minnie was real proud and high-strung an' she wouldn't stand much. She wouldn't give in an inch, and that was the end on't.

I reckon she felt it some, but she never let on. Dunno what her ma and me would hev done without her ef she had got married and gone away, though."

The Dunn house had been originally one of the finest and most pretentious in the village. Now the returning son viewed it with a pang. It was suffering, as human dwellings seem actually to suffer, from premature old age. Gorham Dunn had built the house before his beloved son had come of age. The son knew well enough that it represented his poor father's old proud hopes of him and their decline. The returning man looked at the house, and seemed to see in its dingy walls from which the glossy white paint had either disappeared or was evident in blisters of decay, in its sagging roof from which a zigzag weather stain of some old, fierce storm came down the south wall, in a chimney which needed topping, in the doorstep which creaked beneath his unworthy feet, a faithful symbol of himself in his utter failure.

"Go easy on that step," advised his father. "Frank has got to fix it, now you've come. He 'ain't had a minute. That step ain't safe. It'll land somebody with a broken leg ef it ain't fixed."

"I kin fix it," said the new-comer, eagerly. "I'll git up early to-morrer an' fix it, ef you'll give me a hammer an' some nails an' ends of boards."

"Then you're handy?"

"Always was."

The old man sighed. "My other son was," he said. "He was born handy. He went to college an' learned a profession, so he didn't naturally do much with his hands, but he was born handy." The old man pointed to something in an apple-tree near the door. "See that bird-house?" he said. "My other son made that. It's got two rooms, an' the wrens come back to it every year."

The man looked. How he remembered! The memory seemed to tear his heart. Then they entered the house. "Come right in," said old man Dunn.

David followed him. The side-door led into an entry. There was a black-walnut tree for hats and wraps. That black-walnut tree seemed, to the returned wanderer, a menace of memory. How many times he had hung his hat on it as he hung it now! On the left of the entry was the dining-room. David heard the clink of dishes.

"Minnie is gettin' supper," old man Dunn remarked. David understood there was no maid. He remembered two, always, before he had dissipated the family fortune.

On the right was the sitting-room. David followed his father in there. His mother sat beside the window.

"We've got a new man to work in the store, Ma," said Old Man Dunn. "He's used to tendin' store, an' it's goin' to take a heap off Frank and me."

The old woman beside the window looked up, and her returning son saw in her something very exquisite. The mother of them all had changed the most, but she had changed for wonderful beauty, surpassing that of youth and prime. The son, who had not seen her for twenty years, started and paled. He would not have known his mother. All her pleasant, matronly curves were gone. She looked shorter. She was not such a very old woman, but she seemed to represent age fixed beyond any change until the final one, death. She was very slight. Her features were very small and clear. Her hair, still abundant, covered her little head like a cap of silver. She wore a soft black dress with a little pearl brooch at the throat. Her hands, in her lap, were not wrinkled, but so delicate and thin that they looked like pale flowers. The old woman suggested at once the most fragile loveliness and a wonderful strength that could enable such fragility to exist at all. She was like some delicate field-flower which, even to the winter winds and storms, will not completely yield up its personality, but still stands, a silvery semblance of its summer self, yielding yet unyielding.

The man's mother looked up at him, and he dropped his eyes before the dim blue outlook of hers.

"I'm glad you've got somebody to help, Pa," she said. Her voice had grown very thin. It was like a sweet wind-whisper through meadow-reeds. Then she added, directly to the man, "I hope you will make yourself at home."

He remembered that his mother had always spoken more correctly than his father. She had been fond of books. He remembered also his unspoken childish conviction that whatever discipline he had came from her, not from his adoring father.

"Thank you, ma'am," he said. Then the two pairs of eyes met. If she recognized her son, she made no sign.

"He says he wants to have the garret room, Ma," said Old Man Dunn.

"I think he will find it comfortable," said the old woman. "I remember Jane liked it. Jane was a hired girl we had for twelve years."

"He has a little dog, but you like dogs," said Old Man Dunn.

"I think there was a bone left from dinner," said the old woman, in her sweet, thin voice.

A bell rang. "Supper's ready," said Gorham Dunn.

David found his hardest encounter where he least expected it. Minnie had changed hardly at all. It was wonderful how little Minnie had changed in twenty years. She had kept her figure and her complexion and her pretty hair. Of course, Minnie was much younger than he. She had been a mere girl when he had left home, but—twenty years of wear and tear upon the fine skin of a woman, upon her silky hair, upon her tender figure—and to find her like this! David, looking at Minnie, and finding her so little changed, except in size, felt that she surely must at once recognize him.

But Minnie did not. If there were a lingering doubt about the mother, there was none about the sister. David sat at the table and ate supper with his own father and mother and sister, and, so far as any outward sign went, was absolutely unknown and unsuspected. However, the strain upon him was so great that he resolved, and was able to carry out his resolve, that in future Frank should eat with the family, and he would be the one to keep store and eat at the second table.

He had never been so relieved in his life as he was to find himself back at the store. Not many customers came before Frank returned from his own supper. By this time David knew that a rival grocery had been established a little farther down the road. He remembered the man who owned it as a fat boy, much freckled. His name was Silas Towns. Gorham Dunn and his son Frank were much perturbed by this competition, which was of recent date.

"Guess there won't be many customers; not so many but you can handle 'em," Frank told his brother as he set out for home. "Silas Towns is getting some of our best ones away. He don't keep any better stuff than we do, and he don't sell no cheaper, but his store is new and sort of fancy, and it don't take much to tole folks away."

Frank's voice rang sadly. He looked old and tired, and had the expression of those who have not tasted the savor of the joys of this life, only its duties. After he had gone David reflected that probably because of him his brother had missed his own birthright; had not married, nor had a glimpse of the world outside the little village and the rank old store.

David walked about the place, and did some thinking. He was a shrewd man, exceedingly quick-witted and full of expedients. It had been so much more to his discredit that he had made such a failure of his life. All the time he had known better and had been perfectly able to do better.

Finally he was disturbed by a customer. A man wanted to buy a bag of flour. David was perfectly competent to conclude that transaction.

"Goin' to clerk it here?" asked the man—a dry, lank fellow who owned a little farm on the river road. David remembered him.

"Reckon I'll make a try at it," he said.

"Well, I'm glad Frank and the old man hev got some help," said the customer. "Old man's been failin' lately, and Frank wa'n't never exactly cut out for storekeepin', though he's as good as they make 'em. He's 'most too good, and he 'ain't never had anything but drudgery. His folks spent everything on that good-for-nothin' John that went off and wa'n't never heard of afterward. Reckon he wound up in state prison. Everything had to go for him. T'other son didn't git nothin' but the hard work, an' nothin for doin' it. And Minnie, she lost her beau because he insinnerated somethin' about that good-for-nothin' brother of hern, an' she flared up. Ain't none of the hull family anybody ever darse say anythin' ag'in' him to; an' it's as much as twenty year since he went to the devil. Bad rubbish!"

The man went out, carrying his flour-bag, and David resumed his examination of the store. It was difficult, because the place was poorly lit with oil-lamps. David found a lantern, and used that. The old store was a species of museum. In it was seen enormous waste. David shook his head. Gorham Dunn's business methods must have sorely slackened since his son John's boyhood, and poor Frank could not have been especially fitted for his task. However, as the man examined, a scheme grew in his head. Suddenly he knew that, had he remained right there, that honorable old store would not have borne its present aspect. In him was the true business instinct. It had lain latent. Now it suddenly reared its head.

"Father's store is going to pay!" said John Dunn. And he was right. The little village was fairly agape over the changes suddenly worked in Gorham Dunn's old store. Much was done very early in the morning. Much was done at night. Secrecy was observed as far as possible. It seemed miraculous when Dunn's old country store became spick and span. The very settee for the village loungers was changed for a new one. The sagging roof of the piazza showed plumb-lines and glistened with new shingles. Vines were planted around the new pillars which supported the roof.

Inside, the change was more marked. By degrees, so as not to interfere with the trade, a new floor was laid. A new board ceiling replaced the hideously bulging one of smoke-blackened plaster. There were even new counters, and an old cabinet-maker who lived in the village had constructed stools and arm-chairs out of the old Congregational pulpit. The new man had visions of a soda-fountain, but for that there was need to wait. All the good stock of the store was arranged in a manner to do credit to an artist. The walls containing tinned goods were studies in color. The dry-goods counter was a revelation to the village women.

Then—came the prize-packages! That was the new man's pet scheme: but he needed assistance, and he got it from his sister Minnie. He privately concluded that Minnie and he were the business heads of the family. One evening he had a long talk with her in the kitchen, and, the next day being Sunday, they made a surreptitious visit of inspection to the store. Minnie looked keenly at the sugar, the flour, the chocolate and cocoa, and other things which had been dismissed from the up-to-date stock. She cocked her pretty brown head on one side, and her bright eyes shone indignantly.

"It takes a woman to run some things," said she. "Land! If I had known Pa and Frank were letting things go to waste so! Here are yards and yards of faded gingham, too. Why did they let it stay in the window so long? And look at all this fly-specked ribbon. It is clear waste."

Her unrecognized brother regarded her shrewdly. "Struck me a woman like you might do somethin' to a lot of this truck so it wouldn't be waste," he remarked.

Minnie looked at him. He explained his ideas. The woman's cheeks bloomed pink. She looked years younger with sheer enthusiasm.

The prize-packages at Dunn's, tied up daintily and given with every dollar's worth of merchandise sold, were from the first a great success. Minnie's little cakes and bags of home-made candies, her aprons, old lady Dunn's iron-holders and knitted washcloths, and so on, all heaped together in a great clothes-basket that was trimmed with fringed pink and green tissue paper, and all tied up nicely with pretty blue tape, met with wild approval. Dunn's customers doubled in a week.

Old Gorham Dunn was tremulous with delight. "That new feller knows jest how to take hold," he told his son Frank, who nodded happily.

There was not an envious strain in Frank Dunn's whole make-up. He was only too glad to have the burden lifted from his faithful but inefficient shoulders.

At the end of some weeks the new man, after a colloquy with Gorham and Frank, sought out Silas Towns in his rival store and made certain propositions to him which were accepted without much hesitation. Silas Towns had the making of a shrewd business man in him. He made a good deal with Gorham for his own stock-in-trade, and became an interested, though silent, partner.

Strangely enough, Old Lady Dunn was the only one who evinced no especial pleasure. When Minnie suggested that Dave be given her recreant brother John's old room, she fairly cowered before her mother's gaze.

"No man ever goes into that room to sleep until he's proved himself worthy," said the old woman, in her sweet, reedy voice.

She was almost uncanny in her fragility and hardness. Minnie reflected that her mother had always been the severe one of the family about the beloved recreant son and brother. The mother had often chastised with that thin, lady-hand of hers when the lad had been a child, Minnie remembered. She had not even defended him when he had fallen from his high estate of proud and honored youth in his father's house. In her own family she was so stern that they had almost considered her unfeeling. Once her husband had taken her to task.

"Anybody would think the poor boy wa'n't your son at all, Ma, the way you act," Gorham had said, and his wife had faced him proudly.

"Anybody would think him my son for that very reason," said she. "Do you think I am going to take the part of my own son when I know he doesn't deserve it?"

"You were always sort of hard with him, Ma."

"I wish I had been harder," John Dunn's mother had said. "If I had been harder it would have proved I loved him better than I loved myself. Now, sometimes, I don't know. But I do know that if I have been a selfish mother, it is no reason for me to shame my son more than he has shamed himself, by denying he has done wrong."

After that John had seldom been mentioned in the family.

Scrupulously, twice a year, the boy's room had been cleaned. Then it was closed, and the curtains drawn, as if some one lay in death behind them.

The man in the store, whenever he passed this closed door, realized a little pang. He could not control it. He had overheard his mother deny his right to his old room. He had admired her for it. He admired the exquisite, strong old woman more and more, and she daily gained more power to give him pain, and she used her power.

Finally her husband, her daughter, and her other son were aghast at her treatment of the person whom they knew as David Mann. Old Gorham talked to Minnie about it.

"You'll have to say a leetle to your Ma, I guess, Minnie," he said. "First thing we know, Dave won't stand so much, an' he'll be leavin'; an' I dunno what Frank an' me would do without him, that's a fact."

Minnie and her father and Frank were in the kitchen after supper, and Minnie was washing the dishes. It was Sunday night, and all were at home.

"I feel sort of worried myself," said Frank. "I can't think what's got into Ma."

With that he took up a great pail of refuse and was going out to feed the pig, when a sweet, reedy little voice came from behind him.

"Just set down that swill," said Old Lady Dunn, and her voice and manner dignified the homely little speech. "Let Dave do it."

Frank stared at his mother. She called, remorselessly: "Dave, Dave, come here. It's time to feed the pig."

David Mann, in his Sunday clothes, heard her. He was sitting on the front piazza. He came around through the side-door, took the pail from the other man's hand, and went out with it.

"Ma, it won't do!" gasped old Gorham.

"Frank has fed the pig long enough. It's another man's turn," said the inexorable old lady.

"He'll leave."

"If he leaves, he's not worth keeping," responded the old lady. Then she went back to her place in the sitting-room. But always after that David Mann did the menial tasks about the place, instead of Frank. Ordered by his mother, he milked, cleaned the barn, chopped wood, and performed the tasks of a servant, although both his father and brother remonstrated.

"It beats all what has got into Ma," Gorham told the man whom he knew as David. "The way she orders you around don't suit the rest of us. We know it ain't your place to do all them chores."

David laughed. "Reckon it's my place to do anythin' I kin do," he said.

"Ma seems to hev somethin' ag'in' you, an' you 'ain't done nothin' but be a godsend to us ever sence you come," said Gorham. "You won't think of leavin' because she seems so sort of queer? Women is queer."

"I ain't likely to leave because she asks me to do anythin' I kin do," said the man.

He and his father had been talking out in the yard. It was six months since he had come. The apple-tree which held the bird-house tossed yellow branches over their heads. The house wherein the Dunns dwelt had been painted, and the roof patched. The un-recognized son could hear his sister singing as she cleared up the supper-dishes. Recently a lover had come to her, a very good man who had loved her always, and she had loved him, making no sign. She had forgotten, years and years, the love of her youth. Minnie had refused to listen while affairs were so adverse with their family. Now it was different. The mortgage would soon be paid. A maid could be kept.

The brother heard the happy little song, and smiled. He went out to the barn to finish the milking. His little dog followed him. He milked and carried the last pail to the house. Then he returned to close the barn for the night.

He started. Old Lady Dunn stood there. Her shawl flew out in the wind like sharply pointed gray wings. Her hair stood up like an aureole around her delicate face, an aureole of live silver. The little dog left his master and wagged affectionately around her. Despite her treatment of David, the dog always left him for her. She patted the silky brown head.

"Here," she said to David, "you haven't finished your chores. Go an' pick some of the windfalls and give them to the cows. They like apples."

The man obeyed. He took off his hat, passed around to the or-chard behind the barn, returned with his hat full of apples, and fed them to the cows.

"Get another," ordered the old lady. David obeyed.

When he emerged from the barn after feeding the cows for the second time he looked interrogatively at the woman. She nodded.

"That will do," said she. "Now you can fasten up the barn."

David obeyed. Then he looked with actual timidity at the frail little woman-creature who dominated him. She lifted her right hand, and a white diamond gleamed. He had given her that diamond when he was a boy. He had saved the money for it out of his allowance. He had never seen her wear it since his return.

She held out her hand and moved toward the house, and the man followed. Minnie saw them coming and opened the door. Gorham and Frank were there. Old Lady Dunn and the man they called Dave entered. Old Lady Dunn looked at them; then she turned and pointed at the man, and the diamond gleamed.

"This is my own son. He has come home," she said, and her voice rang out silvery with triumph, like a fine trumpet.

The others exclaimed. The old woman faced them, dauntless. "I knew him all the time," said she. "None of the rest of you knew him but I am his mother. I knew."

"Is it you, John?" queried old Gorham in a shaking voice.

John bowed his head. His face was working.

Frank sprang forward and took him by the hand. Frank was choking with repressed tears. Minnie came forward and kissed him; then she sank into a chair and wept aloud.

Old Gorham put his hand, trembling as if with palsy, on the man's shoulder. "Is it you, John?" John bowed his head again.

Old Gorham suddenly waxed radiant. "He's come home! My son's come home!" he cried out in a great voice. "My son's come home, an' he's made good! I'll show 'em. I guess nobody's goin' to say nothin' more ag'in' my son. He's the smartest man in these parts, I don't keer who he is!" Old Gorham shook his son John back and forth by his passive shoulders. "He's come home, home!" he shouted. Then he turned to the old lady. "What in Sam Hill made you treat him so durned mean fur, Ma," he demanded, "when you knew all the time?"

Old Lady Dunn lifted her head. She looked like a queen throned upon the trials of her whole life. A lovely color came into her soft old cheeks; her eyes shone with blue light. That old flower of life's field which had remained intact as to its flower-shape, though smitten hard by winds of time and grief, seemed suddenly, by virtue of some fine strength of individuality almost beyond the mortal, to bloom anew. She gazed at her son, and the fragrance of the love and sorrow and infinite patience of a woman for her child sweetened the very soul of the man. She smiled a heavenly smile.

"I wanted to make sure that my son had come back," said she. Then she turned to Minnie. "I opened the windows in your brother John's room this morning," said she. "Now I think you had better go and make up the bed."

EXPLANATORY NOTES

"A NEW ENGLAND NUN"

1. *Young Lady's Gift Book: Young Lady's Gift Book: A Common-Place Book of Prose and Poetry* (Providence, R.I., 1836) or a similar book of the popular antebellum genre, the gift-book anthology.
2. *St. George's Dragon:* St. George, patron saint of England and famous dragon slayer.

"A POETESS"

1. *a veritable Mother Hubbard:* Nursery-rhyme character created by Sarah Catherine Martin and appearing in Martin's *The Comic Adventures of Old Mother Hubbard and Her Dog* (London, 1805).

"THE REVOLT OF 'MOTHER' "

1. *buttery:* Pantry or larder for storing provisions, wines, and liquors; chiefly a New England phrase.
2. *like a Webster:* Daniel Webster (1782–1852), formidable New England orator and statesman, often compared with such natural phenomena as Niagara Falls and Mount Washington.
3. *Wolfe's storming of the Heights of Abraham:* James Wolfe (1727–59), English general who defeated the French in Canada but was fatally wounded in the Battle of the Plains (not Heights) of Abraham.

THE JAMESONS

1. *Choctaw:* Language of the North American Muskogean Indian tribe of that name. Used, derogatorily, to denote gibberish.
2. *her old Leghorn hat:* Hat made of fine, smooth plaited straw, often having a broad, soft brim. The plaited straw was often imported from Leghorn, Italy.
3. *that mad problem of Shakespeare and Bacon:* Literary controversy as to whether Sir Francis Bacon or William Shakespeare wrote Shakespeare's plays.
4. *portières:* Curtain hung in a doorway to replace the door or for decoration.

5. *cloth congress boots:* High shoes with elastic sides, worn by men in the United States in the late nineteenth and early twentieth centuries.

6. *Mammon:* Personification of riches as an evil spirit, from New Testament use of mammon as riches or material wealth.

7. *visions of Philadelphia:* Reference to the International Centennial Exposition, the fair celebrating the centennial of the United States held in Philadelphia in 1876.

8. *Young's "Night Thoughts":* Reference to *The Complaint; or, Night Thoughts on Life, Death and Immortality* by English poet Edward Young (1683–1765). The pious and sentimental strain of the poem's first four sections made it internationally popular in the nineteenth century.

9. *barouche:* Four-wheeled carriage with high front seat outside for driver, facing seats inside for two couples, and a folding top over the backseat.

10. *sulky:* Light two-wheeled one-horse carriage for one person.

11. *Grenadine:* Light fabric of open weave in silk or wool.

"THE LOVE OF PARSON LORD"

1. *American Board:* American Board of Foreign Missionaries, established in 1810 by New England Congregationalists.

2. *Dodridge:* Probably *The family expositor; Or, a paraphrase and version of the New testament with critical notes and a practical improvement of each section,* 6 vols. (1739–56), by the Reverend Philip Doddridge (1702–51), English minister and religious writer.

"THE PARROT"

1. *Baal:* Idol worshiped by people surrounding the Israelites and, at various times, by the Israelites themselves when they forsook the Lord (see, for example, Judges 2:11–14).

2. *Golden calf:* Idol made of gold and that the Israelites worshiped when they doubted Moses and the Lord (Exodus 32).

3. *witch of Endor:* Heathen woman consulted by Saul in I Samuel 28.

"THE LOST GHOST"

1. *Missionary Herald:* Published by the American Board of Commissioners for Foreign Missions, 1821–1934.